The fiery brilliance of th[...] the cover is created by "laser h[...] ss in which a powerful laser bea[...] ts so tiny that 9,000,000 fit in a[...] atch the vibrant colors and rad[...]

So look for the Zebra Hologram Heart whenever you buy a historical romance. It is a shimmering reflection of our guarantee that you'll find consistent quality between the covers!

LOVE'S SWEET KISS

Nothing in Gentle Fawn's eighteen-year existence had prepared her for the thunderbolt of electricity that crashed through her veins as Clay's mouth captured hers.

Clay raised up to look into the wide black eyes that stared up at him. And when Gentle Fawn would have cried out her protest, he smiled. He knew kissing wasn't a common practice among Indians and was touched by the stunned curiosity he had seen in the young woman's eyes. "I can see your education's been sadly neglected," he said. "It's time you learned about the finer things in life, my little Sioux princess. That was a *kiss*. And it's even nicer if you close your eyes," he told her gently. To demonstrate his words, he used his thumbs to gently sweep her heavily lashed lids downward. He kissed her closed eyes.

"Kiss," he said with each feathery contact, making sure she understood the full meaning of her first lesson in love . . .

BESTSELLING ROMANCE
from Zebra Books

CAPTIVE SURRENDER   (1986, $3.95)
by Michalann Perry
When both her husband and her father are killed in battle, young
Gentle Fawn vows revenge. Yet once she catches sight of the
piercing blue eyes of her enemy, the Indian maiden knows that
she can never kill him. She must sate the desires he kindled, or
forever be a prisoner of his love.

WILD FLAME   (1671, $3.95)
by Gina Delaney
Although reared as a gentle English lass, once Milly set foot on
the vast Australian farm, she had the Outback in her blood.
When handsome Matthew Aylesbury met Milly, he vowed to have
her, but only when the heat of his passion had melted her pride
into willing submission.

WILD FURY   (1987, $3.95)
by Gina Delaney
Jessica Aylesbury was the beauty of the settled territory in Aus-
tralia's savage Outback, but no one knew that she was an adopted
part-native. Eric, the worshipped friend of her childhood, now
an outlaw, was the only man who made her burn with desire. She
could never let anyone else teach her the pleasures of womanhood.

TEXAS TRIUMPH   (2009, $3.95)
by Victoria Thompson
The Circle M was most important to Rachel McKinsey, so she
took her foreman as a husband to scare off rustlers. But now that
Rachel had sworn that they be business partners, she could never
admit that all she really wanted was to consummate their vows
and have Cole release her sensual response.

TEXAS VIXEN   (1823, $3.95)
by Victoria Thompson
It was either accept Jack Sinclair's vile proposal of marriage or
sell the Colson Ranch. Jack swore, if it took till dawn, he'd sub-
due Maggie Colson's honey-sweet lips and watch her sea-green
eyes deepen to emerald with passion.

*Available wherever paperbacks are sold, or order direct from the
Publisher. Send cover price plus 50¢ per copy for mailing and
handling to Zebra Books, Dept. 1986, 475 Park Avenue South,
New York, N.Y. 10016. Residents of New York, New Jersey and
Pennsylvania must include sales tax. DO NOT SEND CASH.*

CAPTIVE SURRENDER

MICHALANN PERRY

ZEBRA BOOKS
KENSINGTON PUBLISHING CORP.

ZEBRA BOOKS

are published by

Kensington Publishing Corp.
475 Park Avenue South
New York, NY 10016

Copyright © 1987 by Michalann Perry

All rights reserved. No part of this book may be reproduced in any form or by any means without the prior written consent of the Publisher, excepting brief quotes used in reviews.

First printing: February 1987

Printed in the United States of America

To my mom, Joanne Flanagan, who was always going to write a book but never got the chance;

To Dolores and Joyce at Books N' Stuff for their loyal support from the very beginning;

And to Zebra Books for taking a chance on a new writer a couple of years ago.

Thanks. I love you all!

"Micki"

BATTLE OF THE LITTLE BIGHORN
June 25, 1876

BATTLEFIELD

LITTLE BIGHORN RIVER

CUSTER'S ADVANCE

CRAZY HORSE'S
ATTACK

GALL'S
ATTACK

CLAY DONOVAN'S
IMAGINARY OBSERVATION
POINT

SOLDIERS'
FIRST ATTACK

SOLDIERS' 2nd
STAND

ENTRENCHMENT
OF SOLDIERS

N

1 MILE

DIVERSIONARY
ADVANCE OF SOLDIERS

Prologue

Crouched on his haunches before his small breakfast fire, the man's shoulders tensed. He cocked his head alertly, all of his senses leaping to attention with instinctive readiness. Squinting his eyes in concentration, he turned his head to the side, directing his ear toward the piercing sound that had disturbed the early morning quiet. A second shrill scream penetrated the silence of the forest.

"Help me!" he heard a woman cry. "Someone please help me!"

Springing into action, the rifle at his side now gripped tightly in his hand, the man ran in the direction of the wretched pleas. The closer he drew to the woman the more concerned he became, for he did not hear the growls of a wild animal as he had expected, a wild animal he could easily frighten off with a single shot of his rifle. Instead, mingled with her cries he heard the low murmuring voices and grunts of men.

9

Comanche! Four of them! Three watching and waiting their turns as the fourth dropped on top of the helpless woman. All were unaware their brutal attack was being observed.

Hidden in the brush, the lone hunter crept forward on silent feet.

Suddenly the woman's screams ceased, bringing a stunned stillness to the morning air. The brave on the ground cursed, slapping the woman in a forceful demand that she revive.

The man, who understood the Comanche language, heard one of the Indians say, "She's dead."

The brave on the ground grunted his acknowledgment of the fact. He shrugged his shoulders, then moved as if to complete what he had started. But his was a lost cause. Before he could invade the battered body of the lifeless woman, a shot rang out, hitting its mark in his broad chest. The brave jerked spastically and was flung off her prone form—dead.

Certain their only chance was to make a run for it, the remaining three Comanches grabbed their fallen brother and leaped onto their ponies, but not before two of them had suffered minor injuries in the rapid fire of bullets that seemed to come from all around them.

Breathless after running from place to place to make the rapists believe he was more than one, the lone man stood watching after the retreating Comanches, the look on his face sad and indecisive. He glanced hesitantly at the place where the abused body of the young woman lay. He wished he could do something for her, but what? If he stayed and tried to find her family to tell them what had occurred, he knew he would be the one blamed for her

eath—probably hung before the day was out. He could
t least bury her, he thought. No, there was no time for
aat either. Someone could come for her at any time. And
he was caught anywhere near this spot, he would be
ust as dead as she.

His decision made and his breath somewhat regained,
ae man turned to hurry back to his fire. He had to gather
p his belongings and leave as quickly as possible. If he
as going to live to see another sunrise, he'd better be far
way from here when the woman's body was discovered.

The man had taken only two loping strides before a
aewling whimper from the brush brought his steps to an
brupt halt. But the rustling noises and discontented
queaks in the nearby vine-entangled undergrowth soon
onvinced him he had nothing to fear. Evidently he had
ushed a female fox, or some other four-legged mother,
rom her den. In an attempt to decoy the danger away
rom her cubs, she had left her hungry babies to squirm
nd squeal their displeasure.

Shooting an amused glance toward the thicket where
he litter must be hidden, he started off again, only to be
rought up short by a loud, angry wail—a wail definitely
oo strong to come from any fox, a wail he could not fail
o recognize as that of a human baby.

Immediately realizing the dead woman had probably
idden her child in the bushes to protect it from the
Comanches, the man hesitated again. This definitely
omplicated matters. He had to get away before someone
ame and accused him of the woman's murder. But the
aby . . . *I should just leave it here,* he tried to convince
imself. *Someone will be along soon and see what's
appened and take care of it.* But what if no one came?

11

What if a pack of wolves or a wild boar found the baby before help arrived?

Could anyone with a heart leave the unprotected youngster to face that? *A man would have to be made of iron,* he told himself angrily as he began to hack at the thick vines that hid the crying child. "And I'm only flesh and blood."

Chapter One

Montana Territory
June—The Moon of Making Fat—1876

Clay Donovan mumbled irritably as he shifted his weight in a futile effort to arrange his lanky, five-foot-eleven-inch frame in a more bearable position. "What the hell have I gotten myself into now?" he groaned from his hiding place in the brush, cursing the need to stay flattened out on the hard ground. His aching muscles doubling his frustration, he wondered for the hundredth time since sunrise what he was going to do.

Raising up on his elbows, Clay tried yet another time to count the hundreds of tepees and wickiups spread as far as he could see along the west bank of the Little Bighorn, the river the Sioux called the Greasy Grass. "It's no use," he grumbled aloud. *With women and kids, there could be anywhere from two to five thousand Indians in that camp!* he decided with a groan of disgust.

He concentrated his attention on the giant tepee near what he guessed to be the center of the enormous camp.

Since it was larger than the others, he had decided it mus be the council lodge. But it was empty.

The only way I'm going to get in there to talk to Craz Horse is if I'm invisible, he thought. *Or without my hair!* Ar expression of distaste distorted Clay's unshaven face a he pictured his own blond scalp dangling from the wa staff carried into battle by some proud Sioux warrior. In subconscious gesture of verification, Clay pushed his tar Stetson back on his head and threaded his finger through his wavy wheat-colored hair. It was wet and slic with sweat, but it was still on his head. He chuckle silently at his own action. *For how long? I wonder!*

Intelligence told him to jump on his horse and get a far away from this spot as he could—and fast. If he had lick of sense, he'd run like hell!

Swatting at a cloud of buffalo gnats that swarme around his face, Clay cursed again. He pulled his hat lov on his forehead and covered his nose and mouth with bandanna. But it was no use. The tiny insects were n larger than specks of dust, and they continued to worl their way past every barrier, stinging and biting with vengeance. The whites of his clear blue eyes were alread painfully red, the flesh around them swollen.

"If the Sioux don't scalp me, these damned gnats ar going to eat me alive." He laughed to himself—to kee from crying, he decided. *At least I won't be raw. I'll be goo and cooked,* he thought caustically, squinting his eye against the midday sun. It was already so hot it ha burned off all the wispy clouds which had hung over head earlier.

But despite his aching discomfort, the persistent gnat and sweltering heat—and the possibility he could be dis covered and scalped at any moment—Clay wasn't read

14

o give up yet. He was still unable to admit to himself that his plan to interview the famous Oglala Sioux chief Crazy Horse was insane, maybe even impossible!

Giving up was simply not a part of Clay Donovan's makeup. His mother had called it "stubbornness," his father "spit and vinegar"—or a more colorful term if there were no ladies present! But whatever it was, once Clay had an idea in his head, he was determined to carry it through—or die trying. Unfortunately, in this particular situation, dying was more than a strong possibility. Maybe it was time to rethink his priorities—like staying alive.

But no matter how Clay argued and reasoned with himself, he couldn't bring himself to back down. He had never been one to run away from any kind of trouble. Even when turning and running like hell would be a definite sign of intelligence. Like right now!

If I'd run away every time I've been in a tight spot, I'd still be writing announcements for the "Railroad Workers Report," he reminded himself in an effort to bolster his own confidence, determined to ignore his growing doubts about his sanity. *There's got to be a way I can get in there and talk to him!* But how? Would he even recognize the Sioux chief if he saw him? And even if he knew what the man looked like, how was he going to find one lone Indian out of thousands? Then, if he did get lucky and spot the famous warrior, how would he get past the others to interview him? Still, if he could just pick him out, maybe . . .

Clay's gaze scoured the valley one more time in a stubborn search for a warrior that could be Crazy Horse. All up and down the camp Clay could see Indians—men, women, and children alike—bathing, laughing, and

15

splashing happily in the swiftly moving current of the Little Bighorn. Crazy Horse could be any one of them— or none of them. The fact that this was not one of Clay's better ideas was reconfirmed. It was not only a crazy idea, it was downright hopeless! Crazy and hopeless! He'd never find the Indian.

Jealously longing to take a refreshing dip in the cool water as the seemingly carefree Indians were doing, Clay wiped the sweat from his eyes and rinsed his parched mouth with a sip of tepid water from his canteen. Was Crazy Horse one of the braves frolicking in the water? he wondered as he put the cap back on the metal container, unable to give up hope in spite of the unlikely odds. Or perhaps the great war chief was one of the men lazing casually with other warriors in the shade of a rolled-up lodge. But which lodge? Which man? Then again, he could be one of the dozens of braves dozing beneath the trees that grew along the bank. He could be anywhere.

Realizing the futility of finding Crazy Horse in the crowd, Clay allowed himself to be lulled by the relaxed atmosphere that seemed to wrap the entire camp in a cocoon of leisure and casualness. As he watched the peaceful scene in the valley, his eyelids grew heavy. It was difficult for him to remember these were the same fierce Indians who, under the leadership of Crazy Horse, had so brilliantly defended themselves from General George Crook's troops the week before. Not only had the Sioux protected their main camp on the Little Bighorn from being discovered by stopping the advancing soldiers at Rosebud Creek, but General Crook had literally turned tail and run.

And, too, if this was the great Sioux war camp the Army had been talking about, the one which was supposedly preparing for the out-and-out destruction of the whites, why didn't it look like it? Why weren't war parties out looking for soldiers to kill? For that matter, why did they have their women and children along? And why were young people going from lodge to lodge courting and celebrating instead of putting on war paint and doing war dances? Why were women out on the hills digging for turnips as if they were on a Sunday picnic, their children playing unattended throughout the camp? Why wasn't there a single bit of evidence that would indicate these people were preparing for war?

"Not even one war dance going on," Clay mumbled to himself, no longer fighting his body's invitation to close his eyes and rest them for a few minutes. *It doesn't make a damn bit of sense,* he thought as, for the first time in forty-eight hours, he drifted off to sleep. There he remained undisturbed for the next three hours—Indians, gnats, heat, the hard ground all forgotten.

However, when Clay woke again, everything came storming back to him in a turbulent assault on his hearing as the sounds of panic and alarm in the Sioux camp below jerked him awake.

Instantly alert, Clay raised up on his forearms, blinking his stinging eyes in an effort to fathom what he saw. The peaceful scene of a few hours before had exploded into a madhouse. A vision from a nightmare! Everywhere he looked, brown-skinned Sioux warriors were shouting as they thundered through the camp on horseback; screaming women were running in all directions, snatching up crying children, kicking at the barking dogs that nipped at their moccasins; young braves were herding hundreds of nervous, squealing horses into the main camp from where they'd been grazing; and the women and young people who'd been digging in the hills were racing toward the giant village, their turnips forgotten.

Realizing that many of the frightened Indians were pointing toward the upriver end of the great camp, Clay turned his gaze southward, too.

Then he saw what had the Indians so alarmed. His heart dropped to the pit of his stomach with a sickening thud.

A huge ominous cloud of dust hung like smoke over the hills, like the cloud of dust raised by men on horseback. Many men on horseback. Like the dust made by horses being ridden fast. Soldiers charging! "Oh, my God, they're going to attack a village full of women and children!"

Clay leaped to a crouching position and looked around helplessly, his sky blue eyes darkening with fear—not for himself but for the women and children in the village. He had to do something, had to help them. He couldn't just lie there waiting for them all to be killed. And he knew the soldiers would do exactly that. They would kill every Indian they saw, no matter what the sex, no matter how old or how young. Hadn't they already done that very same thing many times? The bloody statistics from the Washita and Sand Creek massacres exploded vividly in Clay's mind. And just this past March the soldiers had destroyed a sleeping Comanche camp on the Powder River, where they'd killed many and left hundreds more without food or clothing to freeze to death in the snow.

Clay knew he couldn't stand by and witness the destruction of another peaceful village. He had to stop them! But how? What could one lone man do? He wasn't

18

sure, but he knew with total certainty that he had to try! If he stayed close to the ground and in the brush, he might have a chance.

Giving his own safety no thought, Clay left his horse hidden in a copse of trees and began to dash on foot toward the cloud of dust that signaled the soldiers' position upstream.

"Bring your horse herds into the camp circle immediately," the crier ordered as he made his rounds through the combined Sioux and Cheyenne camp that stretched three miles along the bank of the peaceful Greasy Grass River. "Warriors, prepare to fight! Signal the turnip diggers to leave the hills and return to their lodges at once!" he yelled out. "Women, do not be afraid. Stay calm! You will be protected. You must be ready to move at once." The orders droned on, repeated over and over in all the camps along the river. "Stay calm. Prepare to fight! Be ready to move . . ."

However, the young Lakota woman who sat alone in her darkened tepee only half heard the monotone voices calling out the emergency instructions. In fact, she was barely aware of the whir of panic buzzing through the great camp, growing more intense as the pounding of running footsteps, the squeals of frightened horses, and the wails of terrified women and confused children rose to a deafening crescendo.

As though this day were no different than any other, Gentle Fawn walked to the entrance of her tepee and looked up at the sky. Unconcerned with the hectic activity around her, the expression on her oval face was dazed, the light in her tearless, almost black eyes dulled by sorrow and anger.

The sun was high and it was hot. Very hot, she noticed idly. But she was only vaguely curious as to why she didn't feel its heat. In fact, she felt cold, colder than she'd ever been in her eighteen winters. Cold and dead. Like Tall Feathers.

Blocking out the sights and sounds of the hysterical storm of panic that had flooded through the camp, Gentle Fawn turned back to the young brave she had called her husband for only one week. Tall Feathers was still now. He was no longer thrashing with fever, and the expression on his handsome face was no longer contorted with pain from the wounds he'd received in the battle that had taken place on Rosebud Creek the day after he'd married Gentle Fawn.

Woodenly studying the man who had died in her arms only moments before the criers had come with their warning, Gentle Fawn knelt and gently closed his eyes as she began to prepare him for his final journey. She washed his dark skin, still warm with life, then carefully put his most prized possessions beside him: his decorated shield, which had been carefully crafted from the rawhide of a bull's neck, over his heart and midsection for protection, his bow in his hand. Next, she placed Tall Feathers' sheathed knife and war bundle on one side of him, a quiver full of arrows and his rifle on the other. She hesitated only a moment before covering Tall Feathers' face with the hide winding sheet.

Just as Gentle Fawn closed the death shroud around Tall Feathers and began to sew it shut with an awl and buffalo sinew, something she heard outside her lodge finally penetrated her frozen senses. She stopped sewing and listened.

"The soldiers are attacking the Hunkpapas. Already they have killed many of the helpless ones. Warriors, prepare to fight. Women, do not be afraid. You will be protected. Make ready to move."

"The soldiers here?" Gentle Fawn asked aloud, not realizing she had given voice to her question. *The soldiers who killed Tall Feathers? Here?* she repeated silently. The bile of her hatred rose chokingly into her throat, the disoriented expression on her youthful face growing hard and old. *The soldiers who killed my husband have come to kill the rest of the People?*

Gentle Fawn suddenly shouted her protest to the walls of the semidarkened tepee, her anguished cry originating in the pit of her belly, in the center of her soul. "Noooooo!" she wailed. "No more! The *wasicun* will kill no more of the People," she vowed with vengeance as she furiously jerked the hide winding sheet off her husband's dead body and studied the war equipment placed so carefully beside him. "The soldiers have destroyed their last village, murdered their last Lakota child. I swear to you, my husband, I will stop them."

Her features set with determination and hatred, Gentle Fawn quickly crossed the tepee and snatched up a pair of Tall Feathers' leggings. She held them up to her waist, immediately realizing the pants that had belonged to her taller-than-average husband would swallow her own five-foot-two-inch, one-hundred-pound frame. The wave of indecision that crossed her face was only fleeting. Gentle Fawn hurriedly used a hunting knife to cut the long pants down to a size that would accommodate her shorter legs and stepped into the leggings. She yanked them up over her boyishly slim hips and secured them around her waist with a strip of rawhide.

21

Picking up Tall Feathers' shirt, Gentle Fawn knew the garment made for the broad-shouldered brave could not be altered to fit her—would only encumber her with its shoulders reaching to her elbows. Allowing herself a moment of remembering, she hugged the tan shirt to her breast and then threw it down with resolution. She would shorten her own mid-calf-length dress for better maneuverability and wear it as a shirt.

With her clothing taken care of, she crossed back to where Tall Feathers lay, second thoughts about what she was planning to do racing through her mind. But her misgivings only delayed her progress for a brief moment. There was just an instant of regret before she dropped to her knees beside her husband's body and opened the pots of paint she took from his war bundle. "I will avenge your death, Tall Feathers. Yours and those of all the others who've been murdered by the whites," she swore as she wiped a slash of red from temple to temple across her cheeks and the bridge of her nose. "They have pushed the People too far."

With the addition of two similar stripes, one yellow and one blue, Gentle Fawn braided the long red feather and deer tail Tall Feathers had worn into battle into her own black hair and reached for her husband's weapons. Her hands were only shaking slightly now.

Moments later, with a full quiver of arrows slung over her shoulder, a knife strapped to her hip, Tall Feathers' bow and rifle in her left hand and his shield in her right, Gentle Fawn stepped into the afternoon sunlight. Without hesitation, she ran to her mother's lodge, where her brothers and father were preparing to fight, their war horses already saddled and tied to nearby trees.

Stepping into the tepee, Gentle Fawn squinted as she

accustomed her eyes to the semidarkness. "My husband is dead," she announced matter-of-factly, the tearless expression on her face revealing none of the pain slashing at her heart.

Quiet Rain rushed to her daughter's side and wrapped her arms around Gentle Fawn's shoulders. "My poor child," she cried as Hunting Bear's other two wives and their daughters began to moan and keen their sorrow loudly.

"It's only the beginning. The whites will kill us all before this is through," lamented Bright Sunshine, the daughter of Hunting Bear's third wife, Green Skirt. Bright Sunshine had lost her husband in the same battle where Tall Feathers had been wounded, leaving her with three small children.

"You're right," Gentle Fawn said to her older half sister. "This is only the beginning, but it will be the Lakotas who will be victorious this time, not the *wasicuns*. It is the whites who will be destroyed—not the People!" It was then the fact that Gentle Fawn was dressed for battle sank into the minds of her relatives. They all stared at Hunting Bear's youngest child.

"What is this?" Quiet Rain asked, stepping back to examine Gentle Fawn's clothing and the weapons gripped fiercely in her hands. A look of fear and realization twisted the woman's moon-shaped face. She reached out and touched the three stripes of paint that swept cross the bridge of her daughter's finely formed nose and grimaced. "You are not a warrior, child. The women and children must prepare to break camp. The men will protect us."

"You break camp, my mother. I will not. I am no longer a child. I am fully grown and I will go into battle

23

beside my father and brothers."

"But you are a woman," her mother protested weakly, certain that if her only child went to war against the whites she would be lost to her forever. "A woman does not go into battle!"

"Then I renounce my womanhood, Mother. This is something I must do. I can no longer do nothing while Lakota warriors die at the hands of the soldiers. I can no longer sit back and wait to be told if they are dead or alive. I must go with them."

"You should never have let her learn the ways of a brave," Hunting Bear's second wife, Many Faces, goaded with satisfaction.

Hunting Bear, his expression a mixture of pride and sorrow, silenced the vindictive woman with a quelling look, then put his arm around Quiet Rain's trembling shoulders. His voice was gentle with his first and favorite wife. "Let her go, my wife."

"But she will be killed," Quiet Rain whimpered, turning her pleading black eyes upward to meet her husband's understanding gaze. "Forbid her to go! Do this for me and I will never ask another thing of you." The woman's voice was high and desperate.

Hunting Bear smiled patiently at his wife. After all these years he still cared for the tiny woman with a love that caused an aching tightness in his chest. If only she'd been able to have children, he would never have had any need for other wives. "I will not forbid her, my wife. But I promise to keep her close to me. Will that ease your mind?" He looked at his youngest child expectantly.

Gentle Fawn responded by coming to her mother. "I give you my word, Mother. I will stay beside my father."

Knowing there was no more she could say or do to stop

er daughter from going, Quiet Rain patted Gentle Fawn's hand and nodded her head mutely. "I will ready one of your father's ponies for you," she said with resignation.

"Thank you, Mother," Gentle Fawn whispered, making no effort to stop Quiet Rain from leaving the lodge. She knew her mother needed to do this for her.

Suddenly there was no more time for discussion. From far upstream, beyond the camp circle of the famous Sitting Bull's band of Hunkpapa Lakotas, they heard the crackling and exploding of guns. Followed by her sisters and their mothers, Gentle Fawn and her brothers dashed outside with Hunting Bear and directed their eyes southward toward the Hunkpapa camp. The dust of running horses rose in a huge, ominous, gray-brown cloud of death.

"Crazy Horse! Crazy Horse! Crazy Horse!" she heard the excited and fearful people around her shout as the unofficial war chief of all the Lakotas—Oglala, Hunkpapa, Sans Arc, Miniconjou, and Brule—rode past with a party of warriors. Young to be an "old man" chief, in his early thirties still, Crazy Horse was impressive on a yellow pinto. Hailstones painted on his body and a lightning streak down one cheek, he carried no shield—only a war club, rifle, bow, and a quiver of arrows.

Hunting Bear's nostrils flared with the scent of battle. He leaped onto a dun-colored stallion, one of his best war horses, shouting, "Come my sons—and my brave daughter! *Hoka hey!* It is a good day to die!"

Reminded of Tall Feathers' last words to her, Gentle Fawn echoed the traditional Lakota call to battle. "*Hoka hey!*" she agreed with fervent excitement. "It is a good day to die! *Hoka hey!*" With the agility of the bravest

25

warrior, she took the reins and vaulted onto the reddish brown pony her mother had readied for her. "But I will not die, Mother!" she promised the woman who stood by silently as her daughter rode into battle. "Not before I see them all dead for what they've done!" she swore, and sank her heels into the soft sides of her mount. "*Hoka hey, Lakotas! Hoka hey!*" she shouted, joining the war party that galloped up the valley of the Greasy Grass River, her rifle held high over her head.

From his vantage point behind a boulder, Clay paused to catch his breath and survey the situation below. Despite the fact that he had run all the way, taking special care to skirt the open areas, going far out of his way to stay hidden in the brush and hills, he finally admitted to himself he wasn't going to reach the soldiers in time. In fact he wasn't going to reach them at all. He was too late. The Indians and soldiers were already engaged in battle, and there was nothing he could do.

Taking an irritated swipe at the stinging sweat in his eyes, Clay pulled his binoculars from their leather case and flattened himself on the ground. Oblivious to the sharp rocks cutting into his arms, he propped his heaving torso up on his elbows and peered through the glasses.

At first, all he saw were Indians. No soldiers, only Indians. Hundreds of Indians. Then he spotted the soldiers, and his heart dove into his belly with a violent plunge.

A pitiful line of blue amid the breechcloth-clad Indians, about eighty soldiers had dismounted and were making a futile stand against the fierce warriors. Formed in a thin skirmish line, their right flank was anchored in he timber along the river. They were firing their rifles apidly and wildly. But it was no use. The Indians were oo many and had already maneuvered around the left nd of the line to catch the soldiers in a deadly crossfire.

Bunching up, the surrounded soldiers moved to the ight and into the woods that grew between them and the ittle Bighorn. Clay breathed a momentary sigh of relief. t least in the heavy undergrowth of the cottonwood and ox elder woods, they would have a better defensive osition than in the open.

But Clay's relief was momentary. As the soldiers ran or cover, they stopped firing. The Indians took dvantage of the lull to draw in even closer, easily picking ff several of the soldiers in their mad dash for safety. ust when the frightened men had reached the shelter of he trees, Clay spotted another group of Sioux. They vere slipping up the river side of the woods to set fire to he dry river-bottom grass and brush that filled the oldiers' refuge.

His heart sank. The outnumbered soldiers were rapped!

Suddenly a horse and blue-coated rider burst out of the imber, other mounted soldiers following close behind. he soldiers were obviously going to make a run for it.

Frustrated that he was at least a quarter mile from the attle and unable to do anything to help, Clay nervously hifted his position and studied the retreating soldiers hrough the binoculars. The man leading the withdrawal vas an officer! "What the hell's going on?" Clay asked imself. "He's not making any attempt to cover his ear!" *They'll be picked off like buffalo in a hunt!* he ealized, spotting the Indians riding alongside the fleeing nen and doing just that.

27

What the hell were they thinking to attack with such a small number of troops? It doesn't make sense! Their scout must've been aware how big this village is! There's no way they couldn't have known. Unless . . . "Oh, my God!" Clay groaned aloud, turning his binoculars northward toward the downstream end of the massive Sioux camp.

"Unless it's a diversion," Crazy Horse said to several other chiefs who had gathered to consult with one another in a stand of trees out of the soldiers' firing range.

"To attack a village full of women and children from two or three sides is Long Hair's way of fighting," a Cheyenne chief offered, his lip curled with hatred as he held out a blue coat marked with the insignia of Custer's 7th Cavalry. "I found a coat marked like this one in the attack on the Washita where my wife and children were killed by Long Hair's soldiers," he told them bitterly.

"Long Hair," several chiefs spat, as if the hated name left a vile taste in their mouths.

Only half listening to what was being said at the hastily convened war conference, Gentle Fawn stood behind her father, a great deal more timid and uncertain than she had been in her mother's lodge. She frequently cast a nervous glance toward the raging battle, quickly averting her eyes again. It was one thing to think about, even speak about, killing the whites—but something else to actually kill another human being.

Gentle Fawn scolded herself harshly for her cowardice. They deserved it, she told herself over and over. The whites killed Tall Feathers—and Bright Sunshine's husband, and thousands of others. They had no right to

here. The People were defending themselves. They
were not the ones who had attacked. It was the soldiers
who had brought this upon themselves. Still it turned her
stomach to watch the bloody fighting and killing.

The spicy and bitter smell of burning green weeds,
sage, and plum underbrush filled her nostrils as she
remembered the relief—and guilt—she had felt when
Crazy Horse had held the Oglala warriors back from the
battle. He had told them their Lakota brothers, the
Hunkpapas, had the battle in hand and that the need to
conserve ammunition was more important than joining
in. The great chief's followers had all been disappointed
and had groaned aloud, some even sneaking away to join
the Hunkpapas anyway. But Gentle Fawn had been
relieved.

Looking to the north, Gentle Fawn noticed something
tiny flash in the sunlight. Mirrors! Mirrors and
blankets. Scouts east of the river were signaling to them!
Gentle Fawn turned and tugged on her father's arm and
pointed to the hills.

"Soldiers heading north behind the ridges," one chief
interpreted, his deep voice rife with alarm.

Crazy Horse was the first to speak. "So it is as we
suspected," he grunted. "Their plan was to hold our
attention while their main force got into position to
attack, catching us off guard. Well, we will be ready for
them. I will ride through the camps on this side of the
river and beat the soldiers to the pass at the northern end
of our camp."

"And I will leave a few braves here to watch these
soldiers while the rest of my warriors ride down the other
side of the river to keep the bluecoats from turning back
when they realize we've outguessed them," Gall, the

29

Hunkpapa leader announced, pleased with the look o
approval Crazy Horse directed toward him.

"It will be as in Sitting Bull's vision," Crazy Hors
said, reminding the others of the great medicine man'
prediction. "The bluecoats will fall into our camp, and w
will be there to catch them," he said, leaping to his pon
and blowing into his war whistle to call his followers.

Chapter Two

The thunder of hoofbeats rumbled along the floor of
the valley, the volume reaching tornado proportions as
the great war party roared through the Lakota and
Cheyenne camps behind Crazy Horse. Gentle Fawn kept
her eyes focused straight ahead. She took no notice of the
women, old men, and children gathered to cheer for the
growing army of braves. She wasn't even aware that
many of the lodges in the lower village were half struck,
hundreds of their inhabitants already moving to the low
hills in preparation for flight. Despite the equal amounts
of excitement and fear pounding relentlessly in her
veins, she couldn't allow her attention to wander. She
couldn't permit herself to think of anything but staying
near her father as she followed the yelling swarm of
warriors north at a fast gallop.

Hundreds of braves too late for the battle at the
upriver end of the camp had joined Crazy Horse as he
rode through the giant village, more merging with the
huge mass of riders each minute. So, by the time they
turned east to ford the river well beyond the camp,

Gentle Fawn found herself near the point of a massiv
human arrow directed toward the advancing soldiers.

Hunting Bear and Gentle Fawn followed Crazy Hors
up to a broad ravine that was deep enough to concea
their coming from the enemy. When they reached th
head of the gorge, they quickly discovered Gall's warrior
had already pushed the soldiers to the crest of the ridg
and that the outnumbered cavalrymen, some mounte
others dismounted and kneeling in firing lines, wer
making stands in little groups along a half-mile stretch o
the ridge.

Uncertain what she should do, Gentle Fawn hesitate
All around her, Crazy Horse's newly arrived warrior
were whooping and yipping, blowing into their eagl
wing-bone whistles as they rushed toward the line o
soldiers. A sense of frenzied excitement consumed th
young woman, and her earlier misgivings and moment
of weakness were forgotten. All she felt now was pride i
her Lakota heritage, the need to avenge her husband'
death, and the thrill of being part of the battle that woul
stop the whites' persecution of the People once and fo
all.

Gentle Fawn eased her restraining grip on her horse'
reins and narrowed her eyes in an effort to locate he
father in the thick cloud of dust and gunpowder smok
that blanketed the ridge. Spotting him, she held her rifl
high, gave a yell, and followed him into the battle.

Using her legs to guide her horse, as her brothers ha
taught her to do, Gentle Fawn fired her rifle toward th
soldiers' line. However, she quickly realized her talen
with a rifle was obviously limited and that the shots wer
short of their mark. Besides, she could fire several arrow
in the time it would take her to load, fire, and reload th

rifle. With an expression of irritation, she inserted the rifle in the beaded case on her saddle and drew out her bow.

As she was making the change from the unfamiliar rifle to the more traditional bow and arrows, she lost sight of her father for a moment. A second of uncertainty tripped over her. Then, when she saw him again, he was riding into the midst of a group of dismounted cavalrymen, his rifle firing from one hand, his war club swinging from the other. The soldiers, who had made a back-to-back circle to fight the Indians charging them from all sides, were so surprised by Hunting Bear's attack that he managed to bring down two of the whites with his heavy, stone-headed war club before they could react to his presence. Gentle Fawn's uncertainty swelled into pride as she watched her brave father attack the soldiers single-handedly.

However, when her father swung his club toward a third soldier, the expression on Gentle Fawn's face suddenly went from pride to horror. The realization of what was happening hit her violently as she saw blood explode from the bronzed muscle of Hunting Bear's chest. *He's been shot!* she realized as the wounded warrior slumped over on his horse's back, his war club dropping to the ground beside him. Gentle Fawn watched helplessly as her father's nervous horse bolted and made a dash away from the soldiers, its wounded rider bobbing up and down on its back as it galloped up the ridge.

"Ate!" Gentle Fawn screamed, angrily urging her own mount toward the soldiers she'd seen shoot Hunting Bear. Without thinking, she rode right through the stand of men, causing them to divide as she raced after her father's frightened pony. Oblivious to the shots being

fired all around her, she only knew she had to get to Hunting Bear before his horse took him any farther into the battle.

Catching up to the runaway horse, Gentle Fawn drew alongside just as Hunting Bear sat up and looked around, the expression on his face stunned. "Come, Father," she started to say, but Hunting Bear didn't hear. He wobbled and fell sideways.

With strength that would have surprised even her if she'd thought about it, she caught him and pulled him onto her own horse. Holding the half-conscious man before her, she dug her heels into her pony's sides and headed back toward the ravine, determined to get her father back to camp.

Gentle Fawn looked at the smiling white faces staring at her from the large gold locket in the palm of her hand. She curled her lip angrily. When her dying father had given her the useless legacy the day before, her first inclination had been to rip the hated pictures of the man and woman and curly-haired baby from the case and tear them to shreds. But the time hadn't been right. It would have been wrong to show her father how much she resented his last gift to her. But the time was right now. It was time to destroy the ugly reminders of the whites who had killed Hunting Bear and Tall Feathers.

Pulling out a knife to pry the likenesses from the case, she hesitated. Why had he done it? Why had her father bequeathed her the impersonal necklace? With his last breath, he'd given his other sons and daughters things that had been part of him: his shield, his knife, his bow, his war bundle, his buffalo robe, his special horses—all things that had been *his*, things that still breathed with his spirit. But all he had left Gentle Fawn was a necklace that had belonged to some unknown white woman—as if he'd only remembered his youngest daughter as an afterthought. *Plunder from some raid he went on years ago,* she thought bitterly. *He didn't even care enough for me to give me something of his own.*

Gentle Fawn inserted the point of her knife under the edge of the picture with the man and woman in it. She stopped again. The people in the photograph were dressed all in white—like she and Tall Feathers had been on their wedding day. Her heart lurched at the reminder of her dead husband, and she looked more closely at the laughing faces.

They both had dark hair, the woman's worn loose and wavy and topped with a jeweled comb holding a cascade of white lace that fell over her hair and shoulders. The man's was cut short with dark sideburns that reached well past his ear lobes, and there was even a thin line of black hair over his upper lip. The four black eyes in the picture seemed to be laughing at her, challenging her to . . . To what? To wonder who they were?

She snapped the locket shut on the happy faces, refusing to do their bidding. *I will keep them to remind me of the whites who murdered my father and husband,* she suddenly decided, not questioning her inability to destroy the picture. *Every time I feel my hatred begin to lessen, I will open this case and remember!*

Gentle Fawn slipped the gold chain over her head and dropped the locket inside her shirt. She stood up and looked around the deserted Indian camp. Everyone was gone. And it was time for her to be moving on, too. She had promised her mother she would catch up with them and had already stayed far too long. It was well past dark and she knew Quiet Rain would be worried. But she had needed this time alone with her dead loved ones before leaving them in the death lodges that had been hastily erected for the Indian victims of the battle on the ridge the day before.

The battle had lasted only an hour, and all the soldiers had been killed. It had been a great victory for the People, but their elation had been short-lived, for today, another army of soldiers had been spotted coming up the river from the north on foot, this one much larger than the one they had defeated the day before. The order had gone out to break camp, and by sunset the last loaded travois had left the great village as the fleeing Lakotas disappeared into the shelter of the mountains to the south.

Her pony heard the noise only an instant before Gentle Fawn did. His ears swiveling alertly, he turned his head toward the sound and sniffed the air nervously. But before he could answer the muffled whinny they'd both heard with one of his own, Gentle Fawn clamped his flared nostrils shut with two fingers to silence him. "Just a latecomer," she whispered soothingly to the fidgeting horse. "He must've gotten separated from the rest of the herd and left behind."

Even though she was convinced the words she spoke were the truth, Gentle Fawn cautiously led the animal deeper into the shadows of one of the death lodges where she silently waited for the lost pony to show itself. Then, when she had decided there was no other horse and had taken a step to leave, she heard it again. Only this time, the horse's whinny was accompanied by the sound of approaching footsteps. The horse was coming toward the place where she hid. Gentle Fawn froze in mid-step, again pinching her horse's nostrils shut as she did.

The footsteps grew louder as the intruder came closer to her hiding place. *The horse is alone. No human being would be so careless about the noise he's making*, she assured herself. Still . . .

Gentle Fawn dropped her own horse's reins to the ground, securing him to the spot as surely as if she had wrapped them around a tree. Taking her bow and quiver from her saddle, she moved away on moccasined feet as silent as those of a bobcat. Taking care to stay hidden in the shadows—just in case—she relocated in a new hiding place beside a deserted lodge.

The horse came into view and nickered softly. Gentle Fawn held her breath and waited for her own horse to answer. But the animal remained silent. The girl breathed a sigh of relief. Then she saw the embodiment of her worst fears. The fear she'd been unable to voice. And her heart raced alarmingly.

Oh, the intruder was a horse all right. But the horse was not alone. It was being led by a man! A tall, broad-shouldered man dressed in a white man's shirt and trousers and wearing a wide-brimmed hat.

Ignoring her shaking hands, the weak feeling in her legs that was turning them to jelly and the sound of her heart pounding with deafening insistence in her ears, Gentle Fawn snatched an arrow from her quiver and readied her bow. She directed her aim toward the white man and waited. *I'll let him get closer before I shoot*, she decided, realizing that once she fired the arrow she would lose the element of surprise and he would dive for cover. Her first arrow must be the last. It had to hit its mark. There was no room for error. If only her hands would stop shaking.

Slowly she drew back on the taut bow string, a bit more with each step the unsuspecting white man took. *Steady now*, she warned herself. *Do not rush. Wait until he is a little closer.*

At that moment, Gentle Fawn's horse decided to answer the stranger's horse. He let a long neighing call, to which the other horse responded with a jerk on his lead rope. The man paused and turned his head toward the sound. Another instant and he would go for cover. Gentle Fawn could hesitate no longer. She released her hold on the bull sinew bow string and let her arrow go.

Though high, her aim was true and the man's head was struck by the silent arrow. Gentle Fawn breathed a sigh of relief as his hat flew off and he fell to the ground on his face. His horse bolted and ran toward Gentle Fawn's waiting mount. But Gentle Fawn stayed where she was, another arrow in readiness in her bow. The man didn't move again.

Finally able to let out the breath she had unconsciously been holding, she stepped out of the shadows and walked toward the man on the ground. Though she was certain he was dead, she approached with caution, a second deadly arrow aimed at his back. Only when she was standing beside the motionless man and saw he still wasn't moving did she slowly release her grip on the bow string.

Dropping her bow to the ground, she removed a knife from her belt. With one knee in the center of the dead man's back, she grabbed a handful of his bloodied hair and pulled his face up out of the dirt to place the blade on his forehead at the hairline. *This is for Tall Feathers*, she swore silently, trying to muster the stomach to make the cut. *And for Hunting Bear!*

However, she hesitated too long, and the "dead man" beneath her suddenly began to rouse. It was then she realized her arrow must have only grazed his scalp. He wasn't dead. He'd only been knocked unconscious for a few minutes. Well, he'd be dead soon. This time she wouldn't miss.

Go on before he gains consciousness completely, she urged herself. Jerking the man's head back farther, she pressed her knife against the stretched skin at the top of his forehead. She hesitated again. Then the wounded man groaned—not a white man's groan, not a Lakota groan, but simply the groan of a human being in pain—and she knew she couldn't do it. Damning herself for a coward, she loosened her grip on the man's scalp, thinking to be gone before he regained total consciousness.

The first thing Clay Donovan was aware of as he returned to his senses was the throbbing pain in his head, especially the area a few inches above his left temple. It stung, as though he'd parted his hair with a butcher knife instead of a comb. He moaned softly and tried to touch a hand to his aching head. Then he noticed the gritty taste of dirt in his mouth, the tugging on his hair, the boring pressure of something in the middle of his back—and the feel of metal against his forehead. Clay came fully awake.

Suddenly, without warning, two strong bands of steel in the form of the man's hands wrapped tightly around Gentle Fawn's wrists, and she was thrown to her back in one efficient motion. Her eyes rounded with surprise, the feeling in her fingers was cut off immediately, and her hands opened of their own accord to release her grip on the knife and her victim's hair.

"Scalp me, will you?" the man straddling Gentle Fawn's chest breathed angrily. "How does it feel with the moccasin on the other foot?" he growled, snatching up the discarded knife and grabbing one of Gentle Fawn's braids. He put the knife to the base of the thick rope of hair as if to take it off at the scalp over her ear.

Stupid white. You cannot even take a scalp the right way, she said silently, staring up at the angry face that loomed over her. Her expression didn't flinch, though her thoughts were filled with self-accusation. *Neither could you,* a chiding inner voice reminded her. *You are the stupid one! You hesitated and let yourself think of a white as a human being. You do not deserve to call yourself a Lakota brave. You do not even have the right to count yourself as one of the People!*

"What the hell are you doing here anyway? I thought all the Indians had moved out by now. Are you alone? Who's with you?" Clay asked, ignoring the pounding ache in his head.

When he received no answer, he jerked the braid angrily, stretching the skin of Gentle Fawn's scalp so hard that her eyes watered, then narrowed stubbornly. Though her English was excellent and she understood every word he hissed at her, she gritted her teeth with determination and continued to pretend otherwise.

The hate shooting from the depths of his prisoner's black eyes was almost a tangible thing. Clay imagined he could actually feel it boring into his soul, and he fought a shiver of apprehension. It was as though the brave beneath him could read his mind and knew he had no desire to kill another man—Indian or otherwise.

"Answer me, damn it, or so help me I'll cut off this goddamned pigtail of yours and use it to strangle you," he threatened, certain the possible disgrace of losing a treasured braid would loosen the brave's tongue. Didn't they believe losing their hair was the same as losing their soul or some such thing?

Evidently not.

The Indian's expression didn't change.

Maybe he doesn't know English! Clay thought hopefully, exaggerating the sawing motions he was making with his knife at the base of the braid. Even if the Indian didn't understand the words, he couldn't miss Clay's intentions.

Could he?

This Indian obviously could. Either that or his hair wasn't all that important to him.

The Indian's features stayed the same.

Damn! It must be the Chinese who set such store on their pigtails!

Her hate-filled glare never wavering, Gentle Fawn studied the white man who seemed more interested in cutting her hair than in scalping her. He loomed above her, the full moon at his back shining through his hair to create a magical ring of gold around his face. He looked like a god. Was that why her arrow fired at such close range hadn't killed him? Was that why he had come back to life when she'd been so sure he was dead?

He is not a god! she told herself sternly, unable to forget the pleasant silky feel of the thick golden hair when she'd held it in her hands. It had been like no hair she'd ever felt. *Gods do not bleed,* she reminded herself suddenly, remembering the blood in the man's hair.

She forced her thoughts away from his hair. If he was going to kill her, why didn't he get it over with? And if he wasn't, what was he going to do? She wished she could see his face for some clue to what he was thinking.

However, as Gentle Fawn was considering her

41

immediate future, Clay was doing the same thing. Though the moon behind him hid the details of his features from her, it illuminated her face completely. And Clay was shocked by what he saw. He released his hold on her hair and sat back.

"You're just a kid!" he exclaimed in disgust. "Now what the hell am I going to do?" he muttered, standing up and roughly yanking Gentle Fawn to her feet. It was bad enough when he thought he had captured a full-grown Sioux brave—but a child! He couldn't kill a child! "How old are you, boy? Twelve? Thirteen?" he asked, certain the youngster didn't understand him, but asking his questions aloud anyway. "What are you doing here alone? Where's the rest of your tribe? Why'd they leave you behind?"

Gentle Fawn stared at Clay, her expression giving away nothing of what she was thinking. Out of the corner of her eye she saw her knife glitter on the ground where the white man had left it. In as long as it took Clay to blink his eye, she dove for the knife landing flat out on the ground. Stretching her reach to its limit, she let a small growl of satisfaction as she felt the knife under her hand. She wrapped her fingers around the handle with purposeful determination.

But Gentle Fawn's freedom was over before it began. No sooner had her hand clamped over the handle than she felt the full weight of the man on top of her. The air expelled from her lungs in a long whoosh as his hand curled over hers on the knife only an instant after she'd grabbed it.

"Look, kid," he grunted, twisting her wrist until she dropped the knife. "I don't want to kill you, but if you try anything that stupid again, I will. Now, are you going to be good?" he breathed into her ear, sending a disturbing shiver rippling along her flesh.

Gentle Fawn refused to recognize the odd feeling that tingled over her as fear. But if it wasn't fear, what was it? She just wouldn't allow herself to think about the other possibility. She grew very still. She had to get the man off her before her thoughts became any more insane.

Clay took her sudden acquiescence as understanding and said, "That's better," against her ear. His voice was gentle, as though he were soothing a wild horse. "I'm not going to hurt you if I don't have to."

Fresh chills skittered along Gentle Fawn's neck and arm, gathering momentum as they spread over her body to concentrate in the private spot between her thighs. Horrified by her body's reaction to the white man's hard frame pressing her into the ground, his warm breath on her skin, his masculine scent in her nostrils, she cursed herself anew. What decent Lakota woman would be feeling like this when her husband had been dead for only a day and night? And toward one of the whites responsible for his death?

But Gentle Fawn's body paid no heed to her self-chastisement. Desire surged in her womb, painful and throbbing. Nature had taken control of every part of her but her thoughts, and there was nothing she could do to stop what was happening.

Is this my punishment for hesitating when I had the chance to kill him? she wailed inwardly. *Is this what becomes of a woman who tries to be what she is not?* Tensing the muscles of her inner thighs and buttocks together in an effort to relieve the demands of her body, Gentle Fawn moved restlessly under her captor.

"What the hell?" Clay choked, throwing himself away

43

from her as though he'd been burned. "What do you think you're doing?" he yelled, still able to feel the warm imprint of the round buttocks pressing into his groin—shocked to find that the feeling wasn't at all unpleasant!

The instant the man's weight was removed from her slight body, reason returned to Gentle Fawn. Without hesitation, she leaped to her feet, intent on making a frantic dash for her horse. She was no longer only afraid for her life.

"Where do you think you're going?" she heard him growl at the same time a long arm snaked out and strong fingers wrapped around her ankle. "We had an agreement," he said with a grunt as she pitched forward onto the ground again. "But you didn't keep your end of the bargain," he grumbled, using a hand-over-hand motion along her leg to drag her back to him.

As he pulled Gentle Fawn toward him, Clay became aware of just how small his prisoner actually was. The boy weighed almost nothing, maybe a hundred pounds at the most. And though his baggy leggings made him look sturdy, Clay realized for the first time that the Indian's build was almost fragile.

In fact, now that he thought about it, he recalled the surge of surprise he'd felt when he'd been able to wrap his fingers entirely around the boy's thin ankle. And look how easily he'd taken the knife from the boy—twice. Then Clay thought about the leg he was touching. He squeezed the flesh just above the boy's knee. Though it was firm, it wasn't nearly as muscular as he would have expected a brave's leg to be—even a small brave like this one. *His leg feels more like it belongs to a girl,* Clay decided as his hand neared the top of the slender thigh.

Gentle Fawn lay very still, the tension in her body

building as she realized the next grip on her leg would put the white man's hand at the juncture of her thighs. Without being aware of it, she held her breath, awaiting the man's discovery that she was not a young boy as he had assumed. Surprisingly, the thought of the man touching her so intimately tightened the coiling spring in her womb even more.

But the anticipated next touch never came. And Gentle Fawn fought to convince herself she was relieved—not disappointed.

Clay sat up suddenly and flipped Gentle Fawn over onto her back. "Look, kid," he said, easily holding her slim wrists together above her head with one hand while he fumbled for his bandanna with the other. "I don't know what you're doing here— Damn!" He couldn't loosen the knot. *Some Indian fighter you are, Donovan! You can't even get the damned bandanna off your own neck to tie his hands!* Clay concentrated all his effort on untying the stubborn neckerchief. But it was no use. It was tied to stay.

"Damn! This has got to be the worst two days of my life!" he grumbled, more to himself than to his captive. His eyes raked over Gentle Fawn's still body with only casual interest. What the hell was he going to do with this kid? "All I wanted was a lousy interview with Crazy Horse, and I end up getting—"

Clay's mouth dropped open and his eyes widened in surprise. "What the hell?"

His gaze zeroed in on the narrow expanse of flesh at Gentle Fawn's waist where her shirt had hiked up when he'd dragged her over the ground.

No brave, young or old, ever curved in like that at the middle.

45

Clay's gaze shot up to his prisoner's face again, his questioning expression alarmed.

Just then the full moon appeared from behind a veil of clouds and illuminated Gentle Fawn's face. "I'll be damned!" How had he ever thought the perfectly shaped face with its large round eyes and full lips could belong to a boy?

Clay's eyes automatically moved to the girl's chest for verification of his shocking discovery. And there it was—just as he'd known it would be. There was the ultimate proof that dispelled his last remaining doubt.

Rising rapidly beneath the soft deerskin shirt, Gentle Fawn's small breasts felt as if they were swelling under the heat of the white man's gaze. Unaware what she was doing, she instinctively arched herself toward him.

"Oh, my God," Clay groaned, uncomfortably conscious that his body had recognized the woman's sex and was already responding to her unconscious action. As though he was being controlled by another power, he reached out and cupped his large hand over one firm mound. "Oh, my God," he said again as the girl's breast leaped to life at his touch, the nub of her nipple hardening and pushing against the palm of his hand.

Clay looked helplessly into the dark staring eyes again, as if to say, *I didn't mean for my hand to do that.* But what he saw confused him even more than his own actions. The inky pools of black he gazed into had taken on another dimension. The eyes that had seemed almost dead when he'd first looked into them had come alive with an element so vibrant, so potent, so compelling he was paralyzed, unable to escape. He was suspended in time. No longer the captor, he had become the captive.

The heat from the hand on her breast raged through

Gentle Fawn's body with fever force, rendering her weak and helpless. Yet she felt alive for the first time since Tall Feathers had died. It was as if the man's hand on her body was filling her with new life. She could feel his strength, his vitality flowing into her veins. And she welcomed it.

Maybe he was a god! After all, he'd brought himself back to life, hadn't he? And now her.

The anxiousness swelling in her abdomen reached unbearable proportions, and Gentle Fawn was lost beyond all reason. She was unable to hold a rational thought, but that didn't matter. She was feeling something she'd never known existed, and she eagerly gave herself over to her senses completely. The only thing that mattered now was that she was alive and could feel again.

Able to make out the man's features for the first time, Gentle Fawn's gaze was drawn to Clay's mouth. Slightly parted, his lips were firm and generous, turning up at the corners in a perpetual smile. Visually tracing the shape of his mouth with her gaze, she couldn't help wondering what it would feel like against her fingertips if she reached up and touched it. Her tongue flicked out to drag along her own lips in an effort to moisten their parched lushness. But it did no good. The fever of desire raging through her was too great.

"Oh, my God," Clay said for the third time when her pink tongue appeared with its innocent invitation. He released his hold on her wrists above her head and leaned over her, cupping her oval face in his palm. His other hand still on her breast, his lips came down to touch hers tentatively. "How could I have thought you were a brave?" he mumbled hoarsely, grazing his mouth across hers again and again.

Unmoving, Gentle Fawn watched with fascination as the man kissed her over and over. It was like nothing she had ever imagined in her wildest fantasies about what went on between men and women—this touching of lips. The spring inside her coiled tighter and she could no longer suppress the small animal moan that welled within.

Clay drew back to study her, his passion-glazed expression uncertain.

Though his mouth was only a few inches above hers, Gentle Fawn instantly felt a sense of unbearable loss. Desire and instinct were controlling her actions now. She lifted her head off the ground to bring her mouth up to his. When he didn't immediately meet her lips with his own, her hands came from over her head to burrow into the man's thick hair and pull him back to her.

No longer questioning the wisdom of taking what was being offered to him, Clay kissed the Indian girl again. Only this time he put all the passion he was feeling into the kiss. There would be no holding back. He would take this unexpected gift and think about the consequences later.

Chapter Three

Nothing in Gentle Fawn's eighteen-year existence had prepared her for the thunderbolt of electricity that crashed through her veins as Clay's mouth captured hers. No longer gentle and inquisitive, his kiss was now demanding, proprietary. His mouth rocked back and forth on her supple lips, the insistent tip of his tongue pressing along the seam that marked the entrance into her mouth.

Clay raised up to look into the wide black eyes. And when Gentle Fawn would have cried out her protest, he smiled. He knew kissing wasn't a common practice among Indians and was touched by the stunned curiosity he saw in the girl's eyes. "I can see your education's been sadly neglected," he said. "It's time you learned about the finer things in life, my little Sioux princess. That was a *kiss*. And it's even nicer if you close your eyes and open your mouth," he told her gently, certain she didn't understand what he was saying. To demonstrate his words, he used his thumbs to gently sweep the girl's heavily lashed lids downward. He kissed her closed eyes.

"Kiss," he said with each feathery contact.

"Kiss," she repeated, her eyes popping open again. She liked the sound of the word on her lips and repeated herself. "Kiss."

"Yes, kiss!" he exclaimed, not worrying that she was still watching him as he bent his head to claim her parted lips before she could close them on the word. He would worry about the eyes later.

The man's tongue penetrated the virgin cavern of her mouth, filling its warmth with the essence of this thing he called the *kiss*. Her eyelids fluttered shut against her will. She fought it. She wanted to see everything that was happening and forced them open. But he was right. Kissing was even nicer with her eyes closed and her mouth open. Without further resistance, she closed her eyes and allowed herself to be totally transported into the exotic and sensual world of the white man's *kiss*.

Gentle Fawn moved her hips restlessly and moaned. There seemed to be an invisible cord from the interior of her mouth to the coiling spring in her belly. It was as though each in-and-out thrust of his tongue nudged and tugged at that secret place in her lower body. Her knees bent of their own accord and raised up off the ground, falling gently apart. She tentatively touched his tongue with hers.

"So sweet," Clay murmured against her mouth, shaken by his own reaction to the simple motion. His lips traveled over her smooth cheek to her neck, leaving a burning trail of kisses in its wake. His hand on her breast began to move at last, sliding toward her waist.

Gentle Fawn groaned and arched herself upward, turning her head toward Clay, her mouth seeking his. Though his lips on her neck were sending exquisite chills rippling throughout her body, she couldn't imagine anything more wonderful than his mouth on hers, his tongue touching hers. And she hadn't had enough—not nearly enough. "Kiss," she begged as a person dying of thirst would beg for water.

"How can anything be so sweet?" Clay moaned, returning to Gentle Fawn's inviting mouth.

"Mmm," she sighed contentedly against his mouth as she opened her own to him.

Clay stretched his lithe body over Gentle Fawn, cradling his hips naturally between her thighs. She moved against him with the spontaneous rhythm that matched the pounding in his veins. And he was catapulted beyond the point of stopping.

Acting now on pure instinct, Clay rolled off the slight girl and pulled clumsily at the rawhide belt that tied her leggings at her waist.

Consumed by a matching need to remove all the barriers separating them as quickly as possible, Gentle Fawn reached down and released the tie.

Handling her as gently as his own passion would allow, Clay slipped the deerskin leggings down her slim hips, exposing the dark delta of her womanhood to his anxious gaze. Unable to hold back, he sighed his relief. "So sweet, so delicate," he chanted, his fingers testing the exquisite treasure he'd discovered beneath the deerskin trousers. She was so moist, so ready for him.

How could he wait another minute? He was ready to burst now! Still, he had to see all of her, needed to feast his eyes on all of her dainty body, naked and writhing beneath him. He had to wait. He would wait—at least until he could get her shirt off.

Pulling Gentle Fawn to a sitting position, Clay

snatched the shirt over her head. But he was surprised when she self-consciously crossed her arms over her breasts and looked away from him. Puzzled by her sudden modesty, he gently removed her arms to see what she was hiding. "What is it, little princess?"

Gentle Fawn had always been embarrassed by her small breasts. She'd been certain no man would find them attractive, was afraid no babe would find nourishment in them. Ashamed, she turned her head to the side. She had wanted to be beautiful for this golden-haired god-man who had brought her back to life again. But now he would think she was ugly, unworthy of his golden perfection. She couldn't look at him.

"Why don't you want me to see your breasts?" Clay asked, his voice hoarse with wonder at the lovely sight before him. He cupped a petite round breast gently in each of his hands. "You're beautiful. All of you. The most beautiful thing I've ever seen. Beautiful and perfect." Clay roughed his thumbs over the dusky nipples. The swelling in his groin tensed as, hypnotized, he watched the tiny buds respond to his touch. "Look how they fit in my hands—as if they were created for my hands alone. See how they react to my touch."

Gentle Fawn didn't believe what she heard. There was no hint of disgust in his voice. She chanced a shy glance at the golden-haired man. She was stunned by what she saw. The look on his face was enraptured. Not repulsed, but enraptured.

She watched with stunned fascination as he leaned forward to kiss a breast. Then, when his lips actually touched the tender flesh, every thought of modesty or inferiority was driven from her mind. "Ooh," she groaned helplessly, clutching his golden head to her as the sensual agony of his gentle mouthing left her with only one thought.

Because her body told her it was the prelude to the ultimate release, she didn't protest when Clay left her again to remove his own clothing. But nothing instinct had revealed to her had readied her for the glorious sight of the beautiful god-man when he at last freed himself of the hindering *wasicun* clothing.

His strong, athletic-looking body was covered with a dusting of golden hair—arms, legs, chest—and Gentle Fawn gasped at the enchanting sight. Never had she seen a man with so much hair on his body. Indeed the Indian men had almost no body hair. Glistening magically in the moonlight, it was mesmerizing. And she ached to touch it. She longed to feel the soft fur that sparkled over the broad expanse of his sinewy chest against the palms of her hands. She hungered to run her fingertips along the narrow line of hair that trailed down the length of his slim middle to the triangle of blond curls at the seat of his manhood.

Gentle Fawn reached out to Clay, the invitation in her eyes a plea.

Clay lowered himself over the waiting young woman with an "Aaah," as he allowed himself to luxuriate in the feel of her satiny flesh against his hair-roughened body. "Kiss," he said, bringing his mouth down to claim hers one last time before his body made its ultimate demand of possession.

Moving his lower body against her, he nestled himself between her open thighs, his throbbing maleness pressing and hot against her belly. Caressing his hands along the length of her, Clay lifted his hips slightly and positioned himself as he wrapped her legs around his

53

waist. Then, unable to suffer another instant of unbearable delay, he took the plunge into the heavenly depths.

Gentle Fawn's eyes flew open in surprise. She wrapped her arms around Clay's chest and squeezed hard. She didn't know what she had expected when she became a woman. Pain? Yes, there had been a bit of pain, but nothing compared to the ache that had throbbed in her body until now. But this was glorious beyond pain, beyond anticipation. It was so . . . so . . . complete.

"Are you all right?" he asked her, looking into her black eyes, the pain in his own eyes relieving any she was feeling.

Oh, yes, she was all right. For the first time in her life, the lonely feeling of not really belonging anywhere was gone. At last she belonged somewhere. She belonged with this golden god-man who had made her a woman. "Kiss," she whispered, lifting her head from the ground, straining toward him.

"Oh, yes! Kiss!" he agreed against her mouth, the relief in his voice choking as he began to move within the snug, caressing curve of her body. "All the kisses you can ever want, little Indian princess," he said, claiming her mouth completely.

Clay's tongue in Gentle Fawn's mouth imitated his body's motion as he gently moved in and out of her. It took all the energy he could muster to hold back his own final release, but he was determined to do so until the petite girl beneath him was ready to make the climb and fall to ecstasy with him.

Then, without warning, it was time and there could be no more holding back.

Gentle Fawn suddenly jerked her mouth away from

his. She couldn't breathe, was certain her heart would pound its way out of her chest. The spring that had coiled within her body since the first moment the man had touched her was stretched to the limit. It would snap any minute. Panting raggedly, she rolled her head from side to side.

His pace increased, reaching frantic speed.

Certain she was dying and being taken to live with the spirits in the land of her ancestors, she cried out and clamped her arms and legs tight around the god-man who was taking her there.

"Oh, yes," he groaned, the grimace of a smile on his face. "Come soar with me," he said roughly, emptying his passion into her warmth at the exact moment the spring in Gentle Fawn exploded into a million tiny pieces of light to be scattered in the four directions of the universe.

Long moments later when the only sounds that disturbed the night were the shuffling of horses' hooves, the singing of crickets, and the rustle of the summer breeze, Clay raised up on his elbows and looked down at the beautiful girl who stared at him with wonder in her dark, penetrating eyes. His breathing still labored, he asked, "Did I hurt you? I didn't know you were a virgin." Then, when she didn't answer, he said, "I wish you could understand me. I wish I could tell you how sweet and lovely you are."

"*Wakan wicasa*," Gentle Fawn said softly, reaching up to hold Clay's face between her small hands, the awe in her voice apparent. She liked the feel of the bristly beard stubble that pricked her palms and rubbed her hands back and forth over his face.

Clay reached up and wiped a hand over his chin. "Does

that mean 'you need a shave'?" he chuckled. "Did it burn your face too much?" he asked, tenderly running his fingers over her cheeks. "I'm sorry."

Gentle Fawn's dark brows drew together in a frown. She wished he would stop speaking to her in the white man's language, the language of the people who had killed her father and Tall Feathers. Her expression thoughtful, she removed her hands from Clay's face and studied it. A disturbing thought suddenly occurred to her. A real god would understand and speak to her in the language of the *ikce wicasa*—the People. He wouldn't use the language of the hated *wasicun!*

Gentle Fawn pointed at Clay and said it again. "*Wakan wicasa?*"

Though he didn't know what she was saying, the test in her tone was obvious, and Clay sensed how important his reaction was. He thought for a minute, nervously aware of the way the girl studied him. "Seems like I remember *wakan* means god," he said slowly. "Yeah, that's it. *Wakan* means god. *Wakan Tanka* is the name of your Great Spirit," he told her excitedly. Gentle Fawn's expression didn't change. "Now for *wicasa.* Hmmm. Man?" he asked hesitantly. "Does *wicasa* mean man? Is that it?"

"*Wakan wicasa!*" Gentle Fawn insisted one last time, refusing to believe the sickening truth. She had actually allowed the full moon and her imagination to convince her that this *wasicun* was a god! A white man! Her stomach roiled. She was going to be sick.

"No, no," Clay denied vehemently, amused that anyone could have thought Clay Donovan, a street-wise Irish kid from New York City could be any kind of god—a devil yes, but a god? Definitely something to write about.

"No *wakan wicasa*, little princess," he chuckled, shaking his head vigorously. "No god-man. Just a man. A very human man who just had the most wonderful experi— Oof!"

Gentle Fawn's balled fists hit the man in his relaxed belly with all the fury she felt. A *wasicun!* He was just an ordinary man! Not a god. Just a man. And she had given herself to him!

Able to roll the man off her with the unexpected blows, she scrambled to her feet, grabbing her deerskin shirt and leggings as she ran for her horse.

"Hey," Clay called after Gentle Fawn, leaping to his feet and running after her, his gait a clumsy hop as he tried to step back into his pants as he followed her. "What'd I say? I didn't mean to laugh! Come back here."

Humiliated beyond endurance, Gentle Fawn reached her pony's side before she realized she was still naked. Rational enough to know she couldn't ride into the night with no clothing on, she quickly dressed herself.

Just as she took a step to leap onto her horse's back, two large hands suddenly appeared, one on her arm and one on the pony's reins.

"What the hell happened?"

"*Wasicun!*" she spat, glaring at him as she kicked out with a small foot. She missed.

Clay could almost feel the hot sparks of hatred fired from her eyes as they pinged over his bare chest, and his own anger exploded. "Is that what this is all about?" he said, the disbelief evident in his tone. "You just noticed I was white? Tell me, when did you first begin to suspect I wasn't an Indian?"

Gentle Fawn silently stared straight ahead, trying to ignore his words. He'd fooled her. He'd made her think he was a god. He'd taken advantage of her. And she swore anew to kill him for what he'd done.

"Was it when you were begging me to kiss you?" he muttered bitterly as he dragged her back to where the rest of his clothing was. "Or was it when you wrapped your legs around me so tight I couldn't have gotten away if I'd wanted to? Or—I know! It was when you moved under me like a wild tigress while I was inside you, wasn't it?" He shoved her to the ground and picked up his shirt. "That's it," he went on grumbling. "I should have realized all those moans and cries and little kitteny sounds you made were sounds of protest."

Gentle Fawn eyed her knife that still lay where they had left it after their earlier scuffle. She looked at Clay to judge her chances of getting to it before he could stop her.

"Don't even think about it," he said, his voice gravelly. "I'm not in the mood for another wrestling match with a little spitfire Indian squaw. In fact, I've had about all of this I can take. If you so much as blink an eye some way I don't like, I'm going to use that knife on you!"

Gentle Fawn studied the white man, still pretending she didn't understand him. But she did, and she wasn't so sure he didn't mean what he was saying.

"Now," he said, putting his hat back on his head and her knife in his belt. He stood over her, his feet apart. From where she sat on the ground, he looked like a giant. "I want to talk to Crazy Horse, and you're going to take me to him."

He noticed a flicker of surprised recognition that crossed Gentle Fawn's face at the mention of Crazy Horse's name. Then it was gone, replaced with the same

58

angry, hate-saturated expression he'd come to expect from her. He had probably imagined it. This wasn't going to be easy. Clay took a deep breath and started over again.

"You," he said, pointing at Gentle Fawn with his index finger. "Me." He tapped his own chest with his thumb. "Go," he said, pressing his open palms together and pointing toward the south with his fingertips. "See." Clay shaded his eyes with his hand and squinted like he was looking into the distance. "Crazy Horse." Oh oh. How could he sign Crazy Horse? "Crazy," he finally said, circling an index finger at his own ear and hoping it would get his meaning across. "Horse," he added quickly, making an upside-down vee with the index and middle fingers of one hand and "mounting" them like a rider on a horse on the inside edge of his other hand. "You—me—go—see—Crazy—Horse," he repeated a second time, his signs and words coming a little more quickly.

"Why do you want to see Crazy Horse?" Gentle Fawn asked, her curiosity making her forget her vow of silence for a moment. The second the words were out of her mouth she cursed herself.

"Because I want to write an article abou— You speak English!" Clay felt like three kinds of fool. Here he'd been doing everything but standing on his head to make the girl understand him, and she'd known what he was saying all along. He yanked her to her feet and glared down into her face, his angry grip digging into her upper arms. "Why didn't you say something?"

"Because the language of the *wasicun* fills my mouth with the taste of dung," she hissed spitefully. To demonstrate her point, she turned her head to the side and spit on the ground—not quite brave enough to direct

59

her spittle where she really wanted it to go.

He hauled her to him roughly, lifting her so that she stood on her tiptoes as he flattened her breasts against the hard wall of his chest. "And the *kiss* of the *wasicun?*" he asked, his face only inches from hers, his eyes focused on her lips. "What taste does the white man's kiss leave in your mouth?"

"The taste of dung and vomit," she answered viciously, ignoring the way the muscles of her throat tried to constrict on the blatant lie.

The cruel words hurt more than he had expected, igniting his anger even more. "You're a real little charmer, aren't you?" he came back, lifting her off the ground and bringing her face to the same level as his, his mouth a fraction of an inch from hers. "And you're a liar, aren't you?"

The instant his breath drifted over her face, Gentle Fawn felt the familiar tightening in her loins. *No, no, no. I cannot allow this to happen again!* Clenching her fists, she gritted her teeth to keep from responding to him. But she could still see him and her body cried out for her to close the small gap that separated their mouths. She closed her eyes in a last-ditch effort to block out her tormentor's face. But it was no use. She could still smell the intoxicating scent of him, could still feel the heat of his body coursing through her own.

When she would have given up her fight and leaned toward him—would have admitted she'd lied for just one more kiss—he spoke. And his voice, hard and cold, violently jerked her out of the trancelike moment of weakness and brought her emotions crashing back to reality.

"Now we both know, don't we?" he said, the

expression of vindictive satisfaction on his face telling her he knew how close she'd been to giving in to his magnetism again. He released his hold on her and let her drop, unconcerned when she staggered backward.

"Let's go," he ordered, giving her a push ahead of him just as she had gained her balance. "Take me to see Crazy Horse."

"I will not lead you to Crazy Horse," she choked, suddenly afraid the tears that had been threatening since Tall Feathers had been mortally wounded were about to be shed. And not only would she rather die than have the horrible white man see her cry, but she was afraid that if she ever started she'd never be able to stop. How could she ever have thought he was a god? How could she have betrayed her husband's memory by giving herself to a *wasicun?*

"We'll just see about that," he said, giving her another prod toward the horses.

"You may as well go on and kill me. I am not taking you to Crazy Horse."

"Then I'll turn you over to those—what is it you call them—bluecoats, is it? There are still quite a few of them holed up in the rocks on the other side of the river. We can just sit down here and wait for them. Once they realize the Indians are all gone, it's only a matter of time before they feel safe enough to come out. Then, just as sure as you please, they'll be swarming all over this deserted camp looking for souvenirs. I give them another two hours—tops. Would you like to be one of their souvenirs, princess? Of course, after what's gone on here the past two days, I don't think they'll be too nice to any Indian they meet. What do you think?"

Gentle Fawn looked toward the upriver end of the

camp. She had forgotten about those soldiers. Though the whites on the ridge had all been killed, there were still survivors from the first attack on the Hunkpapas. The Lakotas had kept them trapped on the other side of the river all day and night after the battle on the ridge. But now that the People had pulled out, there was nothing keeping the soldiers out of the camp. The white man spoke the truth. They would be here soon—no later than sunrise she was certain.

"Well?" They were at the horses now. He took her rifle and put it on his own saddle before checking her saddle for any other weapons. "Which is it going to be? Crazy Horse and me or what's left of the 7th Cavalry?"

Gentle Fawn looked toward the river, weighing her chances. Tiny lights glowed red and gold on the other side, reminding her the soldiers were already feeling confident enough to light a few cookfires. As the white man said, it was just a matter of time.

Still, he must be exhausted. If she chose to wait for the soldiers, her lone captor might fall asleep and she could steal away before the bluecoats came.

On the other hand, if he didn't fall asleep, or if the soldiers came sooner than he expected . . .

Almost as if on cue, Gentle Fawn heard the unmistakable sound of horses' hooves and men's voices. English-speaking men's voices! Her head jerked to the side to look at Clay. He'd heard it, too, and was smiling an infuriating I-told-you-so smile she would have loved to slap off his face.

"You'd better make up your mind pretty quick, spitfire!" He laughed, the confidence that he knew what her choice would be oozing from his wide devilish grin.

Oh, how she'd like to see him dead. And she swore she

would. He wouldn't last a day in the camp of the People. Once they saw his white man's clothing and golden hair, he would be dead—and the next time she went to take his scalp, she wouldn't hesitate. "I will show you the way to the camp of Crazy Horse," she said hoarsely.

"Somehow, I thought you'd say that," Clay laughed, too pleased with himself to notice the threatening undertone to her words. Holding the reins to both horses, he lifted her, none too gently, to the Indian pony's back, then leaped into his own saddle and led the way out of the camp.

"Let's make tracks, little spitfire princess." He laughed when they had finally cleared the massive Indian camp and felt safe to let the horses run. "I've got the biggest story of my career waiting for me up ahead."

The story of how you died in the camp of Crazy Horse! Gentle Fawn swore, the expression on her face blank. The only thing that might have given away her inner thoughts was the light that glistened in her black eyes. But the white man didn't see that. He was too caught up in his own success.

Well, let him think he'd been successful. It wouldn't last long!

Chapter Four

It was late afternoon when Clay and Gentle Fawn spotted the lances of the retreating Indian camp's rear guard disappearing over the next hill. Clay reined in his horse and sat back in the saddle. "So, we're almost there," he said, cupping his hand behind his neck and rotating his head wearily. He'd never imagined such a large number of people and horses could cover so much ground in so little time. The Indians had obviously ridden non-stop through the previous night, as well as the day, and they were still going strong. The fear that they would be able to do the same thing a second night nagged at Clay as he marveled at how the scrawny Indian ponies seemed to be tireless.

Clay and the girl had ridden hard all day to catch up with the fast-moving Indians, and he was aching for a rest and something to eat. But he didn't dare stop if the Indians weren't going to. "What do you think? Will they stop for the night, or will they keep on going?"

Gentle Fawn continued to stare after the Indians, her lips compressed into a thin, stubborn line. She'd managed to keep silent all day long, knowing once they caught up with the fleeing village she would have her revenge against the man who rode beside her.

Shrugging his shoulders indifferently, Clay nudged his horse forward, knowing hers would follow. "Have it your way," he said, the irritation in his tone undisguised.

Clay and Gentle Fawn rode on in silence, the man weary and angry, his patience stretched to the limit, the woman exhilarated with the anticipation of revenge.

Then without warning, they were surrounded by fifty Sioux warriors. Clay's heart vaulted into his throat as he reined his horse to an abrupt halt. "Holy sh— Where the hell'd they come from?"

"They've been with us for several miles," Gentle Fawn answered, not bothering to disguise the vindictive smile of satisfaction that spread across her face.

"Why didn't you tell me?" he asked, his eyes wide with unmitigated alarm as the circle of grim-faced warriors closed in on them. "No need to answer that question," he muttered, twisting around in his saddle to confirm there was no avenue of escape open to him. "I should have listened to my father. He always told me no good would come from being a writer," he grumbled under his breath.

Clay glanced nervously from side to side, expecting any minute to hear the girl's voice rise in his defense. She was just keeping mum to be spiteful, he assured himself. She wouldn't really let them kill him.

Gentle Fawn remained silent, the expression on her face telling him he was in a lot of very serious trouble!

"Say something, damn it! Tell them I've come as a friend!"

Gentle Fawn directed a deliberate now-you'll-be-sorry

smile toward Clay. She'd known all along he was riding to his death. And now he knew it, too!

Unfortunately, watching the realization of his fate dawn in his thick-fringed blue eyes, even as his hope faded proportionately, Gentle Fawn felt none of the satisfaction she'd expected to feel. In fact, an unwanted pang of guilt and second thoughts rushed heedlessly through her consciousness when she looked into the eyes of the man she had planned to see dead before the day was out. And her emotions were set in a turmoil again.

Oh, she didn't feel bad because his eyes were wide with fear. *He deserves to be afraid after what he did to me,* she told herself with conviction. *But does he deserve to die for it?* a tiny unbidden voice asked from within. A voice that would not be ignored. *He didn't kill you when he had the chance,* the voice reminded her.

But it wasn't just the fear in his expression that tugged at Gentle Fawn's emotions. It was hurt! The white man was actually hurt, she realized, unable to believe he had the audacity to look as though she had betrayed him! "What did you expect?" she said defensively, fighting the self-accusing thoughts plaguing her. "It is nothing more than you deserve!"

"Look, God damn it! It's not like I raped you. You were more than willing. And you know it! Now tell them I'm a friend!"

It was in that instant Gentle Fawn knew she couldn't say the words that would be responsible for the *wasicun*'s death. As much as she hated to admit it, he was right. What had happened between them had been as much her doing as his. And suddenly, the thought of his beautiful gold hair on a warrior's lance was physically painful to her.

The warriors continued to move closer, their arrows and rifles aimed menacingly toward the white man. She had to make a decision—and fast.

Gentle Fawn raised her hand in a sign of peace and spoke in the language of the Lakotas. When she was through speaking, there was a united grunt of understanding from the warriors. They eased their hold on their bowstrings, but still kept their arrows trained on Clay. One came forward to disarm him and return Gentle Fawn's weapons to her, then they opened their circle to make a path for the two riders to move on, their ranks closing behind Gentle Fawn and Clay like water behind a finger trailed in a still pond.

"What did you tell them?" Clay whispered out of the corner of his mouth.

"I told them I claimed you as my prisoner and I wanted your death to be long and torturous, not quick!"

"You what?" he shouted. Hearing his own voice echoing loudly in his ears, Clay cast an anxious glance over his shoulder at the warriors, who straightened in their saddles at the tone of his voice. "Why in God's name did you do that?" he said, taking deliberate care to control his volume as he reached out and put a restraining hand on Gentle Fawn's arm.

Two warriors were immediately beside him, the scowling expressions on their faces ominous. Clay shot them a sick, hand-caught-in-the-cookie-jar grin and brought his hand back to his own saddle. The two Indians fell back into line. "Why?" he asked again, this time keeping his hands to himself.

"You should be grateful. I just saved your life, *wasicun*," Gentle Fawn said spitefully. She couldn't decide if she was more angry with him for not

68

appreciating what she'd done for him or with herself for doing it.

"Why couldn't you just tell them I was friendly?"

"The People trust no white man these days. They would have killed you on the spot. But it would be bad manners for them to take another warrior's prisoner from him—or her—so they let us proceed."

"Hmph," Clay grunted, tossing Gentle Fawn a suspicious sideways glance, unable to believe she was telling the truth. "I guess I have no choice but to trust you."

"That is right."

"Will you answer one question for me?" Clay asked, not wanting their conversation to end. Perhaps it would keep his mind off the trail of Indians behind him—every one of them patiently waiting for the chance to put an arrow into his back—or worse—if he even sneezed in the wrong direction.

Gentle Fawn studied him for a minute, then nodded her head and looked forward again. "One question."

"How'd you learn to speak English so well?"

"When we lived on the reservation, I went to the Indian school. White teachers taught me."

"Why did your people leave the reservation?"

"You said one question, *wasicun*, but I will answer your second anyway. We had no choice. The People on the reservation were starving. The buffalo are all gone from that barren land, and the food the government sent was bad. There was never enough meat and flour to feed our numbers. And what little we got was rotten when they gave it to us. Man of the People, our chief, tried to keep the peace by living on the reservation. But when his people began to weaken and die from lack of food and the dysentery they got from eating bad meat, we left. We came back to the hunting grounds of our ancestors to survive."

Clay had heard things were bad on the Indian reservations: graft, Indian agents robbing the very ones they were supposed to be protecting, food too rancid or wormy to be edible, promised blankets and clothing never reaching those they were intended for, Indians being charged for food and supplies that was already theirs by law. But hearing about it from someone who'd been there made it more real. He decided right then that if he got out of this mess, his next story just might be an exposé of the conditions on the reservations. His readers in the East would love it. And who knows, it might even do some good. If the public became aware of what was going on, things might be made better for the Indians.

"I will ask you a question," Gentle Fawn said, still puzzled by the white man.

"Shoot!" he came back, thought better about his choice of words, and grinned sheepishly. "Ask away," he corrected.

"Why do you want to talk to Crazy Horse?"

"I'm a writer, and there are many people all over the country who read the words I write about the West. I want to write about him."

"He hates the whites. He will not want them to read about him."

"That may be true, but I believe Crazy Horse is not only a great warrior, but also a wise man. I want to write the story of what happened at the Little Bighorn from his point of view. I think he is intelligent enough to see how that could benefit the Sioux people."

"Lakota," Gentle Fawn corrected.

"Huh?"

"You called us 'Sioux.' Sioux is a *wasicun* word. We are the Lakota."

"That's exactly the kind of thing I'm talking about!" Clay said excitedly, able to forget the army of warriors behind him for a moment. "There are many misconceptions about the Indians, especially the Lakotas, and I want to give Crazy Horse a chance to tell his side of things!"

"What are misconceptions?"

"Lies—wrong ideas," Clay said, reminding himself to be more cautious with his vocabulary. It wouldn't do to insult her—not when he'd finally gotten her attention again.

"Lies," she repeated, nodding her head thoughtfully. She certainly understood that word in connection with the whites.

"May I ask one more question?"

"What is it?"

"What do I call you? I mean, if I'm your prisoner, I should at least know what your name is, shouldn't I?" He tossed her a boyish grin which Gentle Fawn found irritatingly appealing. She bit the inside of her lip to keep from returning the smile.

"I am called Gentle Fawn," she answered curtly, finding it increasingly annoying and frustrating that she was having such a difficult time hating this man. She never should have let herself get trapped into exchanging words with him. The less she knew about him, the easier it would be to think of him as the enemy. But even as she coached herself on what she should do and say, she voiced the question uppermost in her mind. "What do they call you?"

"My name is Clay Donovan."

Gentle Fawn looked at Clay and frowned. "I know the word Clay. It means earth, does it not? But this word Donovan is strange to me. What does it mean?"

"What does it me— Oh, I see." Clay laughed. "It's just my name. White people's names don't necessarily mean anything like Indian names do. Children are given the same last names as their fathers when they're born. Then the sons pass their fathers' names on to their own sons and daughters." When Gentle Fawn didn't respond, Clay assumed by the puzzled expression on her lovely face that she still didn't understand. So he went on. "For instance, my father is named Patrick Donovan, and his father is named Sean Donovan, and his father was a Donovan, too. And so on through the years."

"And your sons and daughters are also called Donovan?" Gentle Fawn interrupted, not questioning why she was curious about the white man's children.

"Yes— That is, they would be if I had any," he answered quickly, studying her inquisitive face and marveling at the many facets of the enigmatic Lakota girl he'd already seen, wondering how many more there were.

Clay reached up and thoughtfully ran his finger over the line of dried blood that parted his hair. He couldn't help smiling as he thought of Gentle Fawn, the petite boy/girl warrior who had shot him and tried to take his scalp. He'd been lucky in more ways than one, he realized. Oh, yes, he'd been lucky, he remembered, reliving the magical moments he'd spent with Gentle Fawn, the sensuous lover of the night before. Then there had been Gentle Fawn, the hellion who had said his kisses tasted like dung before threatening to cut his heart out. He winced. Her words still hurt the part of him that prided itself on being an excellent lover. Well, he wouldn't dwell on that, he decided.

Instead, he would think about the stoic, silent Gentle Fawn who had ridden beside him all day. Or the quick-thinking Gentle Fawn who—if what she said was true—had managed to keep the warriors from killing him on the spot. Now he was seeing another fascinating side to her nature in this intelligent, English-speaking Gentle Fawn who was carrying on a conversation with him. Would it ever be possible for a man to really know such a woman? He'd like to try, he told himself absently.

Recoiling at the turn his thinking had taken, Clay forced his thoughts back to the casual conversation. "I have no children," he said again.

"Oh?" Gentle Fawn said, looking at him curiously. He'd been quiet for so long she'd thought their talk was ended. She had been surprised to realize she felt strangely empty without his voice to warm the approaching night air. And she was even more amazed by the relief she felt when he spoke again.

"Is your wife barren?" she asked bluntly, trying to ignore the pleasant flush that warmed her features. "It is too bad white men do not have more than one wife," she went on quickly. "If the first wife is barren, he can still have children by his other wives. My father had three wives and many child—"

"I don't have a wife," Clay interrupted quietly.

Gentle Fawn felt the ripple of excitement swelling in her heart leap erratically. She tried to ignore it, reminding herself he was a *wasicun* and they were all liars. Besides, what did it matter if he had no wife? It made no difference to her, she insisted inwardly as she studied Clay's open, honest face. "No wife?" she said, unable to stop herself.

"No wife," he repeated.

Startled by the flagrant joy his words sent storming through her veins, Gentle Fawn lashed out. "Good! That means there will be no wife to mourn your death when you die in the camp of the People!"

Clay's eyes widened in surprise, then narrowed angrily. "What the hell did you expect, Donovan?" he grumbled.

"Yes," Gentle Fawn came back, managing to look her prisoner in the eye, despite the confusing sense of loss she felt at the thought of his death. "What *did* you expect, Clay Donovan?"

"Nothing," he shot back. "Not a damned thing— except maybe a little bit of human decency."

"Do not speak to me of human decency, *wasicun!* No white man knows the meaning of the words!" she hissed, kicking her pony so it pulled ahead. Clay had no choice but to follow behind.

During the last minutes of twilight, just as total night descended on them, Gentle Fawn and Clay rode into the camp of the Oglala Lakota Indians. At first, no one noticed the white man riding at the point of the army of warriors. The weary people were too busy settling themselves for the night. They were obviously intending to move on as soon as the livestock could be rested and fed because there were no tepees being put up. And only a few scattered cookfires could be seen as the people bedded down on the ground, many passing up eating altogether for a few extra minutes of sleep.

"*Wasicun!*" a woman's voice suddenly cried out, and

74

Clay's heart dropped to the pit of his stomach. He had begun to hope he would be able to go unnoticed until Gentle Fawn could take him to Crazy Horse.

No such luck! he realized, helplessly surveying the area as the resting camp leaped to life like a disturbed hill of teeming ants.

Within half a minute of the time his presence had been announced, Clay found himself surrounded by a swarm of angry Oglala women. Their faces distorted with hatred, they screeched curses demanding vengeance as they pinched viciously at his legs. One even slashed a knife at him, narrowing missing his thigh when another woman accidentally bumped her arm in an effort to get her own piece of flesh from the white man.

"I'm a friend!" Clay protested loudly, his panicked gaze seeking out Gentle Fawn. But she had disappeared. She had actually left him to die at the mercy of the vicious mob of women! Clay couldn't believe it. Until that very instant, he had been sure she wouldn't *really* let any harm come to him.

Realizing how badly he'd misjudged her, he cursed himself for a demented fool as he made another effort to stop the enraged women. "Friend!" he shouted again, making an unsuccessful attempt to form the hand signal for friend in between swats at the clawing hands that tore at his clothing.

When Clay realized the knife-wielding woman was coming at him again, it was too late for words, too late to maneuver himself to avoid her attack. The woman's blade sank into the flesh just beside his knee. Stinging pain seared up his leg, deafening him to the shrill tremolo of victory the woman sang out. He didn't even hear the rifle shot that rang over the noise. But the attacking women heard it, and at the sound of gunfire, they froze in their grotesque attack positions.

Clay's head began to swim and his vision blurred. He stared at the women, feebly trying to understand what had stopped them. But he couldn't concentrate. He'd been in the saddle too long, had been without food or sleep too long to think clearly. In fact, he could hardly focus his eyes on the horse and rider that rode toward him through the sea of women.

The area around his mouth turned white with the effort to keep from crying out. His grip on the saddle horn tightened anxiously as he pressed his other hand to the wound on his leg and tried to stop the piercing pain. But it was no use. He shook his head hopelessly.

Gentle Fawn urged her horse through the crowd toward the wounded white man, her heart beating wildly with alarm. Why hadn't she thought about how the women would react to seeing Clay Donovan in their midst? This was her fault. She had let her decision to give him a good scare go too far. Now it might be too late to save him!

Brandishing her smoking rifle where all could see it, Gentle Fawn shouted to the women in their language. "Go back to your families," she ordered, doing her best to control the shaking in her voice. "This *wasicun* is my prisoner," she announced sternly. She prayed no one would call her bluff. But what if they did? Could she really shoot one of the People in defense of a white man? "Go on," she shouted angrily, waving the rifle over the women and hoping she wouldn't be tested. "The *wasicun* is mine!"

The murmuring women looked from one to the other, their expressions changing from, *Why should we listen to*

76

her? to *What difference does it make to us?* When the disgruntled women finally dispersed, Gentle Fawn allowed herself the first easy breath she'd taken in the minutes that had seemed like hours since Clay Donovan had been spotted. Then she looked back at Clay, and anxiety leaped in her chest again.

It was obvious he was dizzy and could fall from the saddle any minute. It was all Gentle Fawn could do to keep from rushing to his side. But she couldn't show him any public compassion—not if she expected to protect him. So, instead of hurrying to his side, she straightened in her saddle and watched the blood seep from between Clay's fingers where he gripped his wounded leg.

Overwhelmed with the feeling she was seeing her own blood dripping onto the ground, her heart pounded with fright when she saw Clay wobble precariously, his eyes rolling and looking unfocused, as though he were losing consciousness.

There must have been something on her blade, Gentle Fawn realized with alarm, no longer worrying about who was watching her. She had to get him where she could take care of him before whatever was on the woman's knife blade could work its way into his whole system. "Let it bleed!" she hissed anxiously, knocking his hand away from the wound as she jerked on Clay's horse's reins and hurried her prisoner away from the crowd.

Clay cursed drunkenly, stubbornly clamping his hand over his leg again, almost falling off the horse as he did. "Aren't you satisfied?" he accused. "Or won't you be happy until I bleed to death?"

"You are not going to bleed to death, Clay Donovan, but you had better let that cut bleed if you want to get the poison out of your body," she said, batting his hand away

77

from the wound again.

This time her blow almost made him lose his balance, and he had to grab his saddle horn to stay seated. But he didn't reach for his leg again. What she had said had miraculously penetrated his brain. "Poison?" he repeated dumbly, looking at his bloody thigh with a bewildered expression on his face. "What poison?"

"We will talk about it later," she said, jumping off her pony before the animal came to a full halt and hurrying to Clay's side. "Lean on me," she ordered, reaching around his waist and literally dragging him off his mount.

Clay gave a drunken chuckle at the thought of this pint-sized woman supporting his hundred and seventy pounds. But before he could voice his skepticism, he found himself standing on the ground and leaning heavily on the surprisingly strong girl, an arm draped around her narrow shoulders.

"I can walk by myself," he insisted, his masculine pride refusing to admit his dependence on a female— especially one who'd almost gotten him killed! He released his grip on Gentle Fawn's shoulders and attempted a step away from her. He winced as he put his full weight on his injured leg and stumbled forward, only escaping a fall when Gentle Fawn's arm slipped back around his waist as she caught him.

"I do not think so, *wasicun*," she laughed harshly. "And you will not only let me help you walk, but you will be quiet and do as I tell you—unless you want me to give you back to the women of my tribe."

"I don't get it," Clay went on, refusing to be quiet, but too weak to refuse her help. "Why didn't you just go ahead and let them kill me?" Beads of sweat broke out on his forehead.

Gentle Fawn studied Clay as she lowered him to the ground beneath a tree. Why hadn't she let them kill him? He was white, and all whites deserved to die. Didn't they? "Perhaps I wanted the pleasure of killing you myself," she said, taking her knife and putting it to his leg.

Seeing her action, Clay grabbed for her wrist, but missed as she inserted the blade in the tear of his pants and ripped the material open to the bottom. Gentle Fawn shrugged off his attempt to take her knife.

"I do not believe whatever she had on her knife blade is going to kill you, Clay Donovan," she said as she examined his wound, unaware that her own relief was luminously evident in her expression and voice. She looked up and smiled, forgetting her own vow to see every white she met dead. All that mattered at that moment was that this one was going to live!

Later, as Gentle Fawn sat sucking the marrow from a roasted bone, she studied the sleeping white man beside her. His wound hadn't been nearly as deep or severe as it had seemed. And evidently the knife that had been used on him had been dipped in something meant to cause excessive pain—not death. Again, she wondered at her feeling of terror when she had thought Clay Donovan was going to die.

After giving Clay a sleeping potion to drink, she had treated the four-inch gash with powdered skunk-cabbage roots—*skota*—to stop the bleeding. The herbal styptic also acted as a narcotic, so by the time she had packed the cut with dried sphagnum moss to absorb the excess blood, Clay had dozed off into a painless sleep.

Gentle Fawn glanced at the sleeping man's slightly

opened mouth, unable to blank out the memory of those lips on hers. She wrapped her arms protectively around her own waist. What was she going to do now? She had to do something with him. She looked at his peacefully sleeping face again and gave a sad laugh. How could he sleep when there were ten thousand Lakota and Cheyenne Indians in the camp who all wanted him dead?

Gentle Fawn knew she should try to get some sleep, too. Decisions were always easier to make in the light of day when a person was well rested. But she knew she wouldn't be able to sleep until she had made her decision. So she proceeded with her futile efforts to sort out her options.

Of course she could just leave him here to find his way back to his own people—or die. That's what her mother wanted her to do, wasn't it? That's what all her family members wanted her to do.

As though her thoughts had conjured up Quiet Rain, the woman appeared beside Gentle Fawn where she watched over Clay. "Has your grief caused you to lose your senses, child?" the woman said quietly, squatting down as she resumed the argument begun when she had begrudgingly brought Gentle Fawn the herbs to treat Clay's wound. "Why did you bring him into our camp? Why did you stop the women from killing him? He could be the one who shot your father or killed your husband. Yet you nurse him with the care a mother would give her child. A wife would not show more concern for her injured husband."

"I told you, Mother. He is not one of the bluecoats. He did not kill Hunting Bear or Tall Feathers," Gentle Fawn said, her own fatigue making it almost impossible to disguise her impatience with Quiet Rain. "He is a writer, not a soldier."

"He is a *wasicun*," Quiet Rain argued stubbornly. "They all are evil and deserve to die!"

"All whites are not evil, Mother. Just as all Lakotas are not good. There were bad Lakota braves with the soldiers, and there are many *wasicuns* who would like to fight against the bad things that have been done to the People. I think Clay Donovan is one of those whites."

"Bah!" Quiet Rain spat with disgust. "You are a fool, child! He has bewitched you!"

"Perhaps he has, Mother," Gentle Fawn admitted, unable to avoid flashes of memory of a magical night that assaulted her mind. "But more than once he had the chance to kill me. Why didn't he? Not because I did not give him reason."

Quiet Rain didn't speak. Could she continue her campaign for the death of the man who had spared the life of her only child, the child who had been *Wakan Tanka's* gift to a woman who had been barren for ten years? "If only you had not stayed behind, then you would not have met him," she said, her voice sad as she got up and walked away, leaving her daughter alone with her prisoner—and her thoughts.

"But I did stay behind, Mother," Gentle Fawn whispered, though her mother didn't hear. "And I did meet him. I did."

Chapter Five

"You are willing to what?" Gentle Fawn gasped, her black eyes sparking with indignation and surprise.

"I am willing to marry you," Many Coups, the tall Cheyenne warrior standing before Gentle Fawn, said, his tone patronizing. "I will marry the bride of my dead son. Because I have no other sons, it is my responsibility to take care of you."

"Take care of me?" Gentle Fawn choked, doing everything in her power not to laugh. Who did this pompous old man think he was talking to? She didn't need any man to take care of her, and certainly not one who was offering marriage out of duty. Still, she couldn't be rude to him. "I thank you for the offer, my husband's father. It is very kind of you, but—"

"Good, then it is settled! We will marry today," Many Coups announced to Quiet Rain, who had stood beside him smiling her pleasure during the exchange.

"No!" Gentle Fawn shouted, drawing a stern look of displeasure from her father-in-law and one of embarrassment from her mother. "I cannot marry you!"

"Of course you can, child," Quiet Rain insisted, looking nervously from her rebellious daughter to the outraged Cheyenne chief. "Many Coups has made a very generous offer for you."

Gentle Fawn glared at Quiet Rain. No words were needed to get her point across.

Quiet Rain wrung her hands nervously and told Many Coups, "I will talk to her. If you will give us a small time alone, I am sure she will see things differently."

Many Coups nodded his consent and walked several feet away to wait for the mother to talk sense to the daughter.

"How could you suggest such a thing?" Gentle Fawn accused Quiet Rain before the warrior was even out of earshot. She fought the tears of betrayal that threatened to spill from her eyes. "It was your idea, wasn't it?"

"Yes," Quiet Rain admitted, "but Many Coups was more than agreeable. Why are you so upset? He is very handsome and owns many horses."

Gentle Fawn glared at Quiet Rain with unflinching stubbornness. "If he is so wonderful, then you marry him, Mother."

"But there is no chance that I carry the baby of his only son in my belly, child. Only you can give him back the son he lost."

Alarm leaped in her heart. Gentle Fawn hadn't thought about the possibility of a baby. Or about the fact that any child she could be carrying would not be of Tall Feathers' seed! Without realizing what she was doing, she placed her hands over her abdomen to protect the child that could be growing there and looked back over her shoulder at her father-in-law who waited impatiently for her answer.

Just look at him. He is so sure I will say yes. I wonder if he would still be willing to marry me if he knew I could be carrying a white man's baby, and not his son's. What would Many Coups do if I married him and my baby had blond hair and blue eyes? Gentle Fawn shuddered at the thought. She didn't have to wonder. She knew exactly what he would do. He would kill her baby—and probably her, too. *Well, he will not have the chance,* she swore silently, already loving and wanting to protect the baby that might be in her womb. "I cannot marry him, Mother. I am going to marry the white man, Clay Donovan!" she announced, hurriedly concocting a desperate plan.

"You cannot mean it!" Quiet Rain wailed.

"I mean it, but please do not say anything to anyone yet. Will you promise me, Mother?"

"Of course I will not say anything. How could I tell the People my daughter wants to marry one of the murderers of her own father?"

Gentle Fawn rolled her eyes and patted her mother's arm. "I have told you, Clay Donovan has killed no one. He is a writer, not a killer. Now, you go back to the others. I will explain to Many Coups that I cannot marry him."

The scene with Many Coups hadn't been pleasant. It was obvious Tall Feathers' father was not accustomed to being told no, and even more obvious he didn't intend to accept no for an answer now. Gentle Fawn curled her lip in an expression of disgust when she remembered the conversation with him. The more he'd insisted that she marry him, the more she'd been determined that she would never marry the man—even if there wasn't the possibility of a half white baby to protect. Thinking of the angry chief's last words to her before he stalked off,

Gentle Fawn cringed. *There is no way he can force me to marry him,* she assured herself. *Still, I had better make certain.*

"How are you feeling this morning, Clay Donovan?" she smiled as she approached the blond writer where he lounged against a tree. She nodded to the two young boys she'd had watch her prisoner while she bathed and changed into a beaded dress.

Clay looked up, surprised by the friendly tone. And his visual senses were assaulted by the beautiful girl. Again, he wondered how he could have thought she was a boy— even for a fraction of a second. She was absolutely lovely. And the smile on her face was enough to take his breath away. He started to respond with a smile of his own. Then good sense took over his thoughts and he wiped his hand across his mouth to disguise the grin forming there.

She's up to something, he decided, eyeing her suspiciously, finding it increasingly difficult not to fall under the spell of her smile. "What difference does it make how I feel?" he growled petulantly.

"Not any. I only thought that if you were feeling better you might like to meet Crazy Horse this morning before we leave."

"What!" Clay laughed, sitting up straight. "Do you mean it? Have you really arranged a meeting for me? I knew it! I knew you could do it!" He slapped his leg happily, narrowly missing the deerskin bandage. He winced at the self-inflicted blow, but went on talking excitedly. "When do I get to see him? Will you get my paper and pencil out of my saddle bags? What are we waiting for?" Lumbering clumsily to his feet, he felt totally recovered.

"Wait," Gentle Fawn said, her expression becoming

more serious. "I have something urgent to discuss with you."

"Can't it wait? This is too important to put off another minute. I've waited all my life for an interview like this."

"If I arrange this *important* interview for you, will you be willing to do something for me in exchange?"

"Anything! I'll do anything for you! Just take me to Crazy Horse!" His excitement was laced with impatience.

"Good, then we will be married this morning before you talk to Crazy Horse," she announced matter-of-factly and turned to go.

"*Married?* We can't get married!" Clay barked as he hobbled after her.

"Why not? You have no wife. I have no husband."

"But why do you want to marry me? I'm white! You hate all whites! Don't you remember? You tried to kill me!"

Gentle Fawn turned and poked her finger into his chest, her eyes squinted angrily. She couldn't understand the hurt his vehement refusal caused her to feel, but she was determined he wouldn't know it. "My feelings for you have not changed, Clay Donovan. That has nothing to do with this bargain."

"Well, I won't do it," he came back stubbornly, knocking her finger away from his chest and crossing his arms with finality.

"Then you will not talk to Crazy Horse." She shrugged her shoulders and moved away.

"Why?" Clay shouted, ignoring the stiffness in his bandaged leg as he ran after her. "Why do you want us to be married?"

"It is only until the Cheyennes move out, Clay Donovan. Not for always. A few weeks at the most. Then

87

you can leave, too, and forget you ever knew me. You will have your interview, and I will have my freedom."

"But why me?" Clay insisted, horrified to realize he was actually considering her crazy idea. He wanted that interview more than just about anything in the world—but enough to get married? There was no way! Still, if it was only going to be for a few weeks. "Why not marry another Indian?"

"I do not wish to be married for always. And if I marry a Lakota brave, it will be for always. If I marry you, it will be only for as long as we need each other. Why are you hesitating? It will not be a real marriage in the eyes of the whites."

"Why do you want to get married only temporarily?" Clay asked, confused by the fact that he was irritated by her plan to discard him when she was through using him.

"Because my dead husband's father wants to marry me, and marrying someone else is the only way I can change his mind."

"Your *husband's* father? What husband? You were a virgin when we . . . Weren't you?" he asked, now not so certain anything that had happened to him in the past two days was real.

"My husband went into battle on the day of our marriage. We did not have the chance to truly become man and wife, but my father-in-law does not know that. Many Coups is convinced that I have Tall Feathers' baby in my belly, and he wants to raise it as his own."

"So tell him!"

"That is not possible. He will still insist on 'taking care' of his son's widow. What do you think would happen if the wife of his dead son, his only son, presented him with a grandson that had blond hair or blue eyes,

Clay Donovan?"

"It's not possible!" Clay choked. He had the intense desire to look behind him to see if there was a shotgun—or bow and arrow—in his back. "It's not!"

"But you and I know it is possible. Is that not true, Clay Donovan?"

"You couldn't be pregnant," Clay insisted, fighting the twinge of excitement the idea caused to trip through him. "Could you? I mean, it was only that once."

"Are you willing to take a chance on your child's life, Clay Donovan? Because that is what you will be doing if you refuse to help me and I am carrying your child. My dead husband's father will kill your baby the instant he realizes it does not belong to his son. Is that what you want?"

"No! Of course not. It's just that . . . Damn!" She was blackmailing him and he knew it. But there wasn't a thing he could do about it.

First she dangled the coveted interview with Crazy Horse in front of his nose like the proverbial carrot. Now a death threat against a baby that probably didn't even exist had been added to her ultimatum—added so cleverly, so convincingly that he found himself believing the baby did exist and must be protected at all costs. But marriage? The expression on his face sickened.

Sure, he wanted to get married—someday. Just not *this* day. And certainly not to an Indian spitfire who could smile at him one minute and might pull a knife on him the next. He would just have to find another way to see Crazy Horse. "I believe I'll pass, little lady. I think the stakes in this game are just a little bit too high for an Irish street kid from New York City!"

"It would be only for a few weeks, Clay Donovan,"

Gentle Fawn reminded him, reaching out to stop him from going back.

Her voice contained a barely audible vulnerability that froze Clay in his tracks. He glanced down at the golden, tan hand resting on his arm, and his heart constricted painfully in his chest. So beautiful, so small, so brave, this tiny package of Indian dynamite. How could he deny her request when she looked at him with those big, black doe eyes that fought so gallantly to hide her insecurity from him?

"Just for a few weeks? You're sure?"

Gentle Fawn nodded her head, afraid to speak lest she give away the surge of hope his words sent rushing over her. He was actually considering doing it!

"When we part, there won't be any tearful good-byes or recriminations?"

Gentle Fawn shook her head, wondering what recriminations meant, but not daring to interrupt by asking.

"Just until your father-in-law and the Cheyennes pull out?"

She nodded again.

"No longer?"

"No longer," she agreed, ignoring the stab of hurt that knifed deeper into her heart with each assurance he asked for to guarantee he wouldn't be tied to her permanently.

"When do I get my interview?"

She had to remind herself that she'd been the one to lay down the ground rules. She'd been the one to suggest they use each other to get what they wanted. So why did it hurt so much to think he was marrying her for purely selfish reasons? That was her reason for marrying him.

too. Wasn't it? "We will go to Man of the People to have our marriage blessed on our way to see Crazy Horse."

Clay drew in a long, deep breath, expanding his chest to its full breadth, then let it out in a loud, relaxing woosh of final decision. "Well, then. I guess there's nothing keeping us from getting this show on the road."

"I do not understand 'show on the road.'" She frowned.

"It means, let's do it. Let's go get married."

Every muscle and nerve in Gentle Fawn's body leaped, urging her to throw her arms around Clay Donovan and tell him how happy he had made her. Fortunately, years of being taught to control her emotions paid off, and she was able to stop her impulsive move in time. Instead, she lowered her gaze to the ground and said, "Good. I will get your paper and pencil from your saddle bags and we will *get this show on the road.*"

Clay's blue eyes popped open in surprise. He snorted an unexpected snicker that immediately developed into a full-fledged roar of happiness. Without thinking, he reached out and hugged Gentle Fawn to his hard chest. "Ah, little princess, what will you say next?"

"You are not going to marry me?" Gentle Fawn said, her serious words muffled against Clay's shirt front. "Is that why you laugh at me?" She could feel the sting of tears gathering in her eyes.

"I'm not laughing at you, little one," Clay chuckled. "I'm laughing at everything—at me, at us, at life. Who'd have thought—" Holding her away from him so he could see into her eyes, he told her, "I'm going to marry you just like I said I would. We have a bargain, don't we?"

Gentle Fawn nodded her head and repeated, "A bargain."

"Then let's do it, *Mrs. Donovan*. Let's go see Man of the People and get married."

Mrs. Donovan . . . Mrs. Donovan . . . Mrs. Donovan . . . The strange yet warmly familiar name Clay Donovan had called her repeated itself over and over in Gentle Fawn's thoughts. She kept reminding herself that it was just another one of Clay Donovan's odd ways of saying things. It meant nothing. She wasn't fooled into thinking it did. She knew that Mrs. was the name *wasicuns* gave their *real* wives. Wives they wanted for always. Not wives they would only keep for a few weeks. Still, the name played its sweet melody over and over in her mind, and she could do nothing to stop the ache in her heart that insisted on reminding her that she would not be a real wife to Clay Donovan. *Mrs. Donovan . . . Mrs. Donovan . . . Mrs. Donovan . . .*

Minutes later, Gentle Fawn looked into Man of the People's warm, understanding eyes and began. "This is Clay Donovan, and I would like my chief's permission to marry him," she said right out, knowing the chief of her band of Oglala Lakotas appreciated directness.

Man of the People's gaze shifted from Gentle Fawn's anxious young face to that of the white man. "Why do you wish to marry this young woman who has been like a daughter to me?" the chief asked Clay suspiciously, his English perfect.

"Huh, well I ah—" They hadn't talked about what reason they were going to give the chief for wanting to marry each other, and his expression sagged with confusion.

"Because we care for one another," Gentle Fawn interrupted quickly, surprised by the truth of her words—from her side anyway.

"Right," Clay agreed eagerly. "We care for—" Suddenly the reality of what he was saying hit him with sobering force and he stopped speaking, the expression on his face flabbergasted. He'd actually let the little Indian spitfire get under his skin. How had it happened? When? Could it really be possible? Or was it just another in a chain of bizarre nightmares that had besieged him since he'd first come to with Gentle Fawn on his back getting ready to scalp him. He shook his head to clear away the crazy idea that Gentle Fawn meant more to him than just a way to get his interview with Crazy Horse. But the thoughts would not go away.

"Yes?" Man of the People waited.

"Because I—we—care for each other," Clay said in a rush of words, trying to ignore the effect they were having on him.

"A marriage between a *wasicun* and one of the People will be very difficult at this time," Man of the People warned. "I should refuse your request, my daughter—at least until a better time." He watched Clay for his reaction to the words and was confused by what he saw in the younger man's expression: relief, disappointment, anger, confusion. Odd, very odd.

"You had a white wife. And your own son, Daniel Blue Eagle, is married to a white woman," Gentle Fawn protested, the urgency rising in her voice as she leaned toward Man of the People. "Please, my chief, approve this marriage!"

"Many Coups, your dead husband's father, has already talked to me about a marriage between you!"

"I will not marry Many Coups! I want to marry Clay Donovan! Please, do not deny us!"

"Many Coups has the right to insist," Man of the

People started.

"No!" Clay blurted out. He had watched the panic grow in Gentle Fawn's expression, listened to her frantic pleading as long as he could bear it. "Many Coups does not have the right to insist! Only I have that right. And I do. I insist you give Gentle Fawn and me permission to marry!"

"I see," Man of the People said thoughtfully, the expression on his distinguished face both surprised and amused. "And by what right do you make this claim?" he asked, his bright gaze traveling alertly from the stunned face of Gentle Fawn to the angry face of the white man.

"By the right any man has to marry the woman who may carry his child in her womb!" Clay returned. *Damn! What the hell am I saying?* he moaned inwardly the instant the words were out of his mouth. *Why couldn't I just keep my big mouth shut?*

Man of the People returned his attention to Gentle Fawn, who was gawking at Clay Donovan. "Is this true, Gentle Fawn?" the chief asked.

"What?" she whispered, continuing to stare at Clay, unable to understand his volatile reaction.

"Is it true that you may be carrying this man's child? How do you explain this? Many Coups claims any baby you have is of his son's seed and therefore his?"

Man of the People shook his head helplessly when Clay and Gentle Fawn left him a few minutes later. He didn't know what he was going to tell Many Coups. But he was certain he'd made the right decision. When Gentle Fawn had explained the circumstances of her meeting with Clay—and the fact that she had not been with Tall Feathers at all—he had known he had no choice but to bless her marriage to the white man. Besides, he had to

94

admit he found the *wasicun* rather likable—definitely preferable to Many Coups.

"Thank you, Clay Donovan," Gentle Fawn said as she walked beside Clay. "You were very kind to stand up for me the way you did."

"I didn't do it to be kind," Clay grunted. "I just want to get the wedding over with so I can talk to Crazy Horse. We've got a bargain, and the sooner we get married, the sooner I get my interview."

Disappointment washed over her. Of course that would be it. She hadn't really thought Clay Donovan had been overcome with some miraculous change of heart and suddenly become anxious to marry her, had she? No, of course she hadn't. Gentle Fawn hardened her features, determined not to let him know how his attitude had hurt her.

"So when do we get married? I hope the ceremony won't take too long."

"There is no need for a ceremony," Gentle Fawn answered woodenly. "By giving us his blessing, Man of the People married us. Though for first marriages, a wedding ceremony is common, all we need to do is declare ourselves married and we are. In the eyes of the People, I am your wife and you are my husband."

Clay stopped in mid-step and looked down at Gentle Fawn. Words failed him.

"You have fulfilled your part of our bargain; now I will fulfill mine." Gentle Fawn walked away from Clay, not daring to look into his sparkling blue eyes and see how little he truly cared about her.

Running as best he could on his wounded leg, which was beginning to throb, Clay hop-skipped after his "bride." "Hey, wait a minute. Slow down," he called out.

"You are in a great hurry to meet Crazy Horse," Gentle Fawn answered without slowing her step, her voice oddly strained.

"We don't have to run," he winced, growing aware that the painkilling herbs Gentle Fawn had given him earlier had evidently worn off.

When Gentle Fawn stopped and Clay caught up with her, she indicated an unassuming, serious-faced woman who was loading her pack horses. "That is Black Shawl, the wife of Crazy Horse. Wait here. I will talk to her," she said, walking toward the woman without giving Clay the opportunity to respond.

He waited anxiously as the two women talked, growing more and more apprehensive the longer it took. And when he saw Gentle Fawn walking toward him a few minutes later, he knew even before she spoke that he'd been duped. He could tell by the expression on his "wife's" face that there would be no interview with Crazy Horse today, maybe never; and he was angrier than he'd ever been in his life.

"Black Shawl says he left the camp before sunrise and that she does not know when he will be back. Maybe he will join us on the trail sometime during the day. Or maybe not for a few days," Gentle Fawn explained, hating the fact that she had been unable to fulfill her end of the bargain with Clay Donovan.

"Is it just a coincidence that you made sure we were married *before* we came here? Or was there some other reason, my dear little conniving wife?"

Gentle Fawn raised her gaze, surprised by the anger that filled her new husband's tone. Of course, she'd known he would be disappointed, but she hadn't expected this attitude of total betrayal. "You think I knew he was already gone and deliberately tricked you so you would claim me as your wife?" she asked, swallowing back the tears that threatened to spill down her cheeks.

"Well, didn't you? You had no intention of taking me to Crazy Horse, did you, *little wife?*"

"I did. But if that is what you think, Clay Donovan, if you think you have been cheated by our bargain, I will go to Man of the People and have our marriage ended," she offered, the words hurting her to think, much less say aloud.

"Oh, no you won't! All I need is for the whole camp to find out I compromised your virtue and then wouldn't stay married to you! No, no, little wife, we'll stay *married* until you deliver your end of the bargain! Is that understood?"

"I do not wish to be married to a man who thinks I am a liar and a cheat," Gentle Fawn came back, the fire in her black eyes shooting sparks at him.

"Well, that's just too damn bad, lady. 'Cause you're married to a man who thinks just that. And you're going to stay married to him until you prove otherwise!"

Chapter Six

Gentle Fawn sneaked a sidelong glance at Clay Donovan, annoyed to see that his posture remained as stoic as it had been since they first mounted their horses that morning, his blue eyes as cold and angry as a winter sky. She sighed her frustration.

By the way the area around his mouth had paled, she could tell his leg was hurting again. But it was his own fault if he was suffering. Not hers. She'd already done more than she should have for him. More than once during the day, when she had noticed him shifting restlessly in his saddle, she'd tried to check his bandages, offered to redress the injury. And each time her sincere concern had been met by unyielding rejection.

Let him suffer, she decided with disgust, trying to convince herself that it was no more than he deserved. She forced herself to look straight ahead and concentrate on the mile-long trail of fleeing Indians in front of them, resolving to ignore him from then on. *I'm not to blame if he's too stubborn to accept my help.*

However, as though her eyes were operating of their

own accord, Gentle Fawn was unable to prevent herself from stealing one last secret glance at Clay—just in time to see his eyes guiltily shift back to the rutted trail left by the hundreds of lodge poles that had been dragged over it. He'd been watching her!

Her heart leapt erratically in her chest. But her elation quickly turned to anger. Anger at herself for caring for even a single moment what a deceitful *wasicun* thought. *Anyway, he is only thinking about how much he hates me— and how anxious he is to be rid of me*, she thought hostilely, jerking her own eyes back to the dusty ground ahead. *No more anxious than I am to see the last of him!*

But no matter what she told herself, Gentle Fawn could not shake the peculiar impression that it hadn't been hatred she'd seen in Clay Donovan's blue eyes in that instant before they'd flashed away from her. If not hate, what? Curiosity? Caring? *Don't be foolish. He hates me! And I hate him!*

Clay finally spoke, wresting Gentle Fawn from her thoughts with a jolt. "How long before we stop for the night?"

The obvious strain in his voice stabbed unexpectedly into her heart. As though his pain were hers! As though she could feel the effort it took for him to finally admit his need to stop.

How could this be happening to her? she wondered with revulsion. She didn't care if he was in pain. She didn't even care if he died—as long as he did it *after* Many Coups and the Cheyennes left the camp.

"Not long," she returned evenly, controlling the illogical urge she still had to reach out and check the bandage on his leg even though she insisted she didn't care.

100

"Well, aren't you going to say it?" Clay looked directly at her now, making his angry charge through teeth gritted against the throbbing ache in his thigh.

"What do you expect me to say, Clay Donovan?"

"Aren't you going to throw it up to me that if I'd listened to you, my leg wouldn't be killing me right this minute?" he spit out bitterly. "There's no woman in the world who would pass up the opportunity to say *I told you so.*"

Before she could respond to Clay's open challenge to an argument, Gentle Fawn heard the welcome order to stop for the night. "We will make camp here tonight," she said, keeping her tone cool as she turned her pony and led her pack animals off to the side of the trail. She didn't have to look over her shoulder to know that Clay would stay behind her—unless he wanted to face the vengeful Lakota women again.

Instead of making her feel more secure, the realization that Clay wouldn't try to escape because he had no choice sent another jab of anger and hurt knifing through her.

Without looking back at the object of her fury, Gentle Fawn leaped from her saddle as though pouncing on a hated enemy and, with a vengeance, attacked the travois holding her tepee cover.

Without warning, the realization of just how stiff the long horseback ride had left his wounded leg hit Clay when he tried to dismount. As he started to lift it over his saddle, an explosion of blinding pain ripped through his thigh and calf, rocking his equilibrium violently. He gripped the saddlehorn and waited for the flaming agony in his leg to subside, doing his best to fight the waves of nausea and keep from fainting.

Clay shot an anxious glance toward Gentle Fawn. She

101

seemed to have forgotten him altogether. His irritation with her grew. Judging by the way she was jerking packs off her horses and slapping lodgepoles together, she probably wouldn't help him anyway. In fact, it would no doubt thrill her to know how much he was suffering.

Her apparent unconcern made Clay more unwavering than ever in his resolve to keep his pain a secret from her. He didn't intend to give her the satisfaction of knowing she'd been right about stopping and checking his leg sooner.

After several long moments, the burning in his leg finally ebbed to a bearable throb, and he willed himself to regather the courage to try to dismount again.

With slow, calculated movements, Clay eased his good leg over the horse's back, intending to position himself sideways in the saddle. From there, it would be a simple matter to slide carefully to the ground, catching all his weight on his good leg. It was a good plan, he decided with satisfaction, knowing he wouldn't have to admit to Gentle Fawn how difficult a simple thing like getting off his horse had been.

Unfortunately, Clay's self-congratulations came just a moment too soon.

"Do you need some help?" Gentle Fawn asked just as he began his cautious descent to the ground.

Startled by the feminine voice that cut into his total concentration, Clay shot an angry look over his shoulder. "I don't need any more of your kind of help, lady!" he snapped. "It's your help that got me into this damned mess in the first place!" With that, he made the remainder of his drop to the ground with a defiant jump.

Volcanic pain erupted from his wound and raced haphazardly throughout his body as the bulk of his weight fell on his bad leg. His eyes watered. He ground his teeth together. Then, unable to stop himself from giving voice to his agony, he cried out. "Aagh!"

Gentle Fawn dropped the cottonwood lodge pole she was putting in place in the tepee she was erecting and ran to assist Clay. "You should have let me help you!" she scolded, the concern in her voice impossible to hide.

Clay shook her hand off his arm with an independent shrug. "I knew it!" he grunted, lifting his injured leg with one hand and balancing himself against his horse's hip with single-minded effort. "I knew you couldn't resist saying I told you so!" he accused, the triumphant grin on his face failing to hide his pain.

"I don't need your help," he insisted. Ignoring the beads of cold sweat that popped out on his forehead, the feeling of light-headedness that was swallowing him, he took a determined step away from the horse. "Don't need any help," he mumbled again, his words slurring together as he staggered in no particular direction.

"You are a fool, Clay Donovan" was the last thing he heard as he pitched forward into the blessed void of unconsciousness.

Her eyes wide with panic, Gentle Fawn's brow furrowed with worry as she knelt beside Clay's still form and dipped a square of cloth into a wooden bowl of water and wrung it out. She bathed his face and neck with its soothing coolness, willing him to rouse. He had to be all right. He couldn't die.

But if he wasn't dying, why didn't he regain consciousness? He'd been like this for what seemed like forever. Long enough for her to remove his clothing and

103

change the bandage on his leg. And long enough for Gentle Fawn's mother and sisters to put up her tepee around them while she kept her vigil over him. But still he hadn't revived.

Wake up, Clay Donovan. You cannot die, she urged silently as she sponged the damp cloth over the bare expanse of muscular chest.

How could this be happening again? Was she being punished for some forgotten transgression? Had she committed an unforgivable offense that had angered the Great Spirit? Was that why she was being forced to watch a second husband die in as many days? Not that Clay Donovan was a real husband to her. But still, in the eyes of the People their marriage was real. And the fact remained that if he died she would be forced to marry Many Coups.

"I will not allow it!" she suddenly shouted, tossing down the wet rag. "We have a bargain, Clay Donovan, and I will not permit you to back out of it!" With desperate urgency ruling her actions, she began to splash handfuls of cool water over the unconscious man's face and muscled torso. "You will not die!" she decreed. "You will live!"

"Hey, what's the big idea?" Clay sputtered, struggling to sit up as a wave of choking water splattered into his face. "What the hell are you doing?" he coughed, spitting as he spoke. "Drowning me isn't the way to keep me alive!"

Gentle Fawn's eyes widened with realization, then narrowed angrily. "You were awake all the time!" she accused through clenched teeth.

The sight of the tiny Indian girl spitting fire made him forget his own anger at being doused with water. "Not *all*

104

along," he said, unable to hide the mischievous grin that played on his mouth or the amused twinkle that gleamed in his eyes.

"You let me think you were dying!" she raged, a strange combination of relief and outrage bringing her dangerously close to tears. She raised her hands and shoved angrily at Clay's bare chest.

"Hold on there, spitfire!" he chuckled, wrapping strong fingers around slim wrists and turning what had started out to be a blow into a caress as he brought her palms to rest against him. "What happened to the gentle nurse who was taking such good care of me a few minutes ago?"

Increasingly aware of the taut water-cooled flesh beneath her hands, Gentle Fawn tried to fold her fingers into fists to protect their sensitive tips from the electrical current already jolting through them and up her arms. But Clay was too quick for her and tightened his grip, pressing her open hands harder against his chest.

Everywhere her flesh touched his, from the tip of every finger to the heels of both hands, her skin burned. "Let go of me," she said, meaning to sound authoritative. But all she'd been able to manage was a pitiful croak that was more plea than command.

"So you can hit me?" Clay asked, the infuriating glint in his eyes changing ever so slightly.

"I will not hit you," Gentle Fawn hissed, ready to promise anything in order to end the torturous physical contact, hating him even more for the way he was making her body betray her.

"What guarantee do I have that you won't go back on your word?"

"Guarantee?"

"What are you willing to give me to prove you won't try to use me for a punching bag again?" he explained, falling back on his buffalo robe pallet with a self-satisfied chuckle.

Finding herself forced to kneel over him, Gentle Fawn's elbows locked just in time or she would have found more than just her hands touching Clay Donovan. And her last bit of instinct for self-preservation told her she had to avoid that at all costs. Already she could feel her newly discovered desire building to painful proportions in her belly. How could this be happening again? How could she begin to forget what the whites had done to her people the minute Clay Donovan touched her?

"Give you?" she choked, a frightening suspicion dawning in her thoughts.

"Something to show you really do have my best interest and comfort at heart," he murmured, his gaze focusing maddeningly on her mouth.

His tongue made a lazy journey over his upper lip, and the now-familiar spring in the pit of Gentle Fawn's stomach began to tighten again—exactly like the night when she had thought he was a god. *But he is not a god. He is just a man,* she reminded herself sternly. She couldn't—wouldn't—give in to him again.

In an instinctive reflex of self-protection, Gentle Fawn sucked her own lips into her mouth and held them between her teeth, as though hiding them would destroy her desire to feel them against his one more time.

"Something special," he said softly, his gaze traveling over her face and then back to her mouth. "Something to ease my pain."

Gentle Fawn's eyes widened with concern. "Is your leg still hurting? I will get more herbs!" she offered hastily,

106

trying to free her entrapped hands.

"My leg's just fine. Doesn't hurt a bit."

"But you said you were in pain."

"I am," he assured her with a feigned pathetic expression on his handsome face. "Unbearable pain only you can ease."

Clay released his hold on her wrists slightly. But before she realized what was happening, his hands slipped up her arms, clamping tight above her elbows.

Seeing this slight freedom as a chance to end her own pain, as well as the dangerous contact between her hands and Clay's chest, Gentle Fawn bent her elbows to free her palms and fingers from the magnetic contact with his flesh.

But Clay's reflexes were too fast for her, and without warning, he jerked her toward his prone body, taking advantage of her relaxed elbows. Now, instead of just her hands touching him, she found her breasts flattened against him and her arms from elbow to fingertips pressed in searing contact against his chest. "A kiss might help."

"A kiss?" Gentle Fawn squeaked, her mouth only inches from his now. Though she knew she was dangerously close to being lost in Clay Donovan's spell again and should act now if she hoped to escape, she was unable to muster the will to struggle anymore.

He gave a little tug on her arms and settled her torso over his more securely. "A kiss to make it better," he said, his smile challenging and amused at the same time.

"Kisses are not part of our bargain," she tried weakly, fighting the desire to stop straining against his hold on her, when all she wanted was to give in to his request. But she knew that one of Clay's kisses would be devastating to her resistance. One would never be enough to ease the longing already building in her. She couldn't take the risk.

"You'd deny a dying man his last request?"

He stuck out his bottom lip in a pout so comical that Gentle Fawn almost laughed. Fortunately, she caught herself in time and managed a frown instead. "You are not a dying man." But her serious expression and irritated tone couldn't quite hide the smile that threatened to break her cross facade.

"Just one kiss to show your good faith?" he coaxed, moving his callused hands up and down her upper arms inside the sleeves of her deerskin dress.

She was losing the battle in her struggle to ignore Clay's playful banter, and she hated herself for her weakness. "I showed my good faith when I did not leave you where you fell when you were too stubborn to let me help you off your horse."

"Because you're crazy about me. Right?"

"Crazy not to have left you for the vultures."

"One little kiss," he appealed, tracing his fingertips in circles over the sensitive areas where her arms joined to her body. Then he slipped his hands inside the armholes of her dress to work his magic on the vulnerable flesh above her breasts, and she couldn't hold back the contented sigh that escaped before she could stop it.

She knew she was lost but still she had to fight him— him and her own body's betrayal. "No!" she insisted, adamantly shaking her head from side to side.

"What harm can come from one kiss between friends?"

"We are not friends. We are enemies."

"We could be friends—if we kiss and make up."

"Make up? I do not understand."

Clay chuckled, loving the way Gentle Fawn cocked her head to the side when he used an expression she hadn't heard before. It made him want to spend a lifetime teaching her new words and expressions. Laughing inwardly at his temporary insanity for even thinking such a ridiculous thought, he said, " 'Kiss and make up' means to stop fighting. When whites want to end a disagreement between two people, they tell them to kiss and make up."

"This kiss of the *wasicun* is very useful," Gentle Fawn mused aloud, her own voice containing a playful ring now, despite all her efforts to stay angry. "Kisses to make injuries feel better, kisses to end fighting. What other things do you use these kisses for?"

"Come here and I'll show you," Clay urged, gripping her shoulders and drawing her closer.

Her lips were only a breath from his, but she had lost all the will to struggle and went easily.

"We use kisses to say hello." Clay smiled and feathered a kiss on the tip of her nose. "Or good-bye." He brushed her eyelids closed with gentle kisses. "To seal bargains—like when two people marry." He kissed each of her cheeks in turn. "All sorts of good things," he said, his voice husky as he kissed her chin.

"And what else?" she whispered weakly, maneuvering her face so the next kiss he gave her would fall naturally on her mouth.

Clay smiled warmly at her innocence. Subtlety and coyness, indoctrinated in white females from birth, were virtually nonexistent in Gentle Fawn. And he found himself hating the day he would have to leave and go back to the artificial etiquette of the white world.

But for now he was here, and for the few blissful moments he would enjoy with the fiery Indian girl in his arms, there would be no other world but this. No past, no future, just now. "This," he said, finally grazing her lips with a soft, teasing kiss.

His voice was a warm croon in her ears, his mouth electric on hers, and the last vestiges of her resistance melted like warm honey. "This," she repeated hypnotically, her body relaxing on his, all thoughts of hate and enemies and bargains forgotten.

"And when we have this," he said with another light caress, "there's no need for anything else. It's everything."

"Everything," Gentle Fawn agreed, no longer able to lie to herself or believe this wasn't what she wanted—had wanted from the moment Clay Donovan had first touched her and sent her logic scattering in the moonlight like a covey of frightened quail. This was the reason she had saved him from the warriors, had stopped the women of her tribe from killing him, had cared for his wound, had been willing to go against her mother's wishes and had refused to marry Many Coups.

It was for this that she had entered into a bargain with her enemy, a white man! It was this moment in his arms, this chance to feel his lips on hers one more time, this promise of the heaven their union would bring, this . . . this . . .

"Everything," she expelled jubilantly, reveling in the feel of his breath on her flesh, chilling and warming at once.

"Everything," he said again, sliding one hand, still inside her dress, over her back to catch her at the nape of the neck and bring her mouth the rest of the way down to his.

Her mouth hovered over his for a fraction of a second before their lips met again, as though giving her one last chance to save herself. But it was already too late, the burning inside too intense. She couldn't wait for him to close the gap between their mouths. She pressed her lips hard against his.

The darkened tepee burst into a magnificent vista of brightness as Clay's tongue dipped deep into her open mouth, caressing hers with gentle urgency. As if her hands had a will of their own, they wound around Clay's neck. Snuggling herself closer into his embrace, she gave herself over to total feeling. The condemning inner voice that had chastised her for her feelings about the *wasicun*, Clay Donovan, was at last silent.

Their kiss deepening, Clay's hands blazed a trail of fire as they left the warmth of her dress sleeves to travel down her sides to her hips. Without easing the passionate intensity of their kiss, he lifted her slim body the rest of the way over his, setting her hips snugly between his legs.

"Now isn't this better than fighting?" he murmured, his voice hoarse and sending a warm rush of response spreading along her veins. Moving his obvious masculinity against her, his lips designed a line of passionate kisses along her jaw to her ear lobe.

The flames building in her trembling body were already reaching inferno heights. She couldn't help rotating her hips against his hardness in an automatic answer to his body's invitation. "Mmm," she moaned helplessly, bringing her mouth back to his in an effort to fuel the hunger of the ever-growing fire raging through her.

Tugging at her dress, he pulled it up around her waist

111

and filled his hands with the satiny flesh of her bottom. His hands roved over her back as she moved against him in the natural rhythm of love. There was no stopping the inevitable. Pure instinct ruled their actions now. She no longer even remembered why she'd called him her enemy—or even that she had.

With hands frantic to feel their naked flesh united, they quickly removed Gentle Fawn's dress. Next to go was the deerskin she had draped over Clay's lower body and legs when she had undressed him to care for his wound. All the while their kisses continued in a wild frenzy, breaking apart only long enough to lift the dress over her head, then resuming with renewed fervor.

Clay sucked in a ragged breath at the sight of her exquisite unclothed beauty. He barely noticed the golden locket gleaming between her breasts as his enthralled gaze fell on the dark, inviting peaks of her perfect breasts. He couldn't wait to feel them against his own.

His fingers caught the back of Gentle Fawn's neck, and he drew her back to him, rubbing the aroused tips of her breasts erotically against the hair-roughened muscle of his chest. His searing kiss was gentle, yet savage. He explored her mouth as if kissing her for the first time, delving into every secret crevice, memorizing it. Finally, releasing her mouth, his lips burned across the sweetness of her cheek to her ear where he sucked her plump lobe into the heat of his mouth.

"So sweet," he moaned as his hands kneaded their way up and down her back and over her buttocks, each time holding her closer to the burning hardness of his manhood that pressed against her.

He blazed lavish kisses across her throat from ear to ear as his splayed fingers glided around her to circle her rib cage. "So beautiful," he whispered, pulling her light body upward to bring her small breasts to within inches of his mouth. "So perfect," he murmured.

Drawing a thrusting peak into his mouth, Clay tugged on and tasted its sweetness, savoring it until Gentle Fawn groaned her ecstasy aloud and threw her head back in wild abandon. Clay's tongue and lips worshiped first one erect nipple then the other, until she was certain she would lose her mind.

"I can't wait any longer, honey," Clay rasped hoarsely, suddenly releasing the tight suction he had on her breast and moving her back down his body.

"No more waiting," she agreed, feeling the same fierce urgency ready to explode inside her. Instinctively, she opened her thighs and straddled Clay's slim hips, bringing the center of her womanhood to rest over his burning hardness. She moved against him mindlessly, the need to be filled with him guiding her.

Placing his hands on her hips, he lifted her upward. With one swift, sure plunge, he filled her aching emptiness with his strength, and Gentle Fawn was unable to hold back the cry of rapture that escaped in a long groan of abandon.

Moving slowly, tentatively at first, her hips rose and fell, over and over, faster and faster, until he was deep inside her, filling her petite body to capacity, taking her to grander heights than she'd ever imagined.

It was difficult to breathe. She lost all concept of time or place as he surged into her, filling her with life. And still they traveled higher, until at last they were hurled wildly into the heavens, to float helplessly back to earth on a cloud of contentment.

Gentle Fawn collapsed on Clay's chest. "It was good,

Clay Donovan," she sighed happily, all their differences forgotten for the moment.

"Good?" he huffed, slapping her bottom lightly. "Just good? Don't I rate at least a 'great' or a 'terrific'?"

She raised her head in surprise at his words. His sapphire eyes were sparkling and his mouth was wide with a mischievous grin. She realized that if she was going to spend the next few weeks with Clay Donovan, she was going to have to get used to his devilish way of talking. She would have to learn to tell when he was serious—maybe even how to tease him in return.

"Very good is as high as I can go," she answered, her face totally serious, though a light in her dark eyes gave her away. "Maybe next time you can be 'great' or 'terrific.'" She smiled, pleased with her first attempts at playing Clay's word games.

Then what she'd said hit her full force. Her mouth dropped open, the teasing expression on her face dissolving into one of shock. She'd said "next time!" As if their marriage were real! As if she expected them to stay together forever!

"Oh oh! My little Indian wife gets sassy when she's feeling good!" Clay chuckled, not noticing the change on her face as he hugged her hard against him. "But that's okay. I like my wives a little bit sassy. Makes life interesting. And as far as being 'terrific' next time— Honey, that's a promise! You can count on it! In fact, if my leg wasn't starting to throb again, I'd make that 'next time' right now!"

The sudden realization of how she'd succumbed to her enemy again assaulted her thoughts. Disgust and self-loathing for her own weakness tore at her insides. "Our bargain did not include this," she said against the sweat-swirled hair of his chest, her voice cold, all playfulness gone from her tone. "It should not have happened! And it cannot happen again! It was a mistake. There will be no 'next time' for us!"

She struggled to remove herself from his embrace, not able to bear his closeness another minute without proving herself to be a liar. Not when, in spite of everything, she was still burning to experience his kisses again. Not when every cell in her body was crying out to tell him she wanted a life full of "next times" with him.

"You mean you're not going to give me a chance to be 'terrific'?" Clay teased, still not realizing the game was over. "What about 'next time'?" he said, throwing her careless words back at her.

"I meant when you returned to the world of the whites! Not with me," she said, choking back sudden tears at the thought of Clay Donovan kissing another woman the way he had her. "It was not part of our bargain and will not happen again."

Clay laughed at her serious tone and idly fingered the locket dangling from her neck. "Don't be too sure about that, *Mrs. Donovan,*" he said, the threat in his friendly tone recognizable. "But in the meantime, you'd better see what you can do about carrying out your end of our bargain. Because as long as we stay in this farce of a marriage, every night we spend alone in this tepee has every possibility of being the 'next time'!"

Chapter Seven

Swatting at the annoying fly that had gotten progressively more persistent with each landing on his nose and upper lip, Clay rolled over onto his stomach and put his arms over his head. "Go away," he mumbled sluggishly into the buffalo robe where he slept, refusing to open his eyes.

As though the fly had heard him, it left him alone—just long enough for Clay to drift back to sleep. Then it was back, diving purposefully for his head, buzzing happily in his ear, tiptoeing gaily over his twitching nostril, as if its only reason in life was to agitate this one man.

"Get, damn it!" Clay shouted, jerking a tangle of deerskin sheet over his head.

The giggles that filled his ears brought him to partial alertness. His first thought was of Gentle Fawn, his perplexing Indian wife. *Temporary wife,* he quickly amended. But he rapidly realized the laughter was not hers. Gentle Fawn didn't giggle. She rarely even smiled. Who then?

With cautious movements, Clay removed the covering from his face just enough to expose one sleepy blue eye to the morning brightness. "Damn!" he grunted unhappily, ducking back under the sheet for protection from the glaring sunshine.

The mysterious giggles rose in ear-piercing glee.

"All right! I give up! What the hell's going on?" he roared, giving the sheet over his face an angry toss to his shoulders and raising up on his elbows to investigate.

The giggles turned to high squeals and scurrying footsteps as Clay's sights focused on the small culprits, who together with a sadistic insect had conspired to waken him.

"What're you doing in here?" Clay, who usually liked kids, growled impatiently, silencing the three round-faced Indian children with a bleary-eyed glare.

The brown-skinned youngsters, appearing to be about two, three, and four years old, didn't answer. But the suddenly frightened expressions that covered their faces told Clay that at least his displeasure had been understood, and he felt ashamed for scaring them. He grinned and softened his tone to say, "Go on back to your own tepee now."

The children returned Clay's smile with tentative ones of their own. But none of them moved.

"Go on! Shoo!" he said, losing his patience again. But they stayed rooted to the spot on the side of the tepee that had been rolled up to let in the morning breeze.

Suddenly a young Indian woman, obviously the mother of the wayward urchins, hurried toward the tepee, scolding her children as she approached. But before Clay could say thank you to her, the children began pointing toward him, their giggles resuming the

118

full-scale attack on his nerves.

The woman admonished her children in their own language, but was unable to control a smile that came over her attractive face when she looked in the direction they were indicating. And soon she was laughing heartily with her offspring.

"What the hell's this all about?" Clay bellowed, looking back over his shoulder to see what could be causing all the commotion.

There was nothing there. Nothing but him. Him in all his naked glory! His horrified gaze zeroed in on his long hairy legs and round buttocks, glaringly white at the moment and on blatant display for the world to see!

"Damn!" he shouted, wrestling with the twisted sheet around his neck and shoulders in a useless effort to cover himself. "Get out of here," he ordered, aware of the fiery blush that raged over his skin, turning everything, including his pale bottom, a bright shade of pink. The giggles increased perceptibly.

The smiling woman shushed her children understandingly. But they proceeded to ignore their mother's reprimand as she hurried across the tepee floor to Clay's side. Without bothering to hide her amusement, she snatched the unmanageable sheet out of Clay's hands and shook it out.

"Gentle Fawn!" Clay yelled, his eyes wide with fear. It was one thing to be attacked when you were fully dressed. But to be forced to defend himself in this naked, vulnerable condition was too much. "Gentle Fawn!" he wailed again, making a desperate grab for the deerskin cover.

Laughing at the white man's ridiculous efforts to hide his nakedness from her, the young mother spread the

119

untangled sheet over him, then dropped to her knees beside him. The wide grin never left her face.

In another situation, Clay might have found her attractive. Some would have even considered her beautiful. Her hair and almond-shaped eyes were even blacker than Gentle Fawn's, if that was possible, and her smooth skin darker. Though her teeth were slightly yellow, they were straight and all there, and she seemed reasonably clean. She was several inches taller than Gentle Fawn, her figure more womanly, and he guessed her to be in her early twenties. But when he compared her in his mind to Gentle Fawn, with her small, almost boyishly slim figure, this lovely woman still came up second best.

She seemed harmless enough, though, Clay decided, feeling more secure with his modesty once more intact. He turned over and sat up on the pallet—taking care to keep the sheet wrapped protectively around his waist. "Thank you," he said to the smiling woman.

She said something to him he couldn't understand. He gave her a friendly nod and said, "Where's Gentle Fawn? Where's my wife?"

"Wife," the woman repeated happily, turning to her children, who still watched from just inside the lodge. She said something to them in their language—Clay assumed she was sending one of them after Gentle Fawn.

But instead of leaving, the children squealed jubilantly and ran to where Clay sat on his buffalo robe clutching his sheet to him. The youngest plopped herself down in his lap and smiled up at him, her round face beaming radiantly as she tangled her chubby fingers curiously into the golden hair on his chest and pulled.

"Stop that!" he yowled in pain, the alarm in his voice

rising audibly as he swatted at the child's hand. "Where's my wife?"

"Wife," the pretty woman said again, patting her open hand on her becomingly full bosom. "Babies," she said sweeping her hand over her children proudly.

"Gentle Fawn!" Clay thundered, almost tossing the affectionate two-year-old off his lap in his effort to stand up and escape. "Gentle Fawn!"

"What is it, Clay Donovan?" Gentle Fawn asked pleasantly, appearing suddenly on the open side of the tepee.

"Who is this woman? She acts like she and her kids belong here."

"They do." Gentle Fawn smiled sweetly, her face radiating innocence.

"What!" Forgetting the precariously arranged sheet, he took an angry step toward her. The deerskin slipped down around his hips, coming dangerously close to exposing more than his rear end and legs. He grabbed for it, catching it just in time. He stood glowering down at her unflinching face. "What the hell's going on? Is this your tepee or not?" he hissed in a stage whisper that could be heard but not understood by everyone in the tepee.

"Not," she returned, the light in her dark eyes mischievous and challenging. "It was loaned to me by Firebird, the wife of Man of the People's son Daniel Blue Eagle. My marriage was arranged so suddenly that I had no time to make my own lodge cover. So they offered us its use while they were away."

"Oh," Clay said, thinking he understood. "So this is Firebird and she wants her tepee back." He indicated the other woman with a toss of his head. "It would have been nice if you'd warned me," he said out of the corner of his mouth as he took a playful yank on one of the four-year-old boy's braids and directed a polite smile at the mother. "And a hellova lot less embarrassing."

"No, this is not Firebird. This is my sister, Bright Sunshine. She, too, lost her husband in the battle on the Rosebud Creek."

"Then where's Firebird?"

"Since Bright Sunshine and her children have no man to protect and provide for them and I have no lodge to call my own, you and I will move into her tepee with her so I can return Firebird's to her when she comes back."

"Just exactly who are you expecting to take care of your sister?" Clay stuttered suspiciously, his blue eye furtively sneaking a glance at Gentle Fawn's attractive sister to see how much of the conversation she was comprehending. Evidently almost none because she was still smiling.

"You, Clay Donovan," Gentle Fawn answered.

Clay's mouth dropped open. "What the hell are you talking about? It's all I can do to take care of myself! Besides, I'm leaving as soon as I get my story! What happens to her then?"

"She will still have me when you leave. I will hunt and provide the food for our fire and she will tan the hides and cook the meals. It is a perfect plan."

"Perfect? You don't expect me to live in a tepee with both of you, do you?"

"Are you breaking our agreement, Clay Donovan? Are you leaving before you speak with Crazy Horse?" she asked, reminding him he only had two choices: leave and give up the story of a lifetime, stay and forget about any time alone with Gentle Fawn.

A light dawned in his brain. So that was it. She'd found a way to insure she wouldn't be put in the position of being alone with him again, he realized, becoming aware of the smug expression she was struggling to hide. It would serve her right if he grabbed her and threw her down on the buffalo robe and made love to her right then in front of her whole damn family—the whole damn tribe for that matter!

"I think I'll stick around until I get what I came for," he said with a thinly veiled threat in his voice. "But you'd better line up that interview fast. And Many Coups and his braves better pull out soon or I may come up with a 'perfect plan' of my own, *Mrs. Donovan!*"

Gentle Fawn took an instinctive step backward. She'd never seen Clay Donovan so angry, so frightening. His natural ability to find humor in the most serious situations seemed to have disappeared completely. He definitely wasn't laughing now!

A trickle of fear wormed its way throughout her body. What would he say when he found out Bright Sunshine also would be his wife after he spent the night in her tepee with her?

"Does she know any English?" he asked suddenly.

"Only a few words like—"

"Like 'wife' and 'babies,'" he broke in, nodding his head. "What's that all abou— My God! You told her she was going to be my wife, didn't you?" He took a step toward Gentle Fawn and grabbed her upper arm, dragging her against him. "Didn't you?" he blasted, causing her to turn her head to the side and squint her eyes shut as though receiving a physical blow to her face.

As she tried to think of an explanation to ease Clay's anger, Gentle Fawn received a temporary reprieve when a runner from Man of the People's tepee approached the lodge with a message that the chief wanted to see Clay and Gentle Fawn immediately.

Minutes later, dressed in borrowed buckskin leggings and a beaded shirt that Gentle Fawn had provided for him, Clay walked silently beside his wife toward Man of the People's lodge.

Gentle Fawn peeked warily at him out of the corner of her eye, unhappiness and dread distorting her lovely face. He was so angry about Bright Sunshine and her children. Was he angry enough to give up his plan to write about Crazy Horse and leave the camp without talking to the famous war chief? Would he try to leave before the Cheyennes did? Was he so angry that he would hand her over to Many Coups?

I should not have offered to share him with Bright Sunshine, she admitted to herself, directing another sidelong glance toward the tall golden man beside her. Even angry, his tanned face, now shadowed with a week's growth of reddish-blond beard was the most handsome one she'd ever seen. It was all she could do to keep from putting her hand on his arm and telling him she was sorry. *But it is his own fault. He should never have suggested that as long as we were supposed to be married we would have to act married even when we were alone!*

"I don't suppose you know what this is all about," he finally asked, his mouth twisted in a sarcastic snarl, one blond eyebrow arched knowingly. "How many wives am I going to walk away from *this* meeting with?"

Ignoring his referral to their unceremonious marriage, Gentle Fawn looked straight ahead and said, "I do not know why Man of the People wants to see us."

"I bet!" he mumbled, deliberately increasing his

124

stride, forcing Gentle Fawn to run to keep pace with him.

"You do not have to accept my sister as your wife," she hurriedly explained. "Though it is a Lakota custom for a married woman's husband to marry her sisters if they have no husbands of their own, it is not a law. I thought you would be pleased to have such a beautiful second wife—even for the short time you will be here."

"I didn't even want one wife! If you'll recall! What the hell made you think I would want to be saddled with two of them? And three giggling kids to boot!"

Gentle Fawn was surprised at the sense of relief that washed over her. He didn't want another wife! Even one as beautiful as Bright Sunshine.

Of course, if Clay Donovan didn't marry Bright Sunshine, Gentle Fawn still hadn't solved the problem of being alone with him at night. And she knew she had to think of something. Fast. Already she was too involved with him, finding herself thinking about him all the time, dreaming about him, longing for him. And each time they made love she would forget more and more completely who and what he was. She couldn't let that happen. And the only way to avoid it was to stay out of his arms—and buffalo robe!

As it was, every time he had kissed her, she'd found herself wishing their temporary marriage could go on forever, though she knew it was impossible. Even if he wanted it to—which he didn't. But if she allowed herself to give in to his charms again and again, she might begin to believe the impossible was possible, might even believe there was one white man in the world she could trust and care for. And if she let herself believe that, she would be totally destroyed when he left. *And he will leave!* she reminded herself sternly. *He only married you to get to*

Crazy Horse. He does not want you any more than he wants Bright Sunshine! And you do not want him!

"Then I will tell my older sister you do not wish to take her for your second wife," Gentle Fawn offered reluctantly. "Though she will be hurt by your rejection," she added in an effort to disguise the unexpected happiness her words brought to her heart.

"I'd hate to hurt your sister's feelings," Clay said sarcastically, bitter that Gentle Fawn had so casually agreed to share him with another woman. So much for thinking he might actually mean something to her besides a way out of a marriage to Many Coups. "She can be my wife as long as I stay!"

Gentle Fawn swung around to face Clay, unable to suppress the shocked gasp that burned in her throat or the stunned expression that twisted her face. But Clay didn't even notice her surprise—or so it seemed.

"After all, what difference does it make?" he went on sadistically. "One woman's pretty much like another. The more the merrier I always say! And like you pointed out earlier, she is quite beautiful!" he said, raising his eyebrows appreciatively and winking to be certain she got his meaning—not questioning his compelling desire to make her jealous.

Gentle Fawn stopped dead in her tracks and stared in stunned silence after Clay, who was walking quite well on his wounded leg now. In fact, his steps seemed lighter than before, as if he would break into a joyful leap at any moment.

She was filled with the urge to run after him and kick him, bite him, tear his eyes out. Not only was he going to take a second wife, but he was looking forward to it! How had she allowed herself to forget her hatred for him for even a moment? Had there actually been a wish to stay married to him? Well, that wouldn't happen again, she promised herself, vowing anew that he had touched her for the last time. She would die before she ever let him know that she had almost believed she felt something for him.

Gathering all the coolness she could manage with a roaring fire of anger raging destructively through her, she ran to catch up with Clay—who had actually begun to whistle gaily! "I am very happy you decided to take another wife. And my sister and her children will be happy, too," she said, every falsely sincere word she uttered catching in her throat.

"I'm glad something I've done makes you happy," Clay said snidely out of the corner of his mouth, then resumed his annoying whistling as he sauntered confidently up to the entrance of Man of the People's tepee and waited. Even though the sides of the lodge were rolled up, it would have been poor manners to walk over the threshold without an invitation.

"Come in, my children," the tall, aquiline-nosed chief called out, beckoning to them with a long-fingered brown hand. "Sit here, my son," he said to Clay, patting the place of honor to his left. He indicated that Gentle Fawn should sit to his right.

The young couple took their seats, Clay sitting cross-legged like the chief and Gentle Fawn resting properly on her heels. They waited expectantly for Man of the People to speak, but as with all important matters, no business would be conducted until they had shared a pipe of *kinnikinnick*. Without speaking, Man of the People filled the stone bowl of his pipe with the mixture of aromatic herbs and tobacco, then held the burning tip of a twig to it, puffing on the stem until the contents of the pipe were lit and the rich odor of smoke and tobacco filled their nostrils.

With slow deliberation, Man of the People drew deeply on the mouthpiece, exhaling the smoke leisurely as he handed the pipe to Clay. Imitating the older man, Clay sucked hard on the pipe, filling his mouth with the strong-tasting smoke. Doing his best not to choke, he quickly blew it out to mingle in the air with Man of the People's.

"The pipe is our line to the spirit world," Man of the People explained, taking another long drag of smoke and handing the pipe to Clay again. They would not know why Man of the People had called for them until the tobacco in the bowl of the pipe had all been smoked.

"Yes, sir," Clay said, having learned his lesson and taking a smaller puff on the pipe this time. He continued to fight the increasing need to cough with every bit of self-control he could summon to his aid.

"The smoke we exhale is the breath of our prayers. See how it curls its way upward into the air around us, into the spirit world?"

"Yes, sir. I do see," Clay said hoarsely.

"And that is why we never have an important discussion until we have smoked the pipe," Man of the People said with a smile as he took the last drag of the pipe and let the smoke out slowly.

Clay breathed a sigh of relief. One more puff of the strong-tasting tobacco and he was sure he'd have been sick—or at least two shades greener than he already was.

"What is it you wish to see us about, Man of the People?" Clay managed to ask, hoping the chief didn't notice he was on the verge of choking to death.

The chief smiled at the writer, fully aware how the smoke had affected him and admiring his valiant efforts to overcome it. He couldn't help thinking it was a shame that Clay Donovan hadn't been born a Lakota instead of white. "How is your leg?" he asked the younger man.

"Much better, thank you," Clay answered, realizing this conversation would be conducted on the chief's timetable and nothing he could do or say would hurry it. He relaxed against the beaded backrest behind him and shot Gentle Fawn a disarming grin. "My wife is a very good nurse."

Man of the People looked from the smiling man to Gentle Fawn and was puzzled by the angry sparks he could almost see flying from the girl's dark eyes. "I am glad to hear that," he said, keeping his curious thoughts to himself. "Because Many Coups has challenged you to a fight for your wife."

Clay and Gentle Fawn both gulped and leaned forward in unison, his eyes round with surprise, hers with worry. "Can he do that?" Clay objected.

"Yes." Man of the People nodded sadly.

"You mean to tell me if a man desires another man's wife he can just take her? That's the craziest damn thing I've ever heard of! What if she doesn't want to go?"

Man of the People answered Clay with an understanding smile of helplessness.

"I don't suppose I could talk him into taking Bright Sunshine instead!" Clay suggested with false hopefulness. "No, I didn't think so." He answered his own question with resignation. "Well, when's this fight supposed to take place?"

Certain Clay would not stand a chance in a fight against the larger Many Coups, Gentle Fawn interrupted, her tone desperate. "A fight will not be necessary, Man of the People. I will leave Clay Donovan and go with Many Coups."

Clay's mouth dropped open in stunned surprise, then closed again, his lips stretching tight in a grim, angry line. What was she up to now? Was she trying to make him feel guilty if he turned away from her? He ought to let her go. It would serve her right after the Bright Sunshine incident. But was he really so angry that, in order to protect himself, he was willing to let her become another man's wife, share another man's bed? *Besides, what about my story on Crazy Horse?*

"When do we fight?" he said again, ignoring Gentle Fawn's practical solution to his problem. He told himself the only reason he was considering this insanity was that he had no intention of giving up his excuse to stay in the Lakota village until he'd talked to Crazy Horse. Until he got that interview, Gentle Fawn was his and it was going to stay that way! When he left, anyone mentally unsound enough to want her would be welcome to her as far as he was concerned. But in the meantime . . . "When?" he ground out.

"You cannot fight with him, Clay Donovan!" Gentle Fawn cried, her dark eyes filling with confusing tears. "You will be killed!"

"Your wife is right, my son," Man of the People said, hoping to talk the headstrong white man out of his foolish decision, while respecting him all the more for it. "Many Coups' fight will be to the death."

"Why doesn't that surprise me?" Clay said, directing his angry gaze toward Gentle Fawn. *I must be crazy. She said she'd go with the Indian. What's stopping me from letting her go? The story? What the hell kind of story am I*

130

going to write if I'm dead? Still, despite all of his arguments as to why he shouldn't do it, he knew his decision was already made. He would fight Many Coups for a wife he hadn't even wanted and intended to leave within a few weeks. *Maybe I bumped my head when I fell last night,* he thought in a futile effort to understand his reasoning—or lack of it!

"When do we fight?" he asked, his voice even and determined.

"Many Coups wanted to meet you tonight, but since we will be staying here for a few days to rest and graze our horses, I shall ask him to put off his challenge until your wound is healed."

"No," Clay said with stunned resignation. "Tonight is fine. Tell Many Coups I'll be there." Clay rose and left the chief's lodge, not seeing the looks of dread that passed between Gentle Fawn and Man of the People.

"Why, Clay Donovan?" she said when she caught up with him a minute later. "Why will you fight with a man who will surely kill you when you do not have to?"

Why indeed? he asked himself, stopping in his tracks and looking down at the petite girl, the evasive answer to his question just out of his grasp. "Why do you think, Gentle Fawn?" he asked, gazing intently into her black eyes and seeing himself mirrored there.

"Our bargain? Is that it? If so, I will release you from it!" she suggested desperately, not even curious as to why it made any difference to her what he did. Whether he died in the fight or left before it could occur, she would still be forced to marry Many Coups.

She only knew she could not bear the thought of his death, could not bear the idea of a world, even though it would not be her world, that did not have Clay Donovan

131

in it. All the laughter and color would be gone if he died. The green grass and blue sky would become bleak and gray, and the birds would cease their singing. "Please do not fight with Many Coups."

"I suppose honoring a bargain is as good a reason as any other," he said, studying her intent face for signs of . . . What? "Why is it so important to you that I don't fight?"

"You will be killed!" she shouted. "Can you understand that? He will kill you!"

"And you want to save that pleasure for yourself," he said, throwing her angry words of the day before up to her.

"What difference does my reason make? Perhaps I only hate the idea of a needless death on my conscience."

"What makes you so certain I'll be the one to die? Maybe his death is the one you'll have on your conscience!"

"Do not be a fool, Clay Donovan. Even if you were not recovering from an injury, he would kill you! He is bigger than you. He is a warrior, trained from birth to fight. You are not!"

"Your confidence in your husband is comforting, Mrs. Donovan!" he said coolly, turning away and taking long, purposeful strides toward the tepee.

"I do not want you to die, Clay Donovan!" she whimpered, watching through eyes glassed with tears as he strode away from her. But her words were too late. He had already disappeared into the lodge. "Do you understand? I do not want you to die!"

Chapter Eight

Pungent with the odor of the burning smudge pots already lit to ward off the mosquitoes that plagued the warm summer nights, the early evening breeze tripped energetically through the Indian village. But breezes and smudgepots and mosquitoes were the farthest things from the minds of the people in the combined Cheyenne and Lakota camp. After a night and day of staying in one place, they were well rested and ready for excitement. And this evening promised to fulfill their every expectation.

Gathered to witness a contest of strength between two men sworn to kill each other, the mood of festivity ran high. For these were not just any two men. This was an encounter between one of their own and a man who was an enemy to them all—a *wasicun*.

There was no doubt in anyone's mind that the golden-haired white man would be killed. Three inches shorter and perhaps thirty-five pounds lighter than the powerful Cheyenne chief—and favoring a wounded leg—he didn't stand a chance. And no one wanted to miss witnessing the spilling of a single drop of his hated white man's blood.

Anxiously chewing on her bottom lip, the person who had the most to lose in the ensuing struggle stood in the front line of the circle of spectators. She also was certain Clay Donovan would be killed, and she told herself that the only reason she cared was that it would mean she would be obligated to go with Many Coups. But her body was not so easily convinced as her brain, and at the thought of the white man's defeat, a convulsive knot formed unexpectedly in her stomach.

Gentle Fawn clutched at her midriff in an effort to stop the gripping pain. She told herself the ache had been caused by something she ate—assuring herself again that she didn't care if Clay Donovan lived or died. She had only wanted him alive long enough to keep Many Coups from claiming her. That was why she was so worried about the outcome of the battle. No other reason.

Yet, somehow she could not shake the feeling that if the white man died, part of her would die, too. And she could not tear her eyes from the man who was officially her husband—as though he would stay alive as long as she was able to keep him in sight.

Their faces void of expression, Clay and Many Coups circled the inside perimeter of the ring of expectant people, sizing each other up and planning their strategies. Both men had shed their shirts; and though they had yet to make physical contact, their flesh already glowed with a sheen of perspiration as the firelight danced over the rippling muscles of their powerful backs and chests and arms.

Dressed only in a breechcloth, Many Coups bared his teeth in a ferocious snarl. Imitating an enraged bear, he growled and made several threatening jumps in succession toward Clay. Each time the Indian made one of his menacing lunges at his opponent, Gentle Fawn's heart vaulted with fear. Every leap could be the one that was genuine, could be the one that brought Many Coups close enough to the white man to sink his gleaming knife into Clay's defenseless belly.

Easily sidestepping the short, taunting jabs of Many Coups' knife, Clay suddenly gave his adversary a disarming grin. "Don't you want to talk this over first?" he said. Switching his knife to his left hand, he took a step toward Many Coups and offered his right hand to the surprised Indian in what Gentle Fawn knew to be the white man's sign of friendship.

Confused by his enemy's behavior, Many Coups stopped in mid-lunge and stared at him.

A deathly silence fell over the crowd gathered to observe the bloodletting.

Gentle Fawn watched in horrified silence as the stunned expression in Many Coups' black eyes changed almost imperceptibly to one of malevolent purpose.

His face broke into a wide grin. He, too, switched his knife to his other hand and reached out to take Clay's hand.

It is a trick, Clay Donovan! she wanted to shout but found that her voice was nothing more than a strangled moan. Then it was too late. Too late to save Clay Donovan, too late to stop the horror unfolding before her eyes.

Just as Many Coups gripped Clay's outreached hand, the Cheyenne chief let a blood-chilling yell and jerked Clay toward him. Lifting the lighter man off his feet with the sudden attack, Many Coups lunged at Clay's exposed midsection with his left hand—the hand that gripped his knife as efficiently as though it was the hand the Indian wielded the knife in naturally.

"So much for handling this on a friendly basis," Clay said, twisting his torso to the side, just as the gleaming blade of Many Coups' knife should have disappeared into his belly. At the same time, he wrapped his right leg behind his opponent's ankle and pulled the warrior's foot out from under him as he took advantage of his own forward momentum and knocked Many Coups on the shoulder with the hand the Cheyenne still held.

A look of amazement on his hard features, Many Coups toppled over backward, losing his grip on Clay's hand and expelling a loud woosh of air as Clay landed on top of him. "Ready to call it quits?" Clay grunted, unwisely using his momentary edge to catch his breath, rather than following up his attack and finishing the fight with his knife.

Many Coups bucked suddenly, taking Clay off guard and rolling over on top of him. The look on his dark face was obsessed, and the vengeful gleam in his black eyes burned for blood. His mouth stretched in a savage, prepare-to-meet-your-*wasicun*-god grin, and Many Coups raised his knife for the final blow.

New terror flooded through Gentle Fawn and she couldn't keep from screaming out her fright. "Do not kill him, Many Coups! I will go with you!"

But her plea for mercy was useless—even if Many Coups had been able to hear her terrified voice over the triumphant cheers for blood which had risen to a deafening roar. Resigning herself to the fact that there would be no mercy for Clay Donovan, she took an angry swipe at the tears streaming down her face and steeled herself to continue watching the fight until its bloody conclusion.

With a strength even he didn't know he possessed, Clay blocked the downward thrust of Many Coups' knife with his forearm, managing to roll the larger but slower man off him. Leaping up to a ready crouch, he faced the other man, challenge bright in his eyes.

Switching his knife back into his right hand, the surprised Indian jumped up from the ground, too. Without warning, he bent his head low, let out a loud feral growl, and rushed Clay.

Seeing him coming, Clay gave the charging bull of a man a cocky grin and said, "You don't learn, do you?" His timing perfect, he brought his boot up off the ground, catching Many Coups under the chin. Many Coups' head snapped back and he staggered clumsily, the look in his black eyes dazed. Trying valiantly to regain his forward movement, he managed only one faltering step, then fell gracelessly on his face.

"I tried to warn you," Clay apologized insincerely as he bored a knee into the almost unconscious Indian's back. He grabbed a fistful of black hair and jerked his head up. Knowing what was expected of the victor, he held the gleaming blade of his own knife against Many Coups' forehead at the base of his scalp. "What the hell am I doing?" he suddenly growled angrily. With a disgusted grunt, he dropped Many Coups' face back into the dirt and stood up.

Unaware that the wound on his leg had opened again, he limped away from the helpless man on the ground. He looked around the sea of brown faces that encircled him, seeking out the one face that never seemed to be very far from his mind. What would she think now? Would she be proud of him? Or would she be disappointed that he had beaten Many Coups?

As Clay searched the crowd for the one face he hoped

would be happy he was still alive, the disgraced Cheyenne rallied. His face red with rage, he vaulted to his feet and charged Clay's back, his knife poised for lethal attack.

"Clay Donovan, watch out!" the victor suddenly heard over the crowd's unified gasp of surprise.

But before he could locate the source of the warning, Clay heard Many Coups nearing him. Learned as a child in the streets of New York City slums and now an automatic reflex, his talent for survival did not fail him. Without turning, Clay bent forward at the waist, kicking his boot straight out behind him as he pivoted on his good leg.

The sound of his hard leather sole breaking ribs seemed to reverberate through the air as Clay's foot made purposeful contact with Many Coups' mid-section.

The hushed crowd watched in amazement as the Indian's large body lifted off the ground and was hurled backward.

Clay took a flying leap across the space that separated them, landing on the beaten Indian's chest and yelling at him. "Damn you! Why'd you do that? I don't want to kill you! I've beaten you. She's mine now. Can't we just leave it at that?"

"You must kill me, *wasicun*," Many Coups spat, his command proud.

My God! I'm damned if I do and damned if I don't! Clay thought helplessly. He knew the Cheyenne would be shamed if his enemy took pity on him and spared his life, not to mention the fact that the Lakotas would think the winner a coward if he showed mercy. Clay knew he had no choice. A look of helpless sadness changing his handsome features, he raised his knife with resolve. But still he hesitated.

Time seemed to stand still as black eyes stared unflinchingly into blue and the gleaming blade hovered, as though suspended, over the defeated Indian's chest.

"Do it, *wasicun*," Many Coups taunted, his expression courageous.

"Why couldn't you let it go? Why, damn it?" Clay cursed savagely. Making his decision, he raised the knife higher before he could change his mind. Not allowing himself to vacillate any longer, he brought his knife downward with all the anger he felt for being placed in this position—burying the blade to the hilt in the dirt beside Many Coups' ear.

Disgustedly dragging himself to his feet, he staggered away from the defeated chief. He knew that Many Coups would be his enemy for life—and that the Lakotas would think he was soft for not killing the other man. But at least he would be able to live with himself. And in the long run, that's all a man could hope for out of life.

Though he had not been able to spot her before, now as if he'd suddenly been provided with a magical homing instinct, Clay went directly to where Gentle Fawn stood, his limping gait more pronounced with each step he took.

Surprised to see that she'd been crying, his heart swelled with a warmth he did not try to understand. She had actually been worried about him!

His eyes glowing with wonder, he reached out to gently brush the backs of his fingers over her wet cheek. "Well, Mrs. Donovan, are those tears because I won or lost?" he teased.

"Why did you not kill him, Clay Donovan?" Gentle Fawn asked, her tone more harsh than she realized as she stoically resisted the urge to close her eyes and melt into the sweet caress on her face, too proud to admit how relieved she was that this man she claimed to hate was still alive.

Clay's hand dropped to his side, the smile on his face souring visibly. She hadn't been the least bit happy to see him safe—not even impressed with his ability to defend himself against a Cheyenne warrior. She only wanted to know why he hadn't done a more thorough job!

"I didn't see any point in killing a man I'd already defeated," Clay said, his tone sarcastic.

"But he is your enemy."

"He's a man, Gentle Fawn! And I have no desire to kill a man who is just fighting for what he believes belongs to him," he ground out harshly. "Not even for a lady as beautiful and scheming as you," he added with a sardonic twist to his mouth. "So I guess you'll just have to find yourself another 'husband' to kill off any unwanted suitors when I leave. Because evidently I'm not the man for the job!"

Taking only a few silent seconds to comprehend Clay's insinuations, Gentle Fawn's eyes rounded in indignant surprise. Her mouth dropped open to protest. "You think that is why I marr—"

But before she could defend herself against his insulting accusation by pointing out he had been the one who insisted on accepting Many Coups' challenge, she was interrupted. Bright Sunshine hurried over to Clay's side, chattering happily in her own language, her round face beaming with pride.

"At least *this wife* appreciates what her husband's been through," Clay said to Gentle Fawn, his tone contemptuous as he turned to Bright Sunshine and favored her with his most captivating smile. "I don't understand a word you say, Bright Sunshine, but I sure like the way you say it. And it beats the hell out of the conversation I've been having."

Deliberately turning his back on Gentle Fawn, he put his arm around the other young woman's shoulders and hugged her warmly. "Why don't you and I go celebrate?" He glanced back at the stunned Gentle Fawn and grinned pointedly, then gave his total attention to Bright Sunshine. "Let's go to your lodge and see if we can't get better acquainted."

Gentle Fawn clamped her hand over her mouth in an attempt to silence an enraged gasp that wheezed loudly in her throat.

But she wasn't quick enough to disguise her reaction —the reaction Clay had hoped for. He smiled to himself, her obvious fury helping to ease some of his own hurt and disappointment.

She sure did understand, "Let's go to your lodge"! Gentle Fawn thought bitterly as, rooted to the ground where she stood, she stared after the happy "newlyweds" as they walked away together.

Why was she so upset? she scolded herself. This was what she had wanted. She cared nothing for Clay Donovan. The entire second marriage had been her idea so she wouldn't have to put up with his masculine appetites until she no longer needed to be married to him. She'd accomplished what she'd set out to accomplish. So why was she feeling so lost and sad? She should be pleased with the way things had worked out. She didn't have to marry Many Coups *or* tolerate Clay Donovan any longer. So what difference did it make to her where he spent his nights—as long as she wasn't spending hers with Many Coups! *I am happy about the way things turned out!* she told herself again.

"Gentle Fawn, Gentle Fawn," a high, childish voice appealed in the language of the Lakotas. "Can we go to Quiet Rain's lodge now!"

"All the others have left!" a second young voice pointed out practically.

"What?" Gentle Fawn answered absently, slowly becoming aware of the tugging on her dress and three small expectant faces looking up at her. "Oh, yes," she said, taking a despondent look around at her surroundings.

The area, teeming with people a few minutes before, was still. The disappointed villagers had gone back to their lodges to smoke their pipes and discuss the night's surprising events. Only Gentle Fawn and Bright Sunshine's three small children remained.

Cursing herself for offering to keep her sister's youngsters in Quiet Rain's tepee so Bright Sunshine and Clay Donovan could be alone on their "wedding night," Gentle Fawn scooped the two-year-old up in her arms and smiled sadly. "You are right. Everyone is gone and it is late."

Too late to be wondering what she'd been thinking of when she'd suggested sharing Clay Donovan with Bright Sunshine. Too late to think about how much she wished she were the "bride" in Clay Donovan's arms tonight. And it was certainly too late to change her mind and put things back the way they were!

Clay ran his hand over his freshly shaved cheeks and chin, checking his skin's smoothness for the fifth time. It was no use. There were no whiskers left to remove. Every bit of stubble had been scraped away—not to mention a

142

layer or two of skin. He'd killed all the time he could. It was time to get on with what was expected of him.

He sucked in a deep sigh, and let it out slowly. He'd already failed to live up to the Lakotas' idea of a man once tonight when he hadn't been able to kill Many Coups. He couldn't fail again.

If he didn't make love to Bright Sunshine, by morning it would be all over the camp that the white man was really one of those prissy men who pranced around the camp in women's clothing. Though he realized the Lakotas accepted the effeminate *winktes*, who not only dressed but looked and acted like women, as special people with the gift of prophecy, Clay had no intentions of giving anyone reason to believe he was one of them. *Over my dead body they will!*

Determination ruling his every action, he dried his hands and razor on a fresh bandanna and replaced his shaving equipment in his saddlebags, not admitting to himself that he was taking undue care to refasten the rawhide straps on the flaps more securely than the minimal value of the contents warranted.

What was the big deal? Why was he dragging his feet? It wasn't as if Bright Sunshine lacked appeal. She was one of the prettiest women he'd seen in the camp. And it wasn't as if he hadn't been with dozens of different women during his adult life. Since when had feeling something for them been a prerequisite to giving and receiving pleasure from a woman? Besides, it wasn't as if he was really married to Gentle Fawn. It wasn't even as if he cared for her or she cared for him. They were just two strangers who'd used each other to achieve their goals— and enjoyed a few pleasant moments in the sack together. Nothing more!

"So what's holding you back, Donovan?" he mumbled aloud, stepping resolutely up to the entrance of the tepee where he knew Bright Sunshine waited for him.

Unaware how long she'd been lying there, staring out the open smoke flap at the peak of her mother's tepee, Gentle Fawn took a deep breath and squeezed her eyes shut—again. But it was no use. Though her body was exhausted, she couldn't sleep. Her lids popped open again to resume her study of the star-studded triangle of black sky she could see through the tepee roof.

Her mother's familiar snores, little more than whispery wheezes she'd heard all her life, seemed to resound in the darkness of the tepee like an orchestra of shrill eagle-wing-bone whistles. And the soft whimpers and moans of Bright Sunshine's children, sweet on any other night, were slowly and methodically driving her nerves to distraction.

She couldn't stand it another minute. Turning over onto her stomach, she clamped her hands over her ears to shut out the sounds.

But her obsessive curiosity got the better of her, and she removed her hands. Listening for the sounds that came from outside the lodge, she told herself she wasn't trying to hear what was happening in Bright Sunshine's tepee next door. She was simply trying to see how many night sounds she could identify—as a game to help her relax and go to sleep.

Crickets—it sounded like several million. Mosquitoes with no regard for the smudge pots. A dog scratching itself outside her mother's lodge. A wolf in the distance. The soft hum of men's voices from across the camp. A baby crying. All adding to the infuriating chorus of sounds that had conspired to keep her awake.

And to make matters worse, a tiny voice inside her head kept reminding her that she had no one to blame for her insomnia but herself. If she hadn't been so determined not to be a real wife to Clay Donovan while they were married . . . If she hadn't practically forced him to take Bright Sunshine as a second wife . . . If not for her own foolish stubbornness, she would have been with him right that minute. She would be the one in his arms—not her sister.

He could be kissing her mouth, or adoring her breasts in the way that sent glorious heat soaring through her body. He could be . . .

Gentle Fawn let a low moan of agony and squirmed restlessly on her buffalo robe.

Was that what he was doing with Bright Sunshine now? Kissing her mouth and caressing her large breasts. Was he telling her how beautiful she was? Was he teasing with her? Was his hand, forceful and gentle at once, prying Bright Sunshine's long thighs apart so that he could enter her anxious body, fill her with his masculinity?

Stop! she screamed inwardly, sitting up and looking around hopelessly. What was wrong with her? How could she be lying here having such thoughts about a man? A white man! An enemy. Killer of the People!

She grabbed desperately at the locket around her neck. The gold searing into her palm, she remembered her vow to use the laughing faces inside the necklace to remind her how much she hated the whites—*all* whites. Opening the old piece of jewelry, she ran her fingers over the pictures inside, certain the faces there were so engraved on her memory that she'd be able to imagine every feature, even though she couldn't see them in the dark.

But it did no good. She couldn't conjure up the faces she needed to see to refuel her hatred. They weren't real. Only one face came to her mind. Only that one was real. Only one smiling white face that she couldn't bring herself to hate no matter how she tried.

But it is too late! You told him you did not want him. You gave him to her. You threw him away!

Suddenly another picture came to her mind. She'd seen Clay Donovan go to the stream to bathe. He might not have come back yet. She didn't know how long she'd been here fighting sleep. Maybe it had only seemed like hours. It could have been only minutes! *He may not have gone into Bright Sunshine's lodge yet!*

Disregarding every intelligent thought she'd ever had, Gentle Fawn jumped up and dashed to the lodge entrance. *I will go to the stream and tell him I was wrong. I will tell him I do want him. It must not be too late!*

With her heart lighter than it had been in hours, Gentle Fawn hurried outside.

A movement beside Bright Sunshine's tepee startled Gentle Fawn and she glanced over there, instinctively stepping back into the shadows of Quiet Rain's lodge.

Holding her breath, Gentle Fawn watched as a man—a tall, broad-shouldered man who was unaware of the magical way the moonlight reflected off his golden hair—disappeared into Bright Sunshine's tepee.

The dog continued to scratch, the crickets to chirp, the mosquitoes to ignore the smudge pots. But now Gentle Fawn was oblivious to them. She heard nothing. Nothing but the sound of her own heart exploding in her chest as she stood staring at the empty doorway into Bright

Sunshine's lodge. And for the second time that day, tears streamed down her face because of Clay Donovan.

Inside Quiet Rain's lodge, her mother and sister's children continued to sleep peacefully, totally unaware that right outside the very soul of their daughter and aunt was crumbling into tiny pieces.

A blessed state of numbness washed over Gentle Fawn. She'd almost made a fool of herself and it didn't even matter. All that mattered was that she was too late. There was nothing left for her.

With shoulders slumped, and feet almost too leaden to move, she returned to her buffalo robe in her mother's lodge and lay back down—certain she would never want to rise again.

The moon lit the interior of the buffalo hide lodge with a strange unearthly light, filling Clay with the feeling that he was being controlled by someone, or something, other than his own brain. What was he doing here? When had this craziness begun?

"Husband," a soft female voice murmured from the pallet on the back side of the tepee.

Clay's head jerked up, as though he hadn't expected the tepee to be occupied.

"Husband—Wife!" Bright Sunshine cooed seductively as she raised up her arms to Clay, bidding him to join her on the buffalo robe.

When he didn't respond to the tempting picture she made, her black hair loose and caping her shoulders seductively, her black eyes large and filled with honest desire, she giggled nervously. With a teasing glint in her eyes, she lifted the sheet draped over her voluptuous body to display the rest of her charms and motioned invitingly to Clay.

Still he stood unmoving, his eyes wide with amazement.

"Husband—Wife!" she said, her coo taking on a petulant whine. Her expression becoming more determined, she sat up and tossed the cover aside completely. Sliding her tongue over her lips in an obvious invitation, she held his eyes with her own as she placed her hands tenderly under her heavy breasts, lifting them upward for him to view, offering them to him for his pleasure.

My God! What's wrong with me? She's beautiful! Why don't I feel something? Something besides the need to get the hell out of here!

"That's it!" he suddenly said, crossing to the alluring Indian woman and yanking the sheet up off the ground. "This has gone too far!" he mumbled angrily, cursing himself for a jackass as he jerked her to her feet and wound her protesting frame mummylike in the blanket.

Bright Sunshine's eyes opened wide with hurt and filled with tears. She began to chatter in her own language, begging him not to reject her.

"Believe me, sugar. It's not you. It's me," he said sincerely, knowing she couldn't understand him, but still feeling the need to explain. "Whatever that squaw put on the knife blade she used to cut my leg must've affected my brain! Because there's no way in hell a man in his right mind would turn down anything as pretty and willing as you."

"No husband?" Bright Sunshine asked, her full pouting mouth turned down at the corners.

"Not this one anyway," Clay said, shaking his head

148

regretfully. "I'm sorry." *You'll never know how sorry*, he reiterated to himself, taking one more doleful look at the beautiful face that looked up at him, her pain streaming wetly down her cheeks.

He smiled sadly and kissed Bright Sunshine on the forehead, then gently pushed her back down to the mat. "Go on to sleep now, and things will look better in the morning!" *'Cause they sure as hell can't look much worse!*

Chapter Nine

"Gentle Fawn!" Clay roared. "Get your butt out here right this minute!"

Everyone in the tepee—Gentle Fawn, Quiet Rain, and Bright Sunshine's children—sat up in unison and looked around at one another, their sleepy expressions frightened and confused.

"I'm counting to five and then I'm coming in after you!" There was a slight pause, and Gentle Fawn held her breath, waiting for the word that would surely come in the next instant. "One!"

"What is it, my mother's sister?" the oldest child asked, his eyes round with fear as he put his arm protectively around the shoulders of his younger brother and sister.

"Two!"

Taught from birth not to cry aloud, the two-year-old began to whimper softly as the three scooted closer to their aunt.

"Three!"

Stirrings from the surrounding lodges were beginning

to be heard. She had to do something before the entire village thought it was under attack.

Her feelings a tumultuous mix of anger and fear Gentle Fawn gave the children each an assuring pat, then stood up. Sending her mother an apologetic look over her shoulder, she made a frantic dash toward the entrance of the lodge. "I will take care of this!" she promised, her voice displaying more confidence than she felt.

"You cannot go out there!' Quiet Rain whispered rushing after her daughter and catching her by the arm to hold her back. "He has gone crazy!"

"Four!"

Gentle Fawn looked nervously toward the hide of the doorflap that she knew was the only thing between her and the madman outside. "I have to before he wakes up the whole village!"

"But he will kill you!"

"I have no choice, Mother. Now let me go!" Gentle Fawn said firmly, giving a determined shrug and freeing her arm from Quiet Rain's restraining grasp.

"Five! Okay, lady. That's it! You asked for it!"

"I am coming," Gentle Fawn hissed irritably. "Just quit all that bellowing! You sound like a wounded bull!"

"Let's go!" he said, grabbing her arm and starting to walk away from her mother's tepee the instant she appeared in the doorway, his strong fingers digging painfully into her firm flesh.

"I am not going anywhere until you tell me what this is all about!" she said, planting her feet firmly and refusing to budge.

"Have it your way!" Clay said, tossing her over his shoulder and continuing his long angry strides across the camp.

"What are you doing?" she choked, pounding her fists against his back—which she couldn't help noticing was bare. "Put me down!" she growled, with noticeably less impetus, knowing even as she spoke that she wasn't sure she wanted him to do her bidding.

Warriors began to appear in their doorways, their rifles and bows in readiness, wives and children peeking out from behind them.

Clay smiled and nodded at the curious onlookers as though they were simply passing on the street, as though he hadn't awakened half the Oglala camp circle. As though he wasn't carrying a human cargo of kicking, squirming woman through the middle of the camp.

"It's okay, folks. You can go on back to sleep now. Just a little spat between me and the little woman here. Gotta show 'em who's boss, ya know!"

"Oooh!" Gentle Fawn squealed, renewing her efforts to be free. But her kicks and punches might as well have been against the nonbudging trunk of a large tree for all the good they did. He was oblivious to them.

The roused Indians watched blankly, until one old woman began to laugh. She quickly translated Clay's words for the enjoyment of the others, and soon all the grim faces in the doorways were grinning happily. Laughing heartily and nodding their heads in understanding toward Clay, the braves turned and herded their families back into their lodges. The sounds of their laughter could still be heard after they'd all gone back inside.

"What are we doing here?" Gentle Fawn asked furiously, the sting of the men's laughter still rankling painfully. He ignored her question as if she hadn't spoken. Continuing his purposeful stride up to the empty tepee, he yanked the doorflap aside. "This is Firebird's lodge!" she protested.

"Well, you and I are going to use it until she gets back or you sew us a new one—or I leave!" he said, dropping his objecting package abruptly onto the buffalo robe at his feet.

"I wish you would leave *now!* I wish I had never set eyes on you, Clay Donovan!" she said scornfully as she struggled to sit up.

"That's quite evident, *Mrs. Donovan,*" he ground out. "But, unfortunately, until you uphold your end of our bargain, you're going to see a whole lot of me!" The lines of anger furrowing deeply between his blond eyebrows, his tone implied a more profound meaning to his words than just "seeing" each other.

Hating herself for being afraid, Gentle Fawn couldn't stop herself from instinctively quailing back against the wall of Firebird's tepee to escape the anger of the man who glowered so ominously above her. "Is that a threat?" she returned, doing her best to keep her voice level and look him in the eyes.

"Honey, that's not a threat. It's a promise!"

"Good. Then I will look forward to seeing the last of you tomorrow," she snarled, feeling some of her courage returning and sitting up straighter. "Because Crazy Horse has told his wife he will speak to you then."

Clay stopped and studied the belligerent face that glared resentfully up at him. He cocked a thick eyebrow suspiciously. "Exactly when did you find this out?"

"Tonight, after you and your 'new wife'"—her lip curled and she wrinkled her nose distastefully—"left," she threw at him angrily.

"Why didn't you come tell me right away?"

"I did not think you would appreciate having your time with my sister interrupted," she explained derisively.

Then the full impact of what she'd told him hit full force, and he completely disregarded her sarcastic answer. He was actually going to be able to talk to Crazy Horse in the morning. And then he would be free to go! Free to leave this crazy place where people were married with no ceremony, where women sanctioned their husbands having other wives, where men considered death preferable to the dishonor of losing a fight. And best of all, he'd be free to leave this woman who had brought him nothing but frustration and trouble from the moment he'd first found her!

"Well, that is good news!" he said, still standing over her, his feet wide apart, his fists balled at his lean hips. Somehow his voice didn't sound as happy as it should have—even to his own ears. Why wasn't he more exhilarated by the news? It was what he had come here for, he reminded himself harshly. It was what he'd nearly gotten himself killed for. Not once, but three times! Of course, it *was* good news!

"Yes, it is," she agreed softly, wondering at the sudden feeling of loss that flooded over her.

"So, the great moment is at hand. We'll finally be able to wash our hands of each other," he said, lowering his muscular frame to the buffalo robe to sit beside her. Turning to face her, he cupped her chin in his warm palm and said, "This calls for a celebration, don't you think?"

Remembering he'd said the same thing to Bright Sunshine earlier, the word "celebration" triggered a new surge of rage in Gentle Fawn.

"No!" she shouted, the word exploding from her

mouth as she twisted her face out of his hand and crossed her wrists beside her cheek, as if warding off evil spirits with a protective shield. "You have celebrated enough for one night."

"I haven't even begun," he said, his voice a tempting caress as he leaned toward her, the mischievous smile on his face sending an irritating jab of desire cutting into her vitals.

Paralyzed with an unnamed emotion, Gentle Fawn could do nothing in her own defense.

Taking a slender wrist in each of his hands, he uncrossed them and placed them on either side of his strong neck, holding them there until he felt the resistance melt from them.

"But we have both lived up to our end of the bargain," she protested weakly, her gaze drawn to his in spite of herself. "It is all over now." Her voice was hoarse, uncertain.

"Not yet, Gentle Fawn. It's not all over until I actually talk to Crazy Horse. And until then, you're still my wife."

Like a cat stalking a bird, he moved toward her so slowly she couldn't be sure it wasn't her imagination that his face was several inches closer to hers than it had been.

"Please," she whimpered.

"Please, what?" he teased, moving his lips so close to hers that she could feel his breath on her skin.

"Please, do not kiss me," she pleaded, knowing her last ounce of resistance would be destroyed if he did.

He was so near now that she could feel a magnetic current pulling at her lips, beckoning them to his. "You don't mean that, do you, my little wife?"

"No—" she whispered, shaking her head. "I mean

yes!" she quickly amended, though unconvincingly.

"Poor little Indian princess," he said, his lips brushing against her soft mouth as he spoke. "Doesn't know what she wants, does she?"

Unable to resist his persistant seduction or her own body's screams for respite, Gentle Fawn could deceive herself no longer. This was what she wanted. She could not deny herself the glorious pleasures of his lovemaking this one last night. They would end their marriage tomorrow and go their separate ways. But tonight she would be a wife to him one last precious time.

With every protest removed from her mind and heart, Gentle Fawn's hands stole around Clay's neck. Her slender fingers furrowed into his thick gold hair, still damp from his prolonged bath, and she pulled him gently to her. Aligning her lips sweetly on his, she opened her mouth and licked hungrily along his lips, seeking and finding welcome entrance as his mouth opened under hers.

Pleasantly surprised by her innocent eagerness, Clay remained perfectly still. He allowed her the leisure to explore the moist interior of his mouth with the tip of her tongue. He was thrilled with the observation that she grew braver and more aggressive with each forage into his mouth.

Unable to restrain himself any longer, his arms closed around her as he hauled her hard against him, his own tongue plunging thirstily into her mouth now. His hands traveled demandingly over her back, fitting her soft curves against the harder planes of his body with wild urgency as he lowered her back onto the fur pallet.

She went back easily, the building tension in her lower body finding momentary assuagement with the feel of his weight on her.

He withdrew his mouth from hers, gasping for air, as though his passion had drained his lungs of all their oxygen. Propping himself above her on his forearms, he looked down into her thoroughly serene face and knew he was in heaven. Her eyes were closed, her long black lashes—the longest he'd ever seen—curling against her cheeks, her soft lips slightly parted in a smile. "Ah, little Indian princess," he groaned, "why do we waste the short time we have together fighting?"

Opening her eyes sleepily, Gentle Fawn was at a loss for words. She shook her head in wonder and brought his mouth back down to hers.

Clay pulled her to a sitting position, taking his mouth from hers long enough to whisk her sleeveless deerskin dress over her head. Feasting his eyes on her petite body, her small breasts pointing their hard peaks proudly toward him, Clay reached up to unfasten a braid that hung over one shoulder. When he had unbraided them both, he combed his fingers through her thick hair until it stood out in wild abandon around her face and shoulders.

"You don't wear bear grease on your hair," he noticed for the first time. Lifting a handful, he buried his face in the glorious cloud of braid-crinkled hair.

"I do not like the smell of bear grease," she whispered, throwing her head back and arching her body toward him as he burrowed his face into the curve of her shoulder.

"I'm glad," he murmured, bending to kiss her offered breasts as he kept his hands at her waist, pulling her upward and toward him.

Slowly he lowered her back down to the soft bed. His mouth, watering for the taste of her, captured the stiff

158

point of one of her breasts. He sucked, gently at first, then with more urgency as he felt her hips rotate demandingly against him.

His mouth still nursing at her succulent breast, he moved his hand down to tease and caress the moist, thrusting flesh at the apex of her thighs. Continuing his magic with his mouth at her breast, he manipulated and explored the hardening bud at the core of her sex until she was writhing violently against his hand. Then, when she was certain she could stand no more of his exquisite torture, his mouth moved away from her breast to lick and suck gently at the flesh around her navel, then lower.

Gasping at the delightful thrill that rippled through her body, she raked her fingers into his thick hair and held him hard against her belly.

His fingers kept up their attack on that most private part of her body as his tongue and lips bathed the smooth skin of her abdomen. Then his head slid even further down.

Little groans of protest gurgled in her throat as she felt his breath burning over the dark triangle of hair at the juncture of her thighs. Straining to free herself from the sexual fog that had her trapped in its mist, she raised her head in shock. "No," she whimpered. "You must not."

"Hush, my little Indian wife. Let me love you thoroughly this one last night together," he said, gripping her slender hips in his strong hands and lifting them upward.

Hot flames of heat exploded between her thighs, raging upward over her stomach and breasts, downward along her legs as he ignited that sensitive kernel at the center of her passion with the torch of his tongue.

Suddenly her breathing became erratic, held in one

second, then coming in rapid spurts the next. She squirmed and twisted wildly beneath his artful torture, certain unconsciousness was only a breath away.

Gentle Fawn cried out suddenly as the welcome release shook spasmodically through her small body.

She reached down to clutch at Clay's hair, desperate to bring him up to her and have him inside her. He came willingly, kissing her hard on the mouth, the taste of her unbridled desire still on his lips and tongue.

Gentle Fawn locked her arms around his neck and moved her hips against his swollen manhood, begging him with her body to fill the aching void inside her.

Moving away from her, Clay quickly removed his buckskin breeches, revealing his aroused masculinity.

Mesmerized by the magnificence of his naked body, Gentle Fawn rolled to her knees and reached out to touch the evidence of his arousal, wrapping her fingers gently around the tightly stretched silken flesh. "Oh, lord help me, honey," he moaned, removing her hand and slipping to his knees in front of her. "I'm about to burst as it is. Another second of that and we'll both be disappointed," he apologized hoarsely, lifting her upward to straddle his lap.

With no further delay, he lowered her onto the proud evidence of his sex, pumping into her with a frenzy of need. Gentle Fawn clasped him to her tightly, finding untold joy in the tension she felt building in the muscles of his back, the strained expression of ecstasy on his face.

His mouth stretched in a grimace of total concentration and he cried out her name as his passion exploded within the sweet receptacle of her body at the same instant Gentle Fawn felt her own internal explosion. And she knew in that moment that, until now, she had never before truly known what it was to be a woman.

Still clutching each other, they toppled to the ground in exquisite exhaustion, their breath coming in loud uncontrolled pants, their bodies slick with perspiration. Replete for the moment, both were too stunned to move as they clung to each other murmuring unintelligible words of praise and happiness.

"Wow!" Clay finally said, his breathing slowing slightly as he released his hold on Gentle Fawn and flopped over onto his back, his arms outstretched helplessly, his eyes closed contentedly. "You really are something, Mrs. Donovan!"

"Is Bright Sunshine 'something,' too?" she said shyly, her thoughts out of her mouth before she could stop them.

Clay's eyes blinked open and he turned his head to the side to stare at Gentle Fawn. "What did you say?"

She looked nervously at him, then back to the top of the tepee. "Is my sister also 'something'? Do you call her Mrs. Donovan, too?"

Clay raised up on his elbow, resting his cheek in one hand, and studied her. She was actually jealous. Who would have thought? "You're really serious, aren't you?" he asked, dumbfounded.

"I am sorry. I should not have asked such a personal question. Please forgive me." She turned her head away from him, desperate to hide the tears forming in her eyes.

"Gentle Fawn, look at me," he said, turning her face gently toward him. "After the special moments we've just spent, do you honestly believe I could have come to you from another woman's bed?"

"You did not?" she whispered uncertainly, her bottom lip trembling and making Clay want to hug her to him and protect her always.

"Gentle Fawn, there are only two Mrs. Donovans in my life—my mother and you." Lord! What had he just said? Had he actually talked like he thought theirs was a real marriage?

"But you—"

"Nothing. I did nothing but apologize to Bright Sunshine for hurting her feelings when I didn't want her," he said with a grin.

Realization dawned in Gentle Fawn's eyes. "You mean— Then you and she did not— But you said she was beautiful— I thought you wanted—"

"Nope!" he said smugly, lying back down and pulling her head to rest on his chest. "Remember? That whole crazy idea was yours! Not mine."

"Then I am your only wife?" She raised up and looked into his blue eyes for assurance.

"It looks that way."

"For tonight!" they both added in unison, a confused silence holding them captive for a moment as they searched each other's eyes for answers to contradicting feelings pounding in both their hearts.

"Where'd you get the necklace?" Clay asked suddenly, indicating the dollar-size gold locket he'd noticed Gentle Fawn always wore and using it as an excuse to talk of anything other than marriage.

"Necklace?" she choked, making a protective grab for the golden circle dangling between her breasts.

"I'm not going to steal it from you. I just wondered where it came from!" He laughed, pulling her head back down onto his shoulder.

"Oh."

"Well? Tell me. How'd a cute little white-hater like

you end up wearing a white woman's gold bauble?"

"It was my father's gift to me when he died," she explained defensively, tightening her hold on the locket.

"What do you keep in it? Can I see?" he asked, putting his hand over hers on the locket, more curious about the peculiar way she was acting than about the necklace itself.

"No! I only keep sacred things in here. Personal things! Things I do not want to be seen by other eyes!" She squirmed to sit up, obviously planning to make a run for it.

"All right! Don't get all upset. I'm not going to look in your locket if you don't want me to!" he said, the expression on his face open and guileless. *But sooner or later I'm going to see what's in there,* he added silently, his writer's inquisitiveness intrigued.

Gentle Fawn studied him for a moment. Then relaxed, finally allowing herself to be returned to the security of his embrace. Resting her hand on his chest, she sighed sleepily.

There was a long comfortable silence, then she suddenly asked, "Are all white men's bodies so covered with hair as yours?" Raking her fingers through the thick blond chest hair that fascinated her so much, she giggled playfully.

Clay laughed. "To tell the truth, I hadn't thought just a whole helluva lot about that. But I guess you could say whites—the men not the women—are a pretty hairy lot!" He grinned and touched the tip of her nose with a kiss. "Some of the women, too, now that I think about it!"

Silence resumed, then he spoke again.

"Do all Indian women have such long eyelashes as you

163

do? I noticed Bright Sunshine didn't. In fact, it's hard for me to believe you two are related—you look nothing alike."

"We are really only stepsisters," she clarified, suddenly wanting him not to be reminded of Bright Sunshine in any way when he looked at her.

"I think you've got it wrong," Clay said patiently, certain he'd found a flaw in her almost faultless understanding of the English language. "Though you have different mothers, you have the same father, so that would make you half sisters, not stepsisters."

"Hunting Bear was not my natural father," she said, annoyed that he was speaking to her as if she were a child. "I was born a Cheyenne, not a Lakota."

"Oh?" Clay's interest perked up tenfold. So far everything they'd said had been small talk. But this was different. "How'd you end up here then?"

"When my natural parents were killed by the whites, Hunting Bear brought me to his first wife, Quiet Rain, who had no children of her own."

"How long ago was that?"

"Fifteen winters. I was about three at the time."

"And you never saw or heard from your parents' people again? Have you ever thought about looking for them?"

"Yes," Gentle Fawn admitted hesitantly, wondering why it seemed so natural to be sharing her deepest secrets and longings with, of all people, a white man. Unable to stop the words she'd held pent up inside her for so many years, she went on. "But they would be impossible to locate—if they are even alive. Hunting Bear spoke of them to me only once, telling me he did not know their names and that there were almost no survivors of the soldiers' attack on their tribe. When I asked him more, he silenced me, saying he and Quiet Rain were my parents now and I should put the others from my mind."

"And did you?" Clay asked, feeling sorry for the little girl who had so desperately wanted to know something—anything—about her true heritage.

"For the sake of my stepmother, Quiet Rain, I never mentioned them again—until now. But no, I did not forget or stop wondering who they were or if they were still alive."

"Poor little brave Indian princess," Clay said, almost to himself. "No wonder your hate for the whites is so great—your parents, your stepfather, your husband."

He hugged her to him and rocked her small, pliant body consolingly, holding her in the safety of his arms the rest of the night as she slept, secure for the first time in days.

Chapter Ten

"I understand you wish to speak with me," a man's voice said in perfect English as Clay stepped out of the tepee shortly after dawn the next morning.

Startled, Clay spun around to see an Indian brave, not much older than he—early thirties at the most—approach him. "Are you—" Clay started, unable to believe this soft-spoken man, who was much shorter than many of his fellow tribesmen, possibly five foot eight, was the fierce war leader of the Sioux Nation.

"I am Ta-Sunko-Witko—Crazy Horse. And you are?"

"Clay Donovan," he stammered, wiping his sweating palm on his pants before offering it to the infamous chief.

"Tell me, Clay Donovan, why do you wish to speak to me?" Crazy Horse asked, ignoring Clay's hand and studying the white man who'd dared to come into the camp of a warring Indian tribe as a man of science would study a strange insect he'd never seen before.

Clay couldn't get over his awe of the man. He had expected Crazy Horse to be a huge brute of a man—bigger than life—one whose step almost made the ground shake when he walked, whose voice caused people to tremble when he spoke. He had expected him at least to swagger and brag of his great victories as he'd heard other warriors do in the few days since he'd been with the Lakotas. But this man was not tall, not a swaggering braggart, not even forceful. Instead, he was unassuming and reserved—quiet. And there was an aura of melancholy about him, as though he knew the great victory at the Little Bighorn had been the beginning of the end for the once great Lakotas.

"I'm a writer—things I write are published in the white man's newspapers all over the country," Clay hurried to explain, certain that if he didn't speak up soon, the man would walk away. And so would his story.

"And?"

"Well, whether or not you know it, you're a very famous man, and I wanted to write an article about you for my readers back East."

"Why?"

"So you could explain how the Lakotas"—he was pleased he hadn't slipped and said Sioux, as the whites called them—"are only trying to protect and preserve what is rightfully theirs."

Crazy Horse's eyebrows lifted slightly, but his handsome face stayed sober, showing no sign that he might be interested in Clay's idea. "Go on."

"I could write about how the Lakotas only want to be left alone—to hunt their own lands without the whites coming in and killing all the buffalo and destroying all the good grazing so there's not enough grass for your livestock to eat."

"You are well informed, Clay Donovan. But still you are saying nothing we have not said many times to the bluecoats and longbeards the white father sends to speak to us."

"But my articles would reach the masses—everyone—not just a few Washington bureaucrats. If we could take your cause to the people who put those men in office, things would be completely different. People back East have no idea what's going on out here—except for what the politicians and Army tell them. Together, you and I could give them the truth."

"I think, Clay Donovan, that you are probably a good man with honorable intentions. But it is too late for the truth. The whites will never forgive the Indians for our victory over them when they attacked our camp on the Greasy Grass River. They will say we attacked the soldiers and will not rest until we are all dead."

"But I can write about that, too! I was there!" Seeing the suspicious look on Crazy Horse's face, Clay hurried to explain. "I was coming to talk to you and was watching your camp from the distance, trying to decide how I would find you. That's when I saw the soldiers attack one end of your camp while others circled around to attack from behind. I'll make the whites understand that the Lakotas had no choice but to fight. They were defending their women and children!"

"You are a very brave man, and because of this I will give you this interview you think will make a difference. But first there is something I wish you to see! Have your woman prepare your horse. You will ride with me today while the others rest themselves and their livestock this one last day before we move on." Without waiting for Clay to agree or disagree, the great chief turned on his heel and walked away, leaving a stunned Clay Donovan staring after him.

Suddenly realizing he didn't know when Crazy Horse would expect to meet him, but suspecting he probably had only a few minutes to prepare to ride, Clay ducked back through the entrance of the tepee. "Gentle Fawn! Honey, this is it! He's going to give me the interview!" he babbled excitedly as he grabbed up his saddle, relieved to find that no one had removed his belongings to Bright Sunshine's lodge.

"I will do that, Clay Donovan," Gentle Fawn said softly, the smile on her face oddly sad as she reached for the saddle. "You eat something while I take care of your horse."

Clay protested and kept his grip on the saddle. "You don't have to do it. I can do it. You're not my servant."

"But I am your wife—for now—and it would make you look like less of a man if you did women's work while I did nothing. And it would make me look like a poor wife."

Clay started to object again, but stopped. Remembering the night before when he'd been unable to kill Many Coups, when he hadn't been able to bed Bright Sunshine, he realized bitterly that his masculinity didn't need any more disparagement than it already had suffered. "Okay, but only to protect your reputation." He handed her the saddle and turned to the cook pot that had been simmering all night.

Minutes later, Gentle Fawn stood in the entrance of her borrowed lodge and watched as Clay and Crazy Horse rode out of the camp together. With two fingers, she sadly touched her lips, still tingling with his hurried good-bye kiss, and blew on their tips toward the retreating backs of the riders. "Farewell, Clay Donovan," she whispered. *You have been a good and brave husband to me. But now our bargain is over. You are free to go back to your white world where you belong. And I will— what? I will simply go on as before!* she vowed. *But I will never marry again!*

"Your husband leaves you so soon after your marriage?" a deep voice said behind her, its anger and bitterness sending a sudden apprehension washing over her skin. She'd been so caught up in her thoughts, she hadn't heard or felt the man approach until he was directly behind her.

Taking a moment to collect her composure, Gentle Fawn forced a pleasant expression to her face and turned to greet her surprise visitor. "Many Coups, I did not expect to see you this morning. Will you have something to eat with me?" she offered politely, unable to look at her former father-in-law's swollen chin and tightly wrapped middle.

"I have eaten. I only came to tell you farewell. Man of the People and I have decided to travel on our separate paths." He was saying all the right things, being very polite in fact; but something in his black eyes—a hardness she'd seen when she'd first turned around— made Gentle Fawn take an uneasy step backward.

"I am sorry to hear that, Many Coups," she forced herself to say as her heart bolted with relief. At least he wouldn't be here to force her into marriage when Clay Donovan left.

"Will you walk with me to my horse?" Many Coups asked, his voice sounding defeated and lonely.

Seeing his unhappiness, Gentle Fawn felt ashamed for thinking he'd come to make more trouble the minute her protector was out of sight. And after all, he was Tall

171

Feathers' father. Didn't she owe him a few minutes of her time? Forcing a smile, she nodded her head. "I will walk with you to your horse, Many Coups."

"Gentle Fawn!" a woman's voice called out as she and Many Coups began to walk.

Turning, she saw three women, one crying hysterically, the other two red with anger, followed by three wailing children clinging to the bottom fringe of the crying woman's dress. *Bright Sunshine, her mother and my mother!* she moaned inwardly, knowing what they were all upset about, and feeling only the slightest twinge of guilt that she'd been the one to spend the night in Clay Donovan's arms and not her sister.

"I will be back," she called out to the emotional threesome before they could reach the spot where she stood. Grabbing Many Coups' arm, she propelled them both toward the Cheyenne camp circle.

In no mood to have anything further to do with Gentle Fawn's family, Many Coups ignored the whining women and went eagerly.

When they reached the camp at the end of the giant village where several bands of Cheyennes were camped, Gentle Fawn realized that Many Coups' band was already pulling out. She looked at him questioningly.

"My horse is over there with some of my braves. We will catch up with the others," he said, obviously understanding her confusion, but refusing to take no for an answer. "Come!" he said, leading her toward the waiting warriors and horses.

"We can say good-bye here," Gentle Fawn said, stopping in her tracks, signals of alarm going off in her head.

"We are not going to say good-bye," Many Coups said

172

coldly, all pretense at politeness discarded as he signaled to his men to join them quickly. "You are going with me."

"But you lost the fight!" she exclaimed, looking around desperately and trying to gauge her chances of escape. She took a step toward her own camp, but was brought up short as Many Coups' strong fingers yanked her backward by her braids.

"That white man you call a husband should have killed me, little one," he growled close to her ear, so close she could feel the sickening warmth of his breath on her cheek, could smell the white man's coffee he'd had for breakfast and the stale tobacco of his pipe. "For I am not a man who forgets his shame all that easily. I will take from the white man what he values most—even as he has taken from me what I hold most high. My honor."

"Do not do this, Many Coups!" she pleaded, straining against his eye-watering hold on her hair. "I cannot go with you. I must stay here and care for my mother and sister who have no husbands!"

"Your white husband can take care of them—even as you will take care of me. My offer of marriage is still open!"

"Never!" she spat out.

"Then you choose slavery?" he said, the evil smile in his tone screeching along her spine and causing her skin to break out in prickly bumps.

"You will not get away with this, Many Coups," Gentle Fawn said, ceasing her struggles, hoping to take her captor off guard before it was too late.

"Of course I will." He laughed, scooping the slight young woman up into his arms and tossing her over the horse that suddenly appeared at his side. Then with the

173

agility of a younger man, he jumped in the saddle behind her.

"Someone will come for me!" she protested, flailing out helplessly at the man whose weight at least doubled her own.

"Who will come?" Many Coups asked, banding her tightly across the chest with his muscled arm as he nudged his horse forward, quickly bringing the Indian mount to a brisk gallop to lead the parade of departing Cheyennes. "Your 'husband'? He has gone with Crazy Horse. They may not be back for days—weeks! And by the time they do return we will be too far away and the trail too old for him to follow us."

"He will be back today. And he will find me. And when he does, this time he will kill you, Many Coups!" she threatened in vain.

She knew as well as Many Coups did that Clay Donovan would not come after her. Even if he didn't believe she'd gone with Many Coups willingly, even if he were foolish enough to attack a Cheyenne camp alone, he wouldn't want to waste time on her. He had his story now, and he would be anxious to leave the Lakotas. She meant nothing to him, certainly not enough to risk his life for her—again. He'd done it once because he needed her to get his story, but she couldn't fool herself into believing that now he had what he wanted he would do anything so unwise a second time.

Gentle Fawn let a deep sigh of resignation and leaned back against the broad chest of Many Coups. It was going to be a long ride. Since no one would be coming after her, she would have to conserve her strength as she waited for the earliest chance to escape—a chance she swore would not be too long in coming.

"I am glad to see you understand the hopelessness of struggling against me," Many Coups said, unable to hide the satisfaction in his voice when he felt her relax against him.

Gentle Fawn said nothing. She just stared ahead and planned her escape. It might take a day, or a week, or a year, but she would find a way to escape Many Coups and return to her own people.

"Gentle Fawn!" Clay shouted jubilantly, his enthusiasm that of a young child as he rode up to her mother's lodge and jumped off his horse five days later. He hadn't seen the tepee they'd been living in and assumed she'd stayed with Quiet Rain when the camp had moved, so he had gone there first.

"Gentle Fawn!" he called again, barely able to stand still as he waited for someone to bid him enter the quiet lodge. But no one responded from behind the dropped doorflap.

"Quiet Rain?" he called tentatively, lifting the hide slightly and peeking inside. "Bright Sunshine? Is anybody home?" The lodge was empty.

"Where is everybody?" he mumbled irritably, turning to rake his confused gaze over the surrounding tents in an effort to locate Gentle Fawn or her family.

His reception—or lack of it—was beginning to put a decided damper on his excitement, and he frowned angrily.

He took off his hat and wiped the perspiration from his forehead with a cotton-sleeved forearm, then furrowed callused fingers through wheat-colored hair before putting the hat back on. After the long hours spent on the trail with Crazy Horse, his skin was browner than before, his face covered with a shadow of thick blond beard, his hair curling damply past his collar.

"Where the hell are you?" he asked no one in particular, knowing none of the Indians who curiously watched him could understand English.

"Wife gone, *wasicun*," a woman's voice said in halting English.

Startled, Clay spun on his boot heel. An old woman had approached so quietly he hadn't even known she was there. "You speak English! Am I glad to see you!"

"Nephew's wife, Firebird, teach Prairie Moon," she announced, patting herself on the chest to indicate she was Prairie Moon and giving him a toothy grin that was more gums than teeth. "Pretty good, huh?"

"Very good," Clay complimented the tiny, moon-faced woman, relieved he wasn't going to have to bother with making himself understood through sign language. "Prairie Moon, you said my wife is gone? Do you know where? She's somewhere in the camp, isn't she?"

"Gone away," Prairie Moon said, shaking her head and pointing toward the distant mountains.

A tremor of panic squeezed at Clay's gut. Why would she leave? "I don't understand. Can't you tell me where she went?" He clamped his hands on the woman's plump upper arms and stooped to put his face on the level with hers, the expression in his clear blue eyes beseeching.

Thinking better of being the one to tell the white man that his wife had left with the Cheyennes, Prairie Moon gave him a sad smile. "You talk to Prairie Moon's brother, Man of the People. He tell what you want know."

For a full minute longer, Clay remained stooped over,

holding her arms and silently searching her black eyes for any clue that would shed a light on Gentle Fawn's sudden disappearance. But though the aged woman's eyes gleamed with intelligence and wisdom, he could see by her expression that she had told him all she intended to.

Taking a deep breath in an unsuccessful attempt to override the building alarm twisting in his belly, he released his hold on Prairie Moon and straightened up. "Where is the lodge that belongs to Man of the People?"

"*Hou,*" she said, nodding her head enthusiastically and pointing to the tepee across the camp circle, which Clay now recognized as the one belonging to the chief.

"Thanks for your help," he said with an absentminded pat on the woman's back, his thoughts obviously distracted, his long stride already in motion.

Forcing his demeanor not to give away the sense of foreboding that had enveloped him from the first instant he'd realized Gentle Fawn wasn't in her mother's lodge, Clay hurried toward the Oglala chief's tepee.

Unmindful of the pitying stares he was drawing from the other villagers, he cursed himself for being so upset. He knew he was going to feel like a fool when he discovered she was at the stream washing her clothes or bathing—or visiting in another tepee—or out in the hills digging for wild onions. *There's a simple explanation,* he insisted, deliberately refusing to consider the alternatives that bombarded his thoughts with nagging persistence.

Approaching the chief's tepee, he heard a woman's distraught voice coming from inside. Maybe he should wait until the chief had straightened out whatever crisis was at hand before barging in and asking where Gentle Fawn was. It would be the proper thing to do. And besides, there was no need to look any more foolish than he already felt for worrying so unreasonably.

He waited impatiently, glancing at the sun to gauge the time of day, then confirming it on the large timepiece he kept in his jacket pocket, then drawing idle patterns in the dirt with the toe of his boot. All of that took about thirty seconds. Pacing three steps to either side of where he'd been standing, Clay decided he'd waited long enough. What if she really was in trouble and time was imperative? He couldn't just stand here cooling his heels like some misbehaving schoolboy when Gentle Fawn might be hurt or dying!

"Man of the People!" he announced, loud enough to be heard over the weeping female voice. "It is Clay Donovan and I must speak to you right away."

As though strong hands had clamped over the woman's mouth, all sounds from inside the lodge ceased. There was total silence for an instant that seemed more like minutes to Clay as he waited outside for Man of the People to bid him enter. Then, all at once the silence was broken with the scuffle of hurrying footsteps, the high excited voice of the woman, the anxious lifting of the doorflap, and the deep voice of Man of the People.

"Come in, Clay Donovan!" he called out eagerly, though Clay couldn't get over the feeling the chief's voice sounded extremely uneasy.

Ducking into the dimly lit tepee, Clay took a moment to accustom his eyes to the darkness. The first person he saw was Quiet Rain. Her face, still quite lovely at about forty, was streaked with tears.

His heart lurched violently in his chest. Something terrible had happened! That was why Gentle Fawn's mother and the chief were sitting in a hot, closed-up tepee instead of rolling up the sides to let in the breeze. "What's going on?" he asked, his voice ominous. He looked urgently to Man of the People for his answer. "Where's Gentle Fawn?"

The compassionate expression of sadness that clouded the kind chief's features told Clay what he wanted to know—much more than he'd wanted to know. But still he had to ask, "What is it? What's happened to her?"

"I am sorry, my son."

"Are you telling me Gentle Fawn's dead?" Clay gasped in alarm, not even wondering at the sense of total loss he felt at that moment when he believed his worst fears had come true. "It can't be possible."

"No, Clay Donovan," Man of the People said gently, "Gentle Fawn is not dead, but she is gone from us—from you."

"Not dead but gone? That doesn't make sense! Gone where? I don't understand!" He was shouting now!

"On the morning you left with Crazy Horse, Many Coups' band of Cheyennes left our camp also. She chose to go with them. I am truly sorry, Clay Donovan, but perhaps it is for the best. A marriage between the two of you during these times could never have survived."

"Are you trying to tell me she went with Many Coups of her own free will?" Clay said, his expression accusing. "That's ridiculous! She might not have wanted to stay married to me, but she never would have gone with Many Coups! She couldn't stand the thought of being married to him. To anybo— That's the whole reason she and I—" Clay stopped himself, feeling for an unexplained reason that he mustn't give away their secret. "If she went with him, it was by force," he said certainly.

"Her own mother and sister saw her smiling and

walking toward the Cheyenne camp with Many Coups only a few minutes after you rode off in the opposite direction," Man of the People said patiently, wishing there were some way he could have softened the blow. He, too, had been certain Gentle Fawn was happy with her marriage to the white man.

"I can't believe it," Clay said, not wanting to accept Man of the People's words as true, but finding it difficult not to consider the ego-destroying possibility.

She had evidently preferred Many Coups all along! Was she the type of woman who enjoyed having men fight over her? Had that been why she'd married him? To make Many Coups jealous? Or had her marriage to him just been a ploy to cover her tracks in case she had actually conceived a white baby that first night in the Indian village?

A sickening thought suddenly occurred to him. That had been the reason she'd tried to stop the fight between him and Many Coups—not to protect her husband but to save Many Coups!

Visions of their last hours together when they had made love the entire night, learned each other's bodies totally, flashed cruelly in his mind. How could she have been so sweet, so passionate, so giving, when the entire time she had known she was leaving with Many Coups in the morning? Never had he experienced such pleasure, found such joy in the act of making love. And now to be told it was all just that—an act. Nothing more. She had been planning to go with Many Coups the whole time!

What the hell difference does it make to me where she goes? She doesn't mean anything to me. She was just a way to get my story—nothing else. And I got my story, so to hell with her and her big eyes and soft, loving body!

"Will you ask Quiet Rain what she did with my things when she folded up Firebird's tepee?" he said woodenly to Man of the People, his tone a heartbreaking mingling of bitterness and hurt. "I'll be leaving for Cheyenne as soon as I can get packed."

Chapter Eleven

"Is there any sign yet?" Gentle Fawn heard Many Coups ask the woman who'd been charged with caring for his prisoner.

Though the woman's response was not audible, Gentle Fawn knew what it was. She was telling the chief that his daughter-in-law was not *isnati*—menstruating. She knew because it had been the same ritual every morning since Many Coups had stolen her from her own people—she refused to think of the Cheyennes as her true heritage after the terrible thing Many Coups had done to her. The woman, called Rainbow Woman and who Gentle Fawn knew to be Many Coups' wife and Tall Feathers' mother, had come to her each day to bring her breakfast and to check to see if she had begun her monthly flow.

Gentle Fawn's face twisted into a mask of undisguised hatred when she thought about the dour Rainbow Woman. When she had protested the indignity of being examined so personally, the woman had smiled evilly, as though she had hoped Gentle Fawn would do just that so she would have a reason to punish her. And punish her she had. She slapped Gentle Fawn across the mouth with such vicious force that her head had snapped back as blinding stars burst brightly in her brain, leaving her helpless and groggy for hours afterward.

From that day on, Gentle Fawn had stayed perfectly still as each day Rainbow Woman had lifted her dress and scrutinized her most private parts and the bedding where she'd slept. Wisely, she realized it would do her no good to struggle and would only leave her weak and unable to think. And she needed to be able to stay alert every minute so she could plan her escape and revenge.

Willing to do anything to keep a clear head, she had been able to remove her mind from what was happening each morning. She had submitted placidly to the examination. The unfeeling expression on her face never once gave away the tortures she planned to perpetrate against the two who'd caged her like an animal and treated her so cruelly.

She remembered when Many Coups had first tossed her like so much garbage into this lodge the day the Cheyennes had arrived at their new campsite, and her lip curled bitterly. That was the last time she'd seen him, though she'd heard him talking to his wife each day at this time.

"You will stay here until we know if you are carrying a child," he had said threateningly. "Then if we find that you are with child, you will remain here until you give birth. If the child belongs to my son, you will give it to me to raise. But if the child is of your white lover's seed, I will take its life in exchange for my son's life."

As if trying to wipe out the memory of his words, Gentle Fawn squirmed restlessly on the mat where she spent her days and nights. She tugged at the leather collar around her neck. She was desperately anxious to see evidence of her monthly flow—though what Many Coups had in mind for her future if it did come was terrible, too. But not nearly so terrible as witnessing the murder of her own child—Clay Donovan's child. Besides, no existence could be worse than this one— lying here day after day with a heavy rawhide strap looped through the torturous collar that constantly chafed at her neck while the ends of the leash were securely attached to a guarded stake outside the tepee.

"If it becomes evident you are not expecting a child, and since you have refused my generous offer to take you as my wife, then I have something a little more suitable in mind for you. You will become our village whore. The young, unmarried braves, as well as the married braves whose wives are indisposed, will come to you to satisfy their needs. That should please a slut like you, catering to the desires of many men, rather than just one."

Gentle Fawn could still hear his vindictive laughter at the expression of shock that had darted across her face. She'd been caught by surprise by his vicious plan and she hadn't recovered quickly enough to hide her fear behind the mask of indifference she'd affected since she'd been his prisoner.

When my monthly time does start, she thought positively, *I will have four or five days to carry out my escape.* She knew they would move her to the special lodge away from the rest of the camp where the women spent their menstrual periods. No braves would come near her during her monthly time, believing a woman who was *isnati* was a strange and powerful force. It was said that a female in that condition could spit at a rattlesnake and it would die.

Too bad it is only a superstition, she thought regretfully, remembering the time when she was about fifteen when she'd tried to kill a snake by spitting on it. She wished with all her heart it had worked. *I would spit on Many Coups!*

A bitter giggle escaped Gentle Fawn's throat as she imagined the shock on Many Coups' face if she spit on him when she was in her flow. She could see his eyes widen in horror as her spittle ran down his face and he clutched at his chest frantically. She could see him sinking to his knees, choking and gasping for his last breaths until he toppled over—dead at her feet.

It was that thought alone that kept Gentle Fawn from losing her mind during the next few days. So far she had managed to keep her sanity through it all. Through the demeaning examinations. Through the whispered conferences outside the lodge. Through the vicious taunts of Many Coups' wife. Through the hopelessness and boredom she suffered with nothing to do and no one to talk to. Through the burning discomfort of the collar that bit into her neck, rubbing her flesh raw. Even through the humiliating trips to relieve herself when Rainbow Woman led her to the bushes on the leash—as one would lead a trained bear.

Using her fingers to tick off the days since her last flux, she realized she should begin any time now. Two or three days at the most until they removed the collar and sent her to the women's lodge. *Just two or three suns until I make my escape*, she promised herself, closing her eyes and willing herself to sleep again so the time would pass more quickly.

*   *   *

186

Favoring his right leg only occasionally now, Clay followed Quiet Rain with reluctant steps. The woman's posture was defeated and she seemed older than her years. Though he knew Gentle Fawn's mother didn't approve of her marriage to him and would have preferred to have her daughter wed to Many Coups, he couldn't help feeling sorry for her.

Surely she had expected to go with Gentle Fawn if she'd married the Cheyenne. But to be left behind like yesterday's problems must hurt unbearably. The woman had had her entire family wiped out in a matter of days and now she was totally alone.

A new spurt of anger spiraled in Clay's brain. How could Gentle Fawn have done such a thoughtless thing as to leave her mother here to fend for herself? Without even telling her good-bye! He told himself the fact that she'd left him without so much as a good-bye was one thing—she hadn't considered she owed him anything any more than he felt he had a commitment to her. After all, theirs was a business bargain. But to leave her mother like that! What kind of heartless bitch would do such a thing?

The same kind who'd marry a stranger to make another one jealous. The same kind who'd get a kick out of watching one man kill another over her. The same kind who'd be disappointed when the fight was over and they were both still alive! He cursed himself again for the fool he was—for actually letting himself believe she was what she claimed to be.

Preceding Clay into her tepee, Quiet Rain pointed toward a pile of *parfleches*—the beaded bags Gentle Fawn had filled to overflowing with dried fruits and meat for the winter—stacked on top of three large hide-wrapped bundles of household supplies.

Exasperated that the woman would have put his things in with all of Gentle Fawn's belongings, Clay ignored the tiny voice at the back of his mind that asked, *Why would Gentle Fawn leave everything she owned behind?*

"These belong to Gentle Fawn," he growled at a blank-faced Quiet Rain. "Where are my things?"

Quiet Rain pointed again to the packs.

"No!" he said, shaking his head back and forth. "My things!" He patted his chest. "Where are *my* things?"

Quiet Rain indicated the same bundles.

"Can you at least tell me which pack my stuff's in?" he begged, forcing his voice to be more gentle.

Quiet Rain shrugged and stepped through the doorway, leaving an annoyed Clay Donovan to search at his own discretion. He could dig through all the rawhide string-tied packs for his meager possessions, or he could just head out with the borrowed buckskins he had on his back.

If he'd known he and Crazy Horse were going to be gone for five days—or even overnight—he'd have taken all his gear with him in the first place. As it was, he had the important things—his pistol, his rifle, and his pencils and paper. Actually, everything he'd left behind could easily be replaced—his shaving equipment, his bedroll, his cooking supplies and a few pieces of clothing.

Telling himself he could sleep on his horse blanket, as he and Crazy Horse had done the past few nights, and could buy new gear when he got to Cheyenne, he took a step toward the door opening. *Besides, the sooner I head out, the sooner I get back to civilization and mail this story off! Why waste time searching through a bunch of hides and bone utensils to find a few worthless things when I can hit the trail and be miles from here by sunset?*

His decision made, Clay ducked out through the tepee entrance and hurried to his horse. *Still,* he thought, stopping mid-step and shooting an indecisive glance over his shoulder at Quiet Rain's lodge, *if I give my horse a night to rest up, we could cover twice as much ground tomorrow. And while he's resting up, I guess I might as well put my time to use and get my stuff out of those packs,* he conceded, turning back to study the sixteen-foot-high tepee he'd just come from.

"What the hell!" he finally decided, turning back to his horse and unstrapping his saddle. "I've got nothing to lose but a couple of hours if I stay one more night. And as long as I'm going to be here anyway—"

Two hours later, surrounded by the unwrapped hide packs that belonged to Gentle Fawn, Clay sat on the ground in the middle of Quiet Rain's lodge. The sides of the tepee had been rolled up to give him the benefit of the late afternoon breeze, but he was still hot and his anger had not helped a bit.

Shedding the buckskin shirt he'd been wearing and tossing it aside, he deliberately ignored the stares and giggles of the band of Lakota children who'd gathered to watch him. *You'd think none of them ever saw a little hair on a man's chest before!* The mood he was in, he didn't pay attention to the understanding inner voice that said, "They probably haven't."

Standing up, he locked his fingers together and turned his hands inside out as he extended them over his head in a long, muscle-relaxing stretch. "Ahhh," he yawned, bringing his hands down to massage his own shoulders, before walking toward the skin of water hung on a tripod outside the now nonexistent entrance.

He turned back toward the tepee, groaning his disgust as he viewed the supplies and clothing strewn haphazardly over the ground. It had been easy enough to locate his things—after he'd torn open every bundle and scattered their contents all over.

For the life of me, I can't figure out why they couldn't have all been put together in one pack! he thought with distaste, remembering his frustration when he'd found something of his in every pack. His shaving soap, a frying pan, his slicker, and a pair of jeans in one bundle. His sleeping bag, razor strop and brush, a metal drinking cup, a fork, a pair of longjohns and a cotton shirt in the second one. And his coffeepot, razor, two more shirts, and a second pair of pants in still another. The things belonging to him hadn't even been together inside the individual bags, but mixed instead throughout Gentle Fawn's equipment and clothing.

At least I think I've got it all now, he thought wearily as he looked at the mound of his personal belongings he'd stacked outside the lodge. "I ought to just leave all this crap and let someone else worry about it!" But even as he spoke, he knew he couldn't do that. He wasn't mad at Quiet Rain. It was her daughter. But the mother, who'd been hurt, too— Now why did he think he'd been hurt? The mother who'd been hurt—period—would be the one who'd have to do the picking up and repacking.

Working hastily with little concern for how neatly he packed Gentle Fawn's things, he angrily tossed everything onto the three hides. With a grunt of disapproval he gave the ground a cursory examination to be sure he hadn't left anything out. Deciding all was in order, he folded the sides, then the ends of the cured skins over each of the heaps he'd gathered at their centers. Working now as though he were tying up a hated enemy, he yanked and jerked on the rawhide ropes until every packet was tied up as well as it had originally been—well, *almost* as well, he conceded begrudgingly.

He hefted the bundles one at a time, wondering at the time how a small woman like Gentle Fawn or her mother could handle such heavy burdens. *Of course, if they couldn't I would have had to repack twice as many.* When the last had been restored to its original position at the side of the lodge, Clay straightened up with a sigh and turned to go.

What made him glance back at the area where he'd first unloaded the packs he couldn't have said; but he did and his gaze caught on a sliver of something shiny.

"What the hell?" he asked as he squatted down on his haunches. He brushed the dirt from the glimmering metal half buried in the ground, his expression growing alarmed as recognition dawned in his eyes.

"Gentle Fawn's locket!" he said, his voice stunned as he scooped the gold disk into the palm of his hand and stared dumbfoundedly at it. *It must have fallen out of one of the bundles when I opened it. But how'd it get in there? Why would she leave it behind? She treasures this thing!*

Suddenly everything his subconscious had noticed came crashing to the forefront of his thoughts. "She wouldn't!" he shouted out, looking around in every direction for someone to show his discovery. "She wouldn't have left without her locket!" *Or her parfleches. Or her horse. Or her mother. Or her clothing. Or her weapons. Or her household equipment. Not unless she was . . .*

"Forced!" he yelled, leaping to his feet. "That son of a bitch forced her to go with him! Someone's got to go after her . . ."

The realization of what he was thinking hit him in the face like a blast of icy winter wind.

"Hold on there, Donovan," he muttered aloud, shaking his head vehemently. He was oblivious to the fact that his actions had frightened his youthful audience and silenced their giggles. "This isn't your problem, pal! We said our good-byes. Our bargain is ended!"

Let her own people go save her. I'll tell them what I've found and what I know. Then they can handle it from there on. It'll be out of my hands!

"It's none of my goddamned business!" he protested fervently, as though arguing with another person.

The people within hearing distance looked around curiously for the person who was the object of his wrath. Seeing no one, they realized the white man was talking to himself. Shaking their braided heads sadly, they turned their backs on his tepee.

Sensing his neighbors' reactions to his strange behavior, Clay stopped pacing and tried to gain his self-control. "It's none of my business," he said again, more quietly this time, his gaze mesmerized by the gold locket in his hand. Its weight seemed to burn into his palm—as though it had retained some of Gentle Fawn's body heat and he was being branded by it.

Wondering again what secrets she kept hidden inside, Clay slid his thumbnail into the seam between the front and back of the gold circle.

The small clasp clicked with a barely discernible sound.

Suddenly, he felt like an intruder, a peeping Tom. She hadn't wanted him to see the locket's contents, and here he was opening it like a sneak thief when she wasn't here to protect her young girl secrets.

192

With his anger now directed at himself for even considering looking inside without her permission, he snapped the locket shut.

He remembered the exact moment she had removed the treasured piece from around her neck. And a pang of guilt somersaulted through his chest with the realization that it was his fault she was without her good-luck piece.

Clay closed his eyes and tried to blot the memory from his mind, but it only grew more vivid. It had been in the last hours before dawn. Gentle Fawn was straddling his hips, the tight tunnel of her sex sheathing him like a luxurious glove. Her thick black hair had been in wild disarray from their hours of lovemaking and her eyes glittered with her newly discovered power over him as she worked the silken muscles of her body in an instinctive milking motion. Leaning over to rub her small breasts against his male nipples and to kiss him, the necklace had suddenly gotten in the way. Without a moment's hesitation in their lovemaking, she'd drawn the chain over her head and tossed it to the side, returning to lick and nip at the flesh and hair on his chest.

Groaning now as he remembered the most ecstatic moments of his life, Clay closed his fingers tightly around the locket, squeezing it until his knuckles turned white.

There was no longer any doubt in Clay's mind. Gentle Fawn hadn't put her treasured locket back on in the morning because she hadn't known she would be leaving the camp!

His long legs carrying him at a run, Clay was back at Man of the People's lodge in no time at all. This time he didn't worry about manners.

"Man of the People! Gentle Fawn didn't go of her own

free will! She was forced! I have proof!" he announced as he burst into the tepee. Coming to a heel-planting halt inside, his mouth dropped open.

Man of the People was not alone, and the look on his face as he shot to his feet was more troubled than angry at the intrusion. Signing to his visitor that he would be right back, the chief hustled Clay out of the lodge before he could say anything else.

"I am very displeased at your rudeness, Clay Donovan! Do you not see that I have a guest?" the tall Indian scolded, hurrying Clay as far from his lodge as quickly as he could.

"That was one of Many Coups' braves!" Clay said, jabbing his thumb back over his shoulder toward the tepee. "I recognize him from the night of the fight!" His tone was accusing. "What's he doing here?"

"Keep your voice down, Clay Donovan!" Man of the People ordered, his tone granting no disobedience.

"But he knows where they've taken Gentle Fawn. You've got to talk to him and find out where she is. I have proof she was taken by force. You need to send some braves to get her back!" The more he spoke, the more he sounded as if he actually had personal feelings for the girl—even to his own ears.

He changed his tone abruptly. "She wouldn't have left all her belongings behind if she had planned to leave with Many Coups," he pointed out calmly. "Are you going to rescue her?"

"Whatever her reason for leaving, we can do nothing, Clay Donovan. If we went there, it would mean a battle between friends. We are too few, and our ammunition is too low to waste fighting those who have sworn to be our allies."

194

"So you're just going to let him keep her?" He was shouting again.

"It is not up to me, Clay Donovan. Only you can decide what to do."

"Me!" he bellowed. "What the hell am I supposed to do? This is Indian business. Her chief should be the one to handle it! Not a white man!"

"But you are her husband, are you not? And this is between you and Many Coups—not between my band of Lakotas and Many Coups' band of Cheyennes."

This was getting to be a pain in the butt! Every time he thought he had things all worked out, Gentle Fawn and her problems put some sort of new kink in his plans.

Oh, Lord! Why me? Clay groaned inwardly. *Why did I have to be the one to find that damn locket? Why couldn't the dirt have completely covered it? Or why couldn't her mother have found it instead of me—after I was gone?*

"It is a custom among the People," Man of the People went on, "that when one man takes another man's wife, he sends an old man to the husband bearing a pipe. It's an offer for peace between the men. If the husband smokes the offering, it means he releases his wife from their marriage and will take no revenge on the other man."

"Is that what that damned Cheyenne is doing in your lodge? He's brought me Many Coups' pipe to smoke?"

Man of the People nodded his head, his own sorrow for the younger man's misery weighing heavily on his heart. But he could not risk getting his braves involved in a full-fledged battle with the Cheyennes in an effort to straighten out a domestic problem. "Will you smoke the pipe?"

"The hell I will!" Clay bellowed without thinking of the consequences. "Who does that sorry son of a bitch think he is anyway? We fought and I won fair and square. She's mine! He can't just waltz in here the minute my back's turned and take my wife!"

Damn! Had he really said that? Had he talked like he believed their marriage was real?

The gut-knotting thought hit him with a mind-clearing blow.

"I would advise you to think carefully before giving the Cheyenne messenger your answer," Man of the People cautioned, studying Clay and wondering if the white man was aware of how much he cared for his wife. Somehow, he didn't think so.

"And if the husband doesn't smoke the pipe?" Clay said acridly, feeling the jaws of the trap he'd been sure he was about to be free of closing shut on him. "What happens then?"

"You will have to go to Many Coups and take your wife back from him. But do not forget, you will be in his camp next time, surrounded by his braves. You will not defeat him so easily a second time, I am afraid," Man of the People warned, shaking his head sadly. He knew his warning was falling on deaf ears. He could see exactly what Clay Donovan would do. It was there in his determined blue eyes—in the midst of the confusion and anger and frustration. Yes, he would ignore all the warnings and go for the woman he loved—and to his death.

"Tell him I'll smoke his pipe," Clay bit out angrily. Well, why shouldn't he? Why should he get himself killed? He'd already lived up to his end of the bargain. That ought to be enough! He didn't owe it to her to stick around until he wound up dead! Besides, she was probably living the life of a queen by now, sitting on lush furs and wearing beautiful doeskin clothing. *Hell, she'd probably be miffed if someone did come for her!* he assured himself. Now, if he could just make himself believe that.

Man of the People studied Clay for a long moment, then nodded his head in agreement. "Good," he said, wishing he could believe the writer would be able to walk away from Gentle Fawn, but knowing in his heart that he would not.

The two approached the waiting Cheyenne messenger silently. Man of the People signed that Clay would smoke the pipe. The Cheyenne's lined face broke into a wide grin. Nodding his head, he held out the pipe to Clay.

Clay looked down at the pipe, back up at the Cheyenne peacemaker, then to the pipe again. He reached out for the red stem of the offered pipe, but his hand stopped in mid-air, hovering over the old Indian's wrinkled palm where the pipe rested. His angry eyes glanced sideways at the Lakota chief, whose stony face gave away none of what he was thinking.

Man of the People nodded almost imperceptibly, his black eyes understanding and kind as he encouraged Clay to take the pipe.

"What the hell!" Clay grumbled, cursing the fates that had again put him in the position of choosing between saving his own skin and saving somebody else's.

Before common sense could fill his crazed brain with another shred of reason, Clay Donovan snatched the pipe out of the old Indian's hand.

Looking the Cheyenne straight in the eye, he held the stem in both hands, raised his knee upward, and brought the pipe down over his hard thigh.

The sound of the peace offering being broken reverberated throughout the silent lodge as the Cheyenne messenger stared at the broken pieces of the pipe in the white man's fists. The man had just pronounced his own death sentence, yet he continued to stand there proud and strong—and angry. The wise old man's expression was a mix of disbelief and respect.

"You tell Many Coups that I'm coming for my wife!" Clay warned, throwing the pipe to the ground as an ancient knight would throw down his gauntlet to challenge his enemy. It didn't matter that the old Cheyenne didn't understand his words. Clay knew his own actions had said it all.

Chapter Twelve

Gentle Fawn heard the loud excited voices and the sound of hurrying footsteps long before she came fully awake. Cursing whoever, or whatever was responsible for interrupting her pleasant dream, she turned over on her side and tried to recapture it. She and Clay Donovan had been riding horses across the plains, his golden locks ruffling and curling wildly in the wind, her dark tresses loose and streaming out behind her like a glossy flag. They were both laughing and happy, finding pure joy in the day and each other.

"No!" she screamed suddenly, jolting herself to a sitting position and shaking her head. Intent on rubbing out the beautiful scene still so vivid in her mind, she ground the heels of her hands in the hollows of her eyes. "It was just a foolish dream!" she told herself angrily. "He is gone. He will not be back!"

It was the sudden quieting of the normal camp activities that caused Gentle Fawn to drop her hands away from her eyes and sit up straighter. As though a giant pillow had descended on the small village, all the normal sounds she should hear were muffled, seeming very far away. She cocked her head to the side and concentrated on listening. Of course, the silence wasn't total. There was a baby whimpering, women whispering nervously, men speaking in low agitated tones, a dog barking, then yelping when someone kicked it to silence.

There were horses approaching the center of the camp. Two, perhaps three horses.

Her curiosity too much to tolerate, Gentle Fawn stood up and walked to the doorway of her tepee prison. She held the leather leash off the ground so it would not pull any more than absolutely necessary on the collar around her neck.

Lifting a corner of the doorflap, she peeked out cautiously. The sunshine was bright—so bright that it blinded her for a moment, causing her eyes to water. Squeezing them shut against the glare, she wiped at the tears, then carefully slitted her eyes to see.

Everyone in the camp seemed to be interested in something at the center of the encampment. Even her guard, the burly Indian brave whose responsibility it was to see that the end of her leash stayed secured to the stake, had walked several feet away to get a better look at what was happening.

It was then she noticed that *no one* was watching her or the stake that kept her anchored to this tent!

Gentle Fawn stuck her head out of the tepee slightly for a better look. Surely there was someone.

No one was on guard. No one! They were all edging toward the activity in the middle of the camp.

Her mouth grew dry.

Her heart leapt turbulently in her chest as the full importance of the situation finally commuted itself to her brain.

It is time! her mind shouted, mentally shaking her body out of its paralyzed state. *It is time to escape!*

Not giving herself a chance to worry about the consequences if she were caught, Gentle Fawn hurried back to her bed and rolled up a buffalo robe into what she hoped looked like her sleeping form. Acting now on pure survival instinct, she rushed back to the doorway and checked the guard's whereabouts once more.

He had conveniently moved even farther away and had his back to her. Luck was on her side—so far.

Dropping to her stomach, she stretched her arms out the lodge entrance and reached for the stake, breathing a sigh of relief when her hands closed over the ends of her leash. By some miraculous kindness of the gods she managed to untie the knot in spite of fingers that shook violently. She hurriedly pulled the strap ends back inside the tepee.

Biting her lip to keep from crying out in agony as the strap's rough texture scoured off what flesh was left on her chafed neck, she began to ease the long strap through the tight space between her skin and the abrasive leather collar, working as quickly as her raw skin under the collar would allow.

It was off. Stained in places with blood—her blood—the vile thing was off. Gentle Fawn didn't try to stop the tears of relief that sprang to her eyes. Even if they came and killed her now, at least she would have known this moment of blessed freedom.

Coming in rapid gasps, her own breathing suddenly seemed to be roaring loudly. Certainly someone had heard her and would come to see what she was doing. Consciously trying to control her deafening respiration by breathing through an open mouth, she wiped her sweating palms on her dress and listened alertly for signs that her escape had been detected.

But it didn't seem as though anyone was near enough to realize what she was doing. She couldn't believe it.

Not able to trust her own hearing, Gentle Fawn moved the hide over the door aside ever so slightly. Whatever it was that held the guard's attention was still working in her favor. She let a long sigh of relief.

Silently moving about the tepee, Gentle Fawn hastily folded the leash in half and tucked the fold under the buffalo robe about where her head should be. Without another moment's hesitation, she dropped to her belly again and moved to the doorflap. This time it would have to be more than her hands that appeared outside.

She moved the flap away from the opening, checked one final time, then scrambled on all fours to the stake. Crouching on her haunches, she fumbled with fingers so unsteady she thought surely she would never be able to make a believable tie in the leash ends. But again, fortune was on her side and she was able to drop her hands from the stake and survey a perfect knot in just a few seconds—seconds that seemed more like minutes.

Taking a deep breath, she gathered her courage and stood up. If anyone were going to spot her, it would be now. She waited an instant, looking around as casually as her nerves would permit. Then with forced naturalness, she began walking—not fast enough to draw attention to herself, yet not so slowly she would be in the open any longer than necessary.

The few feet to the brush nearest the spot she stood seemed like a mile, but she kept putting one foot in front of the other, looking neither left nor right, as though she had every right to be doing just that.

Just as she neared the merciful safety of the dense foliage, she heard the words that caused her breath to catch in her throat and her heart to beat even more erratically than it had been since the moment she'd realized this was her chance to escape.

"So, Clay Donovan," she heard Many Coups shout in English. "Your wish to die is even greater than I had anticipated!"

Gentle Fawn stopped dead in her tracks and turned slowly back toward the camp, her shock making her unmindful of her own safety.

Looking now to the spot where two horsemen, one an old Cheyenne, the other the man she had thought never to see again, sat amidst the people of Many Coups' band.

Clay Donovan! He had come for her!

It dawned on her with confusing force that he had walked deliberately into a death trap to save her. Gentle Fawn clamped her hands over her lips to stifle the horrified scream that rose in her throat, even as her heart thrilled to the fact that he had come for her.

But the instant of happiness she had felt when she first recognized the rider as Clay was short-lived.

The full impact of his being there collided sickly with the joy leaping in her soul.

Because of this dull-witted stunt he had pulled, she couldn't leave now. Even though they would both be killed, she had no choice but to stay here and help him. Her stomach roiled restlessly as spellbound she continued to watch the drama unfold in the center of the camp.

"Get to the point, Many Coups. You know why I'm here. Where is she?"

"You mean that whore who prefers the bed of the enemy to one of the People's?" Many Coups sneered, spitting his distaste on the ground.

"Where, Many Coups?" Clay Donovan ground out evenly, the thumb of his right hand hooked casually in his holster, dangerously near the handle of the large Colt .45 on his hip. He had never been so thankful for the time he'd spent writing that story about Wyatt Earp and his brothers two years before. With the expert training the infamous lawmen had given him, he knew that he would at least be able to get off one accurate shot before he was killed. And there was no doubt where he would send that shot. *Right between your lying eyes,* he vowed silently as he continued to glare down from his saddle at the arrogant Indian chief.

"She is where she belongs."

"We fought and I defeated you. Is this the way a Cheyenne honors his word? By going back on it the minute he can sneak in and steal what he cannot win fairly?"

Many Coups' black eyes narrowed cruelly and shifted from side to side, as though gauging how the witnesses to this second confrontation were reacting to the white man's words. Fortunately, few of them understood English. But he saw respect for the white man's bravery in many of their faces and his hate multiplied tenfold.

"You should have killed me, white man," Many Coups said, his expression distorted with a loathing sneer. "For now you are the one who will die—and it will be a long and painful death. I promise you that." Nodding his head, he turned on his heel and walked away, leaving Clay alone in the middle of the ring of Cheyennes.

"Don't count on it, you cheating son of a bitch!" Clay

growled, whipping out his gun and aiming at the Indian's back.

But before he could call out his threat, the revolver pitched from his grip, as two lassos dropped over his head a split second apart. They tightened immediately on his arms as they were pulled in opposite directions. Still not sure what had happened, he was jerked back and off his horse to land on the ground in a crumpled heap.

His face dangerously close to the startled animal's hind hooves, he raised his head and looked around groggily— just in time to duck when his mount did a frightened run and kick. Missing him by bare inches.

Witnessing the horrible nightmare, Gentle Fawn felt her own head reel violently at the same time a knotting cramp ripped through her abdomen—as though she'd received the full force of the horse's kick in her belly. Staggering backward, she fell into the dense brush behind her.

Why now? she cried silently, knowing how incapacitating her cramps were with some of her menstrual periods. But this was worse than she could ever remember having. She couldn't function because of it. Unaware of the thorny vines and branches that tore at her flesh, she crawled deeper into the thicket where, like a wounded animal, she curled her suffering body into a ball and waited for her head to clear, for the gut-wrenching spasm to pass.

"I should be helping Clay Donovan," she moaned, wrapping her arms around her knees and pulling them against her middle protectively, praying the pain would pass after a moment or two. "I will just rest a minute. Then I will be fine and will decide what to do," she promised herself weakly.

Unfortunately, the toll of the past week on her body had been too much for the petite girl. Though she was exceedingly strong for her size, she was unable to overcome the totally debilitating cramping of her stomach, a twisting so violent she felt certain her insides were being ripped from her body.

Then with one final instinctive push to expel whatever was causing her pain, she slipped into unconsciousness, her body telling her irrefutably that she was not carrying Clay Donovan's baby, the knowledge leaving her with a severe sense of loss rather than the relief she should have been feeling.

When Gentle Fawn finally roused, it was night. Pitch-black night. At first she thought she was back in the tepee, and her entire body jerked to attention. Her whole escape must have been a dream!

Her vision still clouded by sleep, she sat up, relieved that at least the unbearable pain in her belly had subsided to a dull ache. Even though she knew it was a useless gesture, she ran her finger under the leather collar to relieve as much irritation as possible.

It was then she noticed the leash was gone.

Blinking her eyes to clear them, she anxiously circled the collar with both hands, certain the rawhide strap must have just slipped around to the back. But it wasn't there. It was gone!

As though she'd received a slap across her face, she became totally aware. It hadn't been a dream, she realized, looking frantically around her. She was no longer in the tepee. She was in a thicket of scrub brush, not more than a hundred feet from the lodge that had been her prison—and she was free.

Her elation and relief overwhelming, she crawled on her hands and knees to where she could peek out of her hideout.

The sky was overcast, so there were no stars or moon, and the village was still for the night, the occasional call of a night animal the only sound that interrupted the quiet. She had no idea how long she'd been there, but she was certain it was several hours.

What did Many Coups do when he found that she was gone? Had he gone after her, assuming she would be on the way back to the Lakotas, who according to her calculations were hopefully no more than five or ten miles to the north of the Cheyennes?

Each time Many Coups had moved his village, she'd taken careful note of where he was going; and to the best of her knowledge, they were traveling a parallel trail to that of the Lakotas—if her people were still moving toward the Black Hills as they did at this time of year for as long as anyone could remember.

Yes! Many Coups must have men out scouring the area to the north for her right now. Suddenly her incapacitation of a few hours earlier seemed to be a blessing. He would never think to look in his own village for her!

What she should do is travel east rather than north as Many Coups would expect her to do. Once she was a safe distance from the Cheyenne camp, she could slowly begin to angle northward until she met up with the Lakotas.

But what about Clay Donovan? she suddenly wondered. What had the Cheyennes done with him? She couldn't very well leave without finding the answer to that question. Or could she?

It would serve him right if I just left him, she told herself, not really convinced. She tried to sway her decision again. *Any man so crazy that he would ride alone into the camp of his enemy does not deserve to live! And if I leave now, I might have a chance. But if I go back for him, probably neither of us will see morning.* It was just common sense to save herself.

Still, he had been the one to come for her when he didn't have to. He could have been safe back in his white man's world by now. But instead he had risked his life to come for her.

Frowning her disgust with herself for being so soft— and for worrying about a white man—Gentle Fawn crawled out of her hiding place, then scuttled back to the village.

At least the moonless night would work in her favor in that no one would see her, but it made it difficult to determine where Clay Donovan was—or if he was still in the camp.

In the next second, her worried gaze landed on a tall horse tied to a stake separate from the other horses. There was the answer to at least one of her questions. Alive or dead, Clay Donovan was probably still here somewhere.

Her head turning from side to side to be certain she was not observed, she bent low, her hands almost touching the ground, and ran toward Clay's mount.

When she reached the nervous animal, she pinched his nostrils shut to keep him from nickering to her and alarming any guards who might have dozed off. When she had calmed the horse and felt reasonably certain he would be quiet, she quickly opened Clay's saddlebags. She couldn't imagine why the Cheyennes hadn't already taken all his belongings and put his horse in with theirs, but she would worry about that later. For now she would just be glad everything was here, she decided, discovering what she'd been looking for—a knife, some longjohns to control her bleeding, and a rope to hold the makeshift padding in place.

Hiding in the shadow of the horse, she squinted her eyes, finally spotting what appeared to be a man spread-eagled on the ground, his wrists and ankles tied to four stakes. The bound man turned his head and moaned softly. Her chest constricted with a peculiar mix of alarm and relief. He was alive. But for how long?

Her immediate reaction was to rush to Clay's side, but she hesitated, certain there must be a guard. Finally satisfied that no one was watching over Many Coups' prisoner, she hiked up a pair of borrowed jeans to help hold the padding in place; then she dropped to her belly and crawled lizard fashion to where Clay dozed fitfully.

"I do not know why I am doing this, Clay Donovan," she grumbled in his ear, clamping her hand over his mouth so he could not say anything and give away her presence when he started out of his sleep. "A man as crazy as you are does not really deserve to live."

His eyes wide with fear, then recognition, then relief, Clay quit straining against the familiar hand on his mouth and relaxed, gratitude flooding his face. "Where'd you come from?" he whispered when she removed her hand and began to cut the rawhide thong on one wrist. He raised his head up to follow her efficient actions as she finally cut through the rawhide. "They told me you escaped," he said, shaking his freed hand to bring the circulation back to normal.

"And I would have too if I had not lost my mind and

come back for a *wasicun* fool who will probably get us both killed before the night is over," she muttered, just loud enough for him to hear, as she scooted down to cut at the rope on an ankle.

"Look, I didn't ask you to come for me," he hissed irritably. She could have acted just a little bit glad to find him alive, just a little bit appreciative that he'd come to save her—even if she did end up saving him.

"And what would you have done if I had not come, Clay Donovan? Should I have left you here? If that is what you want, tell me. I will leave right now," she threatened hoarsely. Keeping her stomach flattened to the ground as she worked, she moved over to the other leg in spite of her threat. "Maybe it is not too late to save myself. If I am traveling alone and not saddled with a crazy white man who's determined to get himself killed!" she spat.

"Hurry up, will you?" he urged, ignoring her warning and rotating his ankle to relieve the numbness. "What's taking you so goddamned long?"

Gentle Fawn raised her head and glared at Clay, her look saying it all, then resumed her work with renewed vigor. "Where did you get this useless knife?" she grunted, sawing at the leather strap with the dull blade. Finally, the tie gave way.

"That's a perfectly good knife," he grumbled, taking offense at everything at the moment. "You just don't know how to use it," he said defensively, remembering how he'd kept meaning to sharpen it and just never seemed to get around to it.

Stopping what she was doing, Gentle Fawn held the knife in front of her and waved it forbiddingly in his face. "Not one more word," she ground out slowly, emphasizing each word equally, then went back to work on the last rawhide strap.

When she had finally cut through all the stubborn ties, without another word she began to crawl, still on her belly, toward Clay's waiting horse.

As irritated with her surly attitude as he was relieved to be free, Clay rolled over onto his stomach and followed behind the Indian girl.

Without checking to be certain Clay was behind her, Gentle Fawn jumped to a crouching position as soon as she reached the horse. She looked around cautiously, breathing an unconscious sigh of relief with the confirmation that so far their escape had not been observed. Standing up beside the horse she turned to Clay. "Hurry," she ordered over her shoulder as she leapt onto the roan's back, giving every impression that she would begin to ride without him if Clay wasn't there immediately.

"I can't leave without my boots!" he whispered, drawing her glance down to his wool-sock-covered feet.

"They will not do you much good if you are dead— which is what you are going to be if you do not get on this horse now!"

Realizing the truth in her words, he decided begrudgingly that the boots were expendable. But he wouldn't admit it to her. That was for damn sure.

"I don't know what the hell's got your dander up, lady," he grunted in a hoarse whisper as he mounted behind her. None too gently, he reached around her waist and yanked the reins out of her hands. "But I'm getting real sick of your attitude!"

Venting his frustration on the horse's sides, he kicked the animal a little harder than he meant to. The gray lunged forward, almost unseating his riders.

Clay's arms tightened instinctively around Gentle Fawn to hold her in the saddle.

A wave of warm security washed through her body as she was enveloped in his arms. His beard rasped against her cheek; and instead of shrugging off his support as she had meant to do, she couldn't help relaxing back into the curve of his chest. "We must hurry," she whispered, her words not nearly so angry as before.

Certain he must have imagined the change of tone in her voice, Clay turned his head to cast a questioning look at Gentle Fawn. "Which way?" he said into her ear.

Shivers of excitement shimmied over her skin. Gentle Fawn forced herself to lean forward in an effort to break away from Clay Donovan's magical power over her body, but it was useless. She could not escape his warmth, his unique masculine scent. "Man of the People's village is to the north, is it not?" she said breathlessly.

"About two hours away," Clay answered, nodding his head, "but the whole area must be crawling with Cheyennes. That's the way they headed when they discovered you were gone."

"Then we will go east," Gentle Fawn said, the authority in her voice irritating Clay unreasonably.

"We'll go south," he said, turning the horse in that direction even as he spoke.

"South?" she gasped, twisting to look at him angrily. "We will go east and meet my people in the Black Hills," she said through clenched teeth.

"I said we're going south!" he growled, deciding they were far enough from the Cheyenne camp to chance the noise a galloping horse would make. He kicked the horse into a faster pace.

Gentle Fawn's arms flailed out to grab at the reins and turn the horse. "East!" she spat, the moment of pleasantness in the security of his embrace forgotten.

Unfortunately Clay was too fast for her. Before she could confuse the poor horse any more than it was, Clay managed to wrap his arms over Gentle Fawn's, holding them pinned to her sides as he struggled to keep control over the racing horse. "What the hell's the matter with you?"

"The *wasicuns* are to the south!" She defended her actions, struggling uselessly against his hold on her.

"Exactly! That's my point. Many Coups won't follow us into the area where the Army is!"

"Stop and I will go east alone then. I will not go where the killers of the People are. I can walk back to the Lakotas!"

"Do you think I would leave you to fend for yourself in the middle of nowhere—in the middle of the night? After I risked my life to save you?"

"You saved me?" she screamed, her nerves reaching the breaking point. "You forget, *wasicun*. I was the one who did the saving. Not you! If not for me you would still be lying there waiting for the torture they have probably planned for you! Shall I tell you what they would have done to you if *I* had not saved *you?*"

"Why did you?" Clay said suddenly, his tone noticeably softer, his anger dissipated by the realization that she didn't have to come back for him. As she had said, she probably could have been back with the Lakotas by now if she hadn't. Yet she had come. "Why did you come back for me, Gentle Fawn?"

"Why?" Gentle Fawn gulped, not certain she could answer Clay's question.

213

"I thought you were glad to be rid of me."

"I was," she started, realizing even as she spoke that her words were a lie as she remembered how alone she'd felt when he had ridden off with Crazy Horse. "But when I saw that you were Many Coups' prisoner, I felt I owed it to you to help you." She moved about restlessly, suddenly unable to hold still under the weight of her lie. "Because of our bargain," she added hastily. "That is all."

"That's all, huh?" Clay repeated.

"Yes, and now I have done all I can for you, so you can let me go back to my people while you return to yours."

"I'm afraid I can't do that, Gentle Fawn." His hold on her tightened possessively, though he was not aware that it had. "I can't leave you yet."

"What?" She twisted her head to study Clay's face, her own bright with anger. "You owe it to me to let me go. I risked my life to save you from Many Coups."

"And I risked *my* life to save *you* from him, so you owe it to me to stay."

"But you did not save me! I saved you!" she shouted, renewing her wriggling in his arms.

"It's all in how you look at things, little spitfire. But the way I see it, if I hadn't ridden into that camp and diverted everyone's attention, you'd still be a prisoner there!"

Realizing the truth in his words, Gentle Fawn suddenly lost the energy to fight him anymore. Weak from the days of mistreatment by the Cheyennes and the loss of blood in the thicket, she surrendered to her exhaustion and slumped against the hardness of Clay's chest. If she could just rest for a few minutes, she decided, her eyelids growing heavy, then she would have the strength to escape from Clay Donovan. Later would be time enough to leave.

"That's better," Clay said, the satisfaction obvious in his tone as he felt her lean on him. "It's a long way to Cheyenne, and fighting all the way would just make it longer."

When Gentle Fawn didn't respond, Clay looked down to see her eyes were closed and she was asleep. He couldn't help smiling. She looked so young, so vulnerable, and he wondered at the strong sense of protectiveness he felt for the tiny package of Indian dynamite in his arms.

If ever anybody could take care of themselves, it'd be this one, he reminded himself irritably.

Still, in spite of his confused thoughts, he tightened his hold around Gentle Fawn and adjusted his own position in an effort to make her more comfortable as she slept on the galloping horse.

Chapter Thirteen

Refusing to think about how right it felt to be riding with Gentle Fawn folded securely in his arms, or how afraid he'd been that he would never feel this contentment again, Clay concentrated on the story he was going to write.

Calling to mind his days with Crazy Horse for the first time since he'd discovered Gentle Fawn was missing from the Lakota camp, he quickly lost himself in the mental recounting of the things Crazy Horse had shown and told him about the atrocities committed by the soldiers against the Indians. Certain the people in the East would be up in arms when they were told of the brutal treatment the native Americans had received, Clay knew one article describing the truth about Little Bighorn would never be enough. It would take a series of articles, and even then it would take a long time to cover all he had learned.

Of course, the first piece he wrote would have to be about the Battle at the Little Bighorn. Crazy Horse had told him that it had been learned that the famous Lieutenant Colonel George Custer had led the attack and had subsequently been killed with his men on the ridge when the People had turned the tables on the soldiers. That would be where to begin, Clay decided, since there was no doubt in his mind that the newspaper articles published since the battle would be strongly biased against the Indians. It would be up to him, as the one white witness to the battle, to set the story straight.

Then he would write about Crazy Horse, the strange man of the Oglala Lakotas, whose skin was as light as a white man's, whose eyes had witnessed more horror and sadness than any one man should have to bear. He would tell about the man who could lead a band of warriors on the warpath one day, and the next pass out handfuls of raisins to the children in the camp like a breechcloth-clad Santa Claus.

He would write about the young Crazy Horse, then called Curly for his light-colored hair, who had seen the soldiers brutally gun down an old Brule Lakota chief in the shadow of Fort Laramie. Conquering Bear had been trying to make restitution for a white man's cow that had been killed when it ran wild through his peaceful Indian village outside the fort. The chief had asked the soldiers to offer the owner of the cow five horses or mules from his tribe's herds to make up for his loss. But the soldiers were determined to have the man who was responsible for killing the cow and would settle for nothing else. But when Conquering Bear had said, through an interpreter, that he would go and ask the man to give himself up, evidently the interpreter didn't translate the chief's words accurately. As Conquering Bear turned to go, the soldiers leveled their guns at the old man's back and before the eyes of the men, women, and children gathered there, shot him.

Clay cringed involuntarily, thinking of what it had meant to a boy of twelve to see a man he loved and respected like a father murdered by those who were supposed to be his friends; and he vowed anew that he would not rest until he had exposed the soldiers' treatment of the Indians for what it was. Inhumane and inexcusable!

Several hours later, the sound of approaching horses broke into Clay's mental composition of his articles. At first, he didn't realize what it was. Then when he did, it was almost too late to avoid being seen.

Glancing over his shoulder, the alarm in his face vivid, Clay saw that two riders in the distance were coming toward him.

Damn! he cursed inwardly, reaching automatically for the revolver that should have been on his hip, remembering too late that the Cheyennes had taken it, as well as his rifle. Just his luck. No weapons, no boots, and out in the open like a pair of sitting ducks.

Looking around frantically, a glimmer of relief flashed in his mind as he spotted an outcropping of tall, jagged rocks about three hundred feet to the right, their grotesque shapes the most beautiful things he'd ever seen.

"Hang on, sweetheart," he mumbled to the sleeping girl as he shoved her forward with his own body to lie over her. He dug his bootless heels hard into the horse's sides. "We're going to have to pick up the pace a bit," he breathed into her ear, thankful now that he'd allowed the horse to move at its own speed for the past hour or so. At least the animal had had a chance to regain his strength since the first frantic miles of their escape.

"What are you doing?" Gentle Fawn gasped, coming

awake with a start and struggling to move under Clay's weight.

"Just keep your head down, sugar, and pray this old nag of mine doesn't step in a prairie dog hole."

Then her ears also detected the sound of the approaching riders and her heart raced wildly. "Who is it? Has Many Coups found us?" The panic in her voice was building, and again Clay was overwhelmed by the need to protect her at any cost. He couldn't let them hurt her again. No matter what. She was his!

What he was thinking suddenly hit Clay between the eyes with explosion force. He hadn't thought once about his own safety, only hers! For the first time in his life, Clay Donovan was actually worried about someone else's skin, instead of his own. The realization had a stunning, bewildering effect on him.

Shaking his head at the improbability of the whole situation, he laughed aloud at himself. He really was a madman. "I don't know who it is, honey," he finally answered her question, "but I sure as hell don't intend for us to stick around long enough to find out if I can help it."

Within seconds, Clay reined the heavily breathing horse to a stop between two of the large rocks. If the hunters behind them were Cheyennes from Many Coups' tribe, they would follow them into the rocks. If not, perhaps they would ride on past. "Wishful thinking," he snorted derisively, knowing he had to do something—and quick. But what?

Aware that the two riders were drawing nearer every minute, Gentle Fawn turned to face Clay. In a few minutes the men would catch up to them. "What are we going to do, Clay Donovan?" she asked weakly, as though all her instincts for survival had deserted her, had been totally depleted when she helped him escape from the Cheyenne village.

Clay looked down into the upturned face, her large eyes round with fright, and he died a little inside. In all the time he'd known Gentle Fawn, she'd never revealed a single sign of being afraid. She'd always been so strong, so determined to take care of herself, hiding her insecurities behind her anger. Yet, here she was admitting her own fallibility and turning to him for the answers—and he didn't have any.

Knowing what it must have cost her to let him see how afraid she was, his heart burst painfully in his chest. The one time she had let herself depend on him, he was going to let her down. There was nothing he could do. Not a goddamn thing but hide and wait to see if they were followed into the rocks. He didn't even have a gun!

Pulling her hard against his chest, he held her there and kissed the top of her head. "It's okay, honey. I'll think of something. I'm not going to let them get their hands on you again."

Suddenly madder than he'd ever been in his life, his mind began to swirl with an idea. He knew he didn't have a chance against two armed men, but he sure wasn't going to let them win without a hell of a fight. "Gentle Fawn, I want you to ride on without me," he said, setting her away from him and dismounting.

"I will not leave without you, Clay Donovan," she protested, her expression alarmed. She tugged at his arm. "They will kill you."

"Maybe not!" he said, removing her hand from his arm gently. "You ride on and find another hiding place. I'll stay here and take care of our visitors."

"Then I will stay, too," she argued stubbornly. "We will 'take care of' them together."

Clay smiled patiently. "Did I ever tell you you're the most independent, obstinate darn female I ever met? Now go on," he said, his voice sounding much more confident than he felt. "There's not much time and I've got a plan that just might work," he promised, eyeing the flattish top of the saw-toothed rock that hid them from the intruders, then the shorter boulder about six feet behind them. "But you've got to do your part and ride on ahead to divert them. Okay? Otherwise, it won't work."

When she didn't move, he assured her, "I'll whistle like I do for my horse when it's safe to come out. Okay?"

She gave a tentative nod, but still didn't leave.

"But if you don't hear me whistle after a few minutes, you ride like the devil. Now get the hell out of here," he ordered, giving her no more choice in the matter as he slapped the roan on the rump, sending rider and horse disappearing into the darkness.

"Now, Donovan," he said to himself, beginning to climb up the craggy rock in front of him, "let's just see if we can't show these fellows how a kid survives on the streets of New York."

More than once when he was a child he'd had angry people chasing him, sometimes policemen, sometimes the produce vendor he'd stolen an apple from, and sometimes other kids who were bigger than he was.

But no matter where he was, on the streets of New York or in the hills of Wyoming territory, and no matter who was after him, the theory was the same. Divide and conquer. It had never failed him then and it wouldn't now—he hoped.

Of course the stakes had never been quite so high

before . . . But he wouldn't think about that now. He would just think about getting these two bird dogs off his trail and catching up with Gentle Fawn.

Nearing the summit of the rock, he flattened himself against the rough surface. His body one with the ancient stone, he slithered across the top until he had a clear view of the plains.

"Come on, you bastards," he whispered for his ears only. "I'm ready for you."

The riders were near enough now that Clay could see he'd been right. They were from the Cheyenne camp, and he recognized the two as the same men who'd tied him up and had been charged with staying behind with him when the other Cheyenne warriors had gone hunting for Gentle Fawn.

Apparently, they realized the chance of being ambushed if they rode into the giant rocks and they reined their ponies to a stop. Studying the rock formations ahead of them, they were obviously discussing what to do next.

Let me help you boys out some, Clay offered silently, pitching a small stone behind him and to his left.

The Cheyennes looked up in unison, directing their resolute faces toward the crunching sound. They turned toward each other; and even in the darkness, Clay could see their exchange of smiles. They moved forward slowly.

Think you've got it all figured out, do you? Well, let's see what you think about this. Clay threw a second stone to the right, then another to the left, only farther back into the trail between the rocks this time. He hoped it sounded like two people trying to quietly sneak over the crunching gravel.

The Indians stopped again and spoke in hushed tones,

223

one of them pointing in the direction of the second stone. They knew he was unarmed—since they'd been the ones to take his revolver and rifle—but apparently they hadn't realized they were tracking two people. That meant the rest of the tribe must still be looking for Gentle Fawn to the north and wouldn't be coming over the plains to help them out in the next few minutes.

At least that's in my favor. Clay bolstered his weakening courage feebly as the two Indians dismounted, separated, then started to walk toward the maze of tall rocks where he hid.

Clay flattened himself in a crevice on top of the largest rock and waited for the stalking Indians to pass on either side of him. Everything was going according to plan. *Just like when I was a kid,* he assured himself bravely, doing his best to ignore the deafening pound of his own heartbeat in his ears and the glistening beads of sweat popping out on his forehead.

But when you were a kid the fellows coming after you weren't bent on cutting you up and feeding you to the buzzards, an infuriating inner voice pointed out obstinately. *These two are definitely out for blood!*

Good point, he conceded, looking behind him to see if he could confirm that Gentle Fawn had gotten away—and wishing like hell he'd stayed on that horse with her and taken his chances on outrunning the bastards below. As it was, he was locked into this plan and had to see it to the finish. Clay winced at the word "finish."

Well, he'd had a good life. He'd seen more and done more and gone more places than most men twice his age, he comforted himself as the two Indians passed silently on either side of his hiding place, not more than ten feet below and temporarily unable to see each other.

Guns drawn, one carrying a rifle, the other a revolver, they knew he could be behind any of the large rocks ahead of them, so they were moving slowly, their eyes sawing from left to right as they searched the rocky terrain for signs of their prey.

Clay tried to swallow as he waited for the moment to make his daring move, but his mouth and throat were dry, his tongue sticking to the roof of his mouth. His heart was pounding so loudly that he was sure he would give himself away.

Three more steps and it would be time.

Clay sucked in an agonizing gulp of oxygen and forgot to let it out.

Two steps to go.

His muscles tensed painfully, he eased to a crouching position on the edge of the rock, unmindful of the sharp edges cutting into his unprotected feet.

One step left . . .

Now! his mind ordered as he jumped to the ground below—placing himself in full view of both Indians as they rounded opposite sides of the giant rock he'd been on.

"Here I am, you bastards," he shouted as he hit the ground with a bounding leap, his feet only touching the gravelly earth for a split second before he had bounced upward and toward the shorter rock behind the first one.

But in that instant he'd been on the ground between the Cheyennes, he'd seen them both turn their startled gazes toward him and level their guns on the spot where he touched down.

Two simultaneous shots exploded as Clay landed on the ledge of the second rock and scrambled to cover. Then there was nothing. Just silence.

Was it possible that his crazy plan had actually worked and they'd killed each other?

Naagh, he told himself, refusing to get his hopes up. It had just been a bid for more time for Gentle Fawn to escape. There was no way they'd have fallen for such a crazy stunt.

Still, it was awfully quiet.

They're just waiting for me to show myself, he decided, fighting the overwhelming need to peek over the edge and see.

Unable to stand not knowing what was going on another second, he remembered a ploy he'd seen Frank and Jesse James use when they'd let him ride with their gang a few weeks while he wrote a story about them.

Yanking off his hat, Clay put it on the ground and inched it forward slowly to expose it to the men below. The Indians would fire at it if they were still down there.

Nothing happened.

It's a trick, he insisted silently, even as he began to ease his body forward for a peek.

Finally, preferring death to the insufferable waiting— patience had never been one of his virtues—Clay Donovan peered over the edge of the jagged rock.

His mouth dropped open in shock at the sight that greeted him in the gray light of the predawn. He must be imagining things. Shaking his head, he blinked his eyes hard and looked again. The scene hadn't changed.

Both of the Cheyennes were lying where they had dropped, their weapons still in their lifeless hands. "Well, I'll be damned," Clay gasped, straightening up and squinting down on the two for a better look. "Who'd have thought . . ."

Then a wide grin, a blatantly arrogant grin, broke

226

across his unshaved face. "Well, boys, what do you think of us *wasicuns* now?" he asked the dead men as he began his climb down to the ground, the pleased grin never leaving his face.

Giving a whistle that he knew would bring his horse running—if he was still in earshot—Clay quickly limped over to the first Indian, now painfully aware of the cuts and bruises he had sustained in the leap he'd made.

"Sure wish you guys'd thought to bring my boots," he said, holding up one of the Indians' moccasins to his own foot and sizing it. "Guess these'll have to do," he grunted, removing the other moccasin and putting them on his own sore feet.

Giving another loud whistle for his horse, he quickly retrieved both his guns, as well as the Indians' knives— butcher knives, like white women used in their kitchens, he noticed with surprise. When his horse still hadn't come back, Clay hurried to the waiting Indian ponies.

Guess when she heard the shots, she thought they'd gotten me, he realized, irritated with himself for feeling disappointed that she hadn't waited around long enough to make sure he was okay.

"What'd you expect, Donovan? That's what you told her to do, isn't it? You said she should go on without you. She was just following orders."

Shrugging his shoulders, he tried to convince himself the important thing was that she had gotten away safely.

Of course, that's the first time since I've known her that she's ever done what I told her to do! he grumbled inwardly.

With a last hopeful glimpse around, he grabbed the reins of the Indian ponies, mounted one, and turned them toward the south.

"She's probably halfway to the Black Hills by now," he

realized with a regretful glance to the northeast. "It's probably for the best. I don't know what the hell I was thinking of, telling her I was taking her to Cheyenne."

When Gentle Fawn opened her eyes, she was lying on her stomach and conscious of a dull ache in the back of her head. Groaning, she burrowed her fingers into her thick hair to see if she could tell what was causing the pain. Wincing as her fingers came in contact with something warm and sticky, she brought her hand around to determine what it was she felt.

Almost as if only casually interested in the fact that she was bleeding, she studied the wet red stain on her fingertips. She must have hit her head, she decided idly, remembering falling off Clay's horse. But it was as though she had dreamed it. And now that she was awake, what had happened to her didn't even matter.

She'd been riding away from Clay as he'd told her to do, but had known, even as she realized that now was the time she could head for the Lakota camp to the north, that she would not go on. She had turned the horse around and had headed back into the rocks, knowing there must be some way she could help him.

Just as she had gotten back to the far side of the rock maze, she heard Clay shout, followed by two quickly fired shots. Then nothing.

The shots had startled the horse, she remembered, and he had reared, pitching her to the ground. That was the last thing she recalled, the sounds of Clay being killed and the horse throwing her.

They must not have known he had me with him, she realized dully, trying to gather the strength to get up and

228

make a decision about what to do.

She cautiously raised herself and looked around. But the effort was too much. She dropped her head again, oblivious to the sandy gravel abrading the skin of her cheek.

Clay Donovan was dead, the hope of his baby was dead, and she wished that she was, too.

The next time she awoke, it was no longer dark, and the sun was already appearing on the eastern horizon. Rolling over onto her back she flopped her forearm over her eyes to block out the glare of the early morning sun. The effort to rise and go on living too great, she slept again.

"Oh, my God!" she heard a deep voice groan an hour later. "Gentle Fawn, can you hear me?"

She opened her eyes sleepily and smiled, not at all surprised to see him. She had known he would be there to greet her when she passed into the spirit world. "Clay Donovan, are we in the afterlife now?"

"I'm afraid not, love," he said, gently lifting her to a sitting position and holding his canteen to her parched lips. "We're still on good old terra firma."

"Terra firma?" she repeated drunkenly, her brow furrowing as she tried to understand him.

"Solid ground. Earth," he explained. "You're not dead, honey. You're very much alive," he told her. "And you're going to stay that way."

"But I can see you. How can that be if I am not dead also?" she asked hoarsely.

"Gentle Fawn, I'm not dead. I'm just as alive as you are! Neither of us is dead," he said urgently. Scooping her light body into his arms, he moved her to the shade and laid her down.

"Alive? But how? I heard the shots. They killed you."

"No, Gentle Fawn. They didn't kill me. No one's going to kill me. They're both dead and won't bother us again. I promise."

"But how? You had no gun." She tried to sit up, reality beginning to seep into her confused thoughts.

"It's a long story. I'll tell you later. But first you'd better tell me what happened to you," he said, finally noticing her pitiful appearance now that he knew she was all right.

Her hair was matted with blood and dirt, her arms and face were scratched and scraped cruelly, and the dress she wore was covered with dried blood.

"I fell off the horse and must have hit my head," she explained, feeling the back of her head curiously.

"But you're one of the best riders I've ever seen," he protested, checking her head wound and determining it wasn't too serious. "How could that have happened? And this?" he said, indicating the old bloodstains on her dress. "What's all this from?"

The memory of what she'd suffered while lying alone in the thicket came flooding back into her memory and her eyes brimmed with tears. Not wanting him to see her crying, she kept her gaze focused on the stained deerskin. "I am not going to have your child, Clay Donovan," she explained woodenly.

Clay stared dumbly at her, his mouth half open. He didn't know what to think about her reaction to what he had taken for granted all along. He had never believed she was pregnant.

"Is that so terrible?" he finally asked, fighting the ridiculous desire to take her in his arms and tell her they would have other chances for her to get pregnant—

which of course would be a lie since they would be parting company as soon as he could get her back to the Lakotas.

"I lost it," she said pitifully, wiping at the tears streaming down her cheeks.

"Come on, you don't know that."

"I know, Clay Donovan. I always knew," she said certainly, shaking her head from side to side, no longer making an effort to stifle her tears.

"Don't cry, Gentle Fawn," Clay choked, putting his arm around her and pulling her to him, his eyes watering suspiciously. "You'll have other babies," he promised. "Now just wasn't the time. Someday you'll meet the right man, and you'll have lots of babies," he consoled, surprised at how the thought of anyone but him fathering her children tore violently at him.

"Yes, someday I will have many babies," she said stiffly, reminding herself once again that she meant nothing to him. *But they will not be yours, Clay Donovan.*

Chapter Fourteen

"You'll feel better once we get you cleaned up," Clay said more cheerily than he felt. "There's a stream not too far from here," he told her as he lifted Gentle Fawn effortlessly into his arms and stood up. "It's where I found my horse and realized you must've been thrown. If I hadn't seen him grazing there . . ." Clay shuddered at the thought of what could have happened to her. "I wouldn't have known to come back for you."

Humiliated by his reminder of her careless fall, as well as by her tears and spineless behavior, Gentle Fawn fought to regain her pride by struggling in his arms. "Put me down, Clay Donovan. I will walk!"

"And pass out on me? Not on your life!" he refused, tightening his hold on her and smiling down at her angry face. Now, this was the Gentle Fawn he knew—spitting and hissing like an angry kitten. He suddenly felt light-headed. He could handle her this way. It was when she was all weepy and helpless that he felt so disarmed, so completely inadequate. "Quit arguing and let me take care of you for a while."

"I can take care of myself," she declared, even as she fought the desire to relax her head against his chest. "I do not need any man to care for me." But despite her words, she stopped her fighting, admitting at least to herself that she was still very weak from her ordeal. But she'd die before she let him know that.

Pressing her lips into a thin line, she folded her arms over her chest and looked off into the distance, the stubborn expression on her face impenetrable, making certain he knew that she hadn't given in altogether.

It was not until Clay put her on his horse and mounted behind her that she broke the silence angrily. "I can ride alone," she demanded, seeing the two riderless Indian ponies and moving to dismount.

"Huh huh," he grunted, wrapping a strong arm around her small waist and nestling her securely in the curve of his body as he kicked his horse forward. "Not till I'm sure you've fully recovered from that fall you took and—and—and the other," he added, obviously not caring to talk about the baby.

"I am recovered from both the fall *and* 'the other'," she spat out bitterly, hurt that he could slough off her loss so easily, as though he were relieved to know she was not pregnant. She felt the humiliating tears building in her throat again, and her bottom lip began to tremble helplessly.

Suddenly desperate to get away from Clay Donovan before the disgusting wetness that welled in her eyes began to slide down her cheeks, she said, "Just give me one of the Cheyennes' horses and I will trouble you no more. I will go north and join my tribe in the Black Hills. You will be rid of me for good."

Wondering why he couldn't bring himself to take her

up on her offer to ride out of his life permanently—she'd been nothing but trouble from the moment they'd met, and getting away from him was what she obviously wanted more than anything—Clay shook his head and laughed. "How far do you think you'd get alone in your condition?"

"I am strong," she insisted. "Just let me go." She sounded out each word carefully, making the supreme effort not to give herself away.

"We'll talk about it later," Clay said gruffly, realizing that keeping her against her will would put him in the same category with Many Coups. Besides, what was he going to do with her if he kept her? It was different when they'd only had one horse and letting her go would have meant putting her afoot. But now that they had the extra horses, there was really no reason not to head in their separate directions. Sooner or later he was going to have to let her go back to her people. It might as well be sooner.

"We'll get you cleaned up and find you something to eat first. Then after you get some rest, if you feel okay I guess you might as well head north," he said, wishing even as the words were being spoken that he could recall them.

"Do I have your word, Clay Donovan?" she asked, looking off in the distance, afraid to turn and face him for fear he would see the hurt in her eyes.

"You have my word," he said, adding quickly, "that I'll think about it."

"Good," she returned, digging the heel of a hand into one of her eyes and giving a sniff.

"Hey, are you crying again?" Clay asked, cupping her chin in his strong hand and turning her face toward his.

"I am not crying!" Gentle Fawn denied, in spite of the

235

evidence to the contrary. "There is dust in my eyes. That is all." She twisted her face out of his hold and leaned forward in an attempt to end as much physical contact with Clay Donovan as possible. "Is that the stream you spoke of?" she asked anxiously, her relief at being able to change the subject obvious.

The look on his face puzzled, Clay studied her profile for a long moment, then followed her gaze in the direction she was pointing. "Yeah, that's it," he returned disinterestedly.

How was he supposed to know what she wanted? *She's done nothing but tell me how anxious she is to be rid of me since that first night. Yet she risks her life to save me, telling me the whole time that she should have left me to die. Then she cries because she's not going to have my baby when she should be relieved. And to top it off, she then makes it perfectly clear that she can't wait to get away from me. But when I say okay you can go, she starts crying again! Women! Who the hell can figure them?* he grumbled inwardly, nudging his horse toward the tree- and brush-lined bank of the stream.

"I think I've still got a piece of soap you can use," Clay said, his back to Gentle Fawn as he dug in his saddlebags a few minutes later. "Then I'll put some salve on those cuts on your arms and face."

Turning to face the girl who stood silently behind him, Clay could see that she had no intention of doing as he told her. *Orneriest, stubbornest, contrariest . . .* he cursed silently. But when he spoke aloud, he managed to keep his voice even, coaxing. "Come on, take off that dirty dress, and while you're taking your bath I'll wash it for you. You're going to feel so much better."

"I will not take off my dress," she said, her fight

236

beginning to return. "And you will not wash it!"

"Take off the dress, Gentle Fawn," Clay commanded, his tone barely disguising his impatience now.

"I will not!" Her fists balled on her hips, she jutted her chin out and glared at Clay belligerently.

"Take off that damn dress, or I'll take it off for you," Clay shouted, taking a menacing step toward her.

Unconsciously, she took a step backward. "No! Not with you standing there watching me," she refused, her tone indicating she *might* consider the idea if she had some privacy.

Clay grinned at the picture she made. She reminded him of a bedraggled mountain lion cub challenging a bear—and thinking she could win. Well, this time he would let her—after a fashion. "You can take it off in there," he conceded, pointing to a clump of bushes that grew right up to the bank of the stream.

Gentle Fawn looked at the thorny undergrowth skeptically, then back to Clay.

"Well, which is it going to be?" he offered, his smile wide, his blue eyes gleaming. "There or here? The choice is yours. But you better make your decision quick, or I'm going to make it for you." He took another step toward her.

What are a few more scratches, Gentle Fawn decided irritably. Shooting him a quelling glance, she ducked into the screen of green vines.

"Just toss your dress out to me when you get it off. I'll wash it and you can wear one of my shirts until it's dry."

"I will wash it myself!" she yelled defiantly.

"Gentle Fawn . . ." Clay said, his indulgent tone a more effective warning than the loudest command. It wasn't as if he cared who washed the dress, it was the fact that she had to learn when he told her something he meant what he said.

Clay managed to catch the soiled deerskin dress as it came flying out of the bushes, accompanied by very angry Lakota words. He couldn't understand the exact meaning of the words she was saying. But he suspected that was probably for the best.

"Good girl," he called out as he dug a clean shirt out of his saddlebags. "I'll hang the shirt right here," he told her, flinging the red plaid over a branch. His only answer was another string of expletives, which easily made their universal meaning known—despite the language barrier. "Don't forget to wash behind your ears!"

I should have let the Cheyennes keep you, she grumbled to herself, tugging at the irritating leather collar that still rubbed and burned around her neck. *And I should have kept that knife,* she scolded, as she tried again to untie the tangle of fine rawhide knots that held the collar in place.

Her pride refusing to allow her to ask the domineering white man to help her, she stepped into the cool stream after deciding, *It will not be so terrible if I can clean under it.*

When she had washed her hair and scrubbed her skin until it tingled, Gentle Fawn quickly rinsed out the borrowed longjohns and draped them over a shrub to dry. Then making a pad of absorbent sphagnum moss she'd gathered on the bank, she resecured the borrowed blue jeans with the rope and reached for Clay's shirt.

Feeling remarkly better already, she used her finger-nail to separate the fibers in the end of a green stick to make a toothbrush and cleaned her teeth with it to complete her toilet. Then using her fingers to comb her waist-length hair, she stepped out of the bushes, the pleased smile on her face impossible to suppress.

238

But her happiness was brief. An unexpected rush of panic vibrated through her body and the smile slid off her face as her head swiveled from side to side looking for Clay.

He was gone.

Alarm sounding loudly in her ears, she turned in a small circle, her dark eyes wide with terror.

Then the unmistakable sounds of splashing water and a man's deep baritone voice broke the silence. And her heart skipped an anxious beat.

He was singing!

Directing her stunned gaze toward the stream, her fear rioted into anger. Anger at him for frightening her. Anger at herself for not being able to control her feelings for him.

Turning her anger on the collar that still chafed at her neck, she roughly pulled it away from her skin and twisted her head. *I must get this off my neck!*

"Those Cheyennes must have had knives," she murmured, knowing she would need a blade sharper than Clay's if she was going to cut through the rawhide knots very easily. "And hopefully he was smart enough to take them," she grumbled derisively.

"Aha!" She laughed out loud when she discovered a Cheyenne knife and sheath near the top of the saddlebag. "This should do it," she mumbled to herself, checking the blade's sharpness with her thumb as she walked over and knelt in the shade.

Carefully twisting, she slid the tight leather band around her neck so that the knots were in the front. Her fingertips acting as her eyes, she cautiously inserted the tip of the knife under a few of the ties and started to slice outward.

It was at that moment that Clay stepped into the clearing, shirtless and barefoot and fumbling with the buttons on the fly of his jeans.

"What the hell do you think you're doing!" Clay shouted, covering the space that separated them in two easy strides. Grabbing her wrist, he wrenched the knife from her hand and threw it aside.

"What is the matter with you?" Gentle Fawn screamed, scrambling on all fours away from Clay, certain now that he was mad.

Thinking she was going for the knife, Clay took a flying lunge and landed on top of her, flattening her to the soft ground. "I'm not going to let you do it."

"What difference does it make to you?" she grunted, finding it hard to catch her breath under his weight.

"What difference does it make?" he echoed loudly. "Damned if I know," he said, voicing his frustration at the panic that had raged through him when he'd seen her with that knife against her neck. "But it does," he admitted, "and I'm not going to let you kill yourself." He rolled off her and sat up, taking care to keep his hand on her so she wouldn't try to go for the knife.

Gentle Fawn turned over onto her back and stared at Clay incredulously. Able to see the genuine concern in his expression, she lost herself in his intense blue eyes. Now it was her turn to parrot him. "Kill myself? You thought I was going to use the knife to kill myself?"

"Well, weren't you?" Clay said, his blond eyebrows drawing together suspiciously. An inkling of self-doubt was making itself known in his thoughts.

Gentle Fawn shook her head, her black eyes bright with wonder that he could think such a thing—and that he cared.

"Then what were you doing? Don't tell me you were shaving," he joked lamely, relief flooding his heart as he looked down at the delicate woman. Dressed as she was in his clothes and without her braids, she looked more white than Indian and Clay felt as though he were seeing her for the first time. Her hair, still wet from her bath, was loose and fanned out around her face like a wild black halo and he fought the insane desire to bury his face in it.

Gentle Fawn couldn't resist smiling. "No, I was not shaving, Clay Donovan," she said, wishing she could reach up and smooth away the worry lines that were marring his broad forehead. Her fingers ached to touch the beard he'd grown since their last glorious night together. But she resisted the foolish desire with an insistent shake of her head.

"I was trying to cut this off my neck," she explained, tilting her head back to expose the torturous leather collar to him.

Shock and horror clouded Clay's eyes, turning them gray and stormy.

And Gentle Fawn was sorry she had shown him, because she couldn't bear to see the pain in his happy eyes. It hurt her more than the leather collar did, she realized, the knowledge hitting her with a forceful blow to her equilibrium.

"What the hell is that?" he shouted, leaning across her and snatching up the knife, beginning to work at cutting away the offending collar even as he spoke.

"It was how they kept me tied so that I could move around—as far as my leash would allow," she explained bitterly. Clay's gentle concern for her was already easing the bad memory of her time in Many Coups' camp.

"If I ever see that bastard again, I will kill him this

241

time," Clay swore, using every bit of control he could muster to cut each of the tiny strips of tied rawhide separately so he wouldn't chance nicking the vulnerable flesh of Gentle Fawn's neck.

"Oh, honey," he groaned, finally removing the collar and seeing how it had ravaged her skin. It was red and irritated all the way around, open and oozing in several spots. "I didn't know. Why didn't you say something?" he gasped, gathering her into his arms and holding her head against his bare chest, his fingers burrowing into her dark hair.

Gentle Fawn nuzzled her face into the soft, slightly damp blond hair that covered Clay's body. Breathing in deeply to absorb all the headiness of his special scent, she could think of nothing but the glorious feel of his arms around her again.

When she didn't answer his question, though, Clay gripped her shoulders and held her out from him so he could see her face. "Why, Gentle Fawn?" he asked, jarring her contentment.

Still lost in the power of his imploring gaze, Gentle Fawn couldn't look away. "I did not think you would care," she confessed.

"Not care! How could you have thought that?"

Gentle Fawn's eyes widened with surprise and her heart bounded in her chest.

"Don't you know by now that I can't stand to see anyone suffer?"

Her heart plummeted to the floor of her stomach. So that was it. He felt sorry for her. Nothing else. What a fool she'd been to think otherwise.

"I do not need your pity, Clay Donovan," she spat, turning her head to the side and struggling to free herself

242

from his grip on her shoulders.

Her bottom lip began to tremble and she could feel the tears begin to burn in her eyes and throat again. *Stop it!* she ordered herself silently, fighting the threatening tears. *What is wrong with you? You have cried more in the past few hours than you have in the last ten years!*

Oh God, there she goes again, Clay realized, torn between hugging her to him and crying with her or . . . "You're right, you don't need my pity, Gentle Fawn. What you need is a paddling on that butt of yours. And I think I'm going to give you what you need!"

Gentle Fawn swung her head around, her black eyes wide with anger, and raised up on her knees to face him. Her indignant fury had staved off the tears, causing them to dissipate before they could fully form—just as Clay had anticipated. Hands on hips, she dared him, "Just you try it, Clay Donovan!"

Clay hid a smile of self-satisfaction behind a cough. Only when he was certain he could keep a straight face did he speak again. "But first we're going to put some salve on that neck and those cuts of yours," he said, turning his back on the irate girl and walking over to his horse to dig in his saddlebags.

Knowing that fighting him was useless, she sat back on her calves and waited. "Then I will return to the Lakotas," she said purposefully. "And when I see Many Coups again, I will put an arrow through his heart!"

Clay turned and studied her set expression. How could one tiny female contain so much spunk and determination? Even when she was crying, there was a strength about her. She was like no other woman he'd ever known. If any woman in the world could find her way back to the Lakotas and kill Many Coups all alone, he had no doubt it would be Gentle Fawn.

"You need to eat and get some rest before you embark on such a dangerous venture," he said, deliberately avoiding giving her a definite answer.

A tin of ointment and a brown bottle of carbolic in his hands, he knelt beside her and considered the raw skin on her neck again. Even viewing the evidence of Many Coups' cruel treatment a second time, the assault on his emotions was devastating. His anger rose chokingly. And the unexplainable need to protect the small Indian girl he'd known so intimately, yet didn't know at all, clawed at his heart anew.

Clay cleared his throat nervously. "This might sting a little bit, but it will help you heal," he promised, indicating the medical supplies in his hands.

"Then I will leave," Gentle Fawn said, her words sounding more like a question than the determined statement she'd meant them to be.

"We'll talk about it after we eat," he said, the confusion he was feeling making his tone curt and angry.

"You gave me your word, Clay Donovan," she reminded him, fighting the desire to ask him to let her stay with him just a little longer.

"I gave you my word that I'd think about it," he growled. "Now shut up and let me take care of this doctoring so I can find us something to eat!"

"But you—" she started.

Clay's eyes narrowed threateningly.

Gentle Fawn clamped her lips together and glared at him, refusing to be afraid of him. But she was quiet—for a minute anyway.

"Take off the shirt so I can get all those scratches," he said.

Gentle Fawn's eyes widened with alarm. "I will not!" she gasped, clutching the front of the shirt protectively.

"What are you trying to hide? You forget who this is. I've seen you before."

She shrank away from him, her grip on the red shirtfront tightening. "But—but—"

"But what?" he said, even as his inadvertent reminder of their lovemaking caused his own body to tense painfully.

"But it was dark then," she whispered, the embarrassment on her face tugging at Clay's heartstrings.

"Tell you what. I'll turn my back while you take off the shirt and cover up whatever it is you don't want me to see. Okay?"

"All right," she answered cautiously, not doubting that if she didn't accept this concession he would take the shirt off for her. She fumbled nervously with the top button.

Clay turned his back and waited, very aware of the sounds of her clothing rustling as the shirt slid off her shoulders then was wrapped securely around her bosom. The ache in his loins tautened.

You bastard! he berated himself for what he was feeling. *After what she's been through, only an animal would be thinking like that!* "Ready?" he said loudly, the tension evident in his voice.

"Ready," Gentle Fawn answered timidly.

Clay spun around angrily, only to be assaulted by Gentle Fawn's natural beauty. His breath caught in his throat.

The epitome of innocence and sensuous woman, she held the red shirt tightly across her breasts. Glistening with uncertainty and fringed with those long eyelashes

245

he loved, her large eyes seemed bigger than ever before and he felt himself drawn irresistibly into the deep inky pools. The gentle slope of her shoulders curved down to slender arms that were graceful and lovely despite the cuts and scratches that marred their perfection.

And her hair! Had she really been hiding all that luxurious satin in the tight braids she'd always worn? Long and thick and black, it fell almost to her waist, one exquisite lock dropping forward over a pale shoulder.

Unable to stop himself, he groaned aloud. How was he ever going to touch her to take care of her injuries without making love to her? "Your skin is lighter where it hasn't been exposed to the sun," he said woodenly, dabbing at the cuts on the closest arm and trying to remove himself from the fiery contact.

Gentle Fawn frowned and looked down at her shoulder. "So is yours," she returned, noticing the band of white at his waist that his jeans didn't quite cover when he leaned forward.

"But I'm—" Clay's eyebrows drew together and he looked more closely at the pale flesh above the red shirt. "And you're— Are you certain your parents were Cheyennes?" he said, continuing to doctor the cuts.

"Of course they were!" Gentle Fawn returned indignantly.

"Could one of them have been white? That would explain a few things."

"You are insane. Anyone can look at me and know that both my parents were Indians!" she protested vehemently. "My hair, my eyes, everything about me is Indian!"

"Your eyelashes aren't like any I've ever seen on an Indian before," he pointed out. "You could have nherited them from a white mother or father. And what bout your skin? Look at it! It's as light as mine!"

"That proves nothing. Look at Crazy Horse! His skin is ight and his parents are both Lakotas. Whites are not all he same color, so why must Indians be? Some are much ighter and others are much darker. I have even seen ome white soldiers with skin that is black! It means ιothing. They are still *wasicuns* and I am still Indian!"

Clay smiled at her description of the Negro soldiers, nd decided to let the subject drop. It was only agitating ιer, and there was no way to find out if one of her parents vere white anyway. But at least the conversation had erved its purpose. It had brought his lusts to bay by ;iving him something to think about besides his own lesire. "Yeah, I guess you're right. It was just a crazy ιotion."

"Very crazy," she agreed, relaxing as he continued his ;entle ministrations. But once planted in her mind, Clay)onovan's insane suggestion began to grow, slowly at irst, then more persistently, until she began to ask ιerself questions.

Was it possible? Could she be part white? *No*, she ιnsisted. *It is not true.*

Still, long after she had eaten the *pemmican*, a ιourishing, high-protein pressed cake of dried meat and ruit, that Clay had produced from the parfleche he'd thought to bring with him from the Lakota village, the questions continued to plague her.

Chapter Fifteen

"It's time to go, Gentle Fawn," Clay whispered, giving her shoulder a light shake.

Gentle Fawn rolled over onto her back and smiled up at the man who was hunkered beside her. She'd slept so well, snuggled against Clay in the curve of his arm. "It is still night," she protested, covering his hand with her own and tugging on it gently. "I wish to sleep longer."

"We can sleep when we've put a few more miles between this place and us. Now come on and let's get going."

The sudden realization that the time had come for them to part hit Gentle Fawn, bringing her fully awake with a rude jolt.

She sat up and looked around, her expression a mix of sadness and sleepiness. Raking her fingers through her disheveled hair, she stood up. "I will be ready soon," she said, beginning to braid her hair into the tight ropes she always wore.

"I'll get the horses," Clay said, watching with fascination as her slender fingers nimbly twisted the dark silk and finally brought it under control. *Funny, most Indians' hair is coarse, not soft,* he thought, remembering the feel of her hair as it draped across his arm and chest while they had slept. Actually, *she'd* slept; he hadn't. He'd been too aware of her vulnerable warmth touching him from shoulder to foot to get more than a few minutes of sleep.

"It's a shame to hide it in braids," he said, more to himself than to her as he forced himself to concentrate on the task at hand. But she didn't hear him.

"How long will it take to get to Cheyenne?" she asked a few minutes later as she stepped out of the bushes where she'd gone to take care of her personal needs. She had put her own dress back on, though she still wore his jeans under it, and once more she resembled the Indian she was.

"I figure we're about two hundred miles from Cheyenne, so it ought to take about ten days—if there's no more trouble between here and there," he answered, then changed the subject. "Is your neck any better? If not, I'll put some more salve on it before we leave."

Gentle Fawn had forgotten her neck for a while. She reached up to touch it tentatively. "It is much better. Your *wasicun* medicine is very powerful."

"Then I guess we'd better get going." Circling her waist with his strong hands, he lifted her onto one of the Cheyennes' horses. "You do feel strong enough to ride alone, don't you?"

"I feel strong enough," she returned, studying his face quizzically. He seemed not the least unhappy that this was the last time they would ever see each other.

"You're sure you're going to be all right?"

Gentle Fawn nodded her head silently.

"Good. Then let's ride," he said, mounting his own horse and kicking the gray southward toward Cheyenne, leading the riderless pony behind him.

Gentle Fawn watched as he rode away, not even bothering to wipe away the lone tear that trailed down her cheek. He could have at least said good-bye. But what had she expected? He had taken care of her until she was well enough to travel alone—as he had said he would do. She had no reason to wish for more. They had served each other's needs and were parting friends. What more could she ask? She should be glad he had let her go without another argument, she decided.

With a determined shrug, Gentle Fawn turned her mount northeast toward the Black Hills. In two or three days she would be back with the Lakotas and would be able to put Clay Donovan and the past out of her mind completely.

"Hey, where the hell are you going?" Clay shouted over the pounding of horses' hooves as he raced the roan toward Gentle Fawn. "I thought you were right behind me!" he scolded, drawing alongside her and yanking on the reins in her hand.

"Let me go," she screamed angrily, clutching desperately at the horse's mane to keep from coming unseated as the Indian pony swung his rear around in reaction to the surprising pull on his mouth.

"You're not going anywhere without me—and I'm going to Cheyenne!" Clay said, turning his own horse toward the south, refusing to relinquish his hold on her pony's reins.

Unable to understand the surge of happiness that his words caused to explode through her, Gentle Fawn said, "But you said I could go back to the People after

I rested."

"I said I'd think about it," he said angrily, watching her out of the corner of his eye, certain she would make another move to escape any minute.

"But—"

"And I thought about it. There's no way in hell I'm going to let you take a chance on running into Many Coups again."

"If I travel only at night, I will be safe until I reach the Lakotas. Then once I am back in my village, my people will protect me from Many Coups."

"Like they did last time?" he asked with disgust. "If you'd been there when I was trying to convince them to go after you, you wouldn't make such a dumb statement! Hell, they'd turn you back over to him just to keep from having to fight their allies!"

"That is not true!"

Clay turned in the saddle and gave her a long, hard look. "Hell, Gentle Fawn. Why do you think no one came any sooner? They all believed you left with him of your own free will!"

The sudden realization that he had come for her when no one else would churned wildly in her head. "All except you, Clay Donovan," she said softly, her eyes glistening with the knowledge.

"Yes, dammit. All except me!"

Realizing his emotions were edging on betraying him, Clay looked away and started the horses forward. Why didn't he just go on and let her go? She'd be fine. And when they found out how Many Coups had treated her, the Lakotas wouldn't let him have her again. But no matter how he argued with himself, as he'd done all through the sleepless night, he just couldn't leave her without knowing for certain that she was safe.

"You're going to Cheyenne with me!" he said, silently cursing his insanity as he spoke.

"And after Cheyenne, what?"

"Then after I've written my stories about the battle and Crazy Horse and put them on a train to New York, I'll take you back to the Lakotas," he promised, giving voice to an insane idea he'd been fighting all night long. *Anyone lucky enough to get out of there all in one piece deserves to lose his hair if he's dumb enough to go back!* he had told himself again and again. But he couldn't think of any other solution. "I guess I'm just stuck with you until then."

"Yes, stuck with me," Gentle Fawn agreed, forcing her voice not to tremble with disappointment. Refusing to admit how hurt she was by his words, she tried to tell herself that her let-down feeling was caused by the fact that she wasn't going home, nothing else.

During the next five days, Clay and Gentle Fawn covered nearly a hundred miles of rough terrain. Though they had come across no evidence of Indians in the area, on the chance they still were being followed, they had traveled only at night, falling into exhausted sleep during the daylight hours.

Feeling safer with so many miles behind them, Clay looked around at the shady grove of trees where they'd slept since dawn. The horses were quietly grazing on lush grass, the late afternoon sun glistening on their backs, and he couldn't bring himself to saddle up for another long night of riding. "I think we'll stay here an extra day," he said suddenly.

Gentle Fawn eyed the blond man who sat propped against the trunk of a cottonwood tree. One of his long legs was stretched lazily out before him while the other was bent at the knee, serving as a prop for one arm. She felt that same tightening in her chest she experienced every time she caught him in an unguarded pose. And as always, the feeling made her angry with herself. He was a white man, the Lakotas' enemy, her captor. He was one of those she'd sworn to hate and to kill, a man who was taking her farther and farther from her people every day. She knew she should vault on her horse and leave him right now before he could get up and give chase. But somehow she couldn't bring herself to try to escape.

He did promise he would take me back to the People after he was through in Cheyenne. And since we are already halfway there and I have never been there, I might as well stay and see the white man's town, she told herself, refusing to admit to the desire to spend a few more days in Clay Donovan's company.

"Then I will take the opportunity to bathe," she said to him, using every effort not to let her actions betray her inner turmoil.

"Don't go too far," Clay called out as he watched her walk toward the stream, knowing she would do her best to assure her privacy. Gentle Fawn's only answer was an annoyed wave of a hand. But he noticed she entered the stream at the first bend, well within hearing.

Grinning to himself, Clay went to his saddlebags for paper and pencil. Perhaps he could get some writing done now that he had some time alone and was relatively certain he wasn't going to be attacked by avenging Cheyennes at any moment.

As he was rummaging in the bottom of the satchel his

hand brushed over the locket that had sent him in search of Gentle Fawn. His need for a pencil instantly forgotten, his fingers closed over the smooth, round metal, and he brought it into view.

Warm from where the sun had shone on the bag it had been in, the locket held him entranced. He realized with a pang of guilt that he should have given it to Gentle Fawn sooner. But at first he'd been too concerned with their escape. Then her neck had been so raw she couldn't have worn the chain. Then he had simply forgotten.

Clay shook his head vigorously, as if to free himself of a trance. "I'll give it back to her when she's through with her bath," he mumbled aloud. Forcing himself to return his concentration to locating a pencil, he moved to place the shiny piece into the pocket of his vest. But something stopped him.

What do you suppose she keeps in here that's so private? he asked himself, again studying the locket in the palm of his hand.

Probably something crazy like a rabbit's toenail or a dried lizard's earlobe. Something she believes has magical powers, he decided, starting to put the locket away again. And again he stopped short of putting it into his pocket.

What would it hurt if I took a peek? She won't know the difference, he tried to convince himself, slipping a thumbnail into the clasp. The almost silent click as the catch on the locket gave sounded loudly in his ears, making him feel ashamed. *What the hell, if she wants me to know what's in here, she'll show me!* he decided, snapping the locket closed with resolve and jabbing it toward his pocket with disgust.

Almost as though the secret contents of the locket were determined to remain confidential no longer, the

255

necklace sprung from his hand. It dropped to the ground with a soft thump. Lying open at his feet, its clasp broken, the locket seemed to say, "Now can you put me in your pocket and refuse to look?"

"Pictures?" Clay squatted down on his haunches to examine the exposed secrets of the locket. "No magic Indian charms, but pictures!"

His curiosity overcoming any guilt he might have felt, he gently picked it up. Cupping one hand in the other, he held the open locket to examine the three smiling faces that looked out of the two gold frames at him.

The black-eyed, curly-haired baby looked like any pretty baby so he gave that picture little thought. The man was obviously a bridegroom, judging by the clothes he and the woman wore. He looked like the rich Spanish caballeros he'd seen in New Mexico when he'd done a story on the problems between the Spanish-American Catholics, who'd been there first, and the Protestant, Anglo ranchers from Texas who swarmed there after the War Between the States.

But it was the woman who fascinated him. She was exquisite, the most beautiful woman he'd ever seen. And he was overwhelmed with the feeling that this was not the first time he'd seen her lovely features. But where? When? "Who are you?" he asked the happy face in the locket. "And what are you doing in Gentle Fawn's possession?"

She said her father gave it to her when he died. Where did he get it? Did he steal it in a raid? And why is it so special to her? "Were you killed in that raid, pretty *señorita?*"

"What are you doing with that?" a shrill voice asked.

Startled, Clay looked up in time to see Gentle Fawn, fresh from her bath, her hair unbound and wet, coming

A special offer for Zebra Historical Romance readers…

Now You Can Enjoy
Zebra
HISTORICAL ROMANCES
As Never Before And…

GET A FREE BOOK

(a $3.95 value)
NO OBLIGATION

Nothing else approaches Zebra Historical Romances

(turn page for details)

ZEBRA HISTORICAL ROMANCES BURN WITH THE FIRE OF HISTORY. ACCEPT YOUR *FREE* GIFT WITH NO OBLIGATION AND EXPERIENCE TODAY'S BEST SELLING ROMANCES!

Now that you have read a Zebra Historical Romance we're sure you'll want to get more of the passion and sensuality, the desire and dreams and the fascinating historical settings that make these novels the favorite of so many women.

GET A *FREE BOOK*

Zebra has made arrangements for you to receive a FREE Zebra Historical Romance (a $3.95 value) to introduce you to the Zebra Home Subscription Service. Each month you'll be able to preview 4 brand new Zebra Historical Romances *free* for ten days with no obligation to buy even a single book. We'll send them to you as soon as they come off the printing press, so you'll always be assured of being one of the first to get them. You may even get them before they arrive in the book stores.

FREE HOME DELIVERY— AND $AVE ON EVERY BOOK

By joining our Home Subscription Service you'll never have to worry about missing a single new title. You will never miss any of the epic passion that make Zebra books so special.

Each month we'll send you the four newest novels as soon as they are published. You may look them over *free* for ten days. If you are not satisfied with them simply return them and owe nothing. But if you enjoy them as much as we think you will you'll only pay $3.50 each with *NO SHIPPING and Handling charge*. You save $1.80 each month over the cover price. There are no other hidden charges.

MAIL THE POSTAGE PAID COUPON TODAY!

**START YOUR SUBSCRIPTION NOW AND
START ENJOYING THE ONLY ROMANCES THAT
"BURN WITH THE FIRE OF HISTORY."
YOUR GIFT OF A *FREE* BOOK IS WAITING FOR YOU.**

Your FREE Book Offer Card

Zebra

HOME SUBSCRIPTION SERVICE, INC.

☐ YES! please rush me my Free Zebra Historical Romance novel along with my 4 new Zebra Historical Romances to preview. You will bill only $3.50 each: a total of $14.00 (a $15.80 value—I save $1.80) with *no* shipping or handling charge. I understand that I may look these over *Free* for 10 days and return them if I'm not satisfied and owe nothing. Otherwise send me 4 new novels to preview each month as soon as they are published at the same low price. I can always return a shipment and I can cancel this subscription at any time. There is no minimum number of books to purchase. In any event the Free book is mine to keep regardless.

Name _____
                          (Please Print)

Address _____ Apt. No _____

City _____ State _____ Zip _____

Signature _____
              (if under 18, parent or guardian must sign)   2-87

Terms, offer and price subject to change.   PRINTED IN U.S.A.

A FREE ZEBRA
HISTORICAL
ROMANCE
WORTH

$3.95

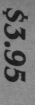

POSTAGE WILL BE PAID BY ADDRESSEE

BUSINESS REPLY MAIL
FIRST CLASS   PERMIT NO. 276   CLIFTON, NJ

ZEBRA HOME SUBSCRIPTION SERVICE
P.O. Box 5214
120 Brighton Road
Clifton, New Jersey 07015

NO POSTAGE
NECESSARY
IF MAILED
IN THE
UNITED STATES

at him.

"That is mine!" she objected, flying across the space that separated her from Clay, her hands bent into claws as they reached out to retrieve her property.

"Whoa there," Clay said, standing up and stepping aside. His long arm shot out in front of her, catching her around the waist and lifting her feet off the ground. "What's gotten into you?" he yelled, holding her back pressed against his strong body.

"Give it to me," she screamed, her arms and legs flailing uselessly in the air. "You had no right to open it."

He tried to explain. "I didn't open it. I dropped it and it opened by itself." His voice was breathless as he fought to keep his hold on the struggling girl in his arms.

"I do not believe you," she said, but ceased her efforts to escape his hold just the same.

Seeing that she was calmer, Clay said, "Will you behave now?"

"Will you give my necklace back to me?" she returned angrily.

"That's what I planned to do when I dropped it." Clay let her down so that her feet touched the ground. But he kept his arm around her waist.

"You looked inside," she said, her chest still rising and falling quickly.

"I told you it was an accident. But what's the big mystery? Why didn't you want me to see what's inside the locket, Gentle Fawn?" he asked, turning her in the circle of his arms to face him.

"Because Hunting Bear gave it to me," she said, keeping her head bent. "For my eyes alone. I hate those smiling white faces, but the locket was all he left me. I would have destroyed the pictures, but I did not have the courage," she admitted, obviously ashamed of her weakness.

"That doesn't make sense. What's any of that got to do with me seeing them?"

"I do not know," she whispered, then finally looked up at him, the expression on her freshly washed face begging him to understand what she herself did not. "I just knew I did not want anyone to see how little my father thought of me—to leave me nothing but a piece of jewelry stolen from a white woman with pictures of the enemy inside. Not when he gave the others—his *natural* sons and daughters—his bow and shield and war bonnet. Parts of himself."

When Clay didn't answer, Gentle Fawn frowned at the stunned expression that had covered his face.

"Holy cow! It's you!" he gasped, holding her out from him and squinting at her as though trying to bring what he was seeing into focus.

"Of course it is me," she answered, the furrow between her dark eyebrows deepening with curiosity.

"I mean it's really you!" he shouted to the confused girl. "Why didn't I see it right away? No wonder the face in the picture was familiar to me! It was you!"

"What are you talking about?" Gentle Fawn asked, managing to take a step back from Clay, her eyes wide with dread as the meaning of his words began to seep into her brain.

"The bride in the picture is you, isn't she?" he accused, so excited about his discovery he wasn't able to reason beyond the fact that the tiny portrait in the locket had come alive before his eyes. "It was the braids that threw me off."

"You really are crazy," she choked, grabbing for her

locket and planning to get on a horse and leave him. "The face in the picture is nothing like mine!"

"Why are you pretending, Gentle Fawn?" he asked, retaining his hold on the locket and the girl. "Tell me what happened? How'd you come to be with the Sioux? Did they kill your husband?"

"Listen to yourself!" she cried out. "Can you not hear how insane this all sounds? I am not the woman in the picture. I could not be her. I have been with the Lakotas since I was a baby. I have never worn a dress like that. And I have never had my likeness put on paper."

Clay released his hold on her arm and studied the picture in his hand, his common sense coming to the fore again after long moments of hibernation. It couldn't be a picture of her. If she were a white captive, why would she deny it? Besides, how would she have been a virgin if she'd been the bride in the picture? One unconsummated marriage was pushing plausibility to the limits. But two? It wasn't possible. Still . . .

"How do you explain the similarity then?" He shoved the locket in front of her eyes.

Gentle Fawn studied the smiling face and grimaced. She knew she did not resemble the woman in the picture. "I explain it easily. You are mad, Clay Donovan! And I am going to leave you before you do something really crazy," she said, snatching the locket out of his hand and making a run toward her horse.

Before she'd gone three feet, she felt a blow to her back. With a loud woosh, the air was expelled from her lungs as she fell to the ground, the weight of Clay on top of her. He moved off her long enough to roll her to her back, then stretched his hard body over the entire length of hers to keep her under control.

Still gripping the locket in her hand, Gentle Fawn beat at his chest and head. But it was no use, and her blows finally subsided.

"Who is she, Gentle Fawn?" he grunted, gripping her wrists and holding them together above her head as he pried the locket from her desperate grasp.

"Give that back to me, Clay Donovan," she said through clenched teeth.

"When you tell me who she is," he said, continuing to hold her hands above her head as he dangled the locket in front of her face. "Who?"

"I do not know," she insisted, glaring at him with eyes narrowed threateningly.

Suddenly Clay rolled off her and sat up, examining the back of the locket. "I didn't notice it before," he said absently, "but this has been engraved."

"Engraved?" Gentle Fawn echoed, sitting up and looking at the locket in Clay's hand. "What is 'engraved'?"

"It means there's writing cut into the gold," he explained, holding it for her to see and pointing to the squiggly lines etched in the precious metal. "It says, 'Francisca, mi querida, Manuel, 1857.' That's Spanish. Do you by any chance understand Spanish?"

Gentle Fawn shook her head, her gaze hypnotized by the strange letters on the locket.

"1857," Clay said thoughtfully, smoothing the pad of his thumb back and forth over the engraved letters as though they would relate the story behind the words if he were persistent enough. "That's nineteen years. So if the bride and groom inside are this Francisca and Manuel, this couldn't very well be a picture of you, could it?"

"I told you I am not the woman in the picture! Now,

you will give me my necklace," she said, holding her open hand out to him. But Clay didn't seem to notice her. It was as if he were talking to himself—as though she no longer existed.

"No, Francisca couldn't be Gentle Fawn," he said, beginning to pace absentmindedly as he gave his full attention to the shiny object in his hand. "On the other hand, Francisca could be—" He stopped pacing and turned to look at Gentle Fawn again. "And Gentle Fawn could be—"

Clay snapped the locket open and looked at the picture of the happy baby he had passed over so quickly before.

"How old are you, Gentle Fawn?" he asked suddenly, taking a penknife from his pocket and opening it.

Puzzled, Gentle Fawn answered without thinking. "I am eighteen winters."

"Eighteen," he repeated, gently insinuating the small knife blade under the narrow gold ring that held the baby's picture in place. "That would mean you were born in '58—a year after this locket was engraved."

The ring seemed to spring from the locket, falling with the picture, turned facedown, into his palm. He studied the writing on the back of the picture, then reread the faded words a second time to be certain he hadn't made a mistake. "And you would have been one in 1859," he said at last, holding the upside-down picture out for her to see the writing on the back.

Her gaze riveted to the words on the round of yellowed paper in Clay's palm, she was unable to stop herself from asking, "What does it mean?"

"It says, 'Camila Elena Delgado, 1 year old, 1859'," he said, his blue eyes wide with discovery. "It means, Gentle Fawn, that if Camila is the daughter of Francisca—" He stopped speaking. Holding his breath, he inserted the knife blade under the gold rim that secured the picture of the people he was certain were Manuel and Francisca on their wedding day. "It means—" he started again. "Oh, my God! It's true!" he said, his voice filled with amazement as he stared dumbfoundedly at the back of the second picture. "I can't believe it! What a story!"

"What is it? What is true? Are they the parents of the baby?"

Clay nodded his head, unable to tear his gaze away from the writing on the back of the second picture. Finally he spoke, reading the tiny words scrawled so lovingly nineteen years before. "'Francisca and Manuel Delgado, 12 December 1857'," he read, his voice barely audible.

"Then the man and woman in the picture are the parents of the baby," she said, curious as to why he was so excited about proving what she had already assumed.

"And baby is—you. You are Camila," he said, studying her large eyes as they widened with surprise.

"Me?" she choked, every knowledge she'd ever had about her past colliding with this insane idea.

"I'm certain of it now. You're Camila Elena Delgado!"

"I am not!"

"Francisca and Manuel Delgado are your parents!"

"Stop!" Gentle Fawn screamed, clamping her hands over her ears and turning her back on Clay. "Why are you doing this to me? Why do you want to hurt me like this?"

Clay wrapped his arms around her from behind and said, "I don't want to hurt you, sweetheart. I just went about it all wrong. Tact isn't one of my strong points, I'm afraid. I should've broken it to you more carefully. But in spite of my clumsy bungling, don't you see it's the only answer? The only way you could look so much like Francisca is to be her—which we both know you're not—or to be her daughter."

"I am not her daughter. Those people are *wasicuns*. I was born a Cheyenne and raised as one of the Lakotas! This is all a co—co—"

"A coincidence?" he helped her out, kissing the top of her head. "I really don't think so, love. All the pieces fit too perfectly to be mere coincidence."

"Suppose you are speaking the truth. Why would Hunting Bear have kept this from me?" she asked, turning in his arms, the look in her dark eyes challenging.

"Only Hunting Bear can answer that. But it would be my guess that, knowing how the People feel about the whites, he thought you would be safer if everyone believed you were one of them."

"Then why give me the locket when it was too late to ask him about it?"

"Maybe when he was dying he could see that the Indians' days of roaming the plains freely were numbered and he wanted to give you a chance to reclaim what you lost as a child—your true heritage. It was his gift to you."

Looking into Clay's deep blue eyes, Gentle Fawn could almost believe the story he had concocted based on a few chance facts. But to accept what he was suggesting for even one moment would mean she had to admit she was one of the people she had hated all her life. And what did that make Hunting Bear? Had he been the one to kill the people in the picture and steal the woman's locket and her baby?

"No! You are lying! It is not true!" she spat angrily, refusing to believe the man she'd known to be a loving father could have done such a thing. "You are just making this up to have something to write on your papers!" she accused, suddenly remembering what he had said. "That is it! You only want another story! Like all the *wasicuns*—the fat takers—you do not care who you hurt to get it, do you?"

Gentle Fawn tore herself out of Clay's arms and began to run. Maybe if she ran hard enough, long enough, she might be able to forget this nightmare.

Chapter Sixteen

"Is it really that terrible?" Clay said, rounding the trees where Gentle Fawn sat hugging her knees and staring off into the distance.

Gentle Fawn looked up at him, her black eyes dry and dull with disillusionment. She had run until she could run no more, finally realizing there was nowhere she could go to escape the seeds of doubt about her birthright that Clay had planted in her mind. "It is that terrible, Clay Donovan."

He bent down to sit on his heels, the tenderness in his gentle blue eyes going unnoticed by the distraught girl. Resting his elbows on his taut thighs, he clasped her hands between his own. "Why?"

"Can you not understand? If what you say is true, my whole life is a lie!" She looked at him beseechingly, seeing in his eyes for the first time the pain he was feeling. When he looked at her like that it almost made her believe he cared about her, and her heart did a wild somersault in her chest.

Irritated with the turn her thoughts had taken with no

warning, Gentle Fawn jerked her hands from Clay's grasp and turned her head to the side so she wouldn't have to look into those hypnotizing eyes. "I would rather be dead than be one of the *wasicuns!*"

"We aren't all so bad," Clay said, cupping her chin in his hand and turning her face back toward his. "Most of us can be pretty nice folks if you give us a chance." He grinned boyishly, a smile that would have melted the coldest heart. And Gentle Fawn's heart was not cold.

"There is nothing 'nice' about the *wasicuns*," she said, making a last-ditch effort to refuel her hatred.

"Are you sure?" Clay's head moved closer to hers, his gaze locked on her lips.

Gentle Fawn nodded her head, her own gaze mesmerized by the mouth drawing nearer and nearer. "The whites take and take and take. They will never be satisfied until they have taken everything from the People. Our lands, our way of life, our pride—our very being!"

"Is that what you think I want, Gentle Fawn?" Clay whispered, his mouth a fraction of an inch from hers, his breath on her face warming her entire body.

Gentle Fawn nodded her head again. "You are trying to steal my Indian blood from me with your vicious lies. You want to destroy me."

Clay smiled and shook his head. "That's not true, and you know it, don't you?"

Gentle Fawn tried to turn her head away, but her chin was still trapped in Clay's strong hand. She looked from side to side nervously. Yes, she knew what he wanted, and God help her, she wanted the same thing. "I do not want you to kiss me, Clay Donovan." Her voice was an uncertain whisper.

"Yes, you do."

"Please stop," she begged, speaking as much to herself as to him, even though she knew that her battle was already lost. How could she proclaim her hatred for all whites one minute, then feel like this for one of them in the next instant?

"I can't," Clay murmured, his mouth brushing hers with a tender kiss that warmed its way past every barrier, real or imagined, that stood between them. All thoughts of the past and her true identity evaporated. All that was left was here, and now, and Clay Donovan.

Had it really been two weeks since she'd felt this contentment, known this feeling of being where she belonged? How could she have thought she could live the rest of her life without this? she wondered as she melted forward into Clay's embrace.

"God, honey, it's been so long," Clay groaned, the fingers of one hand tangling into the confusion of her silky hair as his mouth captured hers in a searing kiss that rocked them both to their very souls.

Lowering her to the ground, his hands roved hungrily over her body. He covered her face and neck with his fiery kisses, returning frequently to her welcoming lips for the sustenance he'd been denied for so long. "Oh, sweetheart, I can't get enough of you. I've got to see you, all of you."

No longer able to resist, Gentle Fawn allowed herself to be drawn to a sitting position. Without an instant of delay, Clay whisked the deerskin dress over her head to reveal her nakedness to his avid gaze. "So pretty, so tiny, so sweet," he whispered, his words a worshipful litany.

As a man dying of thirst would gasp when presented with the cup of water that would save his life, he sighed his relief aloud as he bent his head to taste the sweetness of a rose-tipped nipple.

Gentle Fawn arched her breasts forward and threw her head back, lost to the electricity charging through her body. Her hips began to move of their own accord against the hand which had gently parted her thighs and was stroking the moistness of her femininity.

Desperate now to feel Clay's chest against hers, Gentle Fawn unfastened his shirt with shaking fingers as his hands and mouth continued to fire her desire relentlessly.

Lowering her back down to the ground, he hurriedly shed his clothing and covered her body with his own. Her hips rose instinctively to meet him, her thighs parting to cradle his slim hips between them.

"Oh honey, you're so perfect," he moaned, his tongue trailing along her neck to the bend of her shoulder. "You taste so good." Gently cupping her in his hand, he moved his palm lightly across the nipple, marveling at the way it swelled and peaked under his touch. Using the tips and backs of his fingers, he teased the taut bud, then clasped it between his fingers and gently tugged it as his mouth paid homage to the other breast.

Running the tip of his tongue across the rigid button of her breast, his lips barely touching her, he coaxed the second nipple to a tight peak. When both breasts had been thoroughly adored, he nibbled his way along her ribs, leaving a trail of moist kisses over her flat belly to the silky triangle of dark hair at the top of her thighs.

A low guttural groan escaped from deep in her throat as his mouth touched the tiny center of her sex. The petals of her womanhood immediately flowered under his gentle tutelage, opening up and expanding until the pleasure became almost unbearable.

Suddenly, sweet explosive waves flooded through her. She gasped for air as she burrowed her fingers into Clay's thick hair, holding him to her until the final convulsive spasm had passed.

"I love the way you respond to my loving," he whispered, nipping and kissing his way back up her perspiration-dewed body.

Capturing her mouth in a searing kiss, he plunged his strength into her, gloving himself snugly within the warmth of her womanhood.

Clay rolled over onto his back, carrying Gentle Fawn with him. With her straddling his hips, he held still and waited, curious to see what she would do if she was given the chance. And he was not disappointed.

Able to feel Clay deep inside her, Gentle Fawn stretched her torso over his, lightly rubbing her nipples against his, thrilling to the feel of his chest hair on her breasts. Grasping handfuls of blond hair at each of his temples, she kissed his mouth, long and hard. With only the slightest encouragement from him, she plunged her tongue into his mouth to swab and explore the hidden hollows there.

Her boldness and her enthusiasm for being the aggressor growing by the second, she moved her hips from side to side and up and down as she nibbled hungrily at Clay's earlobe. And when he groaned and grabbed handfuls of her bottom to lift and settle her on him more quickly, she sat up and took his hands in hers. Smiling, she raised his arms over his head and held them there as she bent to kiss a flat brown nipple.

Taking the treasure she had discovered lying in the forest of masculine chest hair into her mouth, she tugged and teased the tiny bud at its center until it was pebble hard. Then, pulling at the wiry curls with her lips, she moved to his other nipple, aware that his movements beneath her were becoming increasingly more restless.

Clay's fingers, entwined with hers and above his head, flexed, his grip tightening on hers as he bucked his hips upward. Then he jerked his hands free. "Oh, God! You're a witch!" he groaned, gripping her waist tightly and lifting her up and down rapidly, his own hips rising to meet her each time.

Gentle Fawn sat up and leaned back against his bent legs, feeling his hardness deeper inside her with every thrust. Then it was happening, that glorious bursting that splintered her soul into thousands of tiny lights as Clay poured his desire into her.

Gentle Fawn fell forward onto Clay's rapidly rising chest, unable to speak. She slid her hands around his neck and just held him, tight, as though she never wanted to let the moment go. And Clay enfolded her slender frame in his arms and hugged her to him as he nuzzled the curve of her shoulder. "Me, too, sweetheart. Me, too."

"Why did you come to Many Coups' camp for me, Clay Donovan?" she asked moments later as they lay together in the last of the fading sun.

Clay's arm tightened on Gentle Fawn's shoulders, but he didn't answer. He couldn't. He didn't know why he'd gone after her. Couldn't imagine why he'd done such a fool thing as to ride alone into the Cheyenne camp. At the time, he had just known she needed him and that he couldn't turn his back on her. Nothing else had been important.

"Why, Clay Donovan?"

"Why did you come back for me when you could've been long gone?" he answered her question with one of his own.

"I owed it to you."

"I guess that's why I came for you, too," he said. "After all, you got me my interview with Crazy Horse."

"But you had already paid your debt for the meeting with Crazy Horse by marrying me. You did not owe me more."

"Yeah, well, I guess I'm just a nice guy." He laughed, uncomfortable with the thoughts that tumbled in his brain. The memory of the fierce sense of possession that had seized him when he had thought of Many Coups knowing Gentle Fawn as he did. The anger that still clawed at him when he envisioned her with any man other than himself.

"I am not."

"Not what?"

"Not nice. I did something very terrible last year. Something the gods are still punishing me for."

She sounded very young and vulnerable and Clay's heart went out to her. He was certain nothing she could have done could be that bad. "What did you do?"

"When our chief's son, Daniel Blue Eagle, brought the white woman, Firebird, to our village and married her I was very angry. Since I was a small girl I had always believed that he would pick me for his wife when I was old enough to marry. But he only thought of me as a child and married her. I hated her very much—because she was white and because she had stolen what I believed should have been mine."

"Jealousy is a very painful thing, Gentle Fawn, but also very human. It's not all that terrible. You shouldn't feel guilty," Clay said, troubled by the twinge of that same emotion that had jerked through him when the

271

woman in his arms had talked of her desire to marry another man—even one who she admitted had not been interested in her.

"But what I did was very bad. I pretended to be Firebird's friend and betrayed her. Because of my jealousy, she could have died when I convinced her to go to Deadwood alone to find other whites who would take her back to her home—and away from Daniel Blue Eagle. And when that failed, I helped white traders kidnap her while her husband and the men were out of our village."

"But evidently that didn't work either," Clay said, surprised by what she was telling him; but her remorse was so sincere, he was unable to bring himself to judge her harshly. "You said she and Daniel Blue Eagle are still together."

"The old men and women of our village saved her before the traders could take her very far."

"What happened then?"

"Though Firebird told no one about my part in the kidnapping, I was exposed. For what I had done, banishment from the tribe would have been just. But the chiefs and Daniel Blue Eagle left my punishment up to her. And instead of asking for revenge, she spoke in my defense. She told them that young people often do foolish things they regret later on and that she thought once I had my own husband I would cause no more trouble." She shrugged her shoulders defenselessly. "That was my only punishment for all the terrible things I did. I was told to choose a husband or one would be chosen for me."

"Is that why you married Tall Feathers?" Clay asked, finding a strange comfort in the possibility that she had not loved her Indian husband.

"Yes," she admitted aloud, and for the first time

272

to herself.

Clay exhaled a long sigh, unaware that he'd been holding his breath waiting for her answer. *Not that it makes any difference,* he told himself sternly. "And evidently you and Firebird became friends again since she let you use her tepee while she was gone."

"Yes, we are friends. She forgave me and said we would forget the past. But I will never be able to forget what I did."

"So what it boils down to is that Firebird could forgive you for being human and making a mistake, but you can't forgive yourself."

Gentle Fawn nodded her head silently.

"You feel guilty because your punishment wasn't more severe, don't you? You'd probably feel better if they'd beaten you or something. But from the sounds of things, you've done enough self-punishing to make up for any penance the chiefs didn't dish out."

Clay sat up and faced her, holding her shoulders in his hands. "Give it up, Gentle Fawn!" he said, searching deep into her black eyes. "It's time for you to forgive yourself. Forget the past like Firebird told you. Accept what happened and learn from it. But don't go on browbeating yourself for what's already happened—for what you can't change. You've got your whole life ahead of you. Don't keep looking back."

"Do you still like me after what I have told you?" she asked, her eyes downcast and her voice making her sound much younger than her eighteen years.

Something deep in the area of Clay's heart tightened painfully. "*Like* you? Oh, honey," he groaned, gathering her into his arms and burying his face in the dark cloud of waves that billowed down her back. "I like you all right.

273

As a matter of fact, I like you just a whole hellova lot."

"This town has sure changed since my dad and I came here with the Union Pacific nine years ago," Clay said, his eyes wide with amazement as he took in the dozens of modern hotels, banks, theaters, saloons, and stores that lined Cheyenne's main street. "It's really something, isn't it?"

Gentle Fawn moved her horse closer to Clay's and nodded her head silently, *her* eyes wide with fear! The street was teeming with animals, wagons, and funny black vehicles Clay had called carriages. And people! Never in all her imaginings had she thought there could be so many white people in one place. Was this what Daniel Blue Eagle had meant when he had argued against fighting the *wasicuns* by pointing out that for every ten of them the People killed, a hundred would come to replace them?

And so loud! Everything was so loud. Her head began to pound as she tried to identify the sounds assaulting her hearing. Booming men's voices, high women's voices. Laughing, shouting, arguing, cursing. Strange music coming from several of the wooden buildings that faced the street. Squealing children running along the wooden walkway that edged the dirt street. Dogs barking. Horses whinnying. Mules and donkeys braying.

"Of course, it's nothing like the cities back East, probably not even a tenth the size of New York City where I grew up, but it's still pretty impressive when you consider how many railroad towns withered away once the railroad workers moved further west. Well, what do you think?" Clay asked enthusiastically, looking at

Gentle Fawn for her reaction.

"I think it is very noisy," she said, unable to hide her distaste; but Clay had already looked away.

"You'll get used to it," he chuckled. "We'll find a place to stay. Then we'll really investigate the improvements that have taken place since my dad and I helped lay that railroad track over there."

Conscious of the curious stares they were attracting, Gentle Fawn stayed close to Clay as he settled the horses in a stable, then led her to a large building on what he said was Eddy Street.

As he approached the large, ornately carved counter of the Rosewood Hotel, Clay glanced around the lavishly decorated lobby.

Growing more nervous by the minute, Gentle Fawn slowed her step to position herself behind Clay, as if standing in his confident shadow would somehow give her the courage she needed in this wild place of Cheyenne. If she could have dissolved into a spot on the plush red rug beneath her feet, she would have in a minute. What was she doing here? Why hadn't she fought Clay Donovan harder when he wouldn't let her return to her own people alone? Surely she would have been safer in the mountains and on the plains by herself than she could possibly be in this place.

"Clay Donovan, with the *New York Tribune,*" she heard Clay announce. "We'll be needing your best room for the next few days—one with a big bathtub if you've got it."

"Yes sir, Mr. Donovan!" the balding man behind the counter answered, his face breaking into a smile of recognition at the mention of Clay's name. "Been readin' your articles in the *Trib* for years. You've really had some adventures, haven't you? What ya doin' in Cheyenne? Ya gonna put us in one o' your pieces?"

"Could be," Clay laughed and sent the man a conspiratorial wink. "Could be. But right now all I want to do is get these dirty duds off and take a bath." He reached for the key the man had put on the counter in front of him.

"Room 206. Best in the house," the hotel manager warbled. "And when ya git ready to do your story 'bout Cheyenne, ya come talk to Homer Penn—that's P-E-N-N—and I'll give ya enough information to fill your whole newspaper."

"I'll sure do that, Mr. Penn," Clay said, giving the man his friendliest smile and turning back to Gentle Fawn. "Ready?" he asked, taking her arm.

"Is *she* with you?" Homer choked, his eyes bulging with shock as his friendly smile seemed to melt off his face.

"Yes, she is," Clay said, the smile on his own face growing cold as he took in the meaning of Penn's words. His eyes narrowed challengingly. "Is there some problem, Homer?" He emphasized the man's name.

"Well—ah—not—ah—actually—there is," he stuttered, his face reddening under the steely glare of Clay Donovan's blue eyes.

"Oh?"

"We don't 'llow no Injuns at the Rosewood," Homer Penn said in a rush of words. "It's against our policy."

Clay's grin broadened, showing his teeth in what Homer realized was anything but a friendly smile. "Then, there's no problem, Penn, since my wife is not an Indian." Clay felt the muscle in Gentle Fawn's arm tense as she turned to deny his words, her mouth hanging

276

open. But he squeezed her arm tightly and for once she was quiet. They could settle her Indian heritage—or lack of it—after they were bathed and rested. Right now a room was the most important thing, and he had no intention of letting the little pipsqueak of a desk clerk force him to waste time looking elsewhere for accommodations.

"Your wife?" The top of Homer's bald head and his forehead were dotted with perspiration. What was he supposed to do? If he asked the reporter to return the room key, he knew he could kiss his chances of seeing his name in the *New York Tribune* good-bye—except in the most derogatory terms, of course. On the other hand, if he let them stay and she really was an Indian, the owner would be furious and Homer could kiss his job good-bye.

"My wife." Clay nodded his head, his eyebrows arched expectantly as he waited for Penn's decision. "That's Penn with two N's. Right?"

"In that case, Mr. Donovan," Penn said, his sweating bald head bobbing up and down quickly. "I hope you'll accept my apologies. Ya can't be too careful, ya know."

"Oh, I know, Homer old boy. Believe me, I know."

Clay turned and prodded Gentle Fawn ahead of him, his barely controlled anger straining to explode any minute. "And I'm learning more everyday, you self-serving son of a bitch," he mumbled through clenched teeth as he scooted her across the lobby to the wide staircase leading to the second floor.

"Who's that prissy little bastard think the land under this fancy hotel belonged to before he got here?" he growled as he inserted the key into the lock to their room. He had kept up his angry monologue all the way up the stairs and down the long hall of the second floor.

"Wants his name in the *Trib,* does he? Well, I'll put him in the paper all right. Him and this whole bigoted hotel!"

Clay gave Gentle Fawn a push into the room, then followed her inside, slamming the door behind him. "Then I'll send him his copy special delivery so he can roll it up real tight and shove it up his sanctimonious little—"

"Why did you lie to that man?" Gentle Fawn asked, wheeling around and glaring accusingly at Clay.

"It wasn't a lie as far as I'm concerned. You're no more Indian than I am! And sooner or later you're going to realize it, too."

"Not about that!" she said, confused by the way her heart had reacted when Clay had claimed they were married. "I understand he would not have let me stay here if you did not say I was white. But why did you tell him I was your wife? Our marriage was only temporary. We agreed that it was to be ended when we each got what we needed from the other."

Dumbfounded, Clay studied the woman facing him. Damned if he knew why he'd done it. Whether or not they were married wouldn't have made any difference to Homer Penn. Clay was certain that the Rosewood, like any other expensive hotel in the country, catered to men with mistresses all the time. So why had he done it?

Suddenly, with mind-destroying clarity, it hit him. From the moment they'd walked out of Man of the People's lodge that morning, he'd thought of Gentle Fawn in no other way but as his wife—as his woman. How had he been able to accept the unceremonious wedding as real when his brain had not acknowledged the divorce they had agreed on?

"I didn't like the insulting way he was looking down

278

his snooty little nose at you," he finally admitted, knowing that was part of the answer anyway.

Gentle Fawn waited for him to say more, not certain why his answer disappointed her. "Oh," she finally said, turning to view the hotel room.

"How long will it be until you can take me back to the Lakotas, Clay Donovan?"

Stunned by her question, Clay rolled his eyes heavenward and plopped himself down in an upholstered chair beside the bed. He had no intention of taking her back to the Lakotas after what he'd discovered in her locket, but he hadn't gotten around to telling her yet. He aleady had ideas on where to look to find out about her true parents. Who knows, one or both of them might still be alive. He could already see the headlines of the story: FAMILY REUNITED AFTER DAUGHTER SPENDS FIFTEEN YEARS WITH THE SIOUX.

"Why are you in such a hurry to leave?" he hedged.

"I do not like it here. This *wasicun* village is dirty and noisy, and I do not wish to stay." She wandered over to the window and looked down on the busy street.

"Well, it will take me a few days to write my story and get it in the mail," he said slowly, as though he was figuring out when he could take her back to the Lakotas. "I guess we should be able to leave in five or six days." There he hadn't lied, had he? He'd just avoided giving her a real answer. "Can you stand it here that long?"

"Where will I cook?" she asked, looking for something that could be used for a cookfire.

"Where will you *what?*"

"Cook. We will have to eat if we will stay here for five or six days."

Clay stared incredulously at the serious girl. Here he'd

279

been preparing himself for another knock-down-drag-out fight over the pictures in the locket or about why he'd said she was his wife when she considered them divorced, and she was worrying about where to cook.

The tension on his forehead was ironed away and his face split into a wide grin. His laugh rich and deep, he crossed the room in two easy strides and threw his arms around her. Hugging her tightly, he lifted her feet off the ground and swung her in a circle. "Ah, my little spitfire Indian princess, what in the hell am I going to do with you?"

"You are laughing at me!" she accused, struggling to free herself from his enthusiastic hug.

"I'm not. Really, I'm not."

"Then tell me where I will cook and I will begin our supper. I will wait until you are through with your business here. Then I will return to my people as you promised."

Her words having a sobering effect on him, he eased her back down to touch her feet to the floor. "Tell you what," he said, kissing her nose lightly. "You just take a little vacation. I'll worry about our food. No cooking for you while we're here. And then in a few days I'll take you back to your people" *Wherever they might be, Camila Elena Delgado!*

Chapter Seventeen

Lying back in the rose-scented bath water that filled the large tub dominating a screened-off corner of their room, Gentle Fawn sighed contentedly. Never in her life had she imagined anything so luxurious and soothing as the feel of hot water lapping over her skin. Her limbs felt weightless, her eyelids heavy, and she slid deeper into the glorious water until even her chin was submerged. Not only was it removing the dirt and grime that had ground into her pores over the past few days, but it seemed as though the water had the power to soak away all of her concerns and problems.

She inhaled deeply, dragging the sweet-smelling steam into her lungs, and smiled happily. "This is one thing that is good about a *wasicun* village," she admitted to herself, wondering how she had lived all her life without knowing the pleasure of a hot bath, and wondering how she could ever go back to bathing in cold streams. Gentle Fawn was certain she now knew why Firebird had the small round wooden tub she kept in her lodge—and why she prized it so highly. Though it was not nearly large enough for a whole person to fit in—as was the one Gentle Fawn lazed in now—it could still be filled with warm water and she could sit in it.

"Aren't you out of there yet?" Clay asked, bumping loudly through the door to their room an hour later. "You're going to turn into a prune!" he said, peeking around the screen after plopping his packages down in a chair.

"I think I fell asleep," Gentle Fawn answered sheepishly. Her dark eyes dreamy and confused, she sat up in the now-tepid water and looked around for her towel.

"Allow me," Clay offered, snatching up the towel and walking over to stand beside the tub with it opened wide.

Without any false sense of modesty, Gentle Fawn stepped out of the tub and allowed herself to be enfolded in the thick white bathsheet and Clay's arms. "I did not mean to stay in so long," she explained. "The water is all cold now."

Clay laughed at her disappointed expression. "They're bringing more hot for me. If you want, you can use it, too," he teased, rubbing the towel briskly over her back and shoulders. "Though I'm not certain you're at your best all wrinkled like this." He held up her hand to show her what he meant. Her water-soaked fingers and palms were puckered and ugly. And white!

The shock of seeing her own skin so pale had the same effect on her as if she'd just had ice water splashed over her naked body.

She jerked her hand out of his and spun away from him, taking the towel with her. "I will dry myself, Clay Donovan," she insisted, wiping the towel over herself vigorously.

"I was just trying to help," Clay laughed, unable to understand what had caused the sudden change in her mood. He bent over and unplugged the tub to let the water drain. He wondered if Gentle Fawn appreciated, or had even noticed for that matter, the Rosewood Hotel's modern way of getting rid of old bath water.

"I do not need your help," she spat angrily, rubbing at her hands to bring them back to their normal color. *I am not white. I am not!*

"Well, when you're through stewing about whatever it is that's got you riled this time, you can put this on," he said to her back. He stepped out from behind the bath screen and tossed a yellow wrapper over the top of it to her.

"I will wear my own dress," she said stubbornly, eyeing the bright-colored cloth covetously, curious as to what such softness would feel like against her skin. "I will not wear *wasicun* clothing! I am not white and do not wish to dress that way!"

"Do whatever you want, but you'd better get something on pretty quick because I think I hear them coming down the hall with my bath water. And red, white, or purple, I doubt you want to have them see you dressed in nothing but your birthday suit and a wet towel!"

Gentle Fawn glanced around hurriedly, looking for her deerskin dress which she was certain she'd left on the stool in the corner of the bathing area. "What have you done with my clothing?"

"It's out here on the bed," Clay said, his insincere effort to sound guiltless failing. "Here, let me—" A knock vibrated the door to the room. "Oops! Too late. My bath's here. I'd better let them in," he said, hurrying to

283

open the door before Gentle Fawn could protest.

Her startled gasp and the sound of the yellow silk wrapper being whisked to the other side of the screen were unnoticed by the two maids and teenage boy who entered the room. But Clay heard, and his face broke into a smug smile. "Come on in," he invited the servants warmly. "I'm really looking forward to this!"

Just as the three approached the screen, their buckets brimming with steamy water, Gentle Fawn stepped out from behind it, her dark eyes shooting shards of black at the smirking blond man. Clutching the silk dressing gown tight at her waist and neck, she slithered past the three water carriers and stood at the window with her back to the others.

"That's great," she heard Clay say as he escorted the threesome to the door. "And can you get this cleaned up for us?"

"Sure thing, mister!" the boy agreed. "I'll have it back to ya in the mornin'."

"Don't worry about rushing," Clay said, laughing at the boy's exuberance when he'd seen the size of the tip Clay held out to him. "Any time in the next couple of days will be fine."

The instant the door closed behind the three, Gentle Fawn wheeled around to face Clay. The desire to fly across the space separating them to scratch his eyes out battled with the tears that threatened to spill down her cheeks. "Why did you shame me like that?" she asked.

"Just exactly how did I shame you?" he asked, making no effort to hide the fact that he wasn't in the mood for another fight. He sat down on the bed and tugged off his moccasins, then began to unbutton his shirt. "Well?"

She was unable to remove her gaze from his hands as

each movement of his fingers widened the vee in his shirt to expose his chest. The familiar tightening in her belly began again. How could she continue to be so intrigued by his body? she wondered angrily. She'd been around bare chests and near-naked men all her life, and she had never had one of them affect her as Clay Donovan did. Why was he different? Why were her feelings about him different?

"You moved my dress so that I had to put on this ugly white woman's garment," she accused, continuing to gaze at him as he removed his shirt to reveal his lean and muscular chest and shoulders.

"Don't you like the gift I bought you?" Clay asked, giving her a lopsided smile that tugged at her anger. "I thought you would like it because it's the color of sunshine."

"Gift?" Gentle Fawn repeated, looking down at the bright yellow that clung to her tiny frame. She felt ashamed of herself.

"Sure. What'd you think it was?" He removed the rest of his clothes and, unabashed by his nakedness, ambled around the screen to step into the newly filled tub. "Ah, now that's what I needed," he groaned, his pleasure obvious as he eased himself down into the stinging hot water.

"I did not know it was a gift," she murmured, allowing herself to become aware of the way the glossy material glided over her flesh and the way it seemed to change color when she moved. "I thought it was one of your tricks to turn me into a *wasicun*." Without realizing what she was doing, she lifted the yellow sash and held it to her lips, then rubbed her cheek against the softness of one robe-encased shoulder.

Clay laid his head against the rim of the bathtub and smiled. He'd known no woman would be able to resist the luxury of the feel of silk. "Why would I do that? You are what you are, aren't you? And no amount of *wasicun* clothing can make you be white if you're not." *And no deerskin dress is going to make you into an Indian, little one. But before you put that hide dress back on you're going to at least know what it feels like to be white. By the time we leave Cheyenne, you may not believe yourself to be white, but you're going to be giving the possibility some pretty serious thought!*

"Then I will accept it if it is a gift," she conceded, secretly realizing it might have taken more strength than she could have mustered to have given up the luxurious garment.

"Good," Clay mumbled, seeming to be falling asleep as she had in the soothing water. "I'm glad."

Leaving Clay to his privacy, Gentle Fawn turned back toward the larger part of the room, letting herself imagine for the first time what it might be like to live in one of the white man's box houses instead of a tepee. It would mean sleeping on one of the soft white men's beds that seemed to swallow you up when you lay down on it. To prove her point to herself, she sat down on the bed. Her face wrinkled distastefully as she sank deep into the mattress. No, she could never get used to that, she decided. Standing back up, she resumed her exploration of the room.

Then she remembered her wonderful bath. She smiled to herself. She could certainly live with owning a bathtub. And with all the space the *wasicun* houses seemed to have, she admitted, thinking how much larger this room was than her mother's whole lodge. And she wouldn't mind having the bureau with drawers to keep her belongings in, she decided, opening and closing all the drawers in the tall chest beside the bed.

As she was examining the smaller washstand that faced the bed, a flash of yellow suddenly caught her attention out of the corner of her eye. Turning her head in that direction, she noticed the door of a ceiling-high wardrobe had been left open slightly. Curious, she opened it the rest of the way, discovering a full-length mirror on the inside.

Stunned, she stared at the small dark-eyed woman who watched her from inside the mirror. Gentle Fawn had seen her own face before—reflected in the water and in small mirrors they'd gotten from the agency—but she couldn't get over the surprise of seeing all of herself at once.

She took a step closer to the mirror and gazed intently into her own black eyes. Then she took several steps back, noting with curiosity that if she was farther from the mirror she could even see her bare feet peeking out from under the hem of the yellow robe. Intrigued by her own reflection, she turned from side to side to see herself at every angle. She even turned around and looked at her back over her shoulder.

Facing the mirror again, she opened the slit in the dressing gown to reveal her slender legs. She noted with a pang of annoyance that her upper legs were much paler than her calves. But, she quickly reminded herself, that part of her body had never been exposed to the sun. Everyone was lighter where the sun hadn't tanned them. *Besides, the dim light in here makes things seem different,* she tried to convince herself.

Suddenly remembering what Clay had said about her

eyelashes not being like other Indians', she moved nearer to the mirror again. Pushing her face close to it, she studied her eyes intently. A frisson of panic shot through her. He was right. Where her family and friends all seemed to have short straight eyelashes, hers were long and curled, forming a thick black fringe around each of her startled eyes. Until this moment, she had never thought of them as unusual. But now . . .

It means nothing! she scolded, starting to close the wardrobe.

Then she noticed her hair for the first time. She had washed it and let it hang over the end of the tub while she soaked the rest of her body. Unrestrained and hanging to her waist, it was almost completely dry now.

And it was curling!

Curling like the hair of the woman in the locket!

No! she shouted inwardly, grabbing half of the offensive mass of waves to the side and twisting them into a tight braid, immediately giving the other side the same treatment when she was finished with the first.

"That is better," she murmured aloud, surveying the results of her efforts in the long mirror. *Now, I look as I should.*

But the longer she studied herself, the harder it became not to recognize certain features of hers as those typical of the whites—and not the Indian. It was more than just the lighter complexion, the longer eyelashes, and the texture of her hair. She could see it in the shape of her slender nose, the softness of her cheekbones, even in the tinge of brown in the irises of her black eyes.

The possibility that the people in the locket could be her parents tugged and tore at her thoughts until she could almost imagine the woman in the mirror and the woman in the locket were one and the same. And the face looking at her seemed to be laughing—laughing at her pride in her Indian heritage, laughing at her hatred for the whites, laughing at the trick the gods had played on her.

"It is not true!" she hissed, slamming the door to the wardrobe shut on the mocking reflection. "I am an Indian!" she said, glaring at the large piece of furniture in front of her, as though saying it out loud would make her believe it again. "I am!"

Moving with short, jerky movements, she untied the belt at her waist and yanked the yellow dressing gown off. She hurled the soft silk at the wardrobe and turned her back on it. She would feel like herself once she had on her own clothing.

"What's going on out there?" Clay's voice came lazily from behind the bathing screen. "Are you talking to me?"

She looked around the room frantically. "Where is my dress?" she shouted, suddenly realizing the deerskin garment was not on the bed as Clay had told her it was. She dropped to her knees to look under the bed and furniture.

"What are you talking about?" Clay asked, his question accompanied by the sound of rushing water as he stood up suddenly in the tub.

"My dress!" Her pitch was rising hysterically. "What have you done with my dress?"

"I gave it to the boy to—"

"You gave away my dress? How could you do this to me? Do you wish to steal everything from me?" Now her voice was reaching a shriek. "You cannot do this, Clay Donovan! I must have my dress back!"

Heedless of her state of undress, Gentle Fawn ran to the door to the hall and jerked it open, intent on retrieving her deerskin dress at any cost.

"Hold on there, little one. Where do you think you're going?" Clay asked, jerking her escape to a halt by wrapping his arm around her waist and slamming the door before she could get outside. "Neither of us is exactly dressed for meeting the public!"

"I want my dress. You had no right to steal it from me!" Her whole body thrashed furiously against his hold on her, as he held her back pressed to him, her flailing arms and legs suspended above the floor.

"Nobody stole your dress, Gentle Fawn," he said, not bothering to hide his annoyance as he tossed her onto the bed and glowered down at her. His hands on his lean hips, his strong legs slightly parted, he said, "I sent it out to be cleaned. You'll have it back in the morning."

"I want it back now!" she grated, determined to ignore the effect the naked man looking down at her was having on her senses.

Yet, deny it as she might, tendrils of the familiar warmth that made her weak and helpless began to spread through her limbs and body as she looked up at Clay.

Still wet from his bath, the fascinating gold body hair she loved to feel against the palms of her hands whorled in dark blond curls over the length and breadth of his muscular body: his chest, his arm, his legs, his . . .

She ripped her gaze from him, not wanting to acknowledge the effect he was having on her, not wanting to admit that any man could have such a power over her. It was degrading in itself that he had the ability to make her forget her anger and hatred for the whites so easily. But the fact that her body actually ached to submit to him over and over again was the ultimate humiliation.

No matter what her body felt, she wouldn't give in to its desires again, she swore fervently. She turned away from Clay Donovan, certain she would be stronger if she couldn't see him.

"It'll be back in the morning," Clay said again, resting one knee on the bed and putting his hand on her shoulder. His tone was more patient now.

"Do not touch me!" Gentle Fawn hissed, rolling out of his grasp before she could be consumed by the fire that immediately roared through her when his hand come in contact with her flesh.

Gentle Fawn felt the bed give as Clay lowered himself onto it. Desperate to escape his nearness, she moved to get off on the opposite side.

A strong hand shot out and wrapped its fingers around her arm.

Half sitting, half lying down, one foot already on the floor, Gentle Fawn froze on the edge of the bed. She was unable to move, as though his touch contained some mysterious paralyzing power.

"Let's get this out in the open right now!" Clay said. "You're not getting out of this bed until you tell me what's bothering you."

"I want my dress back," she said again, irritated by the quake that made her voice sound weak. "You had no right to give it away."

"I promise you'll have it back in the morning." His voice coaxing and husky, he teased his hand up and down her arm from elbow to shoulder. "You have my word."

"Your word means nothing to me, *wasicun!*" she said, making her tone as harsh as she could. She was aware that he had released his grip on her arm, but still she was unable to move. "Whites have broken their word to the People too many times. You are all liars!"

"Have I ever lied to you?" Clay asked, fighting the spasm of guilt he felt. He reminded himself that it had actually been a lie when a few hours earlier he had deliberately led her to believe he was planning on taking her back to the Lakotas when he was through with his business in Cheyenne.

Gentle Fawn thought about it and could not remember Clay ever lying to her before. But that didn't mean he hadn't. It just meant she hadn't caught him. "You are all alike. And I hate you!"

"Hate me, do you?" Clay said, his voice taking on a teasing tone as he pulled her over onto her side to face him. "You're sure going to have a tough time getting me to believe that, little one. You know what I think?" he said, resting her head on his shoulder and gliding his hand over the curve of her hip.

"I do not care what you think," she lied, hating the way her lower body had already begun to rock gently toward him.

He went on as though she hadn't spoken. "I think you're in love with me and just won't admit it."

"In love with you?" she huffed, struggling to at least turn her back on him even though she couldn't get away from him. "You *are* crazy! I do not love anything about you! I hate you!"

"Yep, that's it. You love me and—"

"I hate you."

"I don't think so," he murmured, rolling to his side and planting a series of enticing kisses over the nape of her neck.

Tongues of fire burst through her arms and shoulders before spreading to her lower limbs and womb. It was impossible to control the shudder that shook her petite body.

"I do not want you to do that," she protested breathlessly, hunching up her shoulders protectively and swatting at Clay as she flopped over onto her stomach.

"Yes you do." Ignoring her feeble objections, he continued with his bone-melting assault. He nuzzled his way over her back, along the gently prominent ridges of her spine, kissing her pale skin into a quivering mass of submission.

"Such a sweet little rear," he whispered, giving two quick pecks to the inviting roundness that undulated gently against his lips.

A low moan escaped from deep in Gentle Fawn's throat as he continued his titillating exploration along her legs, giving particular attention to the rose-scented dimples behind her knees and the bottoms of her feet.

"I want you to stop," Gentle Fawn whispered, fighting her surrender with her last ounce of strength by squeezing her legs together tightly.

"Don't you like it when I kiss you here?" he asked, dipping his tongue between her thighs at the knees and moving it upward. Higher. Closer to the heart of her sex. Until she thought she would scream with need.

"No, I do not like it," she insisted, her words a choking gasp as, in spite of her efforts, her legs melted open of their own volition.

"Now who's the liar?" Clay asked against the moist warmth of her.

Gentle Fawn's only answer was a low moan that broke from her mouth, a mouth which had gone totally dry. Her breath coming in rapid pants, she ran her tongue along her parched lips and turned her face into the pillow to muffle another groan that was building deep in her throat, even as her hips lifted upward in an instinctive invitation to his body.

Kneeling between her relaxed thighs, Clay spread his hands around her tiny waist and drew her up and toward him. His manhood slid unerringly into her welcoming body.

Evaporating the last fragment of her mental resistance, his presence deep within her called out to her passion. She was unable to think. Instinct controlled her now. The embrace of her sex on his manhood tightened and she began to rock on her knees in the ancient rhythm of lovers. She strained back to accept Clay's thrusts greedily, then leaned away, only to return to coax him deeper into her snug warmth.

His hands were everywhere, matching their bodies' united movement. He caressed her breasts with one hand, his fingers coaxing her nipples to pebble hardness, squeezing and massaging the small mounds that pushed against his hand in beat with her rising and falling hips. His other hand slid between her legs to further fire the blazing inferno in her body by sensuously tugging at the bud of her femininity, made deliciously available to him by their position.

When their fulfillment came, it was with an intensity that was at once exhilarating and frightening. Gentle Fawn collapsed on her stomach, and Clay fell on top of her, his strength totally spent. "Will I ever get enough of you?" he rasped, seeming to be speaking more to himself than to her, as he kissed the nape of her neck.

They stayed that way for several minutes. The only

sound in the room was their panting breathing as, their chests rising and falling rapidly, they fought to recover from their fervid lovemaking.

Finally, he regained enough strength to shift over onto his back. "Come here, sweet little princess," he said, turning her gently to face him.

Settling Gentle Fawn lovingly along his side, her head on his shoulder, a hand on his damp chest, a slender leg over one of his, her foot held between his calves, he chuckled. "Now what were you saying about hating me?"

Gentle Fawn smiled, unable to stay angry with this man who could find something to smile about no matter how serious the situation. She flicked her tongue over the flat male nipple that nested beside her mouth, pleased with the shudder that shook his chest beneath her cheek.

"No, I do not hate you, Clay Donovan," she admitted to him—and to herself. "You are not like the other *wasicuns*. But can you promise me you will never be like them? Can you give me your word that you will never lie to me?"

That spasm of guilt he'd felt earlier tightened in his gut, multiplying into a rib-crushing squeeze.

If he promised to never lie to her, he would have to tell her he wasn't going to take her back to the Lakotas before he'd had time to find out the truth about her rightful heritage.

On the other hand, if he lied and made the vow she asked for, he would eventually be able to find a way to prove she was white and convince her of it. Unfortunately, no matter how justified his lies were, they were still that. Lies. And he knew she would never forgive him for them.

But damned if I'm going to take her back to a life that

holds nothing for her anymore. She has a right to know who her true parents were. No matter how many lies I have to tell her.

"I will never be like them, Gentle Fawn. I swear it," he said, his serious tone causing her to raise up on her elbow and study his grave expression.

"And never lie to me?" she asked, wanting with all her heart to believe this man who'd come to mean so much to her that she was certain she would go anywhere he asked her to go. Even if it meant leaving her people. If he really wasn't like all the other whites and a liar.

"I won't lie to you, Gentle Fawn. You have my word." His voice sounded as if he were reading lines from a book in school. He couldn't quite bring himself to look into her questioning gaze, praying she didn't notice.

Gentle Fawn let a long sigh and smiled, laying her head back on his arm. She wouldn't think about the odd sadness in his tone when he spoke. If there were no lies between them, nothing else would matter.

Chapter Eighteen

Clay glanced up from the papers scattered over the writing desk the hotel had provided for him. "That's it!" he announced, tossing his pencil down and leaning back in his chair.

"Your articles are finished?" Gentle Fawn said, her face lighting with excitement and—something that tore at Clay—relief. He knew she was relieved because she thought she would be going back to the Lakotas now.

"All six of them. The only thing left to do is put them on the train to New York."

"Then we will leave this place?" she said expectantly, her dark eyes bright with anticipation.

Clay's light eyes clouded. His brow furrowed and he nodded his head. Raking his fingers nervously through his unruly blond hair, he said, "Then we will leave."

How the hell was he going to tell her they were going to head south? Not north to the Black Hills as she believed, but south to Texas. He had put off telling her for almost two weeks now. He'd written three more articles about the Lakotas than he'd planned to write, certain that if he gave her enough time she would begin to accept living like the whites. But his plan had failed at every turn.

She had stubbornly clung to her belief that she was not a white and had no intention of becoming one. For eleven days he had watched her pace the perimeter of their hotel room like a corralled deer seeking a way back to the wild. And his guilt for taking her from the life she knew and loved had mushroomed even more. She hadn't complained once. She just quietly paced while he wrote—and while he tried to think of a way to help her adjust to the life to which she had been born.

Maybe if I could've gotten her to quit wearing that damned deerskin dress, Clay thought with an odd combination of irritation and understanding. He had tried that first day in Cheyenne. He'd bought her several dresses he'd been certain she wouldn't be able to resist at least trying on.

But he had gravely misgauged the degree of her stubbornness. For she was definitely able to resist—the dresses and everything else that would make her look white, like his suggestion that she wear her hair unbraided. Instead, she continued to refuse to wear anything but her own beaded dress and braids. Even the yellow dressing gown she had seemed to accept had been stuffed into a dresser drawer, never to be brought out again.

Only at night when they made love had he been able to forget how unhappy she was in Cheyenne. Only then, when she lay moaning in his arms, was he able to forget how miserable the thought of being white made her.

Looking at her excited upturned face, knowing the time for telling her could no longer be put off, Clay started to speak. "Gentle Fawn, I just want you to know I realize how much you've missed the Lakotas and how sad being with me in Cheyenne has made you—"

"Sad? I am not sad when I am with you, Clay Donovan."

"But the way you've paced—"

"There is nothing else for me to do here. I am accustomed to a very active life. Indian women work from dawn to dusk. There is always more to do in one day than there are hours in that day—hides to tan, clothes to sew, meals to prepare, food to find and store for the winter. Here there is nothing."

"You're just bored?" Her restlessness had nothing to do with keeping a wild thing in captivity. It had been a perfectly normal human reaction to boredom! Not Indian, not white. Just human! Clay knocked himself on the forehead with the heel of his hand. "How could I be so dumb?"

He crossed the room in two quick strides and enfolded her in his arms, lifting her feet off the floor and holding her face even with his. "Can you ever forgive me for being so thoughtless? I've been so wrapped up in my work, I didn't even stop to think how dull being cooped up in here would be for you!"

"It has not *all* been dull," she said. Smiling mischievously, she wended her fingers into his thick gold hair and gave him a playful kiss on the lips.

"No, it hasn't all been dull," he agreed, giving her a hard squeeze. He kissed the tip of her nose and set her back on her own feet. "But we're going to make up for the part that has been dull. Starting right now," he said, already gathering papers off his desk and stuffing them into a sturdy envelope. "Just let me address this to my editor"—he was already writing—"and we'll be off."

"Where are we going?"

"First, we'll go to the train station and see that this gets on the next train heading east. Then— Well, we'll just let it be a surprise!" he said, placing his hat on his blond head and catching her hand in his. "But for the rest of today we're officially on vacation."

Gentle Fawn's excited smile fell. She hadn't been out of their room since the day they'd arrived in Cheyenne. Suddenly she wasn't ready to leave the secure cocoon that had been her shield from the ugly *wasicun* world she knew waited beyond the door. "I will wait here for you," she said, stopping and trying to remove her hand from Clay's grasp.

"Not on your life, lady. You're coming with me!" He tugged on her hand and smiled charmingly.

"But my dress. They will know I am an Indian."

"You want to change into one of the dresses I bought you?" Clay asked, holding his breath as he waited for her answer.

She hesitated for a split second, her eyes shifting indecisively toward the wardrobe that concealed the dresses. If she were dressed like one of them, perhaps their town wouldn't be so frightening.

After a long moment, she shook her head. "No, I do not want to wear one of those dresses."

Clay exhaled slowly, making every effort not to show his disappointment.

"I am only thinking about how angry the hotel man will be when he sees me. You told him I was white."

"To hell with him. What do we care what a small-minded bigot thinks? I've told you before, you are who you are. And what you wear is nobody's business but yours. Now, are you ready, Mrs. Donovan?" he asked, offering his crooked arm to her as though she were dressed in the finest clothing, rather than animal skins.

Taking a deep steadying breath, Gentle Fawn smiled shyly and took his arm. Nothing bad could happen to her, no matter where she was or what clothes she was wearing—not as long as he was with her. "I am ready, Mr. Donovan."

Though still not to her taste for a way to live, the city of Cheyenne proved to be not nearly so frightening to Gentle Fawn as she had expected. Perhaps it was because she was well rested and not exhausted after many days on horseback as she'd been the first time. Or it might have been because she knew she would be leaving it behind her the next day. But whatever the cause, she quickly became accustomed to the hustle of people and animal-drawn vehicles.

The curious stares she and Clay received as they walked arm-in-arm along the sidewalk bothered her only slightly now. And soon she became so fascinated by the bright colors and busy stores around her that she didn't even seem to notice when one bystander turned to another and made a rude comment about her.

But Clay noticed. And a muscle in his jaw knotted perceptibly. He pressed his arm tighter to his side and placed a comforting hand over Gentle Fawn's where it rested in the bend of his arm. He knew he had to ignore them if it was the last thing he ever did. He couldn't risk getting involved in a fight that might leave him unable to protect Gentle Fawn in this city of Indian haters. But it took every bit of self-control he could muster not to call the man to account for his rudeness.

"What is happening?" Gentle Fawn asked excitedly. She pointed toward the street where people had begun to gather along the sidewalks.

A child nearby answered with a high-pitched squeal as he shoved his way past them. "It's the circus! It opens tonight!"

"Circus?" Gentle Fawn asked, looking quizzically to Clay for an explanation. "What is a circus?"

Clay grinned, his anger with the hecklers forgotten for the moment. "Why, a circus is about the greatest thing around. Everybody loves a circus."

"But what is it?" She stretched up on her toes and strained to see over the heads of the people in front of her. It was useless. She was too short.

"A circus is a show. A wonderful, magical show! People gather to watch brightly dressed clowns and acrobats perform. You can hear brass bands and see trapeze artists who fly through the air doing death-defying acts for the audience below. There are people who walk high above the ground on a tiny rope no thicker than one of your braids. And wild animals performing unbelievable tricks. Animals like you've never imagined in your life—elephants, lions, tigers. There are even performers who can stand on horses' backs as the animals gallop around the ring."

"I do not believe you," she said skeptically, looking upward. "I see no people flying and walking on tiny ropes in the sky! You are teasing me again."

"Not *here!*" He laughed. "This is just the parade that comes the day the show opens. Listen!" He cocked his head and turned her to face the direction the crowd was facing. "That's a calliope. It's a machine that makes that music."

"I must see this." She stood on her toes again. But the press and the height of the crowd was too great.

"I've got an idea," Clay said, taking her hand and beginning to run away from the crowd.

"But I want to see the wild animals and the music machine," she protested, her shorter legs taking two steps to every one of Clay's.

"You will. I promise. We'll watch from the window of our room. It faces the street and you'll have a perfect view of the whole parade as it comes by the hotel."

"It was wonderful," Gentle Fawn said an hour later, a sad note in her voice as she gazed down the street from the window in their hotel room. The last of the circus parade had disappeared on its way to prepare for the show that would open that night in a huge tent on the edge of town.

"I'm glad you liked it," Clay said. He stood behind her, his arms around her waist, his chin resting on top of her head. At least now when he told her he was taking her to Texas to meet the people he was certain were her true parents, she would be able to remember something he hadn't lied to her about.

"I did. I liked it very much." She squeezed his arms on her waist. "It was everything you said it would be."

"Of course the parade's just a teaser to get you to come to the circus. It's nothing compared to the real thing," Clay said, realizing what he'd done before the words were completely out of his mouth.

"Then I must see the 'real thing.'"

Damn! I had to open my big mouth. She was happy with the parade. "You didn't really miss that much—and there

303

will be such a crowd. We probably couldn't even get tickets at this late time!"

"But I did not see the people fly through the air and walk on tiny ropes," she said. She turned in his arms and looked up at him, the expression she wore universally feminine. It was the look every woman since time began has given her man when she wanted to wheedle something special from him—and it was the look no man who cared could ever resist. "Please, take me to the circus, Clay Donovan."

He didn't want to take her into the streets after dark. Dressed as she was, it was too dangerous. Some drunk cowboy or miner might hurt her. The risk was just too great—no matter how he wanted to give in to her. "Why do you always call me Clay Donovan?" he asked, changing the subject.

Gentle Fawn's brow wrinkled. "Because it is your name."

"Actually, my whole name is Clay Aloysius Donovan, but people usually just call a man by his first name—not the whole damn thing."

"Then I will call you by your first name—Clay," she said seriously. "Will that make you happy?"

He grinned sheepishly. Actually he hadn't minded having her call him Clay Donovan. In fact, he realized he might even miss it. But white people didn't call other whites by their whole names, so it was really for the best. "Yeah, that makes me happy!"

"Then because I have made you happy, you will take me to the circus so I can see the 'real thing'—Clay!" She made no effort to hide that she had deliberately maneuvered him into a corner. Her smile was wide and flirting as she toyed with the buttons on his shirtfront.

Clay laughed aloud. "You little minx!" He hugged her to him and spun her around, delighting in her giggles. His expression grew serious again. "Honey, I'd love to take you to that circus. But the streets are just too dangerous at night."

"I could wear one of the *wasicun* dresses you brought me," she said suddenly.

Clay's mouth gaped open. "You really want to go enough to put on one of those dresses?"

Gentle Fawn nodded her head. "If the people do not know that I am an Indian, they will not stare at us and say cruel words."

Clay's gut tightened painfully. He had wanted to spare her any hurt and he'd failed. "You heard them?"

"I heard, but things men such as those say do not affect me—because, as you told me, I am who I am. But I do not wish to shame you among your own people as I did this morning."

"Shame me? Honey, you could never shame me. You're a beautiful woman any man would be proud to be seen with!"

"But the men's words upset you. I saw it in your face and felt it in the tightening of your arm under my hand."

"I was ashamed all right. But not of you. Never of you. It was them. I was ashamed to be of the same white blood as they were."

"You were not embarrassed to be seen with me in my Indian clothing?" She looked at him skeptically. She'd been so certain.

"Nope! And to prove it, we'll go to the circus tonight and you can wear whatever you want. I'll go order us up some supper and see if we can get a couple of tickets. You want me to ask them to bring up some hot water for a bath?"

Gentle Fawn grinned apologetically and nodded her head. She'd just had a bath that morning but, as always, found that the idea of another appealed to her. Next to making love to Clay Donovan—Clay, she corrected herself—it was the single most wonderful experience she had ever had. "I like the *wasicun* custom of hot bathing," she explained needlessly.

"As much as kissing?" Clay asked, his tone teasing.

Gentle Fawn tilted her head to the side and appeared to give thought to comparing the two experiences. She held up an index finger and opened her mouth as though to answer, then shook her head and clamped her lips together.

"I must refresh my memory about kissing before I give you my answer."

"You're getting too cute for your moccasins!" Clay chuckled, grabbing her to him and kissing her long and hard.

"Well? What's the verdict?" he finally asked.

"Definitely, kissing is my favorite," she sighed, giving his lips a quick buss.

"That's more like it, you smart little package. Now, I'm going to go get those tickets and our dinner."

"And my bath," she reminded him, handing him his hat and walking with him to the door.

"And your bath," he chuckled and left the room. She could still hear him laughing as he walked down the hall to the stairs.

Gentle Fawn turned back to the room that had been her home for eleven days, and a wave of regret rocked her. She would leave here tomorrow to go back to the Lakotas. After he escorted her back to her people, Clay would return to this strange white world, and they would never see each other again.

What would life be like for her with no Clay Donovan to talk with, to tease with, to laugh with—to love with? She'd spoken the truth when she'd said she preferred kisses even to hot baths. She knew without a doubt she could go on living without the lazy baths she'd become accustomed to. But the kisses—Clay's kisses—were something she wasn't quite so certain about.

Is this what love is? Am I in love with him as he said I was? Is this feeling of only being whole when he's with me love? Is that why I hurt for him more than for myself when those men called us ugly names?

Gentle Fawn shook her head as though waking from a dream. Yes, of course that was it.

She was in love with Clay Donovan!

But what good did it do to know it? They would leave Cheyenne tomorrow and would go their separate ways in a few days.

All they really had left was tonight.

"But we do have tonight!" she said to herself as the knock announcing the arrival of her bath water came. *And tonight I will give him no reason to be ashamed of me!*

An hour later Clay returned to the room victorious. Waving two yellow tickets in the air triumphantly, he burst through the door. "I had to turn the town upside down, but I did it!" he hollered. "I got your tickets to the circus."

It was then his gaze lit on a slight-figured woman standing at the window, her back to him. The sudden realization of his error hit him between the eyes. He began to back toward the door, his face red with embarrassment. "Excuse me, ma'am. I didn't mean to barge in on you like that. I must be in the wrong room. Mine must be the one next door."

"You are not in the wrong room, Clay Don— Clay," the petite woman said, turning slowly to face the stunned man at the door.

"Gentle Fawn?" he rasped, unable to move.

Her smile was apprehensive. "You do not recognize the flowered dress you bought for me?"

He nodded his head mutely, not even seeing the pink dress.

"Do I look all right?" she asked shyly, her small fists nervously pleating and unpleating handfuls of her skirt.

He nodded his head again and, his voice an awed whisper, said, "You're beautiful."

And she was. Her black hair, tied with a pink ribbon, hung in loose waves down her back. And the simple pink calico dress he'd purchased for her, thinking a plain design would make her transition from Indian to white easiest, was elegant on her petite figure. Nipped in at her tiny waist, the high-necked bodice was topped with a white lace collar, and the skirt hung in full gathers, rounding her slim hips becomingly.

As embarrassed as she was pleased with Clay's complimentary assessment, Gentle Fawn suddenly lifted the hem of her skirt. "Look! I am wearing the drawers you bought!" she announced proudly, as she, too, looked down to view the lace-edged white pants that hit her about eight inches above the leather boots she wore.

"Drawers?" Clay blurted. "How do you know they're called drawers?"

"Firebird wore them. She told me they are very good to have on hand when someone is injured and bleeding," she said seriously. "She said they make very good bandages."

"Bandages?" Clamping his lips together, Clay tried gallantly to swallow the chuckle building in his throat. But it was no use, and it escaped in an ungentlemanly snort. "I guess that's as good a reason to wear them as any I've ever heard!" he said, his snicker building beyond his control to a full laugh.

"You think I am funny in these *wasicun* clothes?" she huffed, dropping the skirt indignantly. Crushed by his laughter, she ignored the sting of tears glazing her dark eyes and started to unbutton her bodice. She had tried so hard to make herself look like the white women she'd seen in the street that day. Just figuring out how the clothing all went together had been an almost impossible task. But she had wanted to please him and make him proud of her so she hadn't given up. But obviously she'd done something wrong and he thought she looked as foolish as she felt.

"I didn't mean to laugh, and I wasn't laughing at you. You're gorgeous in those clothes," Clay said, placing his warm hands over hers on the front of her bodice and stilling her busy fingers. "In fact, you're so gorgeous, I'll be the envy of every man at the circus tonight."

He pushed her hands away and concentrated on redoing the buttons she'd managed to unfasten. "It's just that I never thought of drawers being good for anything but keeping the cold wind off a lady's bottom before. That's all. I promise. Do you forgive me?" He lifted her chin and looked into her eyes, his own filled with remorse.

"I do not look funny?"

"Not a bit."

"Men will not stare at me and make you angry as they

309

did when I wore my own clothing today?"

"Well, I wouldn't say that. If anything, they'll stare more than ever. But it will be because they've never seen anything as pretty as you in their whole lives, and they'll all be jealous as hell because you're with me and not them."

"I will have a lot to tell the People when I return to them," Gentle Fawn said hours later when they got back to their room. "It was the most amazing thing I have ever seen," she chortled, extending her arms out from her sides and whirling across the room to flop onto her back on the bed. "How do you suppose they do it?" she suddenly asked, levering herself up on her elbows and studying him where he stood beside the door.

"Do what?" Clay asked, her exuberance only making him feel more guilty than he had earlier. How could he tell her now? He would ruin the entire day—a day that had been as close to perfect as any he'd ever lived. Still, he had to do it! There was no choice and there was no more time. Their stagecoach would leave for Texas at seven the next morning. If he was going to take her to find her parents, he had to tell her now.

"How do they keep from falling off that tiny rope?"

"I don't know. I guess walking a tightrope is like anything else. You just do what you've got to do." His voice sounded old and tired.

"Thank you, Clay, for everything. I loved the circus. And I lov—" She caught herself just in time. She had almost told him she loved him. "I loved the whole day," she quickly amended.

"I loved it, too," Clay said solemnly. Was he doing the

310

wrong thing? Did he really have the right to disrupt her whole life like this? Maybe he should just take her back to the Lakotas and let it go at that. There were a million more stories he could write. This wasn't the only one. Was one story worth spoiling this perfect day and having her remember him as a liar? Still, story or no story, did he have the right to keep what he'd learned about the Delgados from her? *Talk about being on a tightrope!*

"Did I say something wrong?" Gentle Fawn said, noticing for the first time how serious Clay's expression had become. In fact, now that she thought about it, he'd been unusually quiet since the circus had ended. Of course, she'd been so excited, chattering all the way back to the hotel, that he really hadn't had the opportunity to say much. "What is it, Clay Dono— Clay?"

Stretching out on the bed beside her, Clay laid his head back on the pillow and positioned her along his length. "We have to talk, honey. I can't put it off any longer."

Tentacles of anxiety curled along her spine.

"I never wanted to hurt you, Gentle Fawn."

But you are going to, aren't you, Clay Donovan?

"When this whole thing started, I just wanted to get you as far away from Many Coups as possible so I could protect you from him. I felt I owed you something—for saving my life and for getting me the story with Crazy Horse and for . . . Well, whatever, I owed you, so I brought you to Cheyenne, thinking to take you back to the Lakotas later. But when I found the pictures in your locket and was certain you were white, everything changed. I knew you might be the biggest story of my life. Even bigger than Crazy Horse."

"But you said it did not matter who I was, Clay Donovan." She didn't even bother to correct what she

311

called him. A germ of realization began to grow in her thoughts.

Clay looked into her upturned face and tried to explain. "It doesn't to Clay Donovan, the man. But to Clay Donovan the reporter, you're a story—a story I couldn't resist."

"I do not understand what you are trying to tell me."

Clay took a deep breath and exhaled slowly. "I lied to you, Gentle Fawn. Once I saw those pictures in the locket, I never had any intention of taking you back to the Lakotas." His words came in a wooden rush that sounded rehearsed.

"You lied to me?"

"I thought that once I got you to Cheyenne you'd realize that being white wasn't so bad. Then we could go together to find the Delgados."

"You lied to me." She sat up and studied his pain-racked face for a long time. But she had no sympathy for his suffering. He'd done the one thing that could change the way she felt about him. He'd used her. He had kept her a virtual prisoner in this room until he could write his story about her—as though she was one of the performing tigers in the circus. Caged until it was time for the show.

"Why are you telling me now? Have you decided I am not white and you have no more use for me? Or have you already written the story?" Her voice was hard and bitter and tore at Clay's heart.

"Please, honey, let me explain," he pleaded, holding her arm. "You've got to listen."

"I will listen because I am your prisoner. I really have no choice, do I?"

"You're not my prisoner, Gentle Fawn. You've never

been my prisoner?"

"No? Where would I go if I left this room? I would be just like one of the circus animals who dared to escape the safety of his cage if I decided to leave. Both of us *wild animals* would be defenseless on the streets of this *wasicun* village without the protection of our keepers!"

"The reason I'm telling you now is that I've realized I was wrong. Wrong to lie to you. And wrong to try and make your decisions for you. If you don't want to find out who the people in the locket are, I have no right to force it on you. I just want you to know that I'll take you back to the Lakotas tomorrow, if that's what you want."

"That is what I want. It is what I have always wanted."

"Then we will go. But not before I tell you what I've discovered about the Delgados. Facts I think you won't be able to close your eyes to quite so easily as you have to everything else."

Chapter Nineteen

"I do not want to hear any of your *facts*," Gentle Fawn sneered, swinging her feet off the bed and standing up. She had no intention of allowing him to plant any more doubts in her thoughts with his lies.

"Well, you're going to hear them anyway," Clay said, the anger in his tone matching hers as he followed her off the bed to stand behind her. "Then we'll decide what we'll do about them."

"I have already decided what *I* will do. I am leaving this place and going back to where I belong."

"That's the whole point, Gentle Fawn. I'm trying to tell you I think I've found out where you really belong— and it isn't in the Black Hills with the Lakotas and Cheyennes!"

"I belong with the Lakotas and nothing you can say will make me believe anything else!"

"Are you afraid to hear what I've discovered, Gentle Fawn?" Clay challenged. "That's it, isn't it? You're afraid I'll tell you something that will force you to admit the truth to yourself." He turned and walked over to sit down at his writing desk and rummaged through some of the papers.

She followed him, the expression on her face angry. Her hands flat on the desk, her elbows rigid with anger, she leaned forward and glared down at the smug man across from her. "I am not afraid of your lies, Clay Donovan!"

"Then read these!" he ordered her, flicking two yellow squares of paper in her direction.

Gentle Fawn straightened her back and hesitantly took the papers from him, her expression confused. "What are these?"

"They're telegrams. Read them!"

"You are so determined to tell me your *facts*. You read them," she shouted, thrusting the telegrams back to Clay. She would never admit to him that she couldn't read.

"Fine with me!" Clay returned, snatching the wires from her. "I remembered the Sioux used to hunt and roam down into Texas about twenty years ago. And since Texas has a large Spanish population, I decided to start looking for the Delgados there.

"The first wire is from Johnny McGuire, a Texas Ranger friend of mine in Fort Worth. It says, 'CLAY, OLD PAL. CHECKED OUT MANUEL AND FRANCISCA DELGADO AS YOU ASKED. DON'T KNOW IF SHE IS STILL ALIVE, BUT HE IS A SUCCESSFUL RANCHER IN SAN ANTONIO. VERY RICH. JUST FINISHING SECOND TERM AS A TEXAS STATE SENATOR. YOUR REQUEST FOR INFORMATION FORWARDED TO MATT GRAMM IN SAN ANTONIO. GOOD MAN. SHOULD BE ABLE TO FILL YOU IN BETTER ON THE DETAILS. YOU SHOULD BE

HEARING FROM HIM SOON. LET ME KNOW WHAT HE FINDS OUT. JOHNNY.'"

Clay looked at Gentle Fawn, his eyebrows raised expectantly. "Well?"

"Well, what?" she threw back. "That paper proves nothing."

"Not by itself, but Matt's wire puts the clincher on things. Listen. 'MR. DONOVAN. INFORMATION YOU REQUESTED IS AS FOLLOWS. MANUEL AND FRANCISCA DELGADO MARRIED ON DECEMBER 12, 1857, IN SAN ANTONIO. DAUGHTER CAMILA BORN ON OCTOBER 22, 1858. STOLEN BY INDIANS IN NOVEMBER, 1861. NEVER FOUND. MOTHER SAID TO BE SO DEVASTATED BY TRAGEDY THAT SHE NEVER WENT OUT IN PUBLIC AGAIN. MAY OR MAY NOT STILL BE ALIVE. NO OTHER CHILDREN BORN TO DELGADOS. IF I CAN HELP MORE, LET ME KNOW. MATT GRAMM.'"

Self-doubt swelled cloyingly in her chest, threatening to consume her. "It proves nothing," she protested feebly. "It is more of your lies."

"Think about it, Gentle Fawn. I've only tried to lie to you once and I couldn't go through with it. Why would I lie to you about this?"

"Those people are *not* my parents! My parents were Cheyennes!"

"Are you so sure you're not their missing daughter that you're willing to risk not knowing for certain?"

"I am certain."

"But there will always be that doubt, won't there? You'll always wonder if you did the right thing. And you'll always remember those poor parents who don't know if their daughter, their only child, is alive or dead.

317

You'll think about them waiting there year after year for some word of her, and finally, the not knowing will destroy you."

"I will not think about it."

"You will, and you're lying to yourself if you think otherwise. A person who lies to herself is the worst kind of liar. Unless you come with me to San Antonio on that stagecoach tomorrow morning and find out for sure, you're going to be haunted by the Delgados for the rest of your life. Besides, you can always go back to the Lakotas—after you're completely convinced that's where you belong."

Gentle Fawn's chest rose and fell rapidly, and dots of perspiration began to pop out on her upper lip. Suddenly the snug bodice of the pink dress she wore seemed as though it was squeezing the breath out of her. She longed for the feel of her own deerskin dress against her flesh. "Why are you doing this to me?" she murmured weakly, her trembling fingers fumbling with the buttons on her bodice. "I do not want to be white. I want to go back to the People and nothing you can say will change my mind."

Clay threw his hands up in defeat. "You win. I'm not going to discuss it with you anymore. We'll leave for the north early tomorrow morning." He picked up his hat and plopped it on his head and strode angrily across the room. "Lock the door behind me and don't open it for anyone but me. I'll be back in the morning."

"Where are you going?"

"Out!" he said, jerking the door open and exiting before he could even hear Gentle Fawn's gasp of protest.

"How could I have loved you?" she said to the closed door. "You have used me and lied to me. Even this wonderful day was just a trick to make me go with you to Texas so you could get another story. I never meant anything to you at all. The only thing that mattered to you was your *big story*. You do not care what you have to do or who you have to hurt to get it, do you?"

Turning her back to the door and facing the room, Gentle Fawn began to pace restlessly. The thing that hurt most was that she would have happily gone anywhere with him if he'd cared for her as she did him. But he had admitted he'd only kept her with him to get a story. She should hate him, but . . . *Even now I love him,* she realized with disgust.

Suddenly knowing what she had to do, Gentle Fawn quickly stripped off the pink dress and reached for her own familiar clothing. She wouldn't be here when Clay came for her in the morning. That was the answer. She would be well on her way to the Black Hills by then—alone.

"I do not need your protection to find my way safely back to the People. In fact, I will be more inconspicuous and will travel faster without you to slow me down." Keeping up a continuous conversation with the absent man, she slipped her feet into her moccasins and rebraided her hair. "If I do not give you the opportunity, you cannot hurt me again."

Telling herself that her last longing glance around the room was to make certain she hadn't forgotten anything, Gentle Fawn memorized every corner and piece of furniture.

If only I could see him one more time, just to say good-bye, she thought, experiencing a moment of doubt about what she was planning as she surveyed the bed she had shared with Clay. *If only . . .*

319

"If only he had not lied to me!" she spat, grabbing for the doorknob. "He is a liar and a user—like all whites!"

But he risked his life twice to save me from Many Coups. Would a liar and a user do that? her unbidden inner voice suggested obstinately.

"Of course he would—if he wanted something as badly as he wants his stories!" She turned the knob, determined to block out her doubts.

But what if he is right and I am the missing daughter of the people in the locket? Can I spend the rest of my days with the Lakotas without knowing the truth? She pulled the locket out from under her dress and opened it.

"What is wrong with me? I know the truth already," she fumed. She snapped the locket shut and yanked the door open. "They are not my parents!"

She paused in the doorway, one hand still on the knob, the other gripping the locket tightly, the gold seeming to burn in her palm. *Still, what harm would come from going with him and proving I cannot be the baby in the picture?*

"It would just give him a chance to tell me more lies. And it will only prove what I already know!"

But his lies cannot hurt me if I do not let myself believe what he says to me. And it would put my mind to rest once and for all.

"It would be worth it to see his face when the Delgados laugh at him and explode his 'big story' in his face! Still . . ."

One foot in the hallway, the other still in the room, Gentle Fawn had no idea how long she stood there arguing with herself. Every time she would convince herself to go, she would think of an excuse to stay.

Suddenly the choice was snatched from her hands by the pound of heavy boots coming up the stairs in her direction. Looking down at her deerskin dress, the memory of the hate-filled faces and voices of the men in the street that day flashed through her mind. If she went out of the hotel dressed like this, without even so much as a knife to protect herself, she would have no chance to save herself from men like that—men who hated her for being an Indian.

Her vacillating at an end, Gentle Fawn backed into the dark of her room. She quietly closed the door and slid the bolt lock shut.

Her back to the door, she placed her ear against the cool wood and listened. The footsteps grew louder and louder until she was certain they were right outside her door.

Was it Clay coming back to apologize? A surge of excitement revved up the pounding of her heart. She pressed her cheek to the door harder and stopped breathing. Were the footsteps hesitating outside her door or was she imagining it?

The footsteps continued on down the hall. No one had stopped at her room—unless it had just been for the moment it might take to check a room number. It wasn't Clay. Her shoulders, which had been hunched up in anticipation, slumped.

But she didn't resume her breathing until she heard the scrape of a key being used in the door next to hers. Without bothering to turn up the lamps, she crossed the room and lay down on the bed and stared up at the dark ceiling.

Everything suddenly became clear to her as she lay in that dark room alone with her thoughts and fears. She could not deceive herself any longer. There was a good chance she was white—or at least partly white. And as much as she detested the idea, she had to know the truth before she could resume her life. She had no choice. She must go to Texas with Clay Donovan and learn the truth—no matter how frightening that truth might be.

Her decision finally made, Gentle Fawn drifted into a restful sleep filled with pleasant dreams, only to be awakened several hours later by a loud pounding on her door.

She sat up straight and took a sleepy glance around the room, fully expected to see Clay. The dim half light of dawn filled the room and it took her a moment to remember that he hadn't come back to the room after their fight the night before.

The knocking grew more insistent. "Who is there?" she finally asked.

"It's me," Clay's familiar voice answered gruffly. "Unlock the door."

Her relief causing her to temporarily forget the reason Clay had not spent the night in their room, Gentle Fawn jumped off the bed and ran to the door, the smile on her face wide. She hurriedly slid the bolt out of the lock and flung the door open, the expectant smile on her face erased only a second before Clay would have seen it.

"You are back," she said stiffly, her black eyes devouring the sight of him hungrily. It was all she could do to keep from throwing her arms around him and telling him how glad she was to see him. How could she have ever thought she could go back to the Lakotas and never see him again? Just this one night apart had been the loneliest she'd ever spent in her life. It was then she noticed how bad he looked.

Judging by the blond stubble of beard that covered his face and the dark shadows surrounding his bloodshot eyes, it was evident he had slept very little since she last saw him. And it was obvious to her that he'd been just as unhappy as she had been during the long night apart.

A strange combination of sympathy and triumph rippled through her at the sight of his apparent suffering.

Still wearing the clothing he'd had on the night before, he made no effort to hide the fact that he felt terrible. "I see you're ready to resume your life with the Lakotas," he said sarcastically, raking his gaze over her clothing and braids with chilling scrutiny—as one might examine an unappealing stranger.

Hurt by his angry tone, Gentle Fawn looked down at herself, remembering for the first time changing back into the deerskin dress and having fallen asleep in it.

Before she could explain, he shoved himself away from the doorjamb he'd been leaning on and elbowed his way past her into the room. Tossing his hat on the bed, he tunneled his fingers through his disheveled blond hair, then wheeled back to face her.

"You look as if you did not sleep last night," she said, shutting the door behind her, though she didn't move away from it.

"Obviously a problem you didn't have," Clay returned sarcastically, his disposition not the least improved by her well-rested appearance and calm demeanor.

"No, I did not have trouble sleeping. Once I made my decision, sleep came easily." Why didn't he go on and admit how much he'd missed her? Then she could tell him her decision and they could "kiss and make up."

"I'm glad to hear that because I intend for us to cover a lot of miles today, and I don't want to be slowed down by a tired female." He yanked open the wardrobe and began tossing his personal things into his saddlebags.

Gentle Fawn sucked in a gasp of indignation and took a step toward him, her fists balled on her hips. "Just exactly when have I slowed you down, Clay Donovan?"

"I didn't say you had. I just said I didn't want you to."

"It seems to me that if anyone slows us down, it will be you and your bad disposition. Where did you stay last night that left you in this mood?"

Clay opened his mouth to tell her he'd been in the room next door, but immediately swallowed his words. Damned if he'd let her know how impossible it had been for him to sleep without her beside him. "Are you ready? I want to get started as soon as possible."

"I want to change my dress. Then I will be ready."

"Change your dress? To what?" He stopped his packing and gaped at her.

Now she would tell him her decision and he would tell her what he felt. "I will wear the green one you brought to me. It looks like the ones I have seen the women wear when I have watched out the window and seen them getting in the stagecoaches. If I get too warm, I will take off the jacket."

"What the hell are you talking about? Those dresses have been sitting in the wardrobe for two damned weeks and you wouldn't even look at them! Now you're planning to wear one while you're riding horseback. Why now?" he grumbled, turning his back to her again and attacking his packing with a vengeance.

"I thought we were going to Texas in a stagecoach," Gentle Fawn said, taking the green traveling suit out and holding it up to herself. Now he would turn back to her and gather her in his arms and kiss her. She waited excitedly for her words to sink in.

"You're without a doubt the orneriest, contrariest, most impossible-to-read female I've ever seen," he went on as though she hadn't spoken. "Believe me, the next ten days can't be over too soon for me. I can't wait to get back to living with normal peo—" He spun around to face her, the look on his face stunned. "What did

324

you say?"

"About what?" she asked stonily. She knew what he'd been going to say and his words cut into her heart cruelly. He'd finally said what he really felt, as she'd wanted him to—but she hadn't expected it to be that he was anxious to get rid of her.

She was tempted to forget her plan to go to Texas to find out the truth about the Delgados. But unfortunately, she couldn't put the thought of those two happy faces in her locket out of her mind. If there was the slightest chance she was their missing daughter, she had to let them know she was alive—even if it meant spending more time with a man who didn't love her.

"You know about what!" he shouted, grabbing her by the upper arms and making her look at him. "About going to Texas on a stagecoach!"

"I have decided to go to Texas. So now you can stop acting like a spoiled child who does not get everything he wants. You will be able to write your story—if there is a story." She added the last with a spiteful upturn of her mouth.

"You'd do that for me? You'd go to Texas and see the Delgados so I could have my story?"

Gentle Fawn laughed coldy. "You flatter yourself, Clay Donovan. I am going for *me*, not you. Though I still believe my parents were Cheyennes, I must meet these people in Texas on the slightest chance that your crazy idea is true. I have to know for certain. And I am doing it for them. If I am their missing daughter, I cannot bear the thought of having them not know that I am alive."

At a loss for words, Clay stared into Gentle Fawn's determined face. Would he ever be able to figure her out? Somehow, he didn't think so. Shaking his head, his expression hopeless, Clay dropped his hold on her arms and turned toward the wardrobe.

He pulled out a carpetbag he'd purchased the first day in Cheyenne and tossed it on the bed. "You can put your things in here," he finally said, not certain why her words made him angry. What difference did it make why she was going? Hadn't he been the one to plant the doubts in her mind and give her those reasons? She was going. That was all that mattered. She was going and he would get his story. Besides, if she had changed her mind just to please him, he might have felt obligated to her later. This way was much better. They would both get what they wanted. She'd have the truth and he'd have another great story. No obligations. No ties. He wouldn't think about that nagging thought he kept having that he was already bound to her as surely as if they were chained to each other.

Lost in her own thoughts and unable to trust herself to say anything else, Gentle Fawn carried the green dress behind the bath screen to change clothes. Though her heart recognized her desire to stay with Clay as the other reason she was going to Texas, she swore she would bite off her tongue before she would reveal that to a man who only wanted her for the help she could be in getting another of his precious "stories."

An hour later, carpetbag and saddlebags in hand, Clay and Gentle Fawn waited in front of the Rosewood Hotel as the gleaming red and black Concord coach pulled to a halt in front of them. "Well, this is it," Clay said, his tone admiring as he surveyed the Wells Fargo stage.

"Yes, this is it," Gentle Fawn agreed softly as she looked longingly over her shoulder to the north where she knew the Lakotas waited for her.

Chapter Twenty

San Antonio, August 1876

When the stagecoach pulled into San Antonio eight days later, it was a disheveled and slightly disoriented Gentle Fawn who took Clay's offered hand. She stumbled, rather than stepped, out of the dusty coach into the sweltering Texas heat that could actually be seen rising from the sun-baked clay street in blurry waves.

Clay had told her they were going by stagecoach because it would take at least a month by horseback and no more than a week by coach, but she hadn't begun to fathom what tortures they would be forced to endure in the interest of saving time. If she'd had any idea, she would have run screaming in the opposite direction the minute she had first seen the stage in Cheyenne.

She had quickly learned the reason a stagecoach was so much faster than horseback was that the only thing that mattered was speed. Nothing else. Not comfort, not rest, not health, not food. Only speed. They ran all day and all night, only stopping for about ten minutes at a swing station every hour and a half to change horses. And woe be to the passenger who went to relieve himself and wasn't back in his seat when the fresh horses were hitched to the coach.

Every twelve hours the stops were extended to forty minutes so the passengers could purchase meals, but the food had been of such poor quality that more than once Gentle Fawn had gone without eating. They also changed drivers at these longer home station stops. Then the new driver, well rested after a twelve-hour breather, had driven the next leg of the trip at breakneck speed with no concern for the nine passengers crammed inside the coach. It was as though he had to make up for the "leisurely" forty minutes they'd taken to eat and take care of their personal needs.

Of course, there was no time for bathing, but the worst discomfort they'd been forced to put up with had been the inability to lie down and sleep. Sleeping any way but sitting up was impossible in the close quarters of the stagecoach. Gentle Fawn was fortunate because she'd been able to lean her head against Clay's shoulder to sleep, though she'd done little more than doze the whole time. Clay had been able to rest his head against the side and back of the coach. Others in the carriage hadn't been nearly so lucky. The most unfortunate passengers were the three on the middle bench. Without a back support of any kind, they had only a leather handstrap, which hung from the ceiling, to keep them from being thrown out of their seats each time they dozed off.

The dust and heat had been unbearable. With the leather window shades pulled down, the inside of the coach became a suffocating oven filled with limp, sweating bodies. But if some brave soul raised a shade, thinking to escape the heat and the rank odor that permeated the interior, everyone immediately began to choke on the cloud of dust that billowed through the open window to stick to their perspiration-soaked skin. There had been no escape from the torture.

To allow the horses to move at a speed that would have jolted a normal rig apart, the coaches were suspended between the front and rear axles on two three-inch-thick leather straps that served as shock absorbers and accounted for the rocking rather than bumping motion. Gentle Fawn had heard some of the more experienced passengers compare the motion of a stagecoach to a storm-tossed ship at sea. And though she didn't know anything about the ocean, she swore she didn't want to learn anything about it if traveling on it was like the stagecoach in any way.

"I'll never get into another stagecoach! No matter how long it takes, I'm traveling by horseback next time," Gentle Fawn said, clinging to Clay's arm for support until she became accustomed to being on firm, unmoving land again. Perhaps now that they were finally at their destination, she would stop feeling as though she were trying to retain her balance in the moving carriage when she tried to stand.

Clay smiled down at her. Despite the fact that their already strained relationship had been pushed to the limits of endurance by the trip from Cheyenne, he couldn't help admiring her spirit. During the entire impossible trip, she hadn't complained, even when he'd been certain she would be sick to her stomach until she became used to the pitching sway of the stagecoach.

"Mr. Donovan?" a tall brown-haired man asked as he approached the two who continued to stand beside the stage waiting for their small amount of luggage to be unloaded.

"I'm Donovan," Clay said, giving the man a weary grin and extending his right hand. "I sure hope you're Matt Gramm and you're going to tell me you've already made hotel arrangements for us."

"That I am, and that I have!" Matt clasped Clay's hand and returned the handshake eagerly, his brown eyes gleaming with friendliness. "It's a real pleasure to meet you, Mr. Donovan. I really like readin' your articles in the paper."

About thirty years old, Matt Gramm was at least six inches taller than Clay and fifty pounds heavier. He carried his large, muscular frame with a grace one would not expect to find in a man his size. Though his rugged, mustached face could not be called handsome, it contained a warmth and honesty that immediately put Clay at ease. And he knew Johnny McGuire had been right when he'd said that Matt Gramm was a good man. Clay had an intuitive flair for judging people and sensed immediately that Matt Gramm was a man who could be trusted.

"Call me, Clay, Matt. And it's a pleasure to meet you, too." He tilted his head back in an exaggerated look of awe for Matt's size. "I don't think I ever had a mountain tell me he liked my work before!"

"And I never thought a famous newspaper writer would be so short," Matt teased back, the mischievous twinkle in his eyes making no secret of the fact that he could, and would, give as good as he got.

"Short?" Clay blusterd good-naturedly. "In my boots I'm an inch over six feet! That's not exactly a midget! And where I come from it's sure not short!"

"But you're in Texas now, Clay ol' buddy. And down here, we've got jackrabbits taller than you!"

Before Clay could respond with another quip, the stage driver hollered to him from atop the rig, where the excess luggage was stored that would not fit in the rear or front boots of the coach. "Here you go, Donovan," he said, giving Clay's large saddle a toss over the side before Clay could remove himself from Gentle Fawn's grasp and turn around to catch it.

"Hey, watch what you're doin'," Matt shouted, pulling Gentle Fawn and Clay out of the way of the falling saddle and snatching it out of the air before it could hit them or the ground. "Are you all right?" he asked them both, but his eyes were on the tiny young woman who still clung to Clay Donovan's arm.

Gentle Fawn took an instinctive step back. Never had she seen such a big man. And the fact that he was white frightened her doubly. Except for Clay Donovan, no white man had ever spoken to her and she found herself suddenly at a loss for words. But try as she would, she couldn't make herself hate any man with such a kind and gentle face. Even though it was a white face. She nodded her head and graced him with a slight smile.

"Where the hell are my manners? I didn't even introduce you two. Matt Gram, this is Gen—" *Oh, shit! What am I going to say her name is? If I call her Gentle Fawn, everyone within earshot will think she's an Indian and start to ask questions. And I can't call her Camila Delgado because she'll fly into a rage. Besides, I'm not ready to expose her identity to the public yet. I don't intend to take a chance that someone else will get the story in print before I can.* He would have to tell Matt the whole story later when they were where their conversation would not

331

be overheard.

Freeing his arm from her grasp, he wrapped it around her shoulders and gave her an affectionate squeeze. "This is—uh—Ginnie—uh—Fawns!" he improvised, pleased with his quick thinking.

Gentle Fawn's mouth dropped open on a startled gasp and her head jerked around to stare at Clay. She shook her head, her eyes narrowing angrily. "I am—"

"Going to catch flies in your mouth if you don't close it," Clay interrupted, placing a curved index finger under her chin and closing her slack jaw. "Now, Matt, my fast-moving, fast-talking friend, what were you saying about hotel arrangements?"

Hefting Clay's saddle onto one broad shoulder with almost no effort, Matt picked up the carpetbag and started to walk across Alamo Plaza, his long-legged gait an easy amble. "They're expecting you at the Menger Hotel, over on Crockett Street. It's the finest hotel west of the Mississippi," Matt boasted proudly. "And you'll be right next door to the Alamo."

Unoffended by Matt Gramm's pride in the special things that belonged to Texas, Clay matched his stride to the larger man's. Both of them deliberately shortened their pace to accommodate Gentle Fawn's shorter legs. "Believe me, after the week we've spent on that stagecoach, we'd be happy with a dunk in the San Antonio River and a blanket under a cottonwood tree. But the Menger sounds great. How far are we from the Delgado place? Just as soon as we get bathed and rested and eat a decent meal I want to head on over there."

"The Delgado ranch is about half a day's ride from here by carriage. On horseback you could make it in—"

"We will go on horseback," Gentle Fawn interrupted,

her soft, determined voice a surprise to both men. "I will ride in no more *wasicun* coaches."

Matt looked down at Gentle Fawn, his eyebrows drawn together quizzically. "Did you say *wasicun*? Isn't that a Sioux word for white man?" he asked, his tone rife with suspicion.

Clay rolled his eyes, his mouth twisting wryly to one side. He hadn't wanted to get into this right now. Couldn't she have just kept her mouth shut until they'd gotten some rest? "Yeah, that's their word for us. It means 'fat takers.'" Clay's expression was one of frustration.

"Fat takers?"

"We call you that because the whites kill and destroy the buffalo but only take the good parts, leaving the rest to rot and go to waste. Because of the 'fat takers' there are no longer enough buffalo to feed and clothe the Indians," she said, her anger fed by the fact that she was hot and totally exhausted. And her legs still felt as if they would give way under her with the next step she took.

Matt stopped in his tracks and turned to study Gentle Fawn's flushed face. Then he looked at Clay. "Did she say 'we'? What the hell's goin' on here? Who is she?"

"I was going to explain all this to you once we got someplace where we could talk privately." Clay sighed. He cast a disgusted glance around him. Though the plaza was filled with peddlers and shoppers and wagons, no one was within hearing distance. "I guess here's as good a place as any. This is Gentle Fawn."

Matt's eyes widened. "You're an Indian? I never would have guessed." Then realizing he might have said something wrong, he quickly amended his words. "I mean you don't look like an Indian."

"That's just the point, Matt," Clay said, moving closer to the confused Texas Ranger and speaking confidentially. "I found her living with the Sioux and she's convinced her parents were Cheyennes. But her Sioux parents adopted her fifteen years ago when she was three years old—the same year three-year-old Camila Delgado disappeared." Clay raised his blond eyebrows meaningfully, deliberately pausing to let the full import of what he was saying sink in. Then he went on.

"I'm completely convinced she's the Delgados' missing daughter. She was told that her true parents were Cheyennes who were killed in a raid. But I don't believe it. The Sioux either got her from the Cheyennes as they claimed and believed what they told her, or they lied to her for some reason we may never know—maybe they thought she'd be safer if her white blood was kept a secret."

"It could all just be a coincidence," Matt interjected.

Clay shook his head. "Don't you think I considered that at first? But all the pieces fit too perfectly to be mere coincidence. And look at her features. Can you see a single thing about her that's Indian? Except maybe the fact that she has black eyes and hair—which is curly when she lets it down! Not coarse and straight, but fine and curly. And look at her eyelashes! Did you ever see an Indian with eyelashes like that?"

Gentle Fawn cast a scorching look in Clay's direction and wiped at the telling wisps of hair that hung in sweat-soaked ringlets at her nape and temples where they'd escaped from the braids she had wound around her head in a style she'd seen some white women wear.

"And even though her eyes are the right color, they aren't shaped like Indian eyes usually are," Matt noticed, studying Gentle Fawn, who despite her disorderly appearance was the prettiest thing he'd ever seen. She reminded him of a little doll his sister had gotten for Christmas years ago.

Her black eyes shooting sparks now, Gentle Fawn directed her venomous stare toward Matt.

"And look at her cheekbones!" Clay said, catching her face in his hand. "Are these the cheekbones of a—"

"Stop it!" Gentle Fawn screamed, slapping Clay's hand away from her face and giving him a hard shove. "I will not stand here and be poked at and prodded like a—like a . . . frog! Like a frog two curious little boys found in a stream and are determined to torture. I am not a frog and you will not treat me like one!" she shouted, unaware of the tears that trailed down her grimy cheeks, quickly vanishing as they flowed into the salty perspiration that covered her red-splotched face and neck.

A frog? A corner of Clay's mouth twitched involuntarily, and it required every bit of self-discipline he could muster not to give in to the chuckle building in his throat. He loved it when she forgot all that stoic Indian reserve and let herself just be a woman. Not Gentle Fawn, not Camila Delgado. But just a woman. A beautiful, irrational, emotional woman. "Now, Gen—" Clay started, moving to take her arm again.

"Do not call me that!" she shrieked. She held out her arms, her palms facing him as if she were trying to ward off an evil spirit. She'd been certain he'd been about to call her "Ginnie."

"Whatever you say," he returned, holding out his hands in defeat. He was beginning to worry now. This was more than just female excitability. She was getting hysterical. He had been told more than one story of people who'd been affected by "stage craziness" after spending long, tedious days in the uncomfortable confines of a stagecoach without sufficient sleep. He'd heard of passengers who'd shown signs of delirium being forced to stay over at a swing station to catch up on their rest. Sometimes that worked and the passenger was back to normal when the next stage came along. But occasionally it was too late, and the passenger just went into a daze and wandered away from the station, never to be seen again.

"Just take me to the hotel," she said, blinking her eyes to clear her vision which was suddenly cloudy. "Then you—" She wiped at her eyes but it didn't help. "—you two little—" Now her head was beginning to swim and everything she saw seemed to be double. "—little boys—" With a warm rush, the bones in her legs seemed to melt, and she could feel them dissolving beneath her. "—can talk—"

Reacting automatically, Clay caught Gentle Fawn as she pitched forward into a dead faint. "Get us to the hotel fast," he hollered to Matt, the frantic look in his blue eyes giving away the fact that the girl was more to him than just a big story.

"It's right there," Matt said, indicating an off-white three-story building on the other side of the plaza.

Clutching Gentle Fawn protectively against his chest, Clay took off running toward the Menger Hotel.

"I have the keys to your rooms so you can take her on up and sign the register after we take care of her," Matt called after the frantic man as he stooped to add Clay's dropped saddlebags to the rest of his burden before hurrying to catch up.

Neither of the worried men noticed the curious stares

of the guests and hotel personnel in the lavishly decorated lobby as they dashed through it on their way to the rooms Matt Gramm had reserved. "Somebody get a doctor and send him to 207," Matt ordered the desk clerk as they passed by. "And tell him to hustle!"

"Where's that doctor?" Clay groaned a few minutes later as he gently lowered Gentle Fawn onto a large four-poster bed. He leaned over her and patted her cheeks gently. "Honey, wake up. It's all right now." He turned to Matt, who, despite his tough, take-charge exterior, obviously didn't know what to do next. "Hand me a wet cloth, will you?" Clay said.

"Uh, sure," Matt mumbled, looking around the large room for the water pitcher. "Is she goin' to be all right?"

"I don't know. She's been through an awful lot during the last couple of months."

Matt set the washbowl down on the stand by the bed and filled it with cool water, then wrung out a white washcloth and gave it to Clay. "This ought to help. She looks awful hot."

"I know. She's not used to this kind of heat. Did you see how she was sweating before she— I'll never forgive myself if anything happens to her," he interrupted himself. "Where the hell is that doctor?"

"I'll go see if I can find out what's takin' him so long," Matt offered, jumping at the chance to do something. He opened the door just as the doctor raised his hand to knock. "Are you the doctor?" he asked anxiously, taking in the rolled-up sleeves and open collar of the flushed man's sweat-plastered white shirt.

"That's what the sign over my office says," the balding

man quipped roughly, making no effort to hide the fact that he didn't appreciate having to hurry on such a hot day. "We gonna stand here talkin' all day, or are you gonna show me where the sick girl is?" His black bag preceding him into the room, the doctor gave the larger man an irritated look and elbowed his way past.

"She's right here, Doc!" Clay called out, continuing to swab Gentle Fawn's face and neck with the cool wash rag. "I don't know what happened. One minute she was fine and the next she was fainting! Look how pale she is! What do you think it is, Doc? Could it be 'stage craziness'? We've been on one for over a week and she hated it. Is she going to be all right?"

The doctor waited impatiently for Clay to finish his frantic monologue before he spoke. "Young man, if you would move out of the way, I might be able to answer your questions."

"Uh? Oh, sure." Clay stood up beside the bed, but was loath to relinquish his hold on Gentle Fawn's hand. It seemed so small and lifeless in his. What if she died? How would he live with himself if he'd been the one to cause her death by bringing her here? How would he stand life without her?

The doctor cleared his throat purposefully. When Clay didn't take the none-too-subtle hint and leave, the doctor said, "I'm afraid I'll have to ask you to step out of the room, sir."

"I'll just stand here and hold her hand," Clay said, his determined voice gravelly with unshed tears. He was unable to take his eyes off Gentle Fawn's face. She was so pale, so still; and her long black eyelashes seemed darker than ever against the color-drained translucence of her cheeks.

If she died it would be his fault for bringing her here when all she'd wanted was to go back to the Black Hills. But no, he'd been too concerned with his own desires to pay any attention to what she wanted. So he'd kept after her and planted those doubts in her mind until she'd felt she had no choice but to come. If she would only open her eyes so he would know she was all right. *If she dies, it'll be my fault, just as surely as if I held a gun to her head and fired it.*

"It would be better if you wait in the hall with your friend," the doctor said, taking a stethoscope from his black bag.

"I'm staying right here until I know she's all right. If she wakes up and sees a stranger instead of me, she'll be afraid," Clay said, his grip on Gentle Fawn's hand tightening.

"Do as you wish, but you might as well be some help if you insist on staying. Help me get her out of this jacket and take her corset off. That'll make her feel better right away."

"She doesn't wear a corset. She doesn't need one," Clay answered automatically, relaxing his hold on her hand.

The doctor raised his brows in surprise, then nodded his head approvingly. "Need doesn't usually have anything to do with women's fashions," the older man said disdainfully.

He lifted Gentle Fawn to a sitting position and held her while Clay carefully removed her arms from the sleeves of the green jacket of her traveling suit. Clay flinched when he saw that her white blouse was drenched with sweat and sticking to her slender body. She hadn't worn the jacket in the stagecoach, but had put it back on before they got out. He should have insisted she leave it off.

"She wouldn't be the first woman to collapse from the heat because her corset was too tight."

"Is that what's wrong with her? Is it the heat?" Clay asked anxiously.

The doctor gave him a peevish glance and shook his head. "I don't know what's wrong with her yet. It could be the heat," he said, lowering her back down onto the bed and unbuttoning Gentle Fawn's high-necked bodice. "Then again, it could be something else. But by the looks of the way she's sweatin', it's probably the heat."

"A heatstroke?" Clay rasped. People died of heatstroke. *God, please don't let her die,* he prayed urgently. *I won't write the story about her if you'll just let her live. I won't even take her to see the Delgados if she doesn't want to go. Just don't let Gentle Fawn die!*

"Not a heatstroke. With heatstroke the skin is hot and dry and the temperature is very high. Her temperature's about normal and she's sweatin'. So heatstroke's not too likely." He put the stethoscope to Gentle Fawn's chest and listened intently. "Pulse good. No, it's not heatstroke."

"Then what?"

"You folks from up north?" the doctor asked as he took off his stethoscope and rolled it around his hand before dropping it back into the bag.

"Cheyenne," Clay answered, not seeing any need to go into any more detail than that for the stranger.

"That's what I figured. People from up north aren't used to our Texas summers."

"Then it *is* heatstroke?" Clay's own heart began to beat a rapid tattoo of alarm against his ribs.

340

The doctor gave an exasperated sigh and went on talking. "I think we got us a couple of things here," he said slowly, as though carefully considering each word before saying it out loud. "First of all, I believe we've got us a bona fide case of heat prostration here."

"What does that mean? Is she going to be all right or not?" Clay asked through clenched teeth, his patience with the slow-moving doctor at an end.

"She's gonna be fine. She's dehydrated from so much sweatin'. That's all. But if you just keep her cool and start pourin' the water down her throat, she'll be up and around in no time."

"You said there were a couple of things wrong with her," Clay suddenly remembered. "What else is wrong?"

"Nothin' that can't be cured by a decent night's sleep. People can only go so long without sleep before they drop in their tracks. You did say you've been in a stagecoach for over a week, didn't you?"

Clay nodded his head, wondering if he could trust the doctor or if he should call another one for a second opinion. What if she had some mysterious brain fever? "You're sure all she needs is water and sleep?"

"As sure as any human bein' can be," the doctor snapped, making no secret of the fact that he didn't appreciate having his opinion questioned. "Water and sleep. That'll be a dollar," he said, adding seventy-five cents to his usual charge for a house call.

Not even noticing the doctor's huffiness, Clay dug a dollar out of his pocket and dropped it in the man's open hand. "Water and sleep," he repeated one more time.

"Do you want me to write it down so you can remember?"

Clay didn't hear the edge to the doctor's voice and answered, "No thanks, I can remember. Water and sleep."

"I'll give you some free advice, young man," the doctor said as he scurried to the door.

"What's that?"

"You'd be smart to get yourself some sleep, too, before you wind up in the same kind of shape she's in."

"I'm going to do that." *Just as soon as I know Gentle Fawn's okay.*

Chapter Twenty=One

Gentle Fawn opened her eyes languidly and stared at the beige canopy above her. With a lazy stretch of her body, she rolled her head to the side and took a groggy visual tour of the surroundings. The papered walls around her were covered with a delicate gold and white filigree design, and the gaslights that flickered on each of the four walls cast a golden hue over the entire room.

Looking down at herself, she realized that during the night someone had removed her clothing, leaving her clad only in her chemise and drawers, before covering her with a light sheet. Though she was cooler than she'd been in hours, it was still hot, and she welcomed the night breeze that came through the window. Throwing the sheet to the side so the air could touch all of her, she was suddenly shaken by a chill. It was then she realized her underthings were damp from her own perspiration, and that they smelled sour. She reached up and touched her hair. It was damp and sour-smelling, too. Never in her life had she felt so offensive.

"I need to bathe and get out of these things," she said,

thinking she was alone. She sat up.

A movement in the corner of the room caught her eye at the same time a sleepy male voice grunted, "Huh? What'd you say?"

Startled, she looked in that direction to find that the owner of the voice was already nodding his head again, not even aware that he had spoken in his sleep. A warm feeling of tenderness spread through her heart as she studied the sleeping man.

His chest and feet bare, Clay sat slumped in a tan velvet wingback chair beside the window. His fingers were interlaced on his lean belly, his long legs stretched out in front of him and crossed at the ankles. And his hair, his wonderful golden hair, was rumpled as though he'd repeatedly run his fingers through it.

Her heart exploding with love for him, Gentle Fawn climbed off the large bed. She stood still for a minute to be sure her legs would support her. She was pleased—and surprised—to realize that for the first time in over a week she didn't feel as though the ground were moving beneath her when she stood. In fact, she felt good.

Smiling, she scurried over to kneel beside Clay. "Clay, come sleep in the bed," she whispered, kissing his temple and slipping his arm around her shoulders as she wrapped her own arm around his back.

He snorted, smacked his lips, and, mumbling some unintelligible words, tried to turn over onto his side.

"Come to bed, Clay," she said again, tugging at him.

He opened his eyes and stared at her, his look glassy. "Are we there yet?" he muttered almost incoherently.

"We are there, Clay. And it is time for you to go to bed. Let me help you," she pleaded softly. "Stand up. You do not even have to open your eyes. I will guide you."

"Lemme sleep," he protested thickly, resisting her efforts.

Just when she would have given up and left him there, he suddenly jumped out of the chair and looked around, the expression on his face frantic. "Gotta check on Gentle Fawn."

"Clay, it is me. I am fine," she said, holding him and prodding him toward the bed. "And you will be too once you get into bed."

Clay allowed himself to be walked a few steps, then suddenly stopped and stared down at her. "Gentle Fawn?"

She smiled up at him and said, "Who did you think it was?"

He looked at the empty bed for confirmation, then back to her. "Are you all right?" he asked, his voice rough with anxiety.

"I am fine."

"Oh, sugar," he groaned, gathering her into his arms and burying his face in her hair as he became fully aware. "I was so scared I was going to lose you."

She was caught off guard by the intense concern in his voice. Could it be that he did care for her after all? Was it possible that she meant more to him than only a "story"?

Happiness bubbled in her heart. "Is it not clear to you by now that I am not that easy to lose?" she said, her love for him glistening in her luminous eyes.

"I was so worried when you fainted. I don't know what I would have done if something had happened to you." He smoothed his large hands up and down her back, as though needing to prove to himself that she was real. "I was so set on writing the story of your reunion with the Delgados . . ."

345

"The story," she spat with undisguised contempt. She tore herself out of his arms and walked away from him before he could see the disappointment in her expression. She'd almost done it again. She'd almost made a fool of herself by revealing her true feelings. *Of course the only reason he would be so worried was because of his story.* "I should have known," she said bitterly, not even realizing she had spoken aloud.

Clay studied her rigid back, trying to imagine what he'd said that could have caused such a violent reaction. "Should have known what? What's wrong?"

Gentle Fawn's fists tightened at her sides and her posture stiffened at the sound of his voice. "Nothing is wrong," she said, her chin lifting defiantly.

"Something upset you," Clay said, coming up behind her and placing his hands on her shoulders. "Why did you turn away from me like that?"

It took every bit of resistance she could muster not to lean back against him. Even now when she knew how little she really mattered to him, she wanted to feel safe in his arms.

She closed her eyes and took a deep breath for strength. "It is hot," she said woodenly, taking a step away from him, determined to free herself from his power over her. "Where is the place to bathe in this hotel?"

"Don't try to change the subject, Gentle Fawn," he said, his voice stern. "It won't work. Now tell me what upset you. You were fine until I mentioned my story about you. Is that it? The story?"

She didn't answer. There was no need. He could tell by the almost imperceptible straightening of her spine.

"That *is* it, isn't it? Why?"

No longer able to contain her resentment for the way he intended to use her, she wheeled around to face him, her black eyes blazing with anger. "Yes, it is your 'story.' I hate it. I hate everything about it. I hate the idea of having my private life in a newspaper for people to read and laugh and wonder about. And I hate the way nothing matters to you except your 'big stories.' If I had died today, you would not have had your story, would you? And that would have really upset you. Because that is all you care about. The 'big story'! Bah!" she spat viciously. "It does not matter who you hurt or whose life you disrupt—mine, the Delgados. As long as you get your story, nothing else matters to you, does it, Clay Donovan?"

"That's not true," Clay denied hoarsely, knowing even as he spoke that she was right. He'd been like that all his life. It had been the only way to survive in the poor Irish neighborhood in New York City where he was raised. Scrambling and hustling had been a way of life to get whatever he wanted before the other scramblers and hustlers could get there first. And until this moment, he had never resented the lessons in survival he'd learned almost from birth. He'd always felt they were the reason for his quick success as a writer. But now for the first time he wondered if his success was worth the cost. What kind of a human being had he become? Not a very nice one, he realized.

"Oh, you do not think so?" she said, her black brows arched knowingly.

"I never deliberately hurt anyone to get a story," he said, as much to boost his sinking opinion of himself as to explain to Gentle Fawn. At least that was true.

"What about the way you forced me to think about the

347

possibility that the Delgados were my natural parents when you knew how much I hated the idea?"

"I felt I was doing what was best for you."

Gentle Fawn nodded her head and laughed. "Best for me. Of course. Foolish me. How could I forget? The wise white man always knows what is best for the ignorant savage. Is that so? Tell me, Mr. Donovan, is it best for me to rob me of my heritage? The heritage I love and am so proud of? The only heritage I ever knew? Is it best for me to have a heart full of doubt instead of certainty? Is it best to replace my pride in my heritage with feelings of not belonging *anywhere*? Not with the Lakotas, not with the whites. Because of what *you* think is best for *me*, I am nothing and I belong nowhere!"

"I know you belong with the Delgados."

"Yes, the Delgados. Those poor, unfortunate people who lost their daughter so many years ago. Have you given them and their feelings any thought at all? I doubt it. Do you care how they will feel when I show up at their home claiming to be the daughter they thought was dead? Do you think they will be happy to have you dig up all the old pain they have probably buried by now? Then when they realize that I am not their daughter, do you think they will be able to just tuck away the bad memories we have dredged up? Or do you think it will be as though they are losing their daughter all over again?"

"But they won't lose their daughter all over again. They'll *find* you. It'll put an end to their misery!"

"And *if* I am that missing daughter, how do you think they will like having their private lives written about in your newspapers? But none of that matters to you, does it, Clay? Not the Delgados and not me. Only your story!"

"I've already decided not to write the story no matter

348

how things turn out," Clay announced, finding no pleasure in her stunned reaction to his words.

"I do not believe you."

"Believe what you like, but I've decided it wouldn't make that good a story after all. My readers aren't really interested in sentimental stuff like family reunions. They'd rather read about more exciting things—like battles and gunfights." Damned if he'd tell her the real reason why he'd changed his mind. Not now that he knew what she really thought of him. "As a matter of fact, we don't even have to go see the Delgados if you don't want to. We can head back north tomorrow if you feel like it. But right now I'm going to get some sleep." He turned away from her and lowered himself onto the bed.

Gentle Fawn stood rooted to the spot, staring in disbelief at Clay, who already had closed his eyes and seemed well on his way to sleep. What was she supposed to do now? Her first instinct was to take him up on his offer to return to the Black Hills in the morning. It might even be worth another eight days and nights of torture on the stagecoach to be able to put this entire ordeal behind her as quickly as possible. If Clay wasn't going to write the story, he had no more use for her, so he would be anxious to get rid of her. That's what she should do. Leave Texas tomorrow and go back to where she belonged, to the only life she'd ever known. Still . . .

Spying a washstand, a bowl, and a pitcher of water in the corner, all thoughts of decision-making were erased from her mind for a moment. She snatched up the carpetbag holding her clothing and hurried to the washstand, peeling off her chemise and drawers as she went. It wasn't the luxurious bathtub at the Rosewood in Cheyenne, but it was wet and it was clean, and she was in no mood to be particular at that moment. Besides, she wouldn't have a bathtub when she was back with the Lakotas. She might as well get used to it now rather than wait.

Once she had washed the dirt and grime from her body and hair as well as she could, she dusted her skin with the sweet-smelling powder Clay had bought her in Cheyenne. Inhaling the fragrance of the powder, she slipped a thin white lawn gown over her nakedness and walked to the window.

The garden patio below was almost deserted, though she could hear the music of an unseen Mexican band coming from somewhere inside the hotel. An occasional couple strolled arm-in-arm along the pathways, pausing to steal secret kisses when they passed behind a hedge or tree they thought hid them from their chaperones.

Idly sifting her fingers through her thick hair to help it dry in the breeze, she sighed and smiled sadly. How she envied those young lovers down there. To love a man and know that he loved you in return must be the most wonderful thing in the world. If two people loved each other, it wouldn't matter where they came from or where they lived, or even if they were Indian or white. The only thing that would be important would be that they loved each other and would be together always.

But when one loves and the other only uses . . . She shook her hair vigorously to hurry up the drying process—and to blot out the murmuring voices of the lovers in the patio. "Then it only hurts!" she whispered, moving from wall to wall as she turned out the gaslights.

Finally, she crawled into the large bed beside Clay, taking care not to touch the sleeping man.

"You smell good," Clay mumbled groggily as he rolled

350

onto his side and pulled her back against his chest, neatly shaping her pliable body against the harder planes of his. "That's nice," he sighed, burrowing his face into the softness of her hair, then went back to sleep.

She knew she should move away from his hold on her, but all of her resistance was instantly drained from her body by the feel of his breath on her ear and neck. She was as trapped by her own need for the comfort of his nearness as she was by the muscular arm draped protectively over her body. Besides, if they were going back north by stagecoach in the morning, this would probably be the last night she would know the glorious feel of sleeping in his embrace. How could she deny herself this one final night when the memory of it would have to last her a lifetime of nights without him?

Her decision made, she nestled her bottom snugly in the bend of his hips and allowed herself to be lulled into sleepy contentment by the soft rise and fall of Clay's breathing wafting across her skin.

Hours later, Clay's tongue made soft spirals on her ear as his hand slid lazily over her stomach to her breasts. Even in her sleep, she strained toward his touch as he cupped one of the small mounds in his hand.

Imitating the circling motion of his tongue on the shell of her ear, Clay moved the tips of his fingers slowly around first one nipple, then the other, working each into a tight bud, hard and thrusting. Moving in the same easy circular pattern, his fingers traveled to the gentle curve of her waist, then along the line of her hip.

Her body instinctively responded to his titillating caresses even though she was not fully awake. She tried to turn toward him, but he held her in the same position, her back to him. His hand kept up its arousing trek over her flesh, leaving none of her untouched by his magical fondling—her buttocks, the deep indentation of her navel, the inviting crease where her bent leg curved into her hip, seductively indicating the path to Clay's final destination.

When at last his fingers began their agonizing search of the inside of her thighs, still ignoring the soft feminine delta at their apex, he allowed her to roll over.

Slowly, she turned in his arms to lie on her back, eyes still closed, her hips arching desirously. At last he slipped his fingers into the mysterious folds of moist flesh at the heart of her sex and kissed her mouth.

"Good morning," he whispered huskily against her lips, closing his mouth over her welcoming smile before she could respond.

It was then she remembered where she was and the strain between them. She tore her head away from his, ending their kiss abruptly. "Stop," she whispered.

"It's been a long time. I've missed you," he coaxed, each word accented by a flick of his tongue on her ear.

"I am angry with you," she reminded him weakly, her tone hoarse with desire, despite her knowledge that Clay was only interested in using her to fulfill her own needs.

"Let's kiss and make up," he coaxed playfully, raining a shower of kisses over her cheek to her mouth. He moved his fingertips deliberately over the hardening nub guarding the entrance to the treasure of her body. "Can you think of a better way to dissolve our anger?" he asked, capturing the sensitive pearl of her femininity between his thumb and forefinger and tugging seductively.

Before she could stop herself, a groan of ecstasy escaped from her throat and a convulsive spasm shook

352

her entire body, pitching all her anger out the window.

It didn't matter that he was only using her. The only thing that mattered was the unbearable agony of needing the empty chasm of her spirit filled with his masculine vitality.

She gyrated wildly against his restraining hand, reaching desperately for his manhood, begging him to enter her, demanding that he end her torture.

But Clay continued his relentless attack on her senses with his fingers at the same time his mouth began its descent, following the trail his hand had already blazed— over her breasts, swollen with desire; along her stomach, dipping his tongue deep into her navel; at last arriving at the gateway to her femininity.

Her senses were honed to such heady heights that when his lips touched the place where his fingers had been only seconds before, she moved in a rapturous orgasm against his mouth. Her fingers tangled in his thick hair, she cried out her release in a long, tortured groan, and tried to pull his head upward. But Clay gripped her hips and lifted them higher, continuing his unremitting onslaught as again he brought her to an earth-shattering response.

"Please," she begged urgently, her voice weak with exhaustion and the need to have him fill the void that even his wondrous foreplay could not fill.

He moved his body above hers, his manhood hovering tauntingly above her rocking femininity. She raised her hips and again beseeched him to fill her emptiness. "Please."

"Please what?" he whispered, watching her passion-contorted face in the predawn dimness of the room as the tip of his manhood moistened itself on the rim of her body.

"Please do not torture me anymore," she ground out, certain no punishment ever devised could be as divinely cruel.

"Torture? I thought I pleased you."

"I want you," she groaned. "Now!" she insisted throatily, clamping her hands on his buttocks and forcing him to enter her, putting a stop to his abuse of her pounding senses.

Plunging into her heated depths at last, Clay groaned with relief, ending his own self-denial.

Gentle Fawn rose up vigorously to meet his thrusts, matching her wild motions with his. She soared on wings that took her farther away from reality, into uncharted regions beyond the limits of gravity.

And Gentle Fawn was certain that no pleasure ever devised could be as exquisite.

"Oh, God!" Clay shouted urgently, filling her with the fiery lava of his desire she was crying for when his explosion vaulted her tumultuously over the brink.

When he collapsed on her, she was unaware of his compressing weight in the aftermath as she slowly floated back down into the earth's atmosphere.

When Gentle Fawn finally regained her equilibrium, she spoke, her breathing still a heaving panting as she kissed Clay's cheek. "Good morning to you, too," she whispered, her throat tight, her mouth dry, and her body filled with love for this man.

"Are you still mad at me?" he chuckled softly in her ear, his own breathing ragged and irregular. Propping himself above her on his elbows, he threaded his fingers through her hair and smiled down at her.

"Am I supposed to forget that I am angry?" she

answered, fighting the desire to return his warm grin.

"Yeah, I guess you should," he said, his expression growing serious. He rolled away from her to lie on his back. He threw a forearm up over his eyes. "I just hoped that when you learned I wasn't going to write the story about you that you might see it in your heart to forgive me."

He looked so hurt, so unsure of himself. Gentle Fawn had never seen him like this, and the need to comfort him swelled in her heart. "It is not just this story, Clay," she said, turning onto her side to face him. "It is the way you see me—people—only as stories. It is as though you do not see us as human beings with feelings, only as stories put here for you to write about so you can be more famous than you already are."

"I guess that's one way to look at it," he said, his tone slightly bitter. "But maybe if you understood what my writing has meant to me, you might not think I'm such a selfish son of a bitch. When I was a kid, my writing was my only escape from the miserable existence of the poor in the city. Ma and Da insisted I go to school instead of making me work in the factories like the other kids in the neighborhood had to do. And once I learned to read and write, the written word became my way out of poverty.

"I had to steal my pencils and paper as often as not, because in my family there was barely enough money for food and a one-room apartment in the basement of a building unfit for pigs, much less human beings. The prejudice against the Irish in the city was bad, and my father was out of work more often than not. I watched my mother kill herself working in a clothing factory that had no windows and stunk so badly from the fumes of dye that when she came home at night the stink of that damned dye clinging to her clothes would make my eyes water, too.

"But through it all, I had my writing. Through the hunger, the prejudice, the losses, the rags for clothes, the shoes that were more holes than leather, the digging through rich people's trash for food, I had my writing. And I wrote. God, how I wrote. When I wrote I could be anyone I wanted, go anywhere I desired, eat as much as I wanted, change all the wrongs in the world. It was my escape. My salvation.

"When Ma died, I was sixteen. Da and I decided we would give working on the railroad a try since we'd heard they were hiring. The war with the South was just over and with so many men returning home, there were no jobs in New York so we headed west.

"During the two years I laid track for the Union Pacific, I continued to write in my spare time. Only I no longer needed to write to escape because I was where I wanted to be—in the wide open, clean-smelling West. God, I loved it. I still do. Everywhere I went I saw things and people I wanted to put down on paper—as if I could keep them with me forever if I could capture them with my writing.

"Then I found that keeping all these wonderful things and people I'd discovered to myself wasn't enough. I wanted to share my love and enthusiasm about the West with others. I wanted them to feel what I felt. Anyway, I sent a piece I'd written to a newspaper in Kansas. The editor sent me a dollar and asked for more. An editor in San Francisco happened to come across one of my articles in that Kansas paper and paid me and the Kansas paper for the right to reprint *everything* I wrote. By then, I'd quit the railroad to travel and write all over the West.

"Then six years ago, when I was twenty-two, Horace Greeley was in San Francisco and read one of my articles. He wrote offering me a regular column in the *New York Tribune*—with my articles being sold to newspapers all over the country.

"Suddenly I could afford the best clothes, and everywhere I went people knew my name. Suddenly the ragamuffin Irish kid from the streets of New York could walk into the best hotels and restaurants in the country and be treated like a king. Suddenly people looked up to me, not down on me. And best of all, I was doing what I loved, writing about the West. Can you blame me for not wanting to give that all up?"

"I do not expect you to give up what you love," Gentle Fawn said, sensing that he had told her more about himself than he had ever shared with another human being. "It is just that—"

"I know, I know," he interrupted. "It's just that I let my enthusiasm for a project run away with me. I don't mean to, but I can't seem to help myself. I've never lost that initial excitement I felt for everything about the West, and I get so excited about each new story—like it's the very first—and I forget everything else. But I don't only think of people as stories I can write, Gentle Fawn."

He rolled on his side and propped his head in his hand so he could look into her eyes. "You've got to believe that, honey. You've got to know that I would never deliberately write a story that would hurt you—or anyone else. As much as I love my writing, I'd give it up if I couldn't use it to help people. I want to make them feel good, not contribute to their misery."

"I do know that, Clay—now," Gentle Fawn whispered, confused by the feelings tearing through her. How could

357

she ever have thought this man cared nothing for others. "I did not understand. Thank you for telling me."

"You know, I've never told anyone those things before," he said, staring at her with wonder.

"I think I knew that, too." She smiled. "And now that I understand what it means to you—and why—I will not hold you to your promise not to write about me if I am the Delgados' missing daughter."

Touched by her offer when he knew how much she hated the idea, Clay was tempted to grab at her gift. The old Clay would have accepted—even as late as yesterday—before a tiny dark-eyed vixen had forced him to look at his values and make some drastic reevaluations of his own character. "Thanks, sugar. But the promise stands. I'll find another story to write. We'll just keep this one between us. Okay?" He kissed her on the tip of her nose and lay back on the pillow, pulling her down into the curve of his arm.

She adjusted her body along the length of his and wrapped her arm over his middle. "I was thinking—"

"What?"

"Well, I thought that as long as we have come all this way, and as long as we are so near them, it might not hurt to go see the Delgados," she suggested shyly.

"Just as long as we're here, huh?"

"Just as long as we are here."

Chapter Twenty-Two

"You're sure Delgado's not in Austin right now?" Clay asked Matt several hours later as the two men and Gentle Fawn rode their horses toward the Delgado ranch.

Matt chuckled. For a man who'd decided not to write the story, Clay Donovan sure was getting excited the closer they got to Delgado's place. "I've told you. I checked with people in town and the senator's supposed to be at the Rancho Camila." He looked over at Gentle Fawn and grinned. "Clay's more nervous about this than you are."

Lovely in the new clothes Clay had bought her that morning, she wore a split riding skirt of tan nankeen and a long-sleeved white blouse topped with a short bolero vest. Brown leather knee-high boots and a flat, wide-brimmed hat secured beneath her chin with a cord completed her outfit. "Clay does everything with enthusiasm," she explained, directing a knowing smile toward the subject of their conversation. "It is one of the things that makes him special."

Suddenly feeling like a "fifth wheel," as he watched

Clay and Gentle Fawn exchange understanding glances, Matt looked away self-consciously. "Sure is pretty country out here."

"Very beautiful," Gentle Fawn returned, suddenly overcome by a strange feeling of having seen all this before. Of course, that was a ridiculous notion. Even if she were the missing Camila Delgado, she wouldn't remember anything about her life here. She'd been too young when she went to live with the Lakotas. It was simply her imagination playing tricks on her. There was no way she would remember this place. It just looked like some other landscape she had seen before. That was all. Still . . .

"Does anyone know why we're coming?" Clay asked.

Matt rolled his eyes and pulled a cigar out of his pocket. "Man, how many times do I have to tell you?" He bit off the tip and spit it out before putting the cigar back into his mouth. "I got the wire from Johnny tellin' me to send you any information I could get on the Delgados and their kids. Then the one from you tellin' me when you and a friend would be arrivin' in San Antonio. I didn't even know until you got here that the 'friend' was a lady, and I sure didn't have any idea what you were comin' for."

"Maybe I should have warned him we were coming."

"It's a little late for that, friend." Matt laughed. "But if you're really worried about it I could ride on ahead and give Señor Delgado the word."

Leaving the men to continue their discussion, Gentle Fawn pulled her horse out in front of the others. Everything really did look so familiar.

They rode like that for the next thirty minutes, Gentle Fawn out in front, her head swiveling from left to right, studying everything she saw with a growing sense of wonder, the men behind her lost in their own conversation.

Suddenly, Matt signaled Clay to stop as he reined his own horse to a halt.

"Wha—"

"Shh," Matt interrupted, holding a finger to his lips in a quiet sign. "Look," he whispered, nodding his head toward Gentle Fawn.

Ahead of them and oblivious to the fact that their conversation had stopped, Gentle Fawn had ridden off the main road onto a narrower road that forked to the right. "It's the road to Rancho Camila," Matt whispered, his tone awed. "How'd she know to turn here?"

"My God!" Clay gasped, stunned by what he was seeing. As strongly as he'd been convinced that Gentle Fawn and Camila Delgado were one and the same, there'd always been that niggling doubt that he was wrong and setting everyone—Gentle Fawn, the Delgados, and himself—up for nothing but hurt and disappointment. But now . . . "Do you realize what this means?"

Matt nodded his head, the expression on his face disbelieving. "Of course, it could just be a coincidence," he offered, his voice unconvincing.

"Coincidence, my foot! There's no way in hell a person would have turned off the main road here unless they'd been here before. I wouldn't have, would you? I might not've even noticed it!"

"I missed it the first time I came out here," Matt admitted sheepishly. "I was leadin' a few rangers on a hunt for a bank robber who was supposed to be holed up in the area. We wanted to ask the folks on the Delgado place some questions, but we went about half a mile past

361

that road before I realized we had missed our turnoff."

Clay kicked his mount forward, calling out, "Gentle Fawn, wait a minute!"

Gentle Fawn stopped and turned around in her saddle to wait for Clay to catch up to her, a smile on her face.

"Why'd you turn off the main road?"

"Because it's the way to . . ." she started automatically. A puzzled look wiped the smile from her face. She turned to look up the road to Rancho Camila, her brows drawn together in concentration. She glanced at the main road, then back to Clay. "I do not know why," she explained, an unwelcome blush creeping to her cheeks.

"Don't you?" Clay said softly.

"I was just looking at the scenery and did not notice where I was going."

Clay shook his head. "That's not it, Gentle Fawn. You turned off the obvious main road to this more inconspicuous road for only one reason. You turned off because you've been here before and knew it was the road leading to your family's home."

Gentle Fawn looked up the narrow road again. "That is craziness. How would I have known this was the way there? It was just an accident."

"Or a *coincidence?*"

"Yes! A coincidence!"

"Another coincidence, in a list of coincidences that's getting too long to remember."

She looked up the road to the ranch. Nothing seemed familiar anymore. That feeling of being here before was gone. Now everything she saw looked alien and forbidding. "Yes, another coincidence. I have never been here before. No matter how many coincidences you find!

And the faster I prove that to you the better it will be!" She kicked her horse into a gallop, leaving the surprised men to follow behind her.

An hour later, the three riders rode through massive wooden gates into an enormous courtyard surrounding a sprawling one-story home built of whitewashed ashlar limestone and roofed with red tiles.

Without waiting for Clay to help her down, Gentle Fawn slid off her horse and quickly tied him to the hitching rail at the front of the house. She was angry with herself for giving in to her curiosity and coming here. But now that she had gone this far, she was anxious to get it over with. The only thing left to do was to face the Delgados and let them show Clay that she couldn't be their daughter. And then leave.

She hurried up the steps to the stuccoed arcade that wrapped its way around the front of the house. She had her hand raised to knock on the intricately carved front door before Clay and Matt could catch up with her.

As they joined her, the heavy door swung open to reveal a small gray-haired woman dressed in a loose white blouse, a black skirt, and sandals. *"Sí?"* she said, squinting her dark eyes to study the three strangers standing at the door.

"I'm Captain Matt Gramm of the Texas Rangers and I'd like to speak with Señor Delgado," Matt said, stepping forward, inadvertently blocking the woman's view of the other two visitors. "Is he in?"

"El patrón, he is not here," the woman said brusquely, straining to see around the large man in the doorway. "The young señor is in his study. You will speak with him?"

"Sí," Matt answered with a nod of his head.

"Wait here," she said curtly, shutting the heavy door in Matt's face, leaving the three standing on the shaded arcade.

"That'll be Antonio Delgado, Manuel's nephew," Matt explained, turning to the others. "When his brother and sister-in-law died, Delgado took in their son and daughter. I've met the young Delgado a few times and he seems like a pretty good kid."

When the door was opened a second time, it was by a slender young man, about twenty-two years old. Worn with no part, his thick black hair was pomaded back from his face. Straight black sideburns reached past his ears and a pencil-slim mustache decorated his upper lip. Dressed in a loose white shirt and tight black trousers that clung to his lean hips, he was the perfect picture of the young Spanish rancher in casual dress. "Matt! What a pleasant surprise, *mi amigo!*" he said warmly, his black eyes flashing brightly. "To what do we owe this pleasure?"

"Antonio, it's good to see you again," Matt returned, only vaguely aware of the old woman who had answered the door, as she peeked out from behind Antonio Delgado. "In fact, I think it's best that you're the one we talk to first."

"Oh?"

"I've brought some news to your uncle that may come as quite a shock to him. You may be able to help prepare him."

"You have my curiosity piqued, Matt. But let's not stand here. Come inside and I will have Nana prepare all of you a cool drink. Then we will discuss what to do about preparing my uncle for this distressing news you bring— whatever it is."

Boy, he's a cool one, isn't he? Clay said to himself. *Almost as if he was expecting us.* "Something cool to drink sounds great," he said, stepping up to Antonio and extending his hand. "Señor Delgado, I'm Clay Donovan of the *New York Tribune.*"

Clay was certain a flicker of hatred flashed through the cool, assessing black eyes of Antonio Delgado. But it was gone as quickly as it had appeared. The eyes now were warm and friendly. *Too much sun. I'm beginning to imagine things.*

"Señor Donovan, it is a pleasure," Antonio returned, taking his offered hand.

Clay placed his hand at the small of Gentle Fawn's back and gently brought her to stand beside him. "And this is Gen—"

"Madre de Dios!" the old woman suddenly screamed, frantically tapping herself—forehead, chest, left shoulder, right shoulder—in the Catholic sign of the cross. *"Mi niña, mi niña."*

"What is it?" Antonio asked impatiently, turning to stare at the woman who was clutching her breast with one hand and fumbling in her skirt pocket with the other.

"Mi niña," she whispered, bringing her rosary-gripping hand out of her pocket and pointing at Gentle Fawn.

Antonio looked back at the small woman standing between the two men. His black eyes roved over Gentle Fawn, showing only the slightest twinge of recognition. She was lovely, and he could easily see what had frightened the old *duenna.* The likeness to Francisca Delgado was incredible.

"You must forgive her. She sees ghosts everywhere," he said smoothly, his smile never giving away the fact that the girl's face was familiar to him as well. He put his arm around the old woman's shoulder and guided her into another room. "There, there. You go rest," he murmured.

"Obviously she recognizes the young woman as someone she knows," Clay said, studying Delgado carefully when he returned.

Antonio flashed the writer a white-toothed grin and said, "Now that Nana has brought it to my attention, I do see a certain similarity to my Aunt Francisca."

He held out his arm in a welcoming gesture indicating they should come inside. They followed him through the parquet-tiled vestibule and a large main room into a cool room decorated with dark oak tables and chairs, stained black by years of use and polishing. The wide-planked hardwood floors gleamed to perfection, reflecting the hues of cherry red, burnt orange, and rust found in the upholstered furniture and the rugs that decorated the cream-colored stucco walls.

"Of course, the old woman's eyesight isn't what it once was, but—" He stopped speaking and looked more closely at Gentle Fawn. "Actually, the resemblance is quite remarkable," he admitted. "The closest I've seen."

"What do you mean?" Clay asked, aware of the way Gentle Fawn was studying everything in the room. It was just as well that she wasn't paying attention to the conversation. Clay had a sudden feeling things were going to be a little bit sticky.

Antonio smiled his broadest grin. "That is why you're here, is it not, Señor Donovan? You are here in the hope that you will be able to convince my poor unsuspecting uncle that this amazing look-alike of yours is his missing daughter, Camila. Am I correct?"

366

Clay shot a confused look at Matt Gramm, who pulled a cigar from his pocket and continued to study both men. Looking back to Delgado, Clay said, "I have reason to believe she is more than a 'look-alike,' sir. We have proof she *is* Camila Delgado!"

"Proof?" Antonio said, raising his dark brows doubtfully. "That's what all the others said, but when it came to pass, it was never anything."

"All the others?" Clay repeated, directing his baffled look toward Matt, who held out his hands and shrugged his shoulders.

"Surely you are not so naive as to believe that you are the first to try to swindle money from my uncle by passing off a young woman as Camila. However," he said, turning to Matt, "I must admit I am surprised to see that one of our esteemed Texas Rangers would allow himself to be part of such a scheme."

"Scheme?" Matt said to Clay. "You do have proof, don't you?"

"We have the proof," Clay said, his tone not hiding the fact that he was angered by the way Antonio Delgado had turned the suspicion on him.

"And what is this supposed proof, if you do not mind my asking?" Antonio asked saccharinely.

"We will save it for Señor Delgado—Señor Manuel Delgado. If you don't mind my refusing," Clay said sarcastically. "When will he be back?"

Antonio smiled ingratiatingly. "I only thought to save my uncle some pain," he explained, sitting down in a leather-upholstered chair. "Not to mention saving you the embarrassment of being proven a liar. Won't you have a seat while you wait? I am not certain when my uncle will be back. He may not be back before *mañana*. Or

367

even the day after that. But of course you are welcome to wait."

Clay and Matt sat down on the couch, though neither of them was able to relax. Gentle Fawn continued to wander around the large room, a look of wonder on her lovely face.

"Tell me, Delgado, why are you so convinced that she is not Camila Delgado?" Clay's tone was friendly and as casual as if he were asking how many head of cattle were on the ranch. But his insides were in knots. What if he had jumped to conclusions and the whole damned thing was one great big coincidence? Still, she had the locket. And there had been that incident at the fork in the road. One or the other could be a coincidence, but not both of them. No, she was Camila Delgado all right. And once her father saw her and the locket, he would know who she was, no matter what the smiling Señor Antonio Delgado might believe.

Antonio smiled patiently and let out an exasperated sigh. "I'm sure you realize that my uncle is a very wealthy man— Of course you do, otherwise why would you be here? The sad story of my little cousin's disappearance so many years ago is well known. Over the years there have been many—too many to count— impostors who've come to my uncle claiming to be his missing daughter. Each time he let himself hope that the girl was telling the truth and took her in. And every time, one of them was taking advantage of his trusting nature. None of them could stand up to a thorough investigation by the Pinkerton detectives my uncle hired. Every one of them turned out to be frauds. Until at last, my unfortunate uncle finally gave up believing his daughter was still alive. I, too, am convinced poor Camila is dead.

So you see, your little saloon girl, or teacher, or whatever she was when you found her, can't possibly be my cousin."

"I'm certain you believe what you say," Clay said, his expression making it evident that he believed the contrary, "because you would have no reason to prefer that your cousin was never located. Would you?"

Antonio narrowed his eyes, then his smile was back in place. "None whatsoever."

"I'm glad to hear that. And should I produce the proof I have, you would be happy to see your uncle's long period of mourning ended, wouldn't you?"

"Of course, I would. But I do not believe you have this proof, and until I do— Look, Donovan. We both know why you came here. To spare my uncle the pain of going through this again, I'm willing to pay you to take your little *puta* out of here before my uncle sees her and is hurt again."

"How much?" Clay bit out harshly, wanting to bury his fist in the middle of that grinning face. "How much is it worth to you?"

"I believe the last impostor settled for five thousand dollars."

"Only five thousand?"

"But in this case—since she looks so much more like my aunt than the others—I am willing to make it ten. It is worth the price so that my uncle will not suffer any more than he has."

"How commendable of you."

"So do we have a bargain? Ten thousand dollars and you are gone before my uncle returns."

"I don't think so, Delgado. I just wondered how scared you were. And now I know. Ten thousand dollars is a bunch of money, isn't it?"

"*Sí!* My uncle's happiness and well-being are worth a great deal to me. Perhaps even as much as fifteen thousand dollars." He put taunting emphasis on each syllable of the exorbitant amount. "Are you certain you do not wish to reconsider your refusal?"

"Fifteen thousand, huh?" Clay smiled, thinking how he'd hate to get into a poker game with Antonio Delgado. "That's a hellova lot of happiness and well-being. But I believe we'll have to turn it down, too. Because, you see, I'm also interested in your uncle's happiness. And I'm certain finding his daughter after fifteen years will make him happier than having you send her away before he has a chance to see her."

"What do you say to that, Miss— Uh—what name do you go by?" Antonio said.

"My name is Gentle Fawn," she answered, sitting down on the couch beside Clay and studying Antonio Delgado's handsome face.

"I forgot to mention that Gentle Fawn was raised by the Oglala Sioux Indians," Clay said, pleased that something had finally wiped that cocky look off Delgado's face, even for the briefest instant. "She was adopted by them fifteen years ago, when she was three," he added, knowing that Antonio would see the similarities between that and the time Camila disappeared.

"Well, uh, Gentle Fawn," Antonio said, gathering his composure once more. "Do you understand how much money your friend—or is he something else to you?—has turned down in your behalf?"

"Clay Donovan is my—"

"Friend," Clay interjected.

"Friend," Gentle Fawn continued. "And I do not

370

know how much money fifteen thousand dollars is. But it does not matter because I have no use for money."

"Then why are you here, little 'cousin'?" Antonio asked derisively, leaning forward and resting his elbows on his knees. He looked for all the world as if he were fascinated by her words.

"Because I would like to know my real parents. Clay believes the Delgados are those people, so I must meet them to know for certain."

"But I thought you had proof," Antonio baited.

"There is the—"

"Proof that we will show to your uncle when he returns," Clay interrupted. "In the meantime—"

"Antonio, is it true?" an excited female voice asked as a young woman rounded the corner of the entry to the room. "Oh, excuse me," she said, startled to find her brother entertaining.

"Come in, Anita," Antonio said, standing up along with Clay and Matt. "Gentlemen, this is my younger sister, who has yet to learn how to enter a room like a lady. Anita, this is Clay Donovan and Matt Gramm. And I'll wager you can tell by looking at her who the young lady is supposed to be."

"Pleased to meet you, Miss—uh—Señorita Anit—uh—Delgado," Matt said, obviously enraptured by the dark-haired beauty.

Anita looked up at the large stuttering man and smiled, her smile almost identical to her brother's, yet warm and sincere where his was cold and hollow. "I didn't mean to interrupt, but when Nana told me about our special guest, I forgot my manners. Please forgive me."

"There's nothin' to forgive, ma'am," Matt said, his face breaking into a rosy blush.

371

Tearing her gaze away from Matt Gramm, Anita looked at Gentle Fawn and smiled.

"She goes by the name of Gentle Fawn," Antonio said. "They say she's been with the Sioux for the last fifteen years and that they have proof she's Camila. Though they've yet to produce that proof," he added derisively.

"Don't pay any attention to Antonio," Anita said to Gentle Fawn. "He's just overly protective of our uncle. He's certain everyone is out to take advantage of his sorrow."

"Anita, I will not have you taking sides against me."

"Oh, pooh. I'm not taking sides. It's just that you assume everyone is lying before they even have a chance to tell you the truth."

"And you believe every beggar who comes to the door with a pitiful story."

"We are not beggars, Mr. Delgado!" Gentle Fawn said indignantly, concentrating her scorching glare on Antonio. "Clay Donovan is a very famous and successful man who has no need of your money—or your uncle's money. And I have no use for your money either."

"Oh, you speak English. It will be so wonderful to have a woman my age to talk to."

"Anita!"

"Come with me, Gentle Fawn," she said, shooting her brother a quelling look. "Let's leave the men to discuss whatever it is they have to discuss. You must be exhausted. I'll have Nana arrange a room for you so you can freshen up, perhaps even take a nap if you like." She drew Gentle Fawn to her feet.

Gentle Fawn hesitated and looked back at Clay. He nodded his head and she let herself be led away. "We'll see you gentlemen at dinner," Anita said to them at the

372

door, though her eyes stayed leveled on Matt Gramm.
"Our uncle should be home by then."

"Now, tell me all about yourself," she said to Gentle
Fawn once they were in a bedroom at the end of a long
hall. "How long have you known Señor Gramm?"

Gentle Fawn smiled. She liked Anita Delgado already
and found herself liking the idea of having her for a
cousin. "I only met him yesterday, but he is very nice.
Clay says he is a good and honest man."

"And a very handsome man," Anita added mischievously.

"Yes, very handsome. Almost as handsome as Clay
Donovan."

"Aha! So that's the way it is! I must admit I'm glad to
hear it isn't Matt you have your eyes on!" The Spanish
girl winked at Gentle Fawn. "Do you know if he's
married?"

"'Aha! So that's the way it is!'" Gentle Fawn
mimicked her, returning Anita's wink. "No, I do not
think Matt Gramm is married." Both girls burst into
giggles.

Anita threw her arms around Gentle Fawn and hugged
her. "Oh, Gentle Fawn, I hope you do turn out to be my
cousin. We could have so much fun together!"

A wave of sadness washed over Gentle Fawn. What if
she was indeed Camila Delgado? Would she be able to
adjust to this strange place of Texas, never to roam free
with the Lakotas again? And if she wasn't the missing
daughter of Manuel Delgado, would she be able to forgive
herself for hurting Anita, or for causing further pain and
sorrow to a man who had already suffered gravely? Either
way, she could see that she'd made a mistake by coming.
She should never have given in to her curiosity.

"I am quite tired, Anita," she said, suddenly aware that it was the truth. "Do you suppose I could lie down for a few minutes? We only arrived by stagecoach from Cheyenne yesterday, and I am afraid I have not recovered from the trip as completely as I had thought."

"Oh, of course. I'll get you a robe to sleep in and have one of the servants press your suit while you rest. Would you like for me to order a bath for you before dinner?"

"I would like that," Gentle Fawn said. "Thank you."

"Then consider it done!" Anita crossed to the door. "I'll be back in a minute."

"Anita?" Gentle Fawn called out to the friendly young woman. "Why are you being so kind to me?"

Anita looked puzzled for a minute, then laughed. "I told you I like the idea of having someone my age to talk to."

"But your brother is convinced I am an impostor— like the others."

"The others were such obvious frauds, that no one would have believed them. But you—" Anita stopped speaking and studied Gentle Fawn. "Something about you is different. Perhaps it's because you look so much like your . . . uh . . . Camila's mother, Francisca. There's a portrait in the *sala*— I believe the English word is parlor. I'll show it to you after dinner. Besides, you just don't look like a schemer to me. Or maybe I'm just so lonesome for company that I'm willing to give you the benefit of the doubt."

"Thank you, Anita. I will value the fact that you gave me 'the benefit of the doubt.' You are very kind and it would please me greatly to know that we were related."

"Well, let me get that robe and we'll talk more later."

Chapter Twenty-Three

"I think she's genuine," Anita said to her brother as they stood beneath the large portrait of Francisca Delgado in the main hall of their splendid home.

"Did she tell you what the supposed proof of her identity is?" Antonio asked anxiously.

"No," Anita said, thoughtfully studying the smiling portrait that hung above the ornately carved oak mantel. "She really was beautiful, wasn't she?"

"Who?" Antonio asked, following his sister's gaze up to the portrait. "Oh, yes. Beautiful."

"I wish I had known her when she was happy like she is in the portrait," Anita said wistfully.

"Well, you didn't. Now stop this foolishness and tell me why you think that girl is different than the others," he said impatiently.

"All you have to do is look at her. She looks exactly like Aunt Francisca, even down to the smile and the way she tilts her head. All but the eyes. The eyes are definitely Uncle Manuel's."

"Bah! Looking alike isn't enough. I want tangible proof."

"Tell me the story of Francisca's locket again Antonio," she said, studying the gold necklace gleaming on the bosom of the young woman in the portrait.

Antonio sighed irritably. "I've told you. He had it made and engraved to give to her on their wedding day. He designed it himself. That's all there is to tell."

"You forgot to say that there was only one made and that it disappeared the day our cousin did. Francisca always wore it but she wasn't wearing it when they found her."

"Why should I tell you that when you know the story as well as I do?"

"It's really very romantic, isn't it?"

"Why are we talking about this now? We need to decide what we're going to do about that girl and her friends."

"The first thing, my dear brother, would be to start looking at her differently and calling her by her given name—Camila."

"I refuse to do that until our uncle does!"

"She has the locket, Antonio," Anita said, dropping her discovery on him with deadly accuracy.

His black eyes widened in shock. "What did you say?"

"The girl you believe to be an impostor—and I believe to be our cousin—has Francisca's missing locket."

"How do you know that? You must be mistaken."

Anita noticed the way her brother's suave facade seemed to melt away as beads of perspiration popped out on his forehead. Only two years older than she, he had taken his position as head of their family too seriously; and she found great pleasure in pointing out that he wasn't always right. "I saw it around her neck when she took off her clothes to rest," she announced casually.

"So, big brother, what do you say to that?"

"I say you're imagining things! It couldn't be the same locket."

"Oh, but it is, *mi hermano!* It is exactly the same! So you had better get used to the idea of having her here permanently; and you can begin by not being so rude to her or to her companions." Her tone was smug as she turned and walked away from Antonio.

"You little fool!" he hissed, grabbing her arm and whirling her around to face him. "Don't you see what this means? It means we will no longer be our uncle's heirs! He will throw us out."

"He wouldn't do that, Antonio. And you know it. I thought you wanted him to be happy!"

"I do, Anita," he said silkily, giving his sister his most charming smile. "But I am still not convinced that these people are what they say they are. You must get me the locket so I can decide if it is the real thing or an imitation before our uncle sees it and is hurt even more than he has been."

"I can't."

"Do you want to see him hurt if this whole thing is a clever ruse?" he baited her.

"No, you know I don't. I love him as though he were my own father."

"That's another reason we must be *totally* certain before we accept her as our cousin. How do you like the idea of being replaced in his affections by a *fraud?*"

"But how can I get it? I don't think she'll take it off."

"You'd best think of something!" His voice was an obvious threat.

"Ah, here you are, my children," Manuel Delgado called out, crossing the *sala* with easy strides, a happy smile on his distinguished, tanned face.

"Oh, *tio*, I'm so glad to see you," Anita cried, rushing to the man, who was not much taller than she, and throwing her arms around him.

"Well, now, that's the way a man likes to be greeted after a long day out on the range," he chuckled happily, embracing his niece warmly before setting her away from him. "But until I bathe and change out of these dirty clothes, you may prefer to say hello to me from across the room, *mi cara!*"

"We have guests for dinner, *tio*," Antonio said, his expression tense. "And I must talk to you before you meet them."

"Such a serious face, Antonio. But whatever it is you wish to discuss, it must wait until after I change!"

"Of course, *tio*," Antonio said, the smile on his face worried.

The brother and sister watched as their uncle strode across the polished wood floor to the hallway leading to the bedrooms. When he was out of sight, Antonio turned to her, his smile now an angry scowl. "I want that locket, Anita! If you love him as you proclaim and wish to protect him from another disappointment, you will think of a way to get it for me!"

"I know you love him and don't want to see him hurt, or you would never ask me to do such a thing, Antonio. So I will think about what you ask. But I can't promise you that I'm willing to steal for you," Anita said, her shoulders slumping visibly as she, too, went to change for dinner.

An hour later, wearing her freshly pressed riding outfit and feeling revived by a refreshing bath and pleasant nap, Gentle Fawn entered the main living room, the one Anita

378

had called the *sala*. Realizing she must be the first to arrive for dinner, she wandered around the room, idly absorbing everything about it.

Decorated much like the study where they had been earlier, the *sala* was at the center of the house with all the other rooms and hallways opening off this one. Large and long, it was filled with massive furniture of dark oak and leather. Again, its plain stuccoed walls were decorated with colorful blankets and serapes, and there were big furry pillows of cowhide thrown on the leather couch. A piano took up one corner, but since Gentle Fawn had never seen one and didn't realize it made music, she paid no particular attention to it.

Sitting down on the couch, she picked up one of the pillows and rubbed her hand absently over the brown and white hide.

Suddenly, she felt as though she was not alone. Chills shimmied up her spine and along her arms. Certain someone was watching her, she looked around. But no one was there.

Then she saw it. The portrait of Francisca Delgado looking down at her from her gilded frame over the mantel. Fascinated by the face in the picture, she stood and walked closer. The eyes seemed to follow her. Was this her mother? Was it possible? She moved to the side to examine Francisca from a different angle. Again the eyes followed her. It was as though the woman in the portrait was as curious about Gentle Fawn as Gentle Fawn was about her.

"*Mamá?*" she whispered, unaware that she had spoken aloud and in Spanish. "Is that really you?" she asked, gazing into the black eyes that watched her warmly.

As if in answer to her question, the portrait seemed to

379

force Gentle Fawn's gaze to a flash of gold. There, resting on the pale white skin above the low neckline of Francisca's yellow dress, every detail depicted perfectly, was Gentle Fawn's locket.

Reacting automatically, Gentle Fawn clutched at her blouse to feel the security of her own locket. Panic exploded through her. She wasn't wearing it.

Then, laughing breathlessly at herself, she remembered what had happened. She had taken it off to bathe and had simply forgotten to put it on again. She cast an apologetic smile at the portrait as if to say, *Please excuse my stupidity. I will be right back to show you the locket.*

She hurried to the room where she had bathed and napped. Just as she reached out to open the door, it opened for her to reveal the old woman, Nana, who had been so upset earlier. Gentle Fawn and Nana both jumped back and gasped aloud at the sight of the other.

"Oh, I did not mean to frighten you," Gentle Fawn apologized, her nervous voice anxious. "I forgot something in the room."

Nana, her sagging bosom heaving, didn't respond. Instead, her feet seeming frozen to the ground, she continued to stare silently at the girl.

"May I pass?" Gentle Fawn finally asked, suddenly feeling uneasy under the woman's awe.

Nana looked back at the room and then to Gentle Fawn and nodded her head. *"Sí, señorita,"* she said, suddenly returning to life. Carrying her bundle of dirty linens, she scurried down the hall and was immediately out of sight.

Smiling after the strangely behaving woman, Gentle Fawn entered the room and went directly to the dressing table where she had left her necklace.

When she looked at the top of the vanity and saw that

the locket was no longer there, her first inclination was to panic. But she was able to gain control over her rapidly beating heart and frantic thoughts. The room obviously had been cleaned and the bed changed since she'd left. Evidently, that was why Nana had been there.

The old woman must have moved it, she soothed herself, turning in a slow circle, her eyes roving over every piece of furniture. When she had completed her turn and still hadn't spotted the necklace, a ripple of premonition scurried through her. The thought that she wasn't going to find the locket at all pounded in her head.

"It must be here somewhere," she said aloud, in an attempt to drown out the doubts that were multiplying in her head.

She yanked the two drawers open on one side of the vanity. *Nothing.*

The one in the center below the dropped section. *Not in there either.*

The top drawer on the other side. *Empty!*

She took a deep breath and held it, preparing to open the last drawer of the oak dressing table.

With a desperate jerk on the iron pull, she checked the final drawer.

"It has got to be here!" she said, slamming the empty drawer and dropping to her hands and knees to search the braid-rug-covered floor. "Why would someone take my locket?" she mumbled to herself as she crawled over every inch of the floor, patting under and behind each piece of furniture with frenetic urgency, her panic building with each tick of the clock. "It cannot be gone," she whimpered.

A knock on the door broke her concentration. "Who is it?" she cried out, her voice trembling.

"It's Anita."

"Come in, Anita."

"Nana said you had gone into the *sala* and that she was going to straighten the room. But when I went out, you weren't there. Are you all right?"

"Yes, I am— No, I am not all right, Anita. I cannot find my locket."

Anita's gaze shifted nervously to the side. She was unable to look at Gentle Fawn's unhappy face. "The one you were wearing?" she said, her pretty face sympathetic.

"I took it off to bathe and put it right there." She pointed to the bare vanity. "I forgot to put it back on and was in the main room when I realized what I had done. So I hurried back here and now I cannot find it anywhere!"

"Well, it must be here," Anita said, making a show of looking in the drawers of the vanity. "Perhaps Nana put it somewhere for safekeeping," she suggested with forced optimism.

"I have looked in all the drawers, on the floor, under and behind everything. I tell you it is gone."

"It couldn't just walk away. We'll ask Nana. Maybe while she was cleaning in here she put it in her pocket to return to you when she saw you."

"She saw me and said nothing about having my locket. She was leaving the room just as I returned."

"It must have slipped her mind. I don't think she's really recovered from the shock of your resemblance to my Aunt Francisca. Nana was her nurse from the time she was a small baby, and she was Camila's nurse, too. Come along, we'll ask her. She'll know where your locket it. I'm sure there's a simple explanation."

Taking another dismayed glance around the room, Gentle Fawn followed Anita into the hallway. She had no doubt that someone had deliberately removed her locket from the room. And it wasn't to keep it safe for her! Of that she was quite certain.

But why? Why would someone steal her locket when it was obvious this house was filled with things of much greater value? No one who lived in the luxury of the Delgado household would be tempted by the small amount of gold in her locket. There had to be another reason!

Could it be because someone had recognized it as the same locket in the portrait and wanted to stop her from returning it to Manuel Delgado? But who? Anita? She'd been the only one to see her wearing the locket.

Gentle Fawn studied the young woman who walked beside her. Why would she take it? Why would she want to destroy the one tangible thing that could possibly link her to the Delgado family? *It could not be Anita,* she told herself. *She was too happy for me to be here.*

Then who? Nana? *She had plenty of time to pocket it. She's the obvious person to suspect. She must have gone into the room not long after I went into the sala.*

But somehow Gentle Fawn couldn't bring herself to believe the old woman was a thief. It had to be someone else.

But who else even knew about the locket? Not Antonio. She had worn it beneath her blouse so he couldn't have seen it. But he had certainly made it plain that he would be pleased to see her gone. *And he was so insistent on seeing Clay's proof. Would he have come into my room on the chance he could find something to destroy my story? Of course he would have recognized the locket and picked it up! But why would he take it if it could prove I was truly Camila? Wouldn't he be pleased to find that I am real and not a fraud? If the locket proves anything, wouldn't he*

*be happy to learn that his uncle was not going to be hurt
again? Unless, it is not his uncle he is worried about at all!*

"Gentle Fawn," Anita said, her concern evident in her
voice. "Did you hear what I said?"

"What?" Gentle Fawn asked, giving her head a little
shake and looking at Anita as though she were seeing her
for the first time. Disoriented, she blinked her eyes and
looked around her. They were standing in the doorway
leading into the *sala*. "I am sorry! My mind must have
wandered. What did you say?"

"I said we'll have to ask Nana about your locket after
dinner. Everyone is already waiting for us to go into the
dining room."

Gentle Fawn's heart leapt in her chest. By "everyone,"
did Anita mean Manuel Delgado, too? Was she about to
meet the man who, if she believed Clay's conviction, was
her natural father? Her fists clenched at her sides, she
closed her eyes and sucked in a deep breath, attempting
to force the possibility that she was Camila Delgado from
her mind. But the strange, yet familiar word *papá* kept
pounding over and over in her mind. *Papá . . . Papá . . .
Papá.*

Her gaze darted excitedly to the three men who stood
at the opposite end of the *sala*. Of course, she recognized
Clay and Matt immediately. But who was the other man,
the one with his back to her? He couldn't be Antonio
because he was of shorter stature than the young
Spaniard, so he had to be someone she didn't know.
Could it be *him?* Could it be her father?

Unaware of the two women in the archway, Clay and
Matt were listening to Manuel Delgado expound on his
ideas for improving the profits of the Texas cattlemen,
while improving employment problems at the same time.

"As it is now, we must transport our beef on the hoof.

At great expense, I might add. Because it's not butchered until it reaches its point of destination, the quality of our beef diminishes the farther from Texas it goes. Not only do the cattle lose weight during the shipping process, seriously lowering their per pound worth, but the main profit goes to middlemen butchers like Philip Armour and Gustavus Swift up in Chicago. I plan on bringing that profit back to Texas where it rightfully belongs.

"I'd like to establish slaughtering and meat-dressing plants within the state, then ship the meat in special railcars to cities all over the country. With ranchers receiving better prices for their cattle and the slaughter houses creating more jobs for men, all of Texas will profit!"

"But isn't there a problem with shipping butchered meat long distances, Senator?" Clay asked.

"I've been experimenting with slaughtering some of Rancho Camila's beef here on the ranch and then packing and shipping it in sawdust and ice. But unfortunately, up till now, every attempt has failed because the ice melted too quickly and the meat spoiled.

"However, I'm still optimistic and don't intend to give up. Recently I've recieved reports of a new refrigerated railcar that was introduced in May at the Centennial Exposition in Philadelphia."

"I've read about that," Clay said. "I hope it turns out to be the answer!"

"What a pleasant surprise to have my entrance graced by such lovely ladies," Antonio Delgado said, coming up behind the two who hesitated in the arched doorway. Stepping between the young women, he offered each of them a crooked arm. His brows raised inquiringly, his mouth curved in an expectant smile, he spoke to Anita, "Is everything all right, *mi hermana poco?*"

Anita's mouth spread into a tight-lipped smile. "*Sí, mi hermano*," she returned bitterly through her teeth. Refusing her brother's offered arm with disdain, she shrugged her shoulders and swept into the room ahead of them, leaving Gentle Fawn alone with Antonio.

"Well, my dear, that leaves the two of us," Antonio said to Gentle Fawn, placing his warm hand over hers at his elbow.

"I suppose it does," Gentle Fawn returned, resenting the way his eyes traveled over her face and breasts as he spoke to her. It took every bit of resolve she could muster not to show her disgust at his touch.

"I must admit I'm very pleased to have this moment alone with you."

For a brief instant, she was tempted to jerk her hand away from his arm and yell out to everyone in the room that this smiling man was a thief. He probably had the locket in his coat pocket right that minute. But she couldn't insist on having him searched without reason. And no one would consider her instincts as justification. She would have to have the proof first. However, when she got her locket back and had her proof, she promised herself that she would expose Antonio Delgado for what he was.

She glanced up at Antonio and honored him with a flirting grin, then looked away coyly. "Why, señor, I do believe you are teasing me. I could have sworn you did not like me."

Taken back by the girl's directness, Antonio faltered slightly. "Yes, well, uh, I'm sorry you got that impression. I was terribly rude this afternoon. It is just that I love my uncle very much and do not want to see him hurt."

"Of course, I understand."

Gentle Fawn's smile did not quite reach her black assessing eyes, but Antonio Delgado was unaware of the deadly anger that lurked deep in their cool recesses. He was too enthralled by her beauty to suspect what was going on behind the inky pools.

When Anita joined them, coming to stand between her uncle and Matt, Clay immediately looked past Manuel for Gentle Fawn. Seeing her with Antonio in the archway, his gaze was drawn to her small hand on the man's arm.

An unexpected stab of jealousy tore through him, and the muscles of his body knotted angrily. His brow creased, he took a step to relieve her of the company of the oily Spaniard who dared to touch her. Then he saw her smile up at the man, and he froze. *How could she like that sneaky son of a bitch?*

Furious at the way the two were gazing into each other's eyes, Clay tried to return his attention to what Manuel was saying. But it was impossible. His own eyes kept returning to the scene behind the senator. *Look at her smiling at him,* he thought with disgust.

Then he recognized something in her smile. Something he should have seen right away. Hadn't he been on the receiving end of that same smile more than once? When they had first met, when her only desire was to see him dead, she had smiled at him in exactly the same way. *Hell, she doesn't like that bastard. She sees right through him. She's setting him up, and the poor sap doesn't even know he's being prepared for the kill!*

Unable to take his eyes away from the handsome dark-haired couple as they approached the group, Clay almost felt sorry for the unsuspecting Antonio Delgado— almost, but not quite. After all, the man had been unforgivably rude to them when they first arrived. He deserved whatever he got for calling her a fraud.

Gentle Fawn turned toward him, and blue eyes locked with black as Clay and Gentle Fawn embraced without touching across the space that separated them. "I wondered when you would join us," he said, basking in the warmth of the smile she reserved for him.

"I beg your pardon?" Manuel said, looking first at Clay and then turning to determine what held the younger man's attention.

Manuel's eyes, so much like Gentle Fawn's, opened wide, and he inhaled sharply as he viewed the young woman on his nephew's arm. His mouth began to quiver as though he was trying to speak. But no sound came forth.

Gentle Fawn, likewise, was instantly struck speechless by the sight of the man she'd come here to meet. It was as though time had stopped and the two of them were alone in the room. The only person she could see was Manuel Delgado, the man in the picture in her locket come to life. His waistline a little thicker, his black hair showing strands of gray at his temples, and his face permanently lined by the nineteen years of living since the picture was taken, he was still the way she remembered him and she knew she would have recognized him anywhere.

Papá, a voice in her mind said.

"Who are you?" Manuel rasped, his accusing words barely audible.

"*Tío,* I tried to talk to you about the purpose for our guests' visit," Antonio interjected nervously. "They arrived quite unexpectedly and wouldn't leave until they spoke with you."

Manuel looked at his nephew as though just realizing the girl was not alone. "Who is she?"

Clay stepped forward. "I'm sorry to spring this on you like this, sir. I was certain your nephew would have prepared you."

Manuel looked at Clay, the look in his eyes hard as coal. "What is the meaning of this? Who is this young woman and what is she doing in my home?"

"*Tio*, look at her," Anita insisted. "Can't you see who she is?"

"I see nothing but a very clever imitation of my wife. Am I supposed to accept you as my daughter, girl? Is that what you expect me to believe? Simply because you happen to *look* like my wife?"

The expression on Gentle Fawn's face changed from awe to pain, as though she'd seen a glimpse of heaven and then had it snatched from her sight. "I do not expect you to believe anything, Señor Delgado," she said evenly, her shoulders straightening perceptibly and her head held high. "I know now that you could not possibly be *mi padre*, for he would not be afraid to examine all the facts before he claimed to know the truth!"

Clay and Matt exchanged startled glances at Gentle Fawn's use of the Spanish word for father. Was that another coincidence, or could she possibly remember a few Spanish words?

"Gentle Fawn, show him the locket!"

Her eyes brimming with tears she said, "The locket is gone, Clay." Even more than her disappointment for the way Manuel Delgado had reacted to her presence she ached for the fact that she had let Clay down.

"Gone? What are you talking about?"

"Locket? What locket?" Manuel said at the same time Clay spoke.

Anita intervened, unable to stand seeing Gentle Fawn so distressed. "She has a gold locket that she left in her room for a few minutes, and it was gone when she returned. She's very upset by its loss." Anita directed her words at her brother, not bothering to hide the fact that she blamed him for the lost locket and the girl's unhappiness.

"A guest of ours robbed?" Antonio said indignantly. "This is terrible. Have you spoken to the servants?"

"I do not believe a servant took the locket," Gentle Fawn said purposefully. "I believe it was taken by someone who had much to lose if I could prove I was Camila Delgado."

"Why are you looking at me? Are you accusing *me* of taking your locket?" Antonio raged. "I've never even seen your locket! Why would I take it?"

"I was not accusing you of anything. Besides, it does not matter. I was hoping to return the locket to its owner, but he was not willing to hear me out before he accused me of lying. So where it is makes no difference to me. I am returning to the Lakotas where I belong! No matter what color my skin! And no matter how many 'coincidences' say I belong anywhere else! Now, more than ever, I do not want to be part of this white world of yours where people lie and steal from others while pretending to be friendly, and where they do not wait to hear what a person has to say before accusing them of lying!"

She turned and ran toward the front door, determined to escape. "I will wait for you outside, Clay!"

"Will someone please tell me what's going on? What locket? Who is this girl?" Manuel Delgado shouted.

"You fool!" Clay bit out spitefully. "Don't you realize that was your *daughter* you just chased out of here with your warm welcome! Can't you see that she's Camila Delgado?"

Chapter Twenty-Four

"What's the meaning of this, Donovan?" Manuel Delgado roared. "I thought you were planning to do a story on my bid for the governorship of Texas!"

His nostrils flaring, Clay set his gaze on the elder Delgado. "I was, Senator! But now you and your political career can go straight to hell. I'm sure not going to help anyone get elected who's such a sorry sonovabitch he could turn his back on his own kid who's been missing for fifteen years."

Manuel blustered at the younger man's accusation, but Clay went on.

"You bastard! What you did to her is inexcusable. It was hard enough for me to get her to come here, as it was. She didn't want to believe she was your daughter. In spite of all the evidence to the contrary. But she came because she thought she might be able to end your sorrow if it were true. Not for herself, mind you. She was happy where she was. But for you!"

"I don't need to stand here and listen to this!" Manuel turned as if to leave.

"That's right! Run away! But you can't change the truth. Running away won't change the fact that the moment you've supposedly hoped and prayed for the last fifteen years has finally occurred. And you didn't even have the intelligence to recognize the real thing when you saw it. Does it make you feel happy, Senator, to know that you've insured that your daughter is truly dead to you and that you'll never see her again? I hope so, because that's what you've done.

"I'm certain it pleases your nephew," Clay added, wheeling on Antonio and catching the younger man off guard before he had time to remove the smug grin from his face.

"How dare you suggest that it makes me happy to see my uncle hurt? I tried to protect him from this!"

"I dare what I damn well please, pal. I also suggest that it was you who stole her locket!"

Anita and Antonio exchanged nervous glances.

Manuel's face was livid with rage. "Now you have overstepped your bounds, Mr. Donovan! Why would my nephew steal that young woman's locket?"

"Because it was *that* locket!" Clay shouted, his face contorted with rage as he pointed to the portrait of Francisca Delgado over the fireplace, which continued to smile pleasantly down on the arguing people. "How do you think we traced her to you?"

"Francisca's locket?" Manuel whispered, his stare frozen on his wife's portrait.

"This is too bizarre for words!" Antonio hissed. "Are we supposed to believe you have the locket that could prove that young woman to be my *tio's* daughter?"

"Evidently I don't have it now—since it seems to have conveniently disappeared from her room." Clay's tone

392

was an accusation.

"Don't you mean how convenient for *you* that it disappeared before we could see it and prove that it was a counterfeit. Or was there really a locket in the first place? Who ever saw this locket besides yourself? I know I didn't!"

"Anita saw it!" Matt said, unable to resist joining the verbal fracas any longer.

"Is that true, Anita? Did you see the locket? And is it the same as my wife's missing locket?"

Anita's edgy glance darted from her uncle, to Matt, to her brother, the expression on her face trapped.

"Yes, tell us, little sister. Was it the same locket?"

"I did see Gentle Fawn wearing a gold locket," she started hesitantly, her eyes now on Matt. He was so handsome and she so wanted to please him. "It was . . ."

Out of the corner of her eye she saw her brother tense, reminding her where her loyalties had to remain. No matter how wrong he had been to take the locket, he'd been trying to protect their uncle and she couldn't betray him. "But I didn't really get more than a glimpse of it." Her words came in a hurried rush.

She was certain everyone in the room could hear the relieved expulsion of Antonio's breath, but no one seemed to notice. Her dark eyes darted guiltily from her brother's perspiring brow to Matt. "I'm sorry, but I can't tell you what it actually looked like."

"But I can." Clay's voice was cold and dangerous. If he'd had any idea how unwelcome Gentle Fawn would be in her own home, he never would have brought her here. "It is exactly like the one in the portrait—down to the last scroll and flower."

"It could just be a clever copy," Antonio suggested,

his confidence returning now that he knew his sister was not going to give him away. "Hundreds of people have seen that portrait over the years, people who know the locket disappeared the same day as my poor little cousin!"

"And do all of those people know what words were engraved on the back of the locket, Senator?" Clay asked, not bothering to hide his dislike for Antonio Delgado.

"What words?" Antonio asked haughtily.

"'Francisca, *mi querida*, Manuel, 1857.' Isn't that what you had engraved on the back of the locket to give your wife on your wedding day, Senator Delgado?"

Manuel, who was about forty years old, seemed to age before Clay's eyes, and he knew he had struck a nerve. But he couldn't stop now. When the man didn't acknowledge his words, Clay went on.

"Not conclusive enough for you, sir? What if I could tell you what pictures were inside the locket? Would that be enough to convince you? No? How about if I were to tell you what is written on the back of those pictures?"

"Stop!" Manuel ordered savagely. "What kind of deception is this? Are my political rivals responsible for sending you here? What do you want from me?"

Clay smiled sadly, unable to help feeling sorry for the man. If he was unable to look at Gentle Fawn and not see who she was, then he deserved to spend the rest of his life without knowing her. "No one sent me here, Senator Delgado. And I want nothing from you. I thought I was doing something that would make you happy. But I can see now that I was wrong—all the way around. Please forgive me for disrupting your dinner. We won't bother you again!" He turned away from the stunned group. "No need to see me out. I can find my own way."

The remaining four people watched as he strode across the *sala* and disappeared into the vestibule. No one spoke. Clay Donovan had given them too much to think about."

"Well . . . uh . . . I guess I'd better be leavin', too," Matt said, his eyes on Anita and making no secret of the fact that he would have liked to stay and spend more time with her.

"Must you?" she asked, laying a small hand on his arm.

"They'll be needin' someone to guide them back to town," he said huskily.

"Uncle Manuel! You're not going to let them leave like this, are you? It's already dark and it's several hours to San Antonio!"

"I didn't tell them to leave."

"If you'll forgive me for sayin' so, Senator, you might as well have. Good evenin', Miss Anita. It's been a real pleasure meetin' you." Matt started to leave.

Anita shot her uncle a beseeching gaze, then hurried to catch up with Matt. "Wait, Señor Gramm, I'll walk with you."

"I'd like that, ma'am."

"If you promise never to call me ma'am again!" she teased, placing her hand on his arm.

"I guess I can make that promise, Miss Anita, if you'll stop calling me Señor Gramm and start callin' me Matt." He smiled down at the girl on his arm, his eyes drinking in her loveliness.

"Not Miss Anita either. Just Anita . . . Matt."

"Anita—that's a real nice name."

*   *   *

Clay found Gentle Fawn sitting on an iron bench that encircled a large oak tree. Though her eyes were dry, he could tell she'd been crying, and her cheeks were still damp from the recently shed tears. He sat down beside her and gathered her to him. "I'm so sorry, honey. I had no idea it would be so bad. I really thought it would turn out differently."

Leaning her head against Clay's strong chest, Gentle Fawn wrapped her arms around his waist and clung to him as though she would never let go. "I told you I was not the Delgados' daughter and that they would not want me, Clay. I told you."

"I know you did, sweetheart. I know you did." Tightening his hold around her shoulders, he rocked her. "But don't you see? You are his daughter. Because he's too stupid not to realize it doesn't change a damn thing."

"I want to go back to the People, Clay. I do not want to stay here anymore."

Clay noticed she didn't deny that she was Camila Delgado, and that she referred to the Lakotas as "*the* People," not *her* people. "Oh, baby, what have I done to you? I wanted you to have so much, and now I've left you with nothing. Will you ever forgive me?"

"There is nothing to forgive, Clay. Once I knew what the pictures in the locket meant, I had to come. I had to know the truth. And even if they don't want me, I had to know that, too. It is just that . . ." She buried her face against his shirt.

"Don't cry, honey. Please don't cry," Clay begged, his own eyes filling with tears.

"It is just that I did not know it would hurt so much. When I saw my fath— I mean when I saw—him—he looked just as I knew he would, just as I remembered.

And for a moment, only the briefest moment, I believed he was truly my father. And I thought my heart would burst with love for him."

"Don't think about it, sweetheart. He doesn't deserve your love." Now the tears were coursing freely over his own cheeks.

"In that instant when I believed he was my father, when I loved him and felt as if I belonged to him, I wanted to run to him and hold him in my arms. Then he looked at me with those cold black eyes, and I felt his hatred. And something inside me broke, Clay."

"If only I could change everything back to the way it was!"

Gentle Fawn lifted her head and looked into his glistening blue eyes. She took his face between her palms and brushed her thumbs over his wet cheeks. She smiled. "Once I heard you say, 'There is no use crying over spilt milk.' Is that what we are doing now?"

Clay hesitated, then broke into a rich laugh and tightened his hug. "I believe that's exactly what we're doing, Miss Pris! But no more! We're going back in there and force Manuel Delgado to face the truth! I'm not going to let your cousin run you out of your home and usurp your rightful place in that home."

"No! He does not want me, and I do not want to be where I am not wanted and where people call me a liar!"

"Fine. But first we're going to show the Delgados that you're not a liar. Then if you want to, we'll leave. But not before!"

"I do not know . . ."

"Since when does the Gentle Fawn I know run from a fight?"

Releasing her desperate hold on Clay, Gentle Fawn

straightened and said, "Never. I have never run from a fight and I will not start now!"

"Good girl," Clay shouted, standing and drawing her to her feet. "Now wipe that pretty face on this hanky," he said, handing her a bandanna, "and let's go in there and let those people know what happens to folks who insult an Irishman and his best girl!"

"Am I? Am I your best girl?"

"You bet your sweet moccasins you are! Best and only! Now, let's go in there and show 'em our stuff!" He took her hand and started back toward the house.

She knew there was no battle so terrible that she wouldn't be able to face it—as long as Clay Donovan was at her side. "All right, 'let's go in there and show 'em our stuff!'" she mimicked with a teary smile and a sniff.

As they approached the steps to the arcade, they heard the soft murmur of voices.

"I'm sorry we didn't get a chance to know each other better, Mis— I mean, Anita."

"I am, too, Matt."

"Do you think your uncle would mind if I call again sometime?"

"I think my uncle would be pleased to have you call— and so would I," she added shyly, her voice slightly breathless.

"You would?"

"I would. Very much!"

"Well, I don't know when I'll be back in these parts, but you can be sure it won't be long!"

"I hope not, but I do wish you didn't have to go tonight."

"He doesn't!" Clay announced, stomping into the arcade. "Gentle Fawn and I have decided we're going to stay around for a while. Do you suppose you could put us up for a couple of nights?"

"Of course!" Anita squealed, exchanging shy glances with Matt, who was obviously just as pleased as she.

"But what will your uncle say?" Gentle Fawn asked, still not convinced they were making the right choice.

"You just let me take care of *tio!*"

"No, let me do it," Clay suggested. "Tell you what. If you two don't mind, I'm going to leave Gentle Fawn out here with you for a couple of minutes while I go straighten things out with him. Okay?"

"Okay," Matt answered, the fact that he was happy with this turn of events obvious in his wide grin.

"By the way, Matt, old buddy. Do you think you'll be able to find something to do if we stay over a couple of extra days?" Clay said, his face perfectly straight.

"I s'pose I'll manage," Matt returned with a wink and an even wider grin than before. Without thinking about propriety, he draped a muscular arm around Anita's shoulders and squeezed her to his side.

"Somehow, I thought you'd say that, amigo!"

Slamming the heavy front door, Clay crossed the vestibule and *sala* with long angry strides. "I'm glad to see you're still here, Senator! We have something else to discuss!"

"What are you doing back here, Donovan?" Antonio charged loudly, starting to his feet to meet Clay.

"Sit down and shut up, kid! Or I'm going to be forced to put my fist into that pretty face of yours! My business is with your uncle, and if you want to stay and listen, you're going to have to keep your mouth shut!

Is that understood?"

Antonio glanced uncertainly at his uncle, whose nod indicated he would take care of this matter.

Manuel took a sip of wine and leaned back in his chair. "We have nothing further to discuss, Donovan."

"On the contrary, Senator. We have a great deal to discuss," Clay said, stepping to the serving bar and brazenly pouring himself a glass of the same red wine Manuel was drinking. "I have a deal to offer you, a deal I doubt a man of your ambitions will be able to refuse."

Manuel chuckled. "I doubt any 'deal' you have in mind would interest me, Señor Donovan."

"Only a fool would turn down an offer without hearing it first, Senator." Clay sat down on a hard, tufted leather chair directly across from Manuel and took a testing sip of the wine. "Very nice," he said, lazily licking the wine from his lips. "What was I saying? Oh, yes. Only a fool—but then we haven't determined that you aren't one, have we?"

Antonio, his face reddening, leaned forward in his seat and started to speak, the glare in his eyes murderous.

"Antonio, I will take care of Señor Donovan. After all, we would not want it said that Manuel Delgado would not consider any legitimate offer, would we?" He smiled and said silkily, "I will give you five minutes to make this offer of yours."

"I'm willing to go ahead and write an article expounding on your virtues and proclaiming all the wonderful things you will do for Texas—as was my original plan. I'm sure you can imagine what it would do for your bid for governor if the *New York Tribune* were behind you—not to mention all the Texas newspapers who reprint every one of my articles word for word!"

Manuel put his glass down on the table and leaned forward. "Go on."

Clay grinned smugly. The fish was circling the baited hook. "I would only ask one thing in return."

"Yes?"

"I want you to go outside and apologize to Gentle Fawn for your discourteous reception earlier. Then you will invite her to stay at the Rancho Camila for one month so you can get to know her and determine if you are—or are not—her father."

"*Tio!* Don't you see what he's doing?"

"Shut up, Antonio! Or I'll have to ask you to leave!"

"If at the end of the month you're still certain she's not your daughter, I'll take her back to the Sioux, where she's been since they adopted her fifteen years ago. She won't bother you again."

"And the story about my campaign?"

"I'll still write it. No matter what your decision is. At the end of the month I'll mail the story about what a good governor you'll make to my editor at the *Tribune*. So, do we have a deal?" He held out his hand to Manuel.

"Not so fast, young man. What guarantee do I have that you will write a story favorable to my campaign if I decide at the end of her visit that she is not my daughter?"

"Tell you what. I'll write the story and let you read and approve it. Then we'll give it to Captain Gramm, whom we both trust. He'll see that it gets to my editor when the time is up."

"And if I decide my bid for governor can stand on its own, without the backing of the *famous* Clay Donovan and *New York Tribune*? What then?"

Clay's blond brows drew together and his face twisted

into a grimace of regret. "I was hoping we could settle this without things coming to that, Senator. But if you should decide you don't want me to write that particular story and you send your daughter away without giving her a chance, then I will be forced to write a different story about you. I hadn't planned to write about your reunion with your daughter because I wanted to respect your privacy. Besides it reeks of sensationalism. But if you don't take the month I'm offering before you make your final decision, then I will feel it is my duty as a good citizen to inform the voters of Texas that Senator Delgado is a cold-hearted son of a bitch who tossed his own daughter out into the cold! How do you think the voters will take that? Especially after they read about the terrible life she's suffered, living with the Indians all this time."

"No one will believe you. I'll deny everything you say."

Clay laughed. God, he hated this. But it was Gentle Fawn's life he was fighting for and he wasn't going to give in. "Senator, that's one of the benefits of being who I am. People believe what I say because I've never given them reason to doubt me. And they know I never would. My readers trust me. I only print the facts—as I would be in this case. So for the most part your shallow denials would fall on deaf ears."

"This is blackmail."

Clay shrugged his shoulders. "I call it justice, Senator."

Manuel stared at the clever young man thoughtfully. He wanted that favorable story in the *Tribune* so much he could already see it. On the other hand, how did he know he could trust Clay Donovan? He searched his adversary's open face carefully, and knew in that moment that here sat an honest man. An honest man with convictions—and the means to stand behind them. What a rare and powerful combination!

"All right, Donovan. I will accept your offer," Manuel announced, extending his hand to Clay. "I'll give her one month."

"One month," Clay agreed, unable to control his sigh of relief as he clasped Delgado's hand.

"But, *tio* . . ." Antonio started.

Manuel shot him a silencing glare, then looked back to Clay. "But I will insist that you do not refer to this girl as my daughter while she is here."

"Agreed. And I will insist that *everyone* in your household treats her as a welcome guest, and that you, in particular, will spend as much time as possible in her company, getting to know her. Is that understood?"

Manuel grinned at Clay's perception. The shrewd young man had seen right through his plan to make himself scarce during the girl's visit. "Understood."

"Then shall we go and talk to Gentle Fawn and tell her of your invitation?" Clay said, standing and extending his arm in a sweeping gesture, inviting the older man to precede him.

"Have you ever thought of going into politics, Donovan?" Manuel asked as they crossed the large room together. He'd been bested and for some peculiar reason, rather than being angry, he found he was impressed with Clay's cunning. The young writer would make a worthy adversary, and an even more worthy ally.

"No, sir, can't say that I have. I'll leave that to men like you."

Neither of the two men were aware that Antonio

Delgado stood watching after them, the hate in his black eyes deadly.

"The best thing to do would be put the locket back somewhere, so she would think she overlooked it, Antonio," Anita whispered several hours later. They were in her room, where he'd come after the rest of the household was quiet.

"Don't talk like a fool. We need to destroy that locket and make certain no one ever sees it again. As long as our uncle hasn't actually seen it, he won't believe she ever had it," he said, with more confidence than he felt.

He'd seen the way Manuel Delgado had watched the girl when they had come back inside for dinner; and he'd noticed how all through the meal, in spite of his distrust, his uncle had grown more and more interested in her and her story.

"Why?"

"Don't you see, if he believes her, she's in the position to take everything that is due to come to us when our uncle dies. She's here and we can't do anything about that, but we can discredit her at every turn and make sure she has no tangible proof of her identity—not that I believe she is truly our cousin. I'm sure that Donovan came across that locket and just thought up this clever ruse to swindle Uncle Manuel out of his money. But it's up to us to protect him. There's no other way."

"I think you should put the locket back. If she is our cousin, Uncle Manuel won't disinherit us. She wouldn't let him."

"You're so naive, little sister! You're going to be out on the streets without a cent to your name, and you'll

404

still be swearing that the conniving little bitch and her underhanded companion aren't out to steal what's ours! Now, enough talk. Give me the locket.''

Anita looked at her brother, who had his hand extended toward her, palm up. She'd never seen him like this and he frightened her. "I don't have it, Antonio. Don't you?"

"Whose side are you on, Anita? I'm your brother. You have a duty to stand behind me. I'm not just doing this for my self. I'm doing it for the both of us. Now give me the locket!"

"I told you, Antonio, I don't have it. I thought you took it. Didn't you?"

"You know I didn't. Now stop this lying and give it to me!" he snarled.

"I tell you, Antonio, I don't have it."

"You're going to be sorry for this, Anita. I'm going to find that locket, and when I do . . ."

He strode to her dresser and viewed the assortment of cosmetics and jewelry boxes. One by one he began to pick up and open each jar and box on the dresser, dumping the contents on the floor before tossing the containers aside.

"Antonio! Stop!" she whispered, the expression on her face increasingly more frightened. "I don't have it! Why won't you believe me?"

Before she had time to duck, the back of Antonio's hand came flying up to hit her across the cheek, snapping her head back. A numbing pain shot along her spine, and her vision blurred with the impact of the blow. Her knees seemed to fold of their own accord as she sank to the floor among the clothing and jewelry her brother had strewn there.

"It's here. You might as well tell me where!"

"Antonio, why are you doing this to me?" she whimpered, sitting on the floor, cupping her throbbing cheek. "I swear to you I don't have it. Maybe Nana did take it. Or maybe Gentle Fawn just misplaced it."

"Liar!" he cursed, slapping her again, this time causing her to fall flat out on the floor. Crying softly to herself, she didn't speak again.

He began to open drawer after drawer, throwing all the contents on the floor on top of and beside his sister. Next he went to her closet, searching pockets and hat boxes and shoes.

Finally, when he was convinced that he'd left no hiding place unturned, he stooped down beside Anita and clasped her chin hard in his hand. Using his punishing hold to pull her head upward, he shoved his face close to hers and sneered, "You may think you've outwitted me, but don't get too sure of yourself. I'll find that locket. And when I do I'll have the power to destroy both of them. You've chosen the wrong side, little sister, and I won't forget that!"

Chapter Twenty-Five

Startled by a loud thump in the room next to hers, Gentle Fawn's eyes blinked open wide. She stared up at the heavy lace canopy that matched the cream-colored spread on the bed. Telling herself there was nothing peculiar about the noise, she forced her eyes shut, determined to go to sleep this time.

There it is again! she thought, her eyes popping open as she jolted up in the bed. "What is happening in there? It sounds as if someone is throwing things," she mumbled irritably. "How am I supposed to sleep with all that noise?" she muttered to herself, glancing around her own dark room, which seemed to be closing in on her.

Except for those terrible days in Many Coups' camp and the one night in Cheyenne when she and Clay had fought, she had never spent a night alone, and she hated it! Every creaking sound from inside the house and every night sound outside seemed to jar her nerves. She wished Clay was there to hold her until she fell asleep.

It was ridiculous that they couldn't sleep together in the Delgado household because he didn't want the others to think badly of her. What difference did it make to anyone where they slept? It didn't matter to her that the Delgados didn't consider them married. She and Clay were man and wife as far as she was concerned. So why should she have to spend the night alone? Hadn't Clay told the man in Cheyenne that they were married? Hadn't they ignored the dissolving of their marriage after their bargain had ended? Hadn't he said—just tonight— that she was his "only girl"?

Throwing the sheet aside, Gentle Fawn swung her feet off the side of the bed. Feeling with her toes for the top step that led up to the tall bed, she knocked the mosquito netting out of her way and descended the two steps. "Maybe if I take a walk and breathe a little fresh air."

Not bothering with the slippers Anita had lent her, she tiptoed on bare feet to the double doors that led from her room to one of the small connected patios along a wing of bedrooms. Swinging the doors wide, she stepped outside.

Crossing to the waist-high wall that edged the private patio, she peered through the vine-covered iron grillwork into the darkness surrounding the house and greedily drew in deep gulps of the clean-smelling night air.

It was odd how the darkness out here held no threat for her. Yet in the blackness of the bedroom, she had felt frightened, as though once she fell asleep, she would never wake up. Of course, now that she was outside, she realized how foolish her fears were. Still . . .

Spying a couchlike chair that had the seat extended to support a person's outstretched legs, an idea suddenly occurred to her. She would sleep outside on that odd chair!

Feeling better already, she hurried back into her room and snatched the cover and a pillow off the bed, then dashed outside again.

"Can't you sleep?" a deep voice asked in a low whisper, as a broad-shouldered figure suddenly emerged from the shadows of the next patio.

Letting a startled squeak, Gentle Fawn whirled to face the advancing man who let himself through the wrought iron gate into her patio. Her heart beating a punishing tattoo against her rib cage, she clutched the pillow and sheet to her breast.

"Who is it?" she asked, trying to make her croaking voice sound as normal as possible.

"Shh!" he hissed, drawing close enough for her to distinguish his grinning features. "You'll wake everybody else up."

"Clay Donovan! What do you mean by creeping up on me like that?"

"Keep your voice down," he warned in a whisper, stepping close to her and taking her in his arms, pillow and all. "I wasn't creeping. I just came outside for some fresh air and to think. I didn't mean to scare you."

He nibbled at her ear and neck as he spoke, sending shivers of delight tripping over her skin. "Stop that," she giggled softly, unconsciously moving her head to give him better access to her neck.

"Anyone who goes outside on a summer night wearing no more than a thin scrap of nightgown has to expect to get a few bites," he said. He took the sensitive skin where her neck curved into her shoulder between his teeth and gave a low growl. "Might as well get my share before the hungry mosquitoes munch up all the good parts. Like this sweet ear!" Sucking a plump ear lobe into his mouth, he held his tongue beneath it and pressed it against the roof of his mouth just behind his teeth. Ribbons of delight

409

curled through her.

She made a kittenish show of escaping from him. "The mosquitoes are not out tonight! There is too much breeze for mosquitoes."

"But I'm here. And I'm hungry as hell. For you." Suddenly his playful whisper became an intense plea.

Snatching the pillow and sheet from between them, he pressed his body to hers from chest to knee and walked her backward until she felt the patio chair behind her.

"What about the mosquitoes?" she murmured as he lowered himself into the patio chair, pulling her down with him.

"Let them get their own dinner," Clay growled settling her beside him. His hands, hot through the thin white lawn of her gown, roved over her body, leaving none of her untouched.

Her own need as extreme as his, Gentle Fawn pushed herself away from Clay and began to fumble with the buttons on his shirt.

"I too am hungry, Clay Donovan," she whispered dipping her head to taste of the flat male nipple now bared for her pleasure. Teasing the tiny kernel with the tip of her tongue, she delighted as it sprang to life under her loving tutelage. "Hungry for you," she repeated, nipping at the thick mat of gold chest hair with her lips as she moved her mouth to the other tiny masculine nub.

"Oh, God, what you do to me!" Clay groaned, moving beside her in an effort to position himself so that his throbbing manhood could find some relief pressed against her supple body.

Realizing his need, Gentle Fawn continued her drugging ministrations on his nipple as she slid her hand beneath his waistband.

410

Its satiny skin stretched taut, his erect sex seemed to have a life of its own as it thrust its hot length into her seeking hand. Wrapping her fingers around the pulsating strength, she tightened, then loosened her hold before she began to slowly move her hand up and down.

"Oh, lord!" he moaned, arching his head back and squeezing his eyes closed tight as he succumbed to the magic of her touch.

No longer able to stand the hindrance of his clothing, Gentle Fawn withdrew her hand and quickly unfastened his belt buckle.

A fraction of his common sense returning, Clay grasped her wrists and stilled them against his body. "We'd better stop. Someone might see us."

"Everyone else is asleep," she protested, twisting at his hold on her wrists, anxious to get back to her purpose.

"You're a witch," he sighed, loosening his grip and allowing her the freedom to return to her objective.

Quickly unfastening his trousers, she drew them down his lean hips and along his muscular legs. Kneeling at the foot of the chaise longue, she tugged the pants over his bare feet and tossed them aside. Unable to resist, she bent down to tickle her tongue along his ankle, then took a gentle bite of the fleshy part of his calf.

"Hey!" he cried out, sitting up and reaching for her.

"Ssh! You will wake everybody up," she whispered with a mischievous giggle as she leaned out of his reach. Without waiting for him to respond, she crossed her arms in front of her and grabbed handfuls of her flimsy nightgown. In a flash she drew the light garment over her head and pitched it aside to join the discarded trousers. "Do you still think I am a witch?" she teased, kneeling at his feet and stretching her arms upward to give him a full

411

view of her petite, rose-tipped breasts as she loosened her braids.

Clay nodded his head, entranced by this aggressive and seductive Gentle Fawn. Relaxing back against the pillow, his arms folded behind his head, he watched and waited for what she would do next.

Her hair loose and wild, she bent to nip and kiss one leg from ankle to knee before blessing the other one with a similar treatment. Then, with her teeth and tongue and lips, she began a deliberate assault on his sanity as she kissed the length of his thighs over and over, each forage upward bringing her closer to his desire.

Burying his fingers in her thick hair, he tried to bring her up to him, but she resisted. Finally, when she could stand the waiting no longer, she reached out for his manhood, wrapping both hands around its hardness.

"God, honey. What are you doing?" he groaned, his head twisting from side to side as his pelvis rotated upward against her hands. "I can't take this."

"Do you want me to stop?" she asked, her breath on his throbbing need scorching. Without warning, she flicked her tongue over the sensitive tip.

As though she'd given him an electrical shock, his body jerked upward.

"Do you?" she repeated, taking another taste of him.

"Yes," he answered in a long tortured groan, as his body twitched again. "I mean no— Oh, God, are you sure this is what you want?"

"I want to know all of you, Clay Donovan," she said with conviction as her lips closed over the velvety smoothness of his aroused flesh and drew him into the warmth of her mouth.

Afraid he wouldn't be able to control his body's wildly

ounding ardor much longer if Gentle Fawn kept up her unrelenting attack, Clay roughly pulled her up to cover his body with hers, settling her in a straddling position over his thrusting member.

In one swift movement, he turned her over onto her back and plunged into her. Moving together as one, they rose and fell with frenzied desperation, losing all reason and concept of time or place. And still they ascended higher and higher as he delved deeper and deeper into her warmth. Until at last they were both catapulted into spasms of ecstasy. Until they tumbled, wildly out of control, downward, leaving them both too weak to speak.

When at last Gentle Fawn's ragged breathing slowed and the wild pounding in her heart slackened to a bearable pain, she spoke. "I am so glad you came to me," she whispered, her body still trembling in the aftermath of their lovemaking. She ran the tips of her fingers idly over the dampness of his smooth back.

"Me too," Clay groaned against the curve of her neck. "I'm so used to having you in my bed, I can't sleep very well without you beside me," he confessed.

"I do not sleep without you either. Why can we not just tell the Delgados that we are married? Like we told the man at the Rosewood?"

The muscles of Clay's back and shoulders tensed under her hands, and the part of him that was still deep within her began to shrink away from her even though he did not move.

"What did I say wrong?"

"Nothing, honey," he said, kissing her eyelids and moving his hips against her in a futile effort to stay secure inside her. "It's just that this is different."

"Different?"

"Yeah," he said, giving up and rolling to his side. He repositioned the pillow beneath his head and settled her head on his shoulder, then pulled the sheet over them "In Cheyenne, I knew we would never see that jerk at the Rosewood again, so it didn't matter what I told him."

Gentle Fawn didn't respond to what he said, waiting patiently for him to continue.

"But here, with your family, we can't tell them we're married when we're not. Sooner or later they'd find out and if you ever hope to start a new life with them, then everything would be ruined."

"They do not want me here anyway—except for Anita—so what difference does it make what they think? After our visit will we be married again?"

"I've told you, honey. Just saying you're married and sleeping together may be enough for the Lakotas, just like simply saying you're dissolving the marriage and moving out is enough for a divorce. But in the white world there's a religious ceremony in a church, and the marriage is for life—until one or the other of the two people dies. In the eyes of the whites, you're not my wife. You're my mistress—a woman who sleeps with a man she's not married to. Something a proper young lady is not supposed to do.

"You deserve more than that. Not only do you deserve to claim what's rightfully yours, but you deserve a husband and children and *respect!* And you wouldn't be able to have any of those things if anyone found out about us."

"And what am I in *your* eyes, Clay Donovan? Do you see me as your mistress, too? Do you not have respect for me because I have given myself to a man that I did not marry in this *wasicun* church?"

414

Clay looked down at the upturned face and started to speak. But he couldn't. *What the hell is she to me? No matter how responsible I feel to her, she's not my wife and never has been. I don't even want a wife! I'm not ready to be tied down by a wife who'd make me feel guilty every time I got the itch to see another part of the country. No, she's not my wife. But I don't see her as my mistress either. So what is she to me?*

"I didn't mean that was the way *I* felt, honey. I meant that was the way others would think."

"You did not answer my question, Clay," she said, sitting up and watching him intently. "What am I to *you?* Not the others, but to you! Am I your mistress?"

"No! Not that. You're very special to me. I care for you a great deal."

"I am 'special' to you? You 'care for me a great deal'? What does that mean, Clay? I 'care for' many people 'a great deal'," she said bitterly, knowing she was asking questions Clay couldn't answer without hurting her, but asking them just the same. "And I have had *horses* that are 'special' to me! Is that what I am to you? Nothing more important than a horse—a horse you will use, then get rid of when you have no more use for me?"

"Stop it!" Clay interrupted. "Why are you doing this? Of course you mean more to me than some animal! Why do we have to call what we are to each other anything? Isn't it enough to know that you mean more to me than any other woman I've ever known? Isn't that enough?"

"No, it is not, Clay. I need to know exactly what I am to you. Am I your wife or your mistress?"

"Neither, goddammit!" He sat up and gripped her upper arms and looked into her eyes, his own begging for understanding. "You're—you're—" He released his hold on her and turned away. Swinging his feet to the ground, he propped his elbows on his knees. He burrowed his fingers into his mussed hair and held his head in his hands.

"What, Clay?"

"You're just my Gentle Fawn, and I . . ." *What? I never knew anyone like you? I can't imagine my life without you? I love you?* The unbidden words hit Clay like lightning, shaking every nerve in his body. Had he fallen in love with her?

"You what?"

Clay shook his head in disgust. He'd been so busy hustling up a story and planning a future for her that he hadn't even noticed what was happening to him. But damned if it hadn't happened. Just as surely as the sun would rise in the morning, he'd gone and fallen in love with Camila "Gentle Fawn" Delgado!

"Nothing," he grunted. "We'd better get you back to bed. The breeze has died down and I just felt a mosquito bite me," he said, slapping at his own neck and reaching for his pants. "Besides, the moon is up now and this patio is about as lit up as daylight."

Didn't he know that whatever the others called her, wife or mistress, she only cared what he thought? Evidently not. Or if he did, it didn't make any difference to him. Benumbed by his rejection, Gentle Fawn moved automatically. She took her gown from him and slipped it over her head. Snatching up the pillow and sheet, she started for the doors to her room. "Good night, Clay."

Stepping into his trousers, Clay whispered, "Wait a minute."

"I am tired now. I think I will be able to sleep."

"Is that all I am to you? A sleeping potion?" he tried to

tease, catching up to her and drawing her back into his arms.

"That is the way it seems," she returned, obviously not in a playful mood.

"What'll you do when I'm not around to help you sleep?"

"You are not the only 'sleeping potion' in the world, Clay Donovan!" she returned hostilely. Breaking away from him, she ran into her room, slamming the doors behind her.

"Just what the hell does that mean?" he growled, bursting through the doors. He caught up to her just as she placed a foot on the bottom step to the bed. He spun her around to face him.

"Just 'what the hell' do you think it means, Clay?" It took every effort to keep her voice low so no one would hear her.

Clay's eyes widened in surprise. "What kind of a way is that for a lady to talk?"

"The way you taught me! Is there something wrong with my talking, too? No wonder you are ashamed to have anyone know about us. I talk wrong. I gave myself to a man who did not have this church ceremony with me! And I am not a 'lady'! I am surprised you were even willing to admit knowing me!"

"Don't move, Gentle Fawn," Clay said suddenly, his voice stern and deadly, his eyes focused on the bed behind her.

Accustomed to reacting in an emergency, Gentle Fawn recognized the alarm in Clay's voice and did as he said.

Moving with slow, purposeful motions, Clay slid the belt from his pants and folded it in half. "When I tell you, jump as far from this bed as you can. Understand?"

417

Gentle Fawn nodded her head silently, her eyes shifting uneasily back over her shoulder.

She thought she saw a slight movement on the white sheet behind her. Then everything seemed to happen at once.

"Move!" Clay hissed, giving her a shove to the side as he snapped the belt at the moonlight-drenched sheet, not once, but three times in rapid succession.

"I think it's okay now," he murmured, lighting a lamp and carrying it to the bed to make certain the danger was over.

"What is it?" Gentle Fawn asked, staying behind Clay and peeking around him.

There on her bed, exactly where she would have put her hand had Clay not stopped her, were three dead yellow-brown insects. Each of the ugly eight-legged creatures was over two inches long, their curled tails had deadly-looking stingers at their tips, and Gentle Fawn couldn't help the shudder that shook her entire body.

"Scorpions!" Clay announced, recognizing the insects by their hooked tails and front pincers. But these were different than any he'd seen in Texas before. Not wanting to alarm Gentle Fawn, he said, "They're a lot meaner looking than they really are. They don't usually attack unless they're provoked. But they can be poisonous."

"What are they doing in my bed?"

"Who knows what makes bugs do what they do?" Clay said, his tone disguising his concern as he scraped the dead scorpions into a small enameled box he found on the bedside table.

"What if there are more?" she asked, cautiously glancing around the room.

418

"I doubt there are. They usually stick together," he lied about the solitary scorpions. "I'm sure they're all dead."

"I am not sleeping in that bed!" she announced, snatching up the sheet and pillow she'd tossed on the end of the bed, and shaking them both carefully. "I am sleeping outside."

"No, you take my bed. I'll sleep in here."

She noticed he didn't say she could sleep with him. "I do not want to take your bed. After all, we *Indians* are accustomed to sleeping outside. In fact, I prefer it to sleeping with *insects*," she said with a curled lip that made it obvious she wasn't referring to the deadly Mexican scorpions Clay had found in her bed.

Manuel Delgado was in unusually good spirits the following morning when the family and their guests gathered in the dining room for breakfast. He seemed oblivious to the tension that permeated the air. "I trust you slept well," he said to Gentle Fawn, his voice convincingly friendly.

"Very well, thank you," she lied, directing an angry glare at Clay who sat across from her and beside Manuel.

"And you, Señor Donovan? Did you also sleep well?"

"What?" Clay answered with a jump, his searching gaze jerking away from Antonio and back to his host. "Oh, sure. I slept fine. I always do."

"I assume you were also comfortable and made to feel welcome, Captain Gramm?" Manuel went on.

"Yes, sir, I slept like a log," Matt admitted, not bothering to take his questioning gaze away from Anita, who sat with head bent and concentrating on the food before her. "I hope my snorin' didn't keep anyone awake!" he added, certain he could get her to look up and smile at him. He knew something was wrong, but he didn't know what it was. If only she would glance up at him and tell him with her eyes or a smile that she was still glad he was there.

"I'm glad to hear that." Manuel laughed. "And though I cannot speak for the others, your 'snoring' did not keep me awake. Of course, my rooms are on the opposite side of the house," he added with a hearty chuckle.

There were a few polite smiles at the table, but the senator's levity had done nothing to ease the tension nor to stimulate the conversation.

"What about my beautiful niece? You are unusually quiet this morning. Did you sleep well, *mi cara?* Or did perhaps Señor Gramm's snores keep you awake?" His tone was teasing.

Her black hair loose and hanging forward like a curtain hiding her face, Anita darted a nervous glance toward her brother, raising her head just enough for Matt to catch a glimpse of what looked like a bruise on her left cheek and temple. Matt's heart thundered in his massive chest. Had she been injured? Or was it simply a shadow caused by her thick hair?

"I slept well, Uncle Manuel," Anita said, her voice sounding small and afraid to Matt.

Matt looked anxiously from Clay to Manuel to Gentle Fawn to Antonio, then back to Anita. Hadn't anyone besides him noticed the break in her voice when she spoke? Almost as if she were crying—or about to. The muscles in Matt's jaw tightened with the effort it took not to do anything until he knew what was wrong with the unusually reserved young woman.

"And my nephew. How did he sleep?"

Antonio, who'd been studying Gentle Fawn throughout the meal, looked up at his uncle and smiled. "I slept very well, *mi tio*. And how did you sleep?"

"Actually, I slept very well, too. There is just no replacement for spending the night in familiar surroundings. I am gone so many nights—in Austin and traveling around the state—that I really appreciate a night at home in my own bed."

"I know what you mean, sir," Clay said politely, though he was obviously distracted.

"I plan to ride out to the range this morning to check on my herds," Manuel said, suddenly changing the subject—now that the amenities were over. "Why don't you ride along with me, Señor Donovan? It will give us a chance to know each other and help you get started on your story."

Surprised, Clay glanced around the table uncomfortably. He didn't dare leave Gentle Fawn here with whoever had put those scorpions in her bed.

"That would be a very good idea," Antonio said, his smile smug.

I'm sure you think so, you bastard! "I appreciate the offer, Senator, but I think I got enough last night to start my story about you. I want to get it all down on paper while it's still fresh in my mind. Why don't you take your—I mean Gentle Fawn?"

Manuel's smile slipped for an instant as his attention darted to Gentle Fawn, but he said nothing.

"I know she would enjoy seeing your ranch and getting outside, and it would give you a chance to learn more about each other."

"That's a very tempting suggestion, señor. However,

I'm certain the young lady wouldn't be up to riding all day. It gets very hot here in Texas and I may be gone until after dark. Perhaps tomorrow she and I can take a shorter ride."

Gentle Fawn's head jerked up. Suddenly, she wanted to go for that ride more than anything. Not just to get out of the smothering Delgado house, but to show this man who, behind his disguising smile, was looking down at her. "Señor Delgado, you forget where I have lived for the past fifteen years. I assure you I am more comfortable on the back of a horse than I am in this chair! I am used to riding long distances and long hours. In fact, you will probably tire before I do!"

Clay covered an inappropriate smile with his hand and a feigned cough, as father and daughter stared into each other's eyes, each challenging the other to back down.

Manuel was first to break away with a nervous clearing of his throat. "Then I see no reason why you should not accompany me if you like. After all, you are my guest, are you not?"

His emphasis on the word "guest" bothered Gentle Fawn more than she would have expected. But she refused to show it. She smiled at him, disguising the fact that she was hurt by the realization she probably never would be anything else to him. "Yes, I am your 'guest,' Señor Delgado."

Chapter Twenty-Six

"Anita? Open the door. I want to talk to you."

"Please go away, Matt. I don't feel well."

"That's what I want to talk to you about. What's wrong?" he said, speaking with his mouth close to the door so the entire household wouldn't hear him caterwauling outside her room like some love-starved tomcat.

"Nothing's wrong. I just have a headache. That's all," she said on the other side of the door. Her back to it, she leaned against the solid barrier between them and swayed back and forth. "I'll feel better after I rest. We can talk then."

"Please open the door, Anita," he pleaded softly.

"Go away, Matt. I don't want to talk to you now." She moved away from the door and threw herself across her bed, no longer able to control her tears. "Just go away."

"I can't. Not till I know for certain you're all right!" When she didn't answer him, Matt called out again. "Anita?" No answer.

Finally giving up, he turned to go. Had she changed her

mind about wanting him to stay? Or had he simply misread the friendliness in her words and eyes as more than it was? Whatever had happened, he could see she had decided she wasn't interested in his company after all.

Women! he cursed silently as he entered his own room and flopped down on the bed—a bed too short for his long legs, he noticed irritably. "What could have happened to make her so different this morning?"

Maybe she really does have a headache. "Hell, with five sisters, I ought to be used to unreasonable-actin' females," he said aloud. "One or the other of them was always in a snit about somethin'."

Or maybe she's just playin' hard to get! he considered. Hadn't he seen his sisters play their annoying feminine games with more than one poor unsuspecting swain who pictured himself in love?

But no matter how he tried to convince himself that she was only being moody and unreasonable or playing some game with him, something simply didn't ring true. If it were one of his sisters, yes. But not Anita. Not that friendly, open young woman who lit up a room when she entered it. Not the sweet girl who'd been so sincerely sad when she'd thought he was leaving—and so unpretentiously happy when he'd stayed.

He came off the bed with a burst of anger. "She's not playin' games! Somethin's wrong, and I'm gonna find out what it is if I have to break down that damn door!"

Stomping to the door to his room, he yanked it open with a vengeance. Then a thought suddenly occurred to him. "Why didn't I think of that before?" he mumbled, slamming the door he'd just opened.

Matt hurried to the double doors leading to the patio.

Swinging them open, he stepped out into the sunlight to determine if what he suspected was true.

His room was the last on a row of private patios stretching along this wing of bedrooms. The next set of doors were to Clay's room, the following to Gentle Fawn's. "The next patio must be to Anita's room!"

Giving no thought to the fact that the patios were supposed to be relatively private, Matt crashed through the wrought iron gates one after the other until he came to the fourth patio. He paused only an instant before wrenching open its gate.

A tall wall, so thick with vines that almost none of the limestone beneath showed through, told him this was the last patio in the row—and that it must be hers. Then he stopped again.

What if he'd miscalculated where her room was? These Spanish houses seemed to wander all over the place. He could be mistaken. Mentally recounting the number of doors in the hallway between Anita's room and his, Matt made his decision.

Unless I didn't notice another door between hers and mine, this has got to be it! he assured himself.

Taking a deep breath, he covered the distance between the patio gate and the double doors quickly.

Wild with worry and determination, Matt burst into Anita's room. "I want to know what's goin' on!" he announced in a hoarse voice before his eyes even became accustomed to the dim light of the room.

Startled by the giant who suddenly loomed angrily in the doorway, Anita started up in her bed. "What are you doing in my room?"

"I want to know why you're actin' so different this mornin'," he explained, suddenly feeling very foolish.

425

He should turn around and get out of here before he did anything else stupid. But he couldn't move. He was frozen to the spot, unable to move ahead, unable to leave.

"I told you," she said softly. "I have a hea—"

"Don't give me more of that headache crap!" he growled. Her words seemed to have freed his paralyzed muscles, allowing him to move again. He strode across the room to where she sat in the middle of her bed, her arms hugging her bent knees, her forehead resting on them. "If you've decided you're not interested in gettin' to know me, then say it right out, and I'll leave you alone. But don't give me one of those wishy-washy female excuses!"

Anita buried her face against her knees and locked her hands behind her neck. "I'm not lying, Matt," she said on a muffled sob. "It has nothing to do with you. I just have a headache."

Matt stood beside the bed, gazing down at her, not certain what to do now. He wanted to grab her and shake her until she admitted she'd felt anything special between them from the first moment they'd met. He wanted to wrap his arms around her trembling body and hold her until she told him what had her so upset. And he wanted . . .

God! She was so sweet and vulnerable. So small and lovely. He wanted to lie down beside her and gather her into his embrace. He wanted to kiss her and make love to her, losing himself in her softness. He wanted to know the thrill of feeling her yielding beneath him as she opened her body to him.

Matt closed his eyes and clenched his fists. He'd better get out of here before he did something crazy. Unable to speak, he spun on his heel and strode to the double doors.

His hand on the iron door handle, he had almost made it to safety when she called to him.

"Matt," she cried out, her frightened voice his undoing.

"What?" he whispered, stopping in mid-step.

"Don't go." Her voice was barely audible.

His jaws clamped tight, he inhaled deeply through flared nostrils, his chest expanding painfully. "What did you say?"

"Please stay," she murmured. "I don't want you to leave."

Slowly turning to face the bed again, he expelled the breath he'd been holding in a long relieved sigh.

"Are you sure?" he rasped, taking a step toward the bed.

Her face still hidden in her knees, she nodded her head.

Matt vaulted back to the bed, hesitated only a second, then sat down on it. The soft mattress gave beneath his weight, tilting Anita's slight body toward him. Catching her before she fell, Matt enveloped her into his warm embrace.

"Oh, Matt," she cried, leaning into the security of his nearness. "Hold me. Just hold me," she whimpered.

"What is it, Anita? Tell me what's botherin' you," he murmured, tightening his grasp on her. "Let me help!"

She buried her face against his hard chest and shook her head. "I can't."

"Look at me, Anita," Matt said, making his voice as stern as he could manage as he lifted her chin with a large hand. "Tell me what's wrong so I—"

Matt never finished his statement. It was then he saw the dark bruise on Anita's smooth cheek. His eyes widened with shock. "My God, Anita! What happened?"

Wrenching her cheeks from his grasp, she turned her face away from him. "I didn't want you to see me like this."

"Who did this to you? Tell me. I'll kill whoever it was!"

Anita knew without a doubt that Matt would do just as he said. And she knew just as well that she couldn't let that happen. No matter how wrong he'd been, Antonio was still her brother and she had to protect him. "No one *did* it. It was an accident. I ran into the patio door in the middle of the night."

"You what?"

"I left the door open when I went to bed, but I got chilly during the night and got up to close it. I wasn't fully awake and bumped into it."

"At least let me take a look at it," Matt said, seeming to believe her story. "What have you done for it?"

"It doesn't need anything but time to make it go away," she said, tilting her head so Matt could examine the ugly bruise. "But by the time it's gone, you will be, too. I wanted you to think I was pretty."

"You'd be pretty to me no matter how many doors you ran into," Matt confessed, his head drawing closer to her, his gaze no longer on her bruise, but on her lips.

"I would?" Her black eyes, still glistening with the recently shed tears, gazed deeply into his. "Really?"

"Really," he murmured as he tentatively brushed his lips over hers in a featherlight kiss. "You're so beautiful, Anita."

Unable to resist her parted lips, his mouth closed over hers as he lowered her back onto the bed.

"Oh, Matt," she sighed, wending her arms around his

428

broad shoulders and holding her to him.

"I've wanted to do that since the first moment I saw you," he said, raining kisses over her face and neck.

"So have I," she admitted, moving her face to bring his mouth back to hers.

Her confession burst the dam holding him back. He drew her hard against his masculine length. Molding her pliable flesh against his own, his mouth descended in a deep, fervent kiss, leaving them both breathless.

Anita's world exploded into a panorama of swirling brightness as Matt's tongue caressed hers with gentle urgency. And she returned the kiss with an impassioned zeal she had never imagined possible.

As though her hands had a will of their own, they snaked around Matt's muscled back to pull herself even closer into his embrace. Her fingers dug wildly into the material of his cotton shirt.

She'd never been kissed like this, and the intensity of her own rising hunger frightened her. Anita started to pull away. But Matt's ardent kisses quickened a response that spread through her veins like a warm rush of flammable liquid. And she gave herself over to total feeling.

"So sweet, so good," Matt moaned huskily against her skin as his mouth burned its way down her neck to the low neckline of her dress.

Lying on his side, he cupped his hands around the firmness of her buttocks and brought her harder against him, massaging and kneading her malleable body to the shape of his own.

Suddenly Anita was terribly afraid. Not of Matt. Not of the warm hardness pressing against her legs. But of herself. She was afraid of the desire she felt swelling in her body, the instinctive undulating of her hips against him, and the need to have him closer to her.

"Matt, I'm afraid," she whispered, even as she pressed the aching point of her passion against his strength and held him tightly to her.

"I wouldn't ever hurt you, honey," he soothed, deliberately putting a fraction of space between their bodies. His caresses became tender and gentle as his hands roved over her back and he kissed her ear and neck lovingly. "I'm sorry I got so carried away. It's just that you're so perfect—and I—I . . ."

Anita smiled at the giant man who held her so sweetly. "I know you would never hurt me, Matt." She kissed his eyes and nose. "It's just that I've never—I mean I'm still a—I mean—"

"Don't you think I know that, Anita? And I respect that. I never meant to get so carried away. I promise. Just let me lie here and hold you for a few more minutes. Then I'll go. Is that all right?"

"I'd like that," she said, snuggling closer into his embrace. "I feel so safe when I'm with you."

"I'll always be here for you if you need me," Matt promised, realizing that he meant what he said. He did his best to live up to the trust she was placing in him by letting him hold her like this. But it was no use. With her so close to him, he couldn't stop his body from reacting to her. If he was going to remain true to his word to leave her alone, he'd better get out of her bed. Or trust and honor and her virginity be damned, he wouldn't be responsible for his actions. "I have to go now, Anita," he whispered, his voice thick.

"Must you?" she asked, moving closer to him.

"Honey, you'd better not do that!" he winced. "Now

let me go on back to my room before someone comes and finds me here," he said, prying himself loose from her hug and sitting on the edge of the bed.

"Will you kiss me one more time?"

What's a man supposed to do! "Just one kiss," he said, knowing he was only adding to his own pain, but unable to resist. He turned to her and kissed her passionately, filling her mouth with his tongue, as he longed to fill her body with his manhood. Then, unable to bear another second of the exquisite torture, he tore himself away from her and made a desperate dash for the patio door. "I gotta go!"

"What the hell took you so long?" Clay asked as he strode into Matt's room a few minutes later.

"Uh—" Matt stammered as he stood red-faced and stunned at the door.

"Did you go back to sleep?"

"Uh—yeah—uh—back to sleep."

"Well, I'm sorry to cut into your beauty sleep, but this can't wait," Clay apologized, thrusting the enameled box toward Matt. "Shut the door and look at this. What do you make of it?"

Matt took the small box and walked to the window with with it. Opening it, he whistled his amazement. "Where'd you get these sweet little critters?"

"In Gentle Fawn's bed last night!" Clay said ominously.

"They're Mexican scorpions and very pai̶
like a T̶

"I know that. Why do you think I'm so concerned? Someone put those killers in her bed!"

"Got any ideas who?"

"One! Antonio Delgado's got the most to lose if Manuel's daughter is found alive. My money's on him. What do you think?"

"You're probably right. But it could be the senator, himself. With an election comin' up, he'd have a lot to lose with a scandal."

"You think he's capable of doing that to his own daughter?"

"Remember, he doesn't believe she's his daughter. He still thinks she's a schemer out to take him!"

"Nah! I just can't believe that of him. I don't think he's the type of man who'd do something like that, no matter who the other person was! I really think he's a pretty honorable man who's just playing it safe after being taken more than once."

"You're probably right. But what are you goin' to do about it? How're you goin' to prove it?"

"I thought I'd ask you to keep our pal Antonio busy while I search his room. He might have more scorpions in there for future use. And I just might turn up the missing locket while I'm at it."

"Consider it done," Matt said, fingercombing his unruly brown hair and heading for the door. Then he stopped and turned back to Clay. "You don't think there's anybody in on this scam with him, do you?"

Clay smiled at his smitten friend's worried frown. "Anita? I don't think so, Matt. If I'm any

Señorita

Ranger—a man who shall remain nameless at this time!" he added with a teasing grin.

A blush rose from Matt's shirt collar to fire his entire face. "I was just wonderin'," he explained needlessly.

"I'd say the only thing you've got to worry about with Anita is the fact that your days as a single man might be numbered!"

"I'll go hunt down Antonio and keep him out of the way for a while," Matt growled, leaving a stunned Clay standing in the middle of the room. "Give me five minutes before you go into his room!"

Making a mental note that there were some things you just didn't tease a man about, Clay pulled out his pocket watch and studied it.

But before the allotted five minutes were up, Matt hurried back to the room, the look on his face concerned. "He's gone. The servants told me he decided to ride with his uncle and Gentle Fawn this morning!"

"What?" Clay shouted, forgetting the scorpions and hurrying for the door. "You mean she's out there with one man who wants to kill her and another who's convinced she's a confidence woman? I've got to catch up with them!"

"What about Delgado's room?"

"Can you check it for me, pal? I'll owe you one!" Then as an afterthought, he picked up the enameled box and handed it back to Matt. "And if you think about it, you might leave these in his room for a little surprise!"

.... poisonous. Not
..."Dezexas scorpion that'll maybe just make you a little sick if it bites you. One of these fellers is enough to kill most folks. But three—!"

431

"Over 600,000 acres," Antonio boasted proudly, answering for his uncle. "This is all Rancho Camila for as far as you can see in any direction."

Comparing this lush green land to the arid, rocky land the government wanted the Indians confined to, Gentle Fawn could not disguise the rancor she felt for the whites. "It seems to me that one man should not have the right to claim so much land as his own. The People believe the land is owned by the gods and meant to be used by everyone, not just a few."

"Yes, well, there are many whites who've voiced similar opinions," Manuel said.

"Then why do you fence off the large grazing areas with that ugly 'barbed wire'?" she asked, pointing to the border of the pasture they were viewing, a frown of distaste on her face.

"Since the war ended, Rancho Camila has maintained a systematic program for improving our stock—both cattle and horses," Manuel explained to Gentle Fawn as they rested their horses on a slight rise overlooking one of several grazing herds of longhorn cattle. "We've spared no expense to upgrade our herds by breeding them to the best beef cattle from the East and the finest horses money can buy from Kentucky. And the only way to ensure that our herds will continue to improve is with strictly controlled, fenced-in pastures like this one."

"Also, until we fenced, we lost thousands of cattle to rustlers every year," Antonio said. "In the ten years before we put up the fences, we estimate they stole over a million dollars worth of our stock."

"Rustlers?"

"Robbers and thieves," Manuel explained, finding that he admired the girl's inquisitive mind in spite of his

434

determination to believe the worst about her. "Mostly gangs of Mexicans from below the Rio Grande. Until the Texas Rangers were reformed under Captain Leander McNelly, it was a real problem for us."

Suddenly their conversation was interrupted by a loud noise, drawing the attention of the three on the hillock to a drama unfolding below.

A calf had gotten stuck in a mudhole and was struggling to free himself, bawling angrily as he worked his way deeper into the goo.

Urging his pony toward the trapped calf, the lone cowboy on duty unrolled his lariat as he rode. Circling the loop in the air above him, he tossed it skillfully over the bellowing youngster's head, wrapped the other end of the rope around his saddle horn, and leaped off his well-trained mount.

The sturdy little quarterhorse, his muscles bulging with the strain, leaned back, pulling the rope taut. His hindquarters nearly touching the ground, he began to back away from the mudhole as the cowboy walked toward the calf in the mucky prison.

Everyone was so intent on the rescue going on at the mudhole that no one noticed the calf's mother as she charged out of a grove of trees toward the dismounted cowboy's back.

Gentle Fawn realized what was happening before anyone else did, and without thinking of the danger or the consequences, she reacted with lightning speed. Bending over her horse's neck, she kicked the sorrel hard in the sides and slapped his rump with her quirt. Unconcerned with her own safety, woman and horse raced down the slope toward the distraught mother, determined to stop the charging cow before she could run

435

the defenseless man into the ground.

"Yee-agh!" she yelled, deliberately averting the cow's attention away from the man on the ground as she crossed the animal's path. She snatched off her flat riding hat and waved it in the air, continuing to yell all the time. "Yah-ha! Get cow! Yah-ha! Yee-agh!"

The cowboy glanced over his shoulder for an instant to see what was happening behind him. Determining that the other rider had the angry cow in hand, he returned his attention to the squirming calf on the end of his rope.

The cow veered off her course just as the sorrel and his rider crossed her path. Gentle Fawn stayed with the angry longhorn, deliberately placing herself between the mother and calf until the cowboy could complete the rescue.

"Got him!" the cowboy shouted, pulling the muddy calf free with a loud slurp as the suction of the mud gave way. "Here ya go, mama. Yer baby's jest fine," he said, setting the youngster down on solid ground and removing the lariat from around his neck. His ordeal seemingly forgotten, the young bull scurried to his mother.

"Thanks fer the help, mister—" the young cowboy, not more than seventeen or eighteen, said as he turned to face his helper for the first time. He stopped speaking and simply stared at the other rider. "I'll be g-gadamned! Yer a la-lady!" he stuttered. Then realizing what he'd said, he snatched off his hat and apologized. "B-beggin' yer p-pardon, m'ma'am." He blushed.

Exhilarated by the ride and the meeting of a dangerous challenge, Gentle Fawn grinned widely at the boy's stunned expression. "It was my pleasure."

436

"Where did you learn to ride like that, my dear?" Manuel asked, approaching the stammering cowboy and the beaming Gentle Fawn with Antonio at his side. His first instinct had been to race down the hill after her, but when he had seen that she knew what she was doing, he'd sensed that the girl would resent any assistance. Now he was glad he hadn't interfered. Never had he seen such quick acting and skillful riding and he would have hated to have missed it.

Her face becomingly flushed with excitement, Gentle Fawn's eyes twinkled mischievously, "Why, Señor Delgado, don't tell me you did not believe me when I told you I was raised by the Lakotas!"

Seeing how impressed his uncle was with Gentle Fawn, Antonio realized she would have Manuel convinced she was his daughter before the week was out. She was intelligent, beautiful, and brave. What man would deny her very long?

"You were magnificent, *mi cara*," Antonio joined in, reaching over and taking her hand in his. Lifting it to his lips, he kissed it. "As skilled as you are beautiful."

Before she could stopper it, Gentle Fawn let a derisive snort of half-stifled laughter. "Thank you, Antonio," she managed to say, behind her hand.

But Antonio Delgado was too absorbed by his newly contrived plan, and too impressed with his own charm, to notice that the lovely Gentle Fawn was not the least bit fooled or affected by his pretentious manners. Now that he thought about it, he wondered why the idea hadn't occurred to him before. It was all so simple. There would be no nasty investigation, and it would be so much more pleasant than his original plan. He would guarantee that

Rancho Camila was his when his uncle died, and he would have the pleasure of taming the wild Indian squaw as an added bonus.

Whether or not she was Camila Delgado, he would be the winner in this fight! He was going to marry Gentle Fawn!

Chapter Twenty-Seven

Clay had ridden out of the courtyard that morning in a blind panic when he'd discovered Gentle Fawn was with her cousin. As the day had passed, his worries had grown progressively worse until his nerves were stretched as tautly as one of Gentle Fawn's bows.

His fears mounting painfully with each mile he'd ridden over the vast Delgado ranch, at last he had been forced to give up his search. Distraught, he had returned to the hacienda, hoping they were already there.

However, another hour of restless pacing went by before he heard the sound of horses riding up the circular drive fronting the house.

Only two horses! he realized with heart-stopping awareness, his ears confirming his worst fears. Three riders had left that morning, but only two were returning that evening.

My God! They've killed her!

Clay made a frantic dash for the door, his gun already drawn. Stepping onto the arcade, his eyes were assaulted by a scene that tore at his gut and rocked him down to his toes.

The two riders were not Antonio and Manuel as he'd expected. Instead, it was Gentle Fawn and Antonio who'd ridden into the courtyard.

Gentle Fawn was all right. But instead of being relieved to see her safe, he found himself even more angry than before.

Though she was a bit dirty and disheveled from the long day's ride, she obviously was not in any particular danger at the moment. In fact, she seemed to be enjoying herself!

White-hot rage exploded in Clay's brain.

"Get your slimy hands off her, Delgado," he said, stepping out of the shadowy arcade as Antonio reached up to help Gentle Fawn off her horse.

"I beg your pardon, señor," Antonio said, turning his head toward Clay. However, his hands remained intimately clasped about Gentle Fawn's small waist, his thumbs suspiciously near the lower curves of her breasts.

"Clay, put that gun away!" Gentle Fawn's voice was an incredulous choke. "Why are you acting like this?"

Fueled by the long day of anxiety—and Antonio's hands so close to her breasts—Clay's outrage swelled to murderous proportions.

"I said get your hands off her, Delgado," he ground out through clenched teeth.

"I was simply helping my lovely guest dismount," Antonio explained, his dark eyes laughing at Clay's frustration.

"She doesn't need your kind of help!" Clay growled, remembering the gun in his hand and holstering it before he could use it. He glared a warning glance up at Gentle Fawn, who still had her hands on Antonio's shoulders.

440

"She's perfectly capable of dismounting by herself."

"Ah, but no matter how capable she might be, a lady enjoys the little amenities due her sex. Is that not so, *mi querida?*" he said, smiling warmly at Gentle Fawn.

Gentle Fawn looked uncomfortably at Clay. She wanted to deny that she had any need for such things from any man other than him.

Then she remembered she was still mad at him. And his domineering attitude made her even more angry. Who was he to come dashing out here with his gun drawn and spoil a perfectly pleasant outing with his ridiculous jealousy?

Jealous? Why would Clay be jealous of Antonio? Unless . . .

It was obvious in his glowering expression that though he might be ashamed to claim her as his wife, he didn't want anyone else to have her. But why?

Gentle Fawn studied Clay intently.

Then a peculiar thought occurred to her. He was behaving like a man in love!

It might do him good to see that other men don't consider me a thing only to be used in secret, then discarded when it suits their purposes.

"*Sí,* Antonio," she answered, beaming her most beguiling smile on the young Spaniard. "It is very nice when a man treats a woman like a lady. With respect and pride," she added pointedly, peeking out from under her thick eyelashes at Clay.

The muscles in Clay's jaw bunched noticeably. His fists clenched perceptibly. And Gentle Fawn saw it all. Her grin widened—though only she knew her smile was not for Antonio.

Antonio, basking in the warmth of the lovely girl

441

who'd stood with him against her lover, tightened his hold on Gentle Fawn's waist and lifted her off the horse

That's it, damn it! Without warning, Clay propelled himself across the space that separated him from the cocky Spaniard. He grabbed Antonio by the shoulder, the shoulder where Gentle Fawn's hand still rested. Spinning him around, he sank his balled fist into Antonio's startled face.

The impact of Clay's blow to his head lifted the lighter man off his feet, sending him flying backward. He landed a few feet away with a soft thud and a grunt.

"Clay! Stop it!" Gentle Fawn screamed, rushing at him. Why had she done such a stupid thing as to try to make him jealous enough to admit he loved her? Now he was going to kill a man because of it!

The expression on her face frantic, she flung herself between Clay and the downed Antonio. Gripping Clay's arms, she railed, "What are you doing? He was only being kind to me."

"Kind? About as kind as one of those scorpions he left in your bed last night," he bit out, shaking off her grip and taking a step toward the unconscious Antonio.

Gentle Fawn's horrified glare shot to the man on the ground. Was Clay speaking the truth? Could Antonio actually have tried to kill her? Was he so desperate to be rid of her that he would do that?

Her mind rebelled at the thought. "You are lying, Clay," she growled. "You only want to excuse your own bad actions!" she hissed viciously, moving in front of him. "You are just jealous!" She left him and hurried to Antonio, who was beginning to rouse.

"Jealous? You're crazy! Who'd be jealous of a sneaky little kid who goes down with the first punch?" But his denial rang false even to his own ears.

Her heart soaring with the knowledge that Clay cared for her, whether he was ready to admit it publicly or not, Gentle Fawn knelt beside her cousin. "Antonio? Are you all right?" she asked softly, lifting the dark head and holding it in her lap. She winced at the sight of the ugly bruise already starting to form on Antonio's chin.

Seeing her tenderly care for the fallen man brought back unwanted memories of when they'd first met and he'd been wounded. She had held him that way, too. Another stab of jealousy knifed through him, and this time he recognized it for what it was.

"Mmm," moaned Antonio, rolling his head in Gentle Fawn's lap so that his face was nestled intimately against her midriff.

Jealousy and anger rose anew in Clay's gut. But thanks to his new self-knowledge, he had regained a slight facsimile of control over his actions. He still believed Antonio was the would-be murderer, but he knew now he needed proof before he voiced that opinion out loud again. He took a step toward the two on the ground.

Seeing Clay coming toward them, his expression dark and scowling despite his blondness, Gentle Fawn was sure he meant to kill Antonio Delgado. She couldn't let that happen, as much for Clay's sake as for Antonio's.

"Stop where you are, Clay Donovan!" she shouted, clutching Antonio's bruised face to her bosom protectively. Her eyes glistened with possessiveness.

Clay winced at the sight of her holding another man like that. Had she gone and fallen for the slimy Spaniard's phony manners? Was it possible to fall in love with someone in the course of a few hours? Was that it? Was she in love with Antonio Delgado? Could that be why she

443

wouldn't believe him about the scorpions?

A heaviness descended over him like a black shroud.

He had no one to blame but himself. Hadn't she begged him to tell the Delgados about them? Hadn't she given him every opportunity to admit that he loved her? But no, he'd been too stubborn—and stupid—to give her anything but feeble answers like, "I care for you," and "You're special to me."

"You will need to kill me first!" she swore.

Her words brought Clay's attention back to his purpose. "I'm not going to kill anyone," he said with disgust as he knelt on the other side of Antonio. "I was going to help you get him inside." He slid a strong arm around the groggy man's chest and easily lifted him to a standing position. "You run open the front door for me and tell Nana he needs some nursing."

Sensing that Antonio had nothing further to fear from Clay, Gentle Fawn did as Clay told her.

As soon as she disappeared into the shadows of the arcade, Antonio stopped his halting steps, though he continued to lean on Clay. "You've made a mistake Donovan," he grunted hoarsely, his voice not quite a threat, but certainly not an offer to straighten out the misunderstanding.

"Yeah, well, it won't be my first," Clay answered thinking of Gentle Fawn. He resumed walking, taking the unresisting Antonio with him.

"No one is here, except the cook," Gentle Fawn greeted them as they entered the *sala*.

"Where is everybody?"

"The cook said Anita and Matt went for a ride and took Nana with them. She said Nana was *shap-uh-ro-ning* them. What does this word mean?" she asked curiously

444

s she slipped her arm around Antonio's waist and began
o walk with the two men.

"A chaperone is a person who watches over a young
ady when she's with a man, to be certain the man doesn't
o anything ungentlemanly," Clay explained bitterly.
'All proper young Spanish ladies take one with them
vhen they go out." *Where was your chaperone today,
Gentle Fawn? Who was watching over you while this snake
quirmed his way into your trust?* "Speaking of which,
vhere's Manuel? I thought you went riding with him,"
ne said, barely disguising the resentment rising in his
hroat all over again.

"He wanted to check on a *vaquero* who was hurt
esterday. He told us to come to the house and that he
vould be here shortly," Gentle Fawn explained. She took
no satisfaction in knowing that Clay had just realized she
nad only been alone with Antonio for a few minutes.
Only long enough to ride to the main house from the
vorkers' quarters out back.

"I see." Neither of them spoke again as they continued
o cross the *sala* with the limp man between them. Clay
could have sworn he saw Antonio's mouth jerk in a
leeting smile. But when he looked at him closely, he was
ust as unresponsive as ever. Clay began to suspect the
nan was faking his weakness, but what difference did
hat make? He couldn't tell Gentle Fawn. That bit of
nformation would no doubt receive the same reception
nis news about the scorpions had gotten.

Antonio's room was on the short side of the L-shaped
nallway the bedrooms faced. It was two or three times the
size of the other rooms and decorated with massive,
neavy furniture of dark polished oak.

"Put him on the bed," Gentle Fawn ordered, hurrying

445

to light a table lamp. "The cook is bringing hot water and cloths so I can clean his face."

The glance she shot Clay was irritated, as a mother would look at a child who has spilled a glass of milk all over her freshly mopped floor.

"Can I do anything?" he offered, knowing what he really wanted to do was to feel his knuckles crashing into Antonio's face again. Maybe if he was lucky he'd break the guy's perfect nose next time.

Seeing Antonio's bruised face in the full light, Gentle Fawn was inclined to tell Clay he'd already done enough. But the helpless look on his face told her he was already aware of his errors. "Will you see what is taking the water so long?" she asked gently, wishing she could tell him that she understood how he had felt. She knew how much jealousy hurt, how it made you do things you would never do otherwise. But he wouldn't even admit to her that he loved her, so he certainly wouldn't admit he was jealous. He would just laugh and deny both his love and his jealousy.

Besides, I must clean Antonio's face before Pap—before his uncle sees him!

Returning her attention to her patient, she smoothed Antonio's dark hair back from his face, with a gesture like a mother soothing a sick child would use.

But Clay didn't see it that way. He only saw it as the woman he loved caressing the face of her new love. "I'll get the water," he mumbled, turning on his heel and leaving before he did anything else stupid.

"*Mi cara?*" Antonio asked weakly the instant Clay was gone from the room—his timing so perfect Gentle Fawn suspected he'd been deliberately waiting for such an opportunity to regain consciousness. "Is that you?" he

446

asked, his black eyelashes blinking sluggishly.

"It is Gentle Fawn," she answered, knowing he had meant her, but pretending not to. "Clay has gone for some water so I can clean your face. He is sorry he hit you," she lied, hoping to mend the situation. "I do not think the damage is very serious."

"I feel better already just having you with me, *querida*," he declared, his voice surprisingly strong as he grasped her wrist and brought her palm to his lips.

"Antonio! Stop!" Gentle Fawn gasped in shock, doing her best to free her wrist from his grip. "What have I done to make you believe I would welcome such behavior?"

"I cannot help myself, *amor*. You are so beautiful. You have stolen my heart. Tell me I have captured yours as well," he pleaded against her palm, circling the tip of his tongue over it.

"My heart is not mine to give, Antonio," she admitted gently, repulsed by the feel of his tongue and breath on her sensitive palm but not wanting to hurt his feelings. After all, didn't she know the feeling all too well of being rejected by one she loved? "I have already given my heart to another. So release my hand and we will forget this happened." Her voice was steady, only trembling slightly when she felt his grip tighten when she told him she already belonged to someone.

"Another? Such as Clay Donovan?" he spat viciously, no longer pretending to be disabled.

Before she realized what was happening, his free arm snaked up from his side and around her hips, jerking her over him. "I will make you forget him."

The upper half of her body draped over Antonio's, her feet still on the floor, Gentle Fawn struggled against the

447

unwanted embrace. "Antonio, let go of me!" she said, pushing at his chest. "If Clay sees you, he will kill you this time!" she warned, having no doubt in her mind that he would do just that.

Seeing a movement in the doorway out of the corner of his eye, Antonio smiled. "Oh, *mi amor*, you have made me a happy man." He covered her mouth with a hard, wet kiss before she could say more.

"Here's the water you wanted!" Clay's voice boomed from behind her, followed by the sound of a wooden bowl slamming down on a chest and water sloshing over its sides. "If you need anything else, the cook'll get it," he said, wheeling around and heading for his own room.

Pushing at Antonio with strength she didn't know she possessed, Gentle Fawn freed herself and ran to the door calling, "Clay, it is not what it seems!" But he had already disappeared around the corner of the hall and didn't hear her—or at least he didn't seem to.

Rounding on the grinning Antonio, who still lay on the bed, she stomped toward him. "You swine!" she spat, wiping her sleeve roughly over her mouth to remove the feel and taste of his kiss. "You did that on purpose! You meant for him to see us!"

Antonio's grin broadened. "I cannot lie to the woman I love," he said smugly. "There is a saying that goes, 'all's fair in love and war,' and this is both, *mi cara*. I want you and I mean to have you for my wife no matter what it takes. By the time we are married you will have forgotten all about your Clay Donovan."

"Married? Are you insane? I would never marry you. I'm already ma—committed to another. Besides, you and I are cousins. That is incest! A Lakota would never marry a relative!"

448

"You're either my cousin or a Lakota, Gentle Fawn. You can't be both. But whichever you choose to be, you will still agree to be my wife before this month is out."

"You're mad!" she hissed, turning to leave.

"What about my wounds?" Antonio called after her.

Stopping in mid-step, Gentle Fawn eyed the bowl of steaming water on the chest by the door, then glanced over her shoulder at Antonio. Of course, it would probably only make matters worse . . . Then again, it would be worth it.

"Oh, yes, your wounds. I forgot," she said sweetly, lifting the bowl and facing Antonio again. "We mustn't forget your wounds," she said with wide-eyed innocence as she heaved the entire bowl across the room at the shocked young man.

He was splashed in the face full force by the hot water. He barely managed to duck in time to avoid being hit by the clay bowl as it sailed over his head and crashed into the opposite wall.

Less than a minute later she was outside Clay's door, her knock growing more insistent with each rap. "I am not leaving until you open this door and let me explain." She raised her hand to knock again.

But before her fist could contact the wood, it was snatched out of her reach to expose Clay in the doorway. His arms folded over his chest, he leaned against the doorframe and crossed one foot nonchalantly in front of the other one. "Well?" he said, glowering down at her from under a shelf of frowning blond eyebrows. His blue eyes were a stormy gray color that sent a chill of dread shuddering through Gentle Fawn.

"I w-want to tell you—"

"What? That you've decided to get into the Delgado

family one way or another?"

Her eyes opened wide, flashing her impatience and frustration. "Why are you acting like such a fool?"

"You hit the nail on the head, sweetheart. That's exactly what I've been. I've been a fool from the minute I found you in that deserted Indian camp! I should have run in the opposite direction the minute I saw you."

He stepped back and placed his hand on the edge of the door, starting to close it in her face. "Go on back to your new boyfriend. I've got things to do!"

"I am not going anywhere, Clay Donovan!" she shouted, banging the heel of her hand against the door and barging her way into the room before he could stop her.

"Now wait just a damn minute!" he growled, slamming the door behind him and turning to face her.

"No, *you* wait 'just a damn minute,' Clay Donovan," she said, poking him in the chest with an index finger and shoving her face toward his.

"I've told you a lady doesn't talk like that!" He knew he was being ridiculous, but the words came out anyway.

"We have already decided I am not a lady, so I will talk any way I *damn* well please," she goaded, poking him again and backing him against the door. "Now are you going to let me explain or not?"

Clay held out his hands and shrugged his shoulders in mock surrender. "Explain away!"

"First of all, I was not kissing Antonio—"

"Sure as hell could've fooled me!"

Determined not to lose her temper, Gentle Fawn took a deep breath and let it out slowly. She was tempted to let him believe whatever he wanted to believe, but she couldn't bring herself to do that. Knowing firsthand how jealousy could eat away at a person, she had to straighten this out now. "As I was saying. I was not kissing Antonio—"

"And as I was saying, you could've fooled me!" he interrupted again.

"Clay Donovan, you shut up and listen to me! He tricked me and kissed me. I did not want him to kiss me. And I did not return his kiss!"

"I suppose you weren't lying on top of him either," he commented snidely, the corner of his lip curled. "What happened? Were my eyes playing tricks on me, or did you just trip and happen to fall on him?"

"He suddenly grabbed me and pulled me over him. I thought he was still weak and he caught me off guard!"

"I guess that's as good a story as any!"

"Don't you believe me?" Her voice quivered slightly. "You above all others should know that I would not lie to you about such a thing!"

"Why?"

The one harshly spoken word hit her like a slap in the face, and her entire body seemed to wilt. Her black eyes glistened with tears she barely managed to hold back. She spoke softly, turning away from him as she did. "I will leave you now," she said, stepping to the door. "If you cannot see that I am telling you the truth, then perhaps it would be good if we did not speak for a while."

Tell her now, you fool! Don't let her leave! Tell her you love her. Tell her you want her to stay. "That would be a good idea," he returned in a raspy croak.

Throwing her shoulders back and lifting her chin stubbornly, she left the room with all the dignity she could muster.

Gentle Fawn managed to keep her controlled de-

451

meanor for as long as it took to walk into her own room and lock the door behind her. Then the wavering dam on her reserve dissolved in a rushing torrent of tears as she threw herself onto the lace-covered bed to cry out her misery.

At dinner that evening, everyone was uncomfortably quiet. More exhausted than he cared to admit, Manuel had chosen to take his meal in the master suite, as he often did, so there was no one to instigate pleasant conversation. Anita, though not as subdued as she had been earlier, seemed unaware of anyone at the table but Matt. Matt, in turn, wore the silly look of a lovesick puppy and was oblivious to anyone in the room except Anita.

A surly look on his face, Clay only spoke when spoken to, and then it was more growl than speaking. Gentle Fawn was torn between her love for Clay and her annoyance with him for his stubbornness. *Look at him sitting there pouting like a little boy, shooting his dirty looks at Antonio and me!*

Only Antonio seemed to be in good spirits, smiling and issuing orders to the servants, unconcerned with his bruised and swollen chin. In fact, he seemed to be taking pleasure in showing it off, making certain everyone knew he was the injured—and innocent—party here. "No hard feelings, Señor Donovan!" he offered magnanimously. "I understand your feelings of protectiveness for your charge. That is all our lovely guest is to you, is it not?" he added, his voice oily with innuendo and challenge.

Taken back by Antonio's deliberately spurring words,

452

Clay opened his mouth to tell the Spaniard exactly what Gentle Fawn was to him. Then he closed it again. His blue eyes shifted nervously from Antonio to Gentle Fawn and back to Antonio. Everyone at the table watched him. Watched and waited for his answer. Even Anita and Matt seemed to have put aside their mutual enthrallment for the moment.

"I guess you could say I feel responsible for what happens to her," he mumbled out of the side of his mouth. He was unable to look anyone in the eye as he spoke.

Gentle Fawn's face darkened and she swallowed the tears forming a lump in her throat. How had she let herself imagine she meant anything else to him? She looked around the table helplessly, surprised by the smug smile she saw on Antonio's face.

"Then I suppose it is to you that I should declare my intentions," Antonio said.

"Intentions?" Anita, Matt and Clay voiced in unison.

Antonio threw back his head and laughed. "Oh, they are quite honorable, I assure you! This afternoon I asked Gentle Fawn to become my wife," he announced, dropping his bombshell on the gathering with cruel accuracy.

Gentle Fawn's mouth hung open, her eyes wide with shock. She opened her mouth to deny Antonio's ludicrous claim, but no sound came forth.

"Do we have your blessings, sir?" Antonio went on as though everyone at the table was thrilled with his news.

How the hell was he supposed to answer that question? Did he have the right to say no when this man was proposing marriage? Could he profess his own love when he had no intention of getting married, when he was

453

planning on leaving here as soon as he was sure Gentle Fawn would be okay? Did he have the right to deny Gentle Fawn the security of a place in the Delgado home that was rightfully hers? Did he have the right to . . .

"If Gentle Fawn wants to marry you, I won't stand in your way," he said, rising as he spoke. "In fact, I'll make it easy for you. I'm riding back into town in the morning to pick up a few of our things from the hotel."

The only sound in the room was the sharp intake of air that flooded into Gentle Fawn's lungs.

His black eyes cold and cruel, Antonio turned his broad grin on Gentle Fawn. "There, *cara,* I told you he would not stand in our way!"

That was all Clay heard before he disappeared from the dining room.

"You bastard!" Gentle Fawn hissed, thankful in that moment for the special words Clay had taught her. Somehow, the Indians' use of animal growls and grunts to express their anger had never been enough for her. But with her new vocabulary . . . "You son of a bitch! I told you I would not marry you! I love only one man and will marry no other!"

"My, my, such language! I want you to know I will not permit my wife to use such words once we are married." It was as though he hadn't even heard her.

"The day we are married, Antonio, will be the day of my funeral. Because I would kill myself before I would marry a 'sorry jerk' like you!"

Chapter Twenty-Eight

Gentle Fawn was up long before dawn the next morning. Actually, she'd never gone to sleep. Instead, she had lain awake all night, her eyes focused on the patio doors, as though she could will Clay to come through them any minute. But he hadn't come. Through her window, she'd watched the moon rise and disappear from view, and still the louvered doors had remained closed.

Several times during the sleepless night, she had started to go to him, more than once going so far as to put on a robe and step out onto the patio. But each time, her vow to wait for him to come to her had won out, and she had returned to her bed to stare into the darkness at the window and doors.

He owes me an apology for this afternoon, she told herself. *I will not beg him to believe that Antonio was deliberately misleading him. He would just turn it on me and keep on believing whatever he wants to believe.*

When the first gray light of dawn made itself known in the few minutes each morning when there is no black, no white, no color in the world, Gentle Fawn jackknifed up in bed. To hell with her pride. She was going to Clay! What good was pride when it was a wedge between her and the man she loved? Throwing the covers off her legs, she slipped to the floor.

Running on bare feet across the room, out the doors and through the wrought iron gate separating her patio from Clay's, she promised herself she would convince him to take her away from here. She would tell him that she wanted to be with him no matter what. As his wife. As his mistress. Any way he wanted her. It didn't matter now. She just wanted to be with him.

Stopping just outside his room, her hands on the iron doorpulls, Gentle Fawn took a deep breath and pushed the doors open. "Clay, I cannot go on like this. I want to be with you. If you leave here, I want to go, too," she declared, crossing the room to his bed. "I will go wherever you say."

Her only answer was silence.

"Clay," she whispered. "Are you awake? I must talk to you."

She lifted the mosquito netting and reached out toward the center of the bed. "Clay?"

In the cocoon of the netting, it was slightly darker than the rest of the room. When she put her hand down on the crumpled bedsheets, she jerked it back in alarm—as though she had touched hot metal when she'd been expecting ice. "Clay?" she called out, climbing onto his bed and frantically patting the mattress. "Where are you?"

Kneeling in the center of the empty bed, realization began to dawn in the gray half-light of the morning. He was already gone. He had left without saying good-bye, without making any attempt to mend the split in their relationship. He hadn't even cared enough to tell her when he would be back.

Moving lethargically, she climbed off the bed and wandered to the patio exit. He hadn't been jealous of Antonio at all. He'd been glad to have her off his hands. So glad, he couldn't even wait until daylight to leave. He'd probably left right after dinner, so anxious was he to get back to his own life.

"Well, I do not need him," she professed aloud as she reentered her own room, thankful no one had seen or heard her make a fool of herself just now.

She slammed the patio doors hard behind her, but they immediately bounced open again—as though they were laughing at her.

Using only the light of the predawn, she attended to her morning toilet and dressed in a skirt and blouse Anita had lent her. By the time she was through, the sun had risen, and with the new day she gained determination. If it took every bit of reserve she could gather, she would not let the others know how hurt she was by Clay's desertion. She would hold her head high and pretend he meant nothing to her.

Jutting her chin stubbornly and setting her mouth in a tight smile, Gentle Fawn gave a defiant toss of her glossy black hair and crossed her room to the door.

It was then she saw the white envelope on the floor, radiantly spotlighted in a beam of the newly risen sun. Her dark brows drawn together in a puzzled frown, she bent to retrieve the envelope. Squatting down, she examined it curiously where it lay on the floor. There were two words on the front, and though she could not read what they said, she recognized the familiar scrawl as Clay's. Her elbows propped on her bent knees, she tentatively picked up the envelope and lifted the back flap.

Inside was a single sheet of paper covered with more words in Clay's handwriting. A letter! He had written her a letter! She glanced at the envelope again. The two words on it must be "Gentle Fawn." But what did the letter say? She desperately searched the inked letters on the paper for a word she could recognize. She spotted her name again, but nothing else. If only she could read.

"What does it say?" she mused aloud, her imagination running rampant with possibilities. Jumping to her feet, she jerked the door to her room open. Unmindful of the hour, she ran down the hall to Anita's room.

"Anita! I must speak with you! Please open the door!"

"Who is it?" came a sleepy reply, accompanied by the rustle of bed linens and what sounded suspiciously like a man's irritated voice.

"It is Gentle Fawn!"

"Oh!" More whispers and rustling and a thud, as if someone had jumped out of bed. "What time is it? Is something wrong?"

"I need your help!" Gentle Fawn said against the crack in the door to keep anyone else from hearing her.

"I'll be right there." More rustling. The squeak of a patio door. A long moment of silence. Then the sound of shuffling footsteps hurrying toward the door where Gentle Fawn stood.

"I would not disturb your sleep if it were not very important," Gentle Fawn apologized a minute later as she rushed past Anita into her room.

"That's all right," a flushed and tousled Anita said, tying her robe at her waist as she followed her cousin into the room. "I needed to get up anyway. I didn't mean to leep so late."

"It is still early."

"Yes, well—uh— What is it you need?"

"You must read this!" Gentle Fawn declared, shoving he envelope toward the Spanish girl.

Anita took it, but did not remove the letter. "It's ddressed to you. Are you certain you want me to read t?"

Gentle Fawn had already thought of that. There was a trong possibility that Clay had written to say she would ever see him again, and she hated the idea of sharing her urt and humiliation with another person. But that idea vasn't nearly as terrible as not knowing exactly what the etter said. "I cannot read it myself," she admitted. "I eed for you to tell me what it says."

"You can't read? Your English is so good, I just ssumed—"

Gentle Fawn shook her head mutely.

"Well, that's not so terrible. I'll teach you how. We an begin your lessons today."

"Please read me the letter, Anita." The pitch of Gentle 'awn's voice was rising nervously. "It is from Clay)onovan and he has gone. I must know what it says."

"All right," Anita chuckled warmly. She was certain it vas a love letter. She'd seen the way Clay and Gentle 'awn looked at each other. *Like Matt and I do.* She smiled nwardly, brushing a raven lock of hair off her face and limbing onto the bed. And she'd seen the look on Clay's ace when Antonio had made his ludicrous announce- nent at dinner last night. "Here," she said, patting the nattress beside her, "sit down."

Reluctantly, Gentle Fawn climbed onto the bed with Anita.

"Now," Anita said with a teasing smile, "what do you suppose Mr. Donovan could have to say that was so important he had to write it in a letter? A proposal perhaps? A declaration of his love?"

"Anita, please," Gentle Fawn whispered tersely.

Anita sighed. "I was just building the suspense a little bit!" She pulled the letter from the envelope and opened it in her lap. Unable to resist one last try at drawing out the anticipation, she made an elaborate show of smoothing the stationery.

"Anita!"

"Oh, all right. You're no fun at all. "'Dear Gentle Fawn,'" she began to read. "'I'm going back to the hotel to pick up your things and get a little writing done. I should be back in a few days. Matt will stay here, so if you need me for anything, tell him and he'll get word to me.

"'Honey, I'm sorry about the way I acted yesterday. It's none of my business who you go riding with—or who you marry for that matter. I knew things couldn't go on indefinitely for us the way they were. But it was still a shock to realize that the time for us to go our separate ways was so close at hand. You know me better than anyone, don't you? Old act-now-think-later Donovan! One of these days I'm going to learn!

"'If Antonio Delgado is the man you want, then I wish you both well. In fact, it's probably for the best. He can give you the kind of security someone like me doesn't have to offer. But I sure will miss you.

"'I'll always remember our times together as some of the most wonderful of my life! I'll never forget you, sugar; and no matter how things turn out with the Delgados, you'll always be my best girl, my little Indian princess. Clay.'"

Anita looked up at Gentle Fawn, who stared blankly at the letter she handed back to her. "I don't understand. I would have sworn this letter would have been to ask you to marry him," Anita said, her tone apologetic. "And what was all that about Antonio? Surely Clay didn't believe you were seriously considering my brother's proposal." A sudden look of uncertainty and embarrassment crossed Anita's face. "You aren't, are you?"

Gentle Fawn shook her head and laughed. "No, I am not considering marrying Antonio."

"Does Clay know that?"

Gentle Fawn smiled sadly and nodded her head. "Oh, I think he knows," she said bitterly, remembering the way she'd begged him to listen to her the day before. "He is using this as an excuse to be rid of me once and for all."

"I think you're reading things all wrong. I think he cares for you a great deal."

"Is that why he left the minute he thought I was taken care of?"

"Maybe he thought he was doing you a favor. Did you ever consider that he might love you so much he would give you up if he thought it would be best for you?"

"That is ridiculous! He does not love me! He would have said so. I gave him every chance."

"Tell me something. Have you told him how you feel about him? Have you ever said to him, 'I love you, Clay Donovan'?"

"Not exactly. But—"

"No, of course not. You were waiting for him to tell you first, weren't you?" Anita asked softly, taking both of Gentle Fawn's hands in her own and giving them an affectionate squeeze.

Nodding her head, Gentle Fawn smiled tremulously.

"But I tried to show him in other ways. I came to Texas with him. I wore *wasicun* clothes so I would not shame him. I made lo—" Gentle Fawn caught herself, remembering what Clay had told her about how proper young women behaved.

Anita ignored her cousin's slip with an understanding smile. "But you never told him you loved him in words?"

"I wanted to, but—"

"You were afraid he would reject you. You didn't want to take a chance on that, did you?" When Gentle Fawn didn't answer, Anita went on speaking. "Did it ever occur to you he was afraid to speak up for the same reason?"

Her eyes wide with disbelief, Gentle Fawn denied the possibility with a vehement shake of her head. "Clay Donovan is not afraid of anything. He even rode into a Cheyenne camp by himself to save me from Many Coups."

Anita grinned and scooted closer to Gentle Fawn to slip an arm around her shoulders. "Let me tell you something, *cara*. Men are nothing more than silly little boys who do—and don't do—things for the most ridiculous reasons. When it comes to proving their masculinity, they will face death without a thought, lest someone think they aren't real men. But when it comes to affairs of the heart they are very vulnerable.

"Oh, they strut and brag and pretend things like love and security aren't important to them, but inside they are just little boys afraid of rejection. That's when we girls have to be the strong ones. We have to be the ones to take the chances then."

"Do you really think he was just waiting for me to tell him I love him?" A spark of hope was beginning to grow in Gentle Fawn's heart.

"I'd be willing to bet on it. And do you know what else

think?"

"What?"

"I think you should give him these days away from you to realize just how much he loves you and what an idiot he is if he gives you up without a fight."

"But you said—"

"Then when he comes back, you will rush to him and throw your arms around him and tell him you love him and have no intention of letting him get away. You'll find yourself married to him in no time at all."

"But what if he does not ask me?"

"Then you ask him!"

"He may say no."

"Then I'll get my uncle to bring out his shotgun!" Anita teased, but her joke was over Gentle Fawn's head.

"I do not want him dead if he does not want me for a wife."

"Gentle Fawn, that was just a figure of speech. No one would really shoot him."

"Oh, I see," Gentle Fawn said, nodding her head and smiling, though it was obvious she did not understand at all.

"In the meantime, we will begin your reading lessons to make the waiting go faster. Now, you run along to breakfast and I'll be there as soon as I'm dressed," Anita said, shooing Gentle Fawn off the bed and across the room.

"All right," Gentle Fawn said at the door. She started down the hall, then turned and ran back to Anita. "Thank you," she choked, hugging Anita hard. "You are a wonderful friend."

"That's what family is for, *Camila*."

*   *   *

The next few days went quickly. Between her lessons with Anita and her frequent rides with Manuel Delgado, there was little time to worry that things would not turn out exactly as Anita had predicted. Antonio had been gone for several days, so the entire atmosphere of the hacienda had been very pleasant.

Every day, things on the Rancho Camila seemed more familiar to her, like the day when she'd known exactly where a secluded pond was and had gone there for a private swim without someone to show her the way. Or the way a few Spanish words had crept into her vocabulary when she least expected them. Or the way she had called an old stableman by name when no one had told her who he was. Or the time she recognized a piece Anita was playing on the piano.

She found out later that the familiar melody had been her mother's favorite, and that the pond was where her mother and father had frquently taken their baby for private family picnics and swims. And the old man—well, he had been little Camila's favorite babysitter. He'd taken her on her first horseback ride, sitting in front of him and held securely in his arms, of course.

By noon on the fifth day after Clay had gone, Gentle Fawn knew without a doubt that she was Camila Delgado and longed to ask Manuel about her mother. But Francisca Delgado was the one subject that no one would talk to her about, their expressions becoming closed if any mention was made of Manuel's wife.

And she missed Clay. How she missed him! "I have given him enough time, Anita," she announced as the two women walked together in the courtyard after the midday meal. "I am going back to San Antonio and talk o him."

"I think that's a good idea," Anita said. She, too, had begun to worry that she had misguided her cousin. "In fact, Matt and I will go with you in the morning. I've been wanting to do some shopping and . . ."

Just then a horse and rider came galloping through the open gates, interrupting the conversation. Dismounting before the horse had completely halted, Antonio ran into the house as though he hadn't even seen them.

Knowing something was wrong, both young women burst into a run and followed the obviously agitated young man inside. They could hear loud voices coming from the study and followed the sound. "What's wrong?" Anita asked, never thinking to leave men's business to her uncle and brother.

"Look at this and you tell me!" Antonio roared, snatching an extra newspaper off the desk and shoving it at Anita. "Here's one for you, too!" he said, hurling another at Gentle Fawn.

The only sound in the room was the horrified gasp that escaped from Gentle Fawn's throat. There on the front page was a picture of her in her doeskin dress and braids. She recognized it as the tintype Clay'd had taken of her that morning when they'd explored the city of Cheyenne. "I do not understand. How did the newspaper get my picture?"

"You ask how?" Manuel said evenly, his upper lip twitching perceptibly. "Your friend, Mr. Donovan, seems to have gone back on his word not to write your story," he said bitterly as he tapped the byline under the heading: SIOUX INDIAN PRINCESS IS THE MISSING CAMILA DELGADO.

Gentle Fawn couldn't read all the words, but, thanks to

Anita's diligent teaching, she did recognize Clay's name and enough to understand what the rest of the article must say. "No, it cannot be. Clay would not do that. He gave me his word!"

"What's going on?" Matt Gramm bellowed, stepping into the room. "What's this all about? What wouldn't Clay do?"

No one answered. Instead they let Matt read the story for himself. "That sorry son of a—"

Moving with long, angry strides, Matt hurried toward the front door. Anita followed close on his heels. "Where are you going?"

"To San Antonio. Clay Donovan has some explaining to do!"

"Wait! I'm coming with you!" Manuel chimed in.

"It won't do you any good!" Antonio announced, slapping the rolled-up newspaper against the palm of his hand.

"What do you mean?" Gentle Fawn asked, refusing to quake under Antonio's hard, accusing glare.

"I mean your 'partner' is gone. He's left you to answer for his actions."

"Gone?" Anita, Matt, Manuel and Gentle Fawn asked in unison, as though their response had been orchestrated by a fine conductor.

"The first thing I did when I saw this newspaper was to go the Menger Hotel to find him. I was going to have it out with him and force him to print a retraction. But the desk manager said Donovan checked out four days ago and caught the first stagecoach headed north."

"There must be a mistake," Gentle Fawn said woodenly, knowing even as she spoke that Clay was really gone and that she would never see him again. "He

;ave me his word."

"I guess he decided his story was too hot to give up," Antonio said with a cruel smile, his black eyes transmitting his smugness to Gentle Fawn, despite his attempt to hide his satisfaction from the others.

"I am so sorry this happened, Señor Delgado," Gentle Fawn whispered. "I believed him when he said he would not bring shame on your home and name. It was never my desire to disgrace you and your family. I will go to San Antonio in the morning. And before I return to the Lakotas I will tell the newspaper that I am not your daughter. Now, if you do not mind, I will lie down in my room. I do not feel well." She turned and started to leave.

"*Tio!* Do something!" Anita shouted. "You can't let her leave. What will become of her? Can't you see who she is yet?"

"Wait!" Manuel commanded Gentle Fawn, pain and uncertainty twisting the expression on his face.

Gentle Fawn stopped but did not turn to her father.

"I cannot claim you as my daughter yet," he rasped, fighting every instinct to gather this girl into his arms and proclaim to the world that, yes, this was Camila Delgado, his beloved daughter. But he'd been hurt by convincing frauds before. Never again would he allow himself to experience the heartbreak of learning the girl he hoped was his daughter was nothing more than a clever schemer. No, there would have to be some kind of proof before he would claim her.

"I understand, señor," Gentle Fawn responded, her back straightening, her fists nervously pleating and unpleating the folds of her skirt. She took a step to leave.

"But we agreed that you would stay here for a month before I had to make my decision," he added, cursing

467

himself for wanting her to be what she said she was, for wanting her to be Camila. "The month is only a week gone."

"You want me to stay?" Gentle Fawn asked incredulously, turning to gaze into her father's hurt eyes that were so like her own. "After the disgrace I have caused you."

"You've caused me no disgrace, Gentle Fawn."

"But you were so angry."

"I am hurt more than angry. The one thing I cannot tolerate is a liar. And I believed Clay Donovan when he told me he would not write this story."

Me too, Papá. Me too, she said silently, fighting the need to run to Manuel Delgado and feel her father's embrace for the first time in fifteen years.

Gentle Fawn's eyes opened suddenly. She'd heard something. Something had awakened her from a sound sleep. Lying on her stomach, she lifted her head off the pillow so she could use both ears. She listened intently. But everything was still.

I just went to bed too early, she decided, remembering she had been asleep before dark and had even slept through the dinner hour. It had been the only way she'd been able to escape from thoughts of Clay's betrayal. But now it all came back to her with heartbreaking clarity.

Flopping over onto her back, she studied the dark, trying to understand all that had happened to her and figure out what she could have done differently.

Suddenly her thoughts were interrupted.

There it was again. That same noise! Soft, shuffling, stealthy.

468

"Clay?" she whispered, jolting straight up in bed and cursing the fact that there was no moon that night so she could see better.

Then, in the time it took for her to turn her head toward the window, the mosquito netting was snatched from around her bed and a strong hand was slapped over her mouth.

"It is your *prometido*—your betrothed!" a husky voice hissed into her ear as a man's weight pressed her back into the pillows. "I have come to seal our engagement."

Antonio! Her first inclination was to struggle against him, but she couldn't. The way he had positioned his body, any movement she made would only serve to arouse him further. Already his hips were undulating against her lower body, his erection hard and punishing through the sheet and her bedclothes.

Using every fragment of self-control and instinct for survival she'd ever been taught, she forced herself to go limp beneath Antonio.

"That's better," he grunted, biting hungrily at the skin of her neck. "I knew that you desired me as much as I desire you." His lower body continuing its rapid movements, he struggled to tug the sheet from between their hips with his one free hand. Realizing she was tangled in the sheet, he released his hold on her mouth so he could use both hands.

Before Gentle Fawn could scream for help, Antonio covered her mouth with his in a brutal kiss. His teeth cutting into her lips, he rammed his tongue, thick and tasting of whiskey and stale tobacco, deep into her mouth. Keeping his lips cemented to hers, he lifted his hips to knock the sheet out of the way and wedge himself between her thighs.

Bile churning in the back of her throat, Gentle Fawn knew she had to defend herself. Aware now that he had freed his turgid manhood from his trousers and the only thing that was stopping him from joining with her was the thin white lawn of her nightgown, Gentle Fawn managed to free her hands. Gliding them over Antonio's bare, sweat-slicked back in what she hoped he would take for a caress, she worked them into his pomaded hair.

"Ah, yes, my little hot-blooded savage," he groaned against her mouth. "I knew it would be like this." His hands groped at the neckline of her gown. "When I saw you on the patio with Donovan that first night, I knew then that such beauty and lust were wasted on that *gringo*." A hard hand slipped inside the thin garment, grabbing and squeezing a small breast cruelly. "Every man wants a wife who is a lady in the *sala* and a *puta* in the bedroom. You and I are a perfect match, little Indian *puta*."

Gentle Fawn winced at the cruel treatment of her breast, but Antonio didn't notice. He kissed her lips again. But this time when they separated, she set her plan into motion. Almost choking on the taste of him, she kissed and nibbled her way along his neck until she reached his ear.

Pretending an increasing passion, she grabbed fistfuls of his oily black hair at each of his temples and drew a vulnerable earlobe into her mouth.

Then, when everything was set, her seeming compliance abruptly changed to attack. Tightening her grip on his hair, she bit down on his earlobe. Hard. Vengefully! She showed no mercy.

Antonio's entire body stiffened and he let a piercing yowl of pain. He jerked back in an effort to free himself.

But like a starving dog with a bone, Gentle Fawn hung on, coming up off the bed as Antonio tried to get away.

"Let go!" he screamed, his voice a high-pitched screech. He shoved at her shoulders and batted at her head.

A vicious snarl issued from deep in her throat as her cousin stood up, his fists pummeling her head and shoulders. But she was not aware of the blows and continued to cling to him stubbornly. *How does it feel to be helpless?* she asked silently, exerting a last surge of effort on her bite.

With a sickening crunch, her teeth sank through the fleshy earlobe and met. Releasing her hold on his hair, she raised her foot and kicked him in the gut, spitting the gore from her mouth as she did.

Grabbing desperately at his bleeding ear, Antonio toppled over backward.

Wiping the back of her hand across her lips distastefully, she advanced on Antonio. "Now, get out of here!" she hissed.

"You bitch! You bit off my ear!" he cried, his face wet with tears as he felt for the missing protuberance.

"Just a little bit of it," she corrected with a sneer, hating him all the more for reducing her to a wild animal. "But the next time you touch me, I will not stop at a piece of earlobe." She eyed his now flaccid manhood purposefully. "The next time you'll wish you were dead! Now, leave before I forget that I am your guest!"

"You'll pay for this," he growled, crawling to his hands and knees, then to his feet. He took two staggering steps toward the patio door, still clutching the side of his head.

Without warning, he wheeled around and literally flew

across the space that separated them. Enraged beyond reasonable action, Antonio threw his greater weight at Gentle Fawn and she was hurled to the floor.

A loud thump as her head made cracking contact with the corner of the bed was the last thing she remembered.

It was to this scene that Anita entered the room through the open doors.

"Antonio! What have you done?" she shrieked, horrified to see her brother, his eyes wild with insanity, on top of the unconscious girl.

Holding his ear with one hand, he ripped at Gentle Fawn's bloodied nightgown with the other, as though no one else was in the room. "You'll pay, you whore!" he swore over and over in a deranged litany. "You'll pay!"

"No!" Anita shrilled, instinctively lifting a heavy candlestick holder from a nearby dresser and raising it over her head with both hands. "Stop!" she screamed in a long, tortured wail, bringing the holder down on the back of her brother's head with all her might.

Chapter Twenty=Nine

"Anita?" Gentle Fawn croaked through parched lips. "Where's Antonio? H-he tried to r-ra—" She couldn't go on. Her mouth was too dry and still carried the taste of blood.

"Pfft," Anita spat with aversion as she helped Gentle Fawn sit up and propped pillows behind her. "Do not speak that villain's name to me! He will not bother you again. Here, you can rinse your mouth," she suggested, offering a cup of water and washbowl to Gentle Fawn.

"I've sent my nephew away," Manuel Delgado said softly, his voice rife with sadness. "He has disgraced us all with his actions."

Realizing her father was at her bedside, Gentle Fawn rolled her head toward him. "*Papá?*" she whispered without realizing what she'd said. "Did he . . . ?"

Manuel shook his head, too touched and startled by the unfamiliar word on her lips to deny it. She looked so tiny and innocent in the middle of the large bed. A memory came to mind of another time, the time right after Camila had been stolen. Francisca had lain in a

473

similar bed, battered and bruised from a like situation
And there had been nothing he could do then either.

Though he ached to take this girl in his arms t
comfort her, he settled for picking up a small hand tha
rested limply on the sheet beside her. "Anita arrived i
time, *cara*," he rasped, sandwiching her hand betwee
his. "You mustn't worry about it. Antonio did not— H
did not carry out his evil intention."

When Manuel heard the relieved sigh Gentle Faw
breathed and saw her sink back into the covers, h
realized she'd been holding her breath with dread.

Tears sprang into Manuel's eyes. "There, there," h
said, patting her hand and setting it back down on th
white sheet. He turned his face from hers but went o
speaking. "You rest now. We will talk no more of this."

"Why did he do it?" Gentle Fawn asked, her focu
never wavering from her father's face, even though
was in profile now.

"He had an insane idea that Uncle Manuel woul
disinherit him if you proved to be our cousin." Anita'
tone held no understanding or forgiveness.

"Which was foolish, because I would never hav
turned my back on him," Manuel said. "I would hav
provided for all my family."

"But that wasn't enough for my greedy brother. H
wanted it all. So he decided to marry you so that you
share of the inheritance would come under his control
you turned out to be Camila."

"But raping a woman is not a way to get her to accept
proposal of marriage," Gentle Fawn protested.

"He was so angry when you continued to resist hi
offer, telling him you are committed to another, that
suppose he went mad with frustration."

"Where is he now?" Gentle Fawn asked, looking round the room uneasily. She still couldn't shake that feeling of helplessness she'd felt as she'd been thrown to the floor by Antonio's weight.

"He's on his way to Galveston where he will be put on a ship going to California. I have some land out there that I've deeded to him—on the condition he never sets foot in Texas again," Manuel informed her, his face seeming to age before her eyes.

"Did he say anything about the locket before he left?" Gentle Fawn asked, knowing the answer already. "Did he tell you where it is?"

Manuel and Anita both shook their heads. "I asked him right out what he did with it," Anita said with irritation. "But up until the moment he rode out of the courtyard he continued to proclaim his innocence where the locket was concerned. He still says he didn't take it. I suppose we'll never know for certain what became of it."

"It was never my intention to cause your family such unhappiness, Señor Delgado. But since I came here I have brought nothing but sadness to your house. Now because of me, you have been forced to send your nephew away. I think it will be best if I leave in the morning before I can cause you further trouble. I will ask Matt to take me to San Antonio, then I will return to the Lakotas. I do wish I could have given your wife's locket back to you though."

Suddenly, the realization that Matt was not in the room hit her and Gentle Fawn sat up straighter. "Where is he? Where is Matt?" Her eyes sawed from Anita to Manuel, her gaze confused.

Anita smiled dolefully. She had to tell Gentle Fawn where Matt was. "He has gone to find Clay Donovan and

475

bring him back to Rancho Camila."

Gentle Fawn turned to her father, the distressed look in her eyes betraying her love for the reporter. "But why? Did his story break a *wasicun* law? What are you going to do to him? You must understand Clay Donovan. He does not mean to hurt people. But when a story is 'big' he cannot help himself. His enthusiasm makes him forget to think. He would never hurt anyone intentionally. You must not punish him."

"I'm not going to punish him," Manuel promised with a weary smile. "Antonio confessed that it was he who gave your story to the newspapers under Clay's name in order to destroy his credibility with me."

"But the tintype of me? How did he get that?"

"When Clay left the Menger several days ago, presumably to come back here with your things, he was attacked by Mexican *bandidos* and taken to a village not far from here. One of those bandits was my brother," Anita admitted shamefully. "He found the tintype in Clay's saddlebags."

Sitting up in the bed, her eyes round and large in her small face, Gentle Fawn gasped. "Did they kill him? Is Clay dead?"

"We can be thankful that Antonio's greed did not destroy all that was good in him. He didn't have your friend killed. He had the men hold Clay prisoner until he could convince you to marry him. Then they had orders to escort Clay Donovan out of Texas."

"When will he be here?" she asked anxiously.

"Any time now," Anita said, the gaiety in her tone not fooling anyone. It was obvious that she was worried. "Matt rode out right after you were hurt. That was several hours ago."

"Is there something you are not telling me?"

Anita looked nervously at her uncle, then back to Gentle Fawn. "I don't know what you're talking about."

"What is it? What are you not telling me?" Gentle Fawn questioned anxiously as she swung her feet over the side of the bed and onto the top step. "Do you think Clay is dead? Is that what you are hiding from me?"

"It's not that, *cara*. It's just that my niece is concerned that Matt will be facing several armed men alone. But I am certain Señor Gramm can handle them."

As though in response to Manuel's words, the inside door to the room opened. The threesome turned their heads expectantly.

But instead of Matt and Clay silhouetted in the doorway, they saw the tiny figure of a woman, barely five feet tall. Wearing a flowing white nightgown and holding a candle in her hand, she was in her bare feet, an unruly mass of raven-colored hair curling to her waist.

Gentle Fawn recognized her immediately. It was the woman in the locket! Francisca! Her mother!

Gentle Fawn's eyes rounded with grateful amazement and filled with tears. Even if she had to leave here forever, she knew now that her mother was alive. She'd been given this one glimpse of her.

"*Querida!*" said Manuel, who was the first to recover from the shock of seeing his wife out of their suite of rooms on the other side of the house. He rushed to Francisca's side and wrapped his arm around her frail shoulders. "I told you I wanted you to stay in our rooms until our guests left," he said, his loving tone bearing no trace of anger. Shielding her from the rest of the room, he started to take her back.

"Why didn't you tell me, Manuel? Why didn't you tell

477

me you had found our Camila?" Francisca asked, th[e] hurt in her eyes evident as she looked up at her husban[d]. It was then they all noticed the newspaper gripped in he[r] other hand. She walked out of Manuel's arms toward th[e] bed where Gentle Fawn sat in stunned silence.

"Please, Francisca!" Manuel choked, his own stub[b]born need for tangible proof weakening as he saw the tw[o] women facing each other. Except for the age differenc[e] and their eyes, they could have been identical twins.

"We have no proof that she is our daughter," he sai[d] valiantly trying to hang onto his resolution. Seeing the[m] together like this though, it would be so easy to take th[e] girl at face value and hang the need for more evidence. "[I] didn't want you to see her until we knew for certain tha[t] she was not another impostor."

"Can't you see that she isn't an impostor, Manuel? [I] could the minute I saw the picture in the newspape[r]. She's our Camila," Francisca said, opening her arms in [a] gesture familiar to Gentle Fawn from her forgotte[n] childhood. "Camila."

"*Mamá!*" Gentle Fawn wept, bolting off the bed an[d] into her mother's welcoming embrace. "Oh, *Mamá!* [I] thought you were dead. No one has seen you for year[s] and no one talked about you."

"Dead?" Francisca said tearfully, shooting her hus[s]band a scolding glance.

"She didn't ask about you, and I didn't want you to b[e] hurt. There have been so many impostors and she was s[o] convincing, I thought it would be best if you didn't mee[t]. But now you have . . ." He threw up his hands and smile[d] weakly. What difference did it make if this girl was a[n] impostor or not? Anyone who could bring Francisca ou[t] of her long mourning like this would have his undyin[g] gratitude. And who knows, maybe the girl wasn't lying. Maybe she really believed herself to be Camila. Maybe she even was. "And I want to claim her as our daughter."

"But you aren't really convinced she is, are you, Manuel?" Francisca said with an understanding smile, seeing right through his plan to do anything to make her happy. "But I can give you the proof you wish for."

Her arm around Gentle Fawn, Francisca led her to the bed and sat down. "Put your head in *Mamá's* lap the way you did when you were small," she whispered conspiratorially to her daughter.

Confused, Gentle Fawn did as Francisca coaxed. A sense of homecoming, like nothing she'd ever experienced, swept over Gentle Fawn; and the last fragment of uncertainty was washed from her soul. *It's true. She is my mother!*

Lifting the heavy skein of her daughter's hair away from her neck, Francisca separated the fine hair at the base of her neckline. "There it is. Just as I knew it would be," Francisca announced, the relief in her voice evident.

To Manuel's amazement, his wife exposed a small strawberry birthmark in the hollow at the nape of Gentle Fawn's neck. Though it was almost indiscernible beneath the thick black hair, there was no mistaking that it was identical to the one in his wife's hair. "I'd forgotten the birthmark," Manuel whispered in awe, suddenly mesmerized by the sight of his wife and daughter together for the first time in fifteen years. It was a sight he'd prayed for every day during that fifteen years but had never allowed himself to believe he would really see. Tears streamed unabashedly down his cheeks.

"What birthmark?" Gentle Fawn asked, running her

fingers into her own hair. "I did not know that I have a birthmark."

Francisca drew Gentle Fawn to a sitting position and turned her back to her. "Look very carefully right about here on my head, and you will see what yours looks like."

"I see it!" Gentle Fawn laughed gleefully. "But it is so faint."

"Now. But when we were both babies and our hair was not so thick, they were more obvious. My *mamá*, your *abuela*, told me about mine when she saw the identical mark on you when you were first born."

"Then it is true!" Gentle Fawn whispered, assaulted by the full weight of knowing her real identity at last. "I am really your daughter. I really am Camila Delgado!"

"You really are!" Manuel cried ecstatically, unable to hold off embracing her a second longer. "Can you ever forgive a stubborn old man for not seeing the truth sooner?" Weeping tears of joy, he gathered his wife and child into his embrace and held them hard against him.

"There is nothing to forgive, *Papá*. You were only trying to protect *Mamá*." She paused and laughed. "Besides, who should better understand stubbornness than a stubborn man's stubborn daughter?"

Francisca drew back from her husband and daughter, the smile on her tear-stained face brilliant. "I have something for you, Camila," she said, digging into a hidden pocket in her gown. "I thought it was lost, but I came upon it the other day when I was checking to be certain the guest rooms were in order. Evidently Nana found it and left it on the dresser," she said, producing a gold chain and locket from her pocket.

Unmindful of the paralyzing hush that fell over the group, Francisca went on talking. "She's getting so old and blind that she probably didn't even recognize it as min— Why are you all looking at me so strangely?"

Her innocent question seemed to free their tongues all at once. "The locket!" they chorused, laughing at the marvelous quirk of fate.

"It was you all along!"

"We were so sure Antonio had destroyed it!"

"No wonder he protested his innocence so vehemently!"

"It was your *papá's* gift to me on our wedding day!" Francisca explained with a polite smile and shrug of her shoulders, still not certain what she had missed.

"I know, *Mamá*. I love it!" Gentle Fawn cried, her happy tears mingling with her laughter as she threw her arms around her mother and hugged her. "And I love you! Both of you! So much!"

"What's going on in here?" a familiar voice said from the patio entrance.

"Matt!" cried Anita, who'd stood silently watching the three on the bed. Running into the large man's arms and hugging him, she sobbed, "I was so worried!" Standing on her tiptoes, she kissed his face eagerly.

"Where's Clay?" Gentle Fawn said from the bed, the joy of finding her parents suddenly marred by the fear that she had lost the man she loved.

"Did someone call my name?" a dirty and disheveled Clay asked as he stepped around the embracing couple and into the light. Though his clothes were in tatters and he seemed to have lost some weight during his ordeal as Antonio's prisoner, his clear blue eyes were bright with his ever-present wit and enthusiasm. "Looks like a party! Why wasn't I invited?"

"Because you do not know how to dress for a party!"

481

Gentle Fawn giggled through her tears as she ran to Clay and threw her arms around his neck.

"Don't know how to dress? What's wrong with the way I dress?" he teased, his eyes twinkling mischievously as he returned her hug.

"You didn't even shave!" she scolded playfully, catching his bearded cheeks in her hands and pulling his head down to hers. "And you haven't kissed me," she whispered for his ears alone, not in the least worried about what the others in the room might think.

"A definite oversight on my part," he said, kissing her on the forehead.

"That is not a kiss! *This* is a kiss!" She glued her lips to his and told him with her mouth all the things she'd been unable to say since he left her.

"It would appear that our daughter is being courted, Francisca!" Manuel said, pleased with Gentle Fawn's choice in a man.

"Did he say *daughter?*" Clay choked, jerking his mouth from Gentle Fawn's and staring at the smiling Manuel and Francisca.

"Oh, Clay! So much has happened since you've been gone. They really are my parents. My *mamá* and *papá*. I have a birthmark. Right here!" She took his hand and carried it to the nape of her neck. "You were right all along. I am Camila Delgado."

Suddenly nervous with the way everyone in the room watched for his reaction, and very conscious of the scanty nightgown Gentle Fawn wore, Clay put her from him and smiled. "Well, that is good news, isn't it?" he said with a sick smile, disengaging himself from her embrace.

While he'd been the *bandidos'* prisoner, he'd had lots

482

of time to think. About Gentle Fawn and what he felt for her. About his career. About the future. And he'd come to the conclusion that if he ever got free, he was going to come to Gentle Fawn and beg her to marry him, for better or worse. They would work out the problems with his career later. For then, all that had mattered was that he loved her and didn't want to live without her.

But everything had changed. He couldn't marry her now. Not when she was the rich Camila Delgado instead of the homeless and penniless Gentle Fawn. He couldn't take her away from all this luxury to drag her all over the country chasing down stories with him. What kind of a life would that be for her? She had the right to so much more. This was all justly hers and he couldn't—wouldn't—be the one to rob her of it.

She would have her life as Camila Delgado, even if it meant he would have to give her up.

"In that case, I guess it's okay for me to be on my way. I'm happy for all of you, but I've already spent too much time away from my work. By the way, I finished that story on you, Senator," he said to Manuel. "I think you'll be pleased with it."

"I'm certain I will," Manuel returned, his dark eyes shifting uneasily from Clay's face to Gentle Fawn's hurt expression of shock.

"You're leaving?" she whispered, studying him intently. "Just like that?"

"I've done what I came here for. I've reunited you and your family. There's no reason to stay longer."

Gentle Fawn turned to her parents and smiled politely, her demeanor calm and controlled. Taking care to keep her voice even, she said, "Will you excuse us, please. Clay and I must speak privately."

"Of course," Manuel said, guiding his confused wife toward the hall entrance.

"Should they be left alone? It's not proper," Francisca whispered, glancing back over her shoulder at Clay and Gentle Fawn.

"Something tells me we're a little late to worry about propriety, *querida*," Manuel confided with a purposeful smile.

"We'll just slip out through the patio," Anita said to Gentle Fawn, taking Matt by the hand and pulling him outside.

"With *both* of our girls, it seems!" Manuel added as he and Francisca disappeared into the hallway.

Gentle Fawn rounded on Clay the instant they were alone, the fire in her eyes deadly. "Now, Mr. Donovan! Would you care to explain what you mean when you say there is no reason for you to stay?" She made no effort to keep her voice down.

"Obviously changing your name hasn't done anything for your temper!"

"That's right! Try to change the subject! But you are not going to get out of explaining why you are leaving."

"I have work to do! I don't have a rich new ma and da to support me!"

"Then I will come with you," she shouted just as angrily, her balled fists resting on her hips.

"You can't."

"I can and I will!" Suddenly she lowered her voice the expression on her face softening. "Don't you understand, Clay? Nothing means anything to me i it means losing you. I love you," she said softly.

"You love me?" The anger in his expression disap

peared, to be replaced with a warm smile of happiness.

"Are you so surprised?" She looked down at her hands as they nervously folded and unfolded the clean gown Anita must have put on her when they'd taken care of the bump on her head. She couldn't meet his searching eyes. "You shouldn't be, you know."

"I love you, too, Gentle Fawn." He drew close to her and pulled her into his arms.

Gentle Fawn's head jerked back and she searched his eyes for evidence that he was teasing her. "You do? Really?"

Clay nodded his head. "Really! I think I always have."

"Why didn't you tell me?"

"I didn't want to stand in your way."

"That's foolishness. How could being loved by the man I love stand in my way? You are all I want."

"You mean you'd be willing to leave here?"

Gentle Fawn smiled and nodded her head.

"But this is your home. What about your parents?"

"I would visit my parents from time to time, just as I will visit the Lakotas and Quiet Rain, but neither of those places are my home now. My home is with you."

"I'm not sure I could settle down. I've been on the move most of my life."

Gentle Fawn smiled patiently. It was as Anita had told her. Men really were silly little boys when it came to love. "Have you forgotten who raised me, Clay? I have never spent more than a moon in one place in my life."

"What will your mother and father think?"

"I think they will understand if . . ."

"If what?"

Gentle Fawn let an exasperated sigh. How could one man be so stupid? "If we do what two people who love each other usually do."

When he still didn't seem to understand what she was getting at, she lost her temper. "Damn it, Clay. I asked you to marry me the first time, and I was the first to say I love you. Don't you think you could do the asking this time?"

"I've told you a lady doesn't use words like damn it!"

"Clay!" she ground out threateningly, "Are you going to ask me to marry you in the *wasicun* church or should I have Anita bring my father's shotgun in here?"

"Will you marry me in a *wasicun* church, Camila Elena Gentle Fawn Delgado?" Clay asked, changing his tone to tenderness.

Gentle Fawn's mouth dropped open and she stared at him stupidly. "Do you mean it?"

"Of course I mean it! Why would I say it if I didn't mean it?"

"Are you just asking me because I threatened to have Anita shoot you?" she asked suspiciously.

Clay laughed heartily. He could already see that marriage to Gentle Fawn would never be the least bit dull. "No, my sweet little Indian stick of dynamite. I want to marry you because I love you with all my heart and am only whole when I have you in my arms. So," he said, dropping to one knee and taking her hand, "are you going to marry me or what?"

Her dark eyes glittering impishly, she pretended to be considering her answer. "I would hate to have you be able to say I forced you to marry me—like I did the first time. But because I do not like to think of you living the rest of your life as half a man—yes, I will marry you! If you are sure this is what *you* want."

"Come here, you little minx and I'll show you what I want!"

"To seal our bargain with a kiss?"

"That, too!"

"Then, 'let's get this show on the road, Mr. Donovan'!" she whispered seductively, tunneling her fingers into his shaggy blond hair and plastering her body against his from breast to knee.

"You're something else, Mrs. Donovan."

"You haven't 'seen the half of it,' Mr. Donovan! Not by a long shot!"

"That's what I'm counting on!"

Epilogue

"There they are," Gentle Fawn squealed to Clay, her voice ringing with excitement. "Anita! Matt!" she cried out, waving at the approaching couple as she stepped off the train and started running.

"We were about to give up on you!" Anita chided warmly as Gentle Fawn threw her arms around her cousin. "We were afraid you weren't coming."

"Are you kidding?" Clay laughed, joining Gentle Fawn and the Gramms on the railroad platform. "If I didn't get my wife back to Texas in time to celebrate our mutual wedding anniversary every September, I'd be celebrating the rest of them by myself." He winked at Matt and held out his free hand. "How are you doing, pal?"

"Better, now that you folks finally got here." He wrapped his arm around Anita and gave her a squeeze. "She's been about to drive me crazy worryin' you wouldn't make it this year. You know how nervous expectant mamas get!" He patted his wife's rounded belly affectionately.

Anita gave her husband a reproachful glare and swatted his hand away. Then her pretty face split into a wide grin. "If he doesn't like 'nervous expectant mamas' he's sure married to the wrong woman, isn't he?" She laughed, not needing to remind the others that she'd been pregnant nine out of every twelve months since she'd married Matt five years before.

"What're you trying to do, Matt? Start your own company of Texas Rangers?" Clay asked, ruffling the dark head of Matt's oldest son who stood between his parents. His three younger brothers had been left at the Rancho Camila with the doting Nana and Francisca, who were getting everything ready for the Donovans' annual six-month visit.

"If the next one's not a girl, I may give that some serious thought. But what about you? You're slippin' behind."

"I'm afraid that's one race we're going to concede to you." Gentle Fawn laughed. "Do you realize how hard traveling all over the country for Clay's stories can get with just these two girls?" All eyes focused on the redheaded two-year-old in Clay's arms, then to the spot between them where their four-year-old daughter should have stood. "Where is she?"

"She was right here a minute ago!" Clay returned, his voice a mingle of alarm and exasperated frustration.

"There she is!" Anita said.

They all turned toward the direction in which Anita was pointing. The elusive child, her dark auburn curls bouncing up and down, was talking animatedly to a porter who was helping passengers step off the train.

"See what I mean?" Gentle Fawn laughed with relief as she took the youngest child from her husband, and Clay

490

vent to retrieve their wandering daughter. "Evidently, he wanted to get one last 'interview' before we left!"

"But, Da! How will I be a writer if I can't interview people?" the petite youngster argued logically with her father as the two approached.

Clay rolled his eyes heavenward and covered a laugh with a feigned cough. "But I've told you, there's a time and a place for interviewing people," Clay went on, forcing a stern tone to his voice. "And wandering off alone is not the time!"

"How will I know when it's time?"

Clay looked at Gentle Fawn helplessly.

"She's your daughter," his wife chided good-naturedly.

"That she is!" Clay laughed, swooping his oldest up into his arms and giving her nose a pinch. "And I guess two little redheaded firecrackers are exactly what I deserve for marrying a hot-tempered stick of dynamite!" He hugged his wife with his free arm.

"Exactly what you deserve, Mr. Donovan!" Gentle Fawn said, melting against Clay, the smile on her face beaming. "And the three of us haven't even begun to make things 'hot' for you! Not by a long shot!"

Though the Battle of the Little Bighorn was the greatest victory, Indian or white, in the long history of fighting between the whites and the Plains Indians, it was the beginning of the end of the free, nomadic life of the proud, native American people.

Sitting Bull had predicted the battle and the results of the fighting when he told of his vision, saying he had seen soldiers "falling" into the huge Indian camp. But he had warned that the soldiers were a gift from Wakan Tanka and could be killed, but "If you take the weapons and belongings of the white man, it will prove a curse to the People." However, the Indians, intoxicated by their victory, ignored the great medicine man's prediction and took everything: uniforms, saddles, weapons, and about ten thousand rounds of cartridges.

In the coming months, the People came to see that Sitting Bull had been right. But then it was too late. The die was cast.

The united Indian camp stayed together longer than usual that year, as though huddling together around campfires and reliving their great victory over the whites could put off what they all soon believed was destined to come. But eventually, the individual tribes had to go their separate ways for their annual autumn buffalo hunt.

In September, in a place called Slim Buttes, northeast of the Black Hills on the Grand River, General Crook's soldiers attacked thirty-seven lodges of Lakotas. The village was destroyed and much of the property stolen from Custer's men was recovered. The only people left in the Indian camp were corpses: women, children, babies, old men, young men—all dead, many scalped.

After Slim Buttes, large numbers of tribes gave up and turned themselves in at the agencies. But Sitting Bull led his people into Canada, not to return to the United States until 1881 when he and the last ragged survivors of his band surrendered at Fort Buford, near the Dakota-Montana line.

The Lakotas who had given in at the agencies signed documents relinquishing all claims to the Black Hills (land the government had tried to force the Lakotas to sell for six million dollars and now stole for nothing) and Powder River country—about a third of their land. They'd been given no choice. Congress had suspended their rations until they submitted. It was sign the agreement or starve.

By spring 1877, even Crazy Horse and his followers knew the Indians' cause was lost. On May 6, 1877, dressed in full war paint, singing their war songs, their weapons in plain view, Crazy Horse and fifteen hundred proud Lakotas surrendered to General Crook at the Red Cloud Agency in Nebraska. Weakened by the cold and hunger and admitting total defeat, they still fought to retain their tenuous grasp on the last vestige of the dignity the white man had stripped from the Indian so deliberately and thoroughly.

Supposedly trying to escape a few months later, Crazy Horse was killed by the guards where he had been confined at Fort Robinson. The Sioux wars were at an end—as was a way of life that had survived thousands of years.

SIZZLING ROMANCE
from Zebra Books

REBEL PLEASURE   (1672, $3.95)
by Mary Martin
Union agent Jason Woods knew Christina was a brazen flirt, but his dangerous mission had no room for a clinging vixen. Then he caressed every luscious contour of her body and realized he could never go too far with this confederate tigress.

PASSION'S PARADISE   (1618, $3.75)
by Sonya T. Pelton
Angel was certain that Captain Ty would treat her only as a slave. She plotted to use her body to trick the handsome devil into freeing her, but before she knew what happened to her resolve, she was planning to keep him by her side forever.

TEXAS TIGRESS   (1714, $3.95)
by Sonya T. Pelton
As the bold ranger swaggered back into town, Tanya couldn't stop the flush of desire that scorched her from head to toe. But all she could think of was how to break his heart like he had shattered hers—and show him only love could tame a wild TEXAS TIGRESS.

WILD EMBRACE   (1713, $3.95)
by Myra Rowe
Marisa was a young innocent, but she had to follow Nicholas into the Louisiana wilderness to spend all of her days by his side and her nights in his bed. . . . He didn't want her as his bride until she surrendered to his WILD EMBRACE.

TENDER TORMENT   (1550, $3.95)
by Joyce Myrus
From their first meeting, Caitlin knew Quinn would be a fearsome enemy, a powerful ally and a magnificent lover. Together they'd risk danger and defy convention by stealing away to his isolated Canadian castle to share the magic of the Northern lights.

Available wherever paperbacks are sold, or order direct from the Publisher. Send cover price plus 50¢ per copy for mailing and handling to Zebra Books, Dept. 1986, 475 Park Avenue South, New York, N.Y. 10016. Residents of New York, New Jersey and Pennsylvania must include sales tax. DO NOT SEND CASH.